First Act

Rachel Lynch is a million-copy bestselling author of crime fiction, best known for her gripping DI Kelly Porter series as well as several standalones and the Major Helen Scott military police thrillers. Born and raised in Cumbria, the haunting beauty of the Lake District seeps into every story she tells. After teaching history in London and living across the globe as an army wife, Rachel eventually returned to her greatest passion: writing. Travel and the shared human experience comprise the fabric of her work. She explores the darkest corners of humanity with empathy and edge, weaving gritty realism with unforgettable characters. Alongside multiple standalone novels, she now brings her stories to life in a whole new way, through her podcast *The Killer Storyteller: A Podcast with Rachel Lynch*, where she unpacks every twist and turn, book by book.

Also by Rachel Lynch

The Rich
The Famous

Helen Scott Royal Military Police Thrillers

The Rift
The Line

Detective Kelly Porter

First Act (prequel)
Dark Game
Deep Fear
Dead End
Bitter Edge
Bold Lies
Blood Rites
Little Doubt
Lost Cause
Lying Ways
Sudden Death
Silent Bones
Shared Remains

RACHEL LYNCH

FIRST ACT

CANELO CRIME

First published in the United Kingdom in 2026 by

Canelo Crime, an imprint of
Canelo Digital Publishing Limited,
20 Vauxhall Bridge Road,
London SW1V 2SA
United Kingdom

A Penguin Random House Company
The authorised representative in the EEA is Dorling Kindersley Verlag GmbH. Arnulfstr. 124, 80636 Munich, Germany

Copyright © Rachel Lynch 2026

The moral right of Rachel Lynch to be identified as the creator of this work has been asserted in accordance with the Copyright, Designs and Patents Act, 1988.

All rights reserved. No part of this publication may be reproduced or transmitted in any form or by any means, electronic or mechanical, including photocopy, recording, or any information storage and retrieval system, without permission in writing from the publisher.

No part of this book may be used or reproduced in any manner for the purpose of training artificial intelligence technologies or systems. In accordance with Article 4(3) of the DSM Directive 2019/790, Canelo expressly reserves this work from the text and data mining exception.

A CIP catalogue record for this book is available from the British Library.

Ebook ISBN 978 1 83598 119 1
Hardback ISBN 978 1 83598 121 4
Trade Paperback ISBN 978 1 83598 415 4

This book is a work of fiction. Names, characters, businesses, organizations, places and events are either the product of the author's imagination or are used fictitiously. Any resemblance to actual persons, living or dead, events or locales is entirely coincidental.

Cover design by Dan Mogford

Cover images © Shutterstock

Printed and bound in Great Britain by Clays Ltd, Elcograf S.p.A.

Look for more great books at
www.canelo.co | www.dk.com

Chapter 1

Summer 2008

They arrived at the Hackney pub separately. Three people of advancing years. To anyone watching from across the road or even along the bar, they looked harmless, friendly and benign.

Utterly inoffensive.

To the inquisitive they looked as though they had a story to tell. To the nonchalant Londoner they were slow and in the way. To the surveillance car around the corner they were potentially lethal.

The first to arrive was a gentleman in his seventies, who stooped a little from old age, though seventy-something wasn't 'old' anymore. But Frank had relied on the NHS to keep him healthy rather than take on the responsibility himself because it was too much like hard work. His muscles were withered and his face sagged. His back was kyphotic and he gripped a cane. A young woman held the door for him and smiled. He reminded her of her grandad. Frank pushed his spectacles up his nose and coughed: a rattling, rasping expulsion of bile. The young woman got a whiff of his body as she left the pub and turned up her nose.

Poor bugger, she thought. *No one to look after him.*

The barwoman waved at Frank, and he nodded to her.

'Good evening, Sookie,' he said.

'The usual, Frank?' she asked.

He nodded.

He took a seat by the window to catch his breath and the traffic from the busy road outside buzzed past, rattling the old windows. They hadn't been upgraded to double glazing and much of the pub had stayed the same as it had since Frank drank in there thirty years ago. Hackney itself had changed, of course, but along Mare Street, the same watering holes stood, serving new-fangled super drinks that fizzed and contained odd chemicals. In his day, hops and barley were the only ingredients for booze. Or grapes if you drank that God-awful wine.

The Grain & Grape had stood there for over a hundred years but had swapped names a few times of course, like a lot of things had altered. Nothing ever stayed the same.

Which is why he was here.

To meet his friends who were themselves adapting. Always moving on and staying ahead of anyone who might want to find them and ask awkward questions about the past. But they were also there to remember a dear friend. They used to be a group of four, not three. Before time came knocking.

Dorothy was the next to arrive. She wore a grey cardigan despite the heat of the summer outside the pub. Old London pubs always tended to be built in cavernous cellars which kept out the heat and only let in the occasional gust of gritty oxygen from outside when a new punter walked in. In that sense, the oldest watering holes hadn't changed in hundreds of years, which made Frank feel even older as he smiled warily at the new arrival. Dorothy wasn't a typical London pub-goer. She'd taken better care of herself and was well turned out. But she'd also aged and looked all of her sixty-odd years. Dorothy had always been in control, but as Frank watched her search the pub, nobody paid her any attention, nor did they notice her superiority. Her face was unfriendly and Frank watched with amusement as a man got up to leave and didn't hold the door open for her. Then Dorothy spotted him and her mouth set into a familiar straight gash across her face, like one of those awful puppets at the fair: the ones with garish makeup all over their faces, the ones that scared kids. Poor Dorothy. For a woman who was fastidious in everything else, including her cruelty, she sure couldn't apply lipstick straight, and her cack-handedness gave her an unfortunate smile, but one you weren't likely to forget.

Dorothy wasn't amused, but then Frank didn't expect her to be: she was a bloody teacher now, of all things, and in Leyton of all places, and it was glaringly obvious that her dismal gloom still followed her everywhere she went. None of them had moved very far.

Dorothy ordered a port and lemon from the bar and took it across to where Frank nursed his pint of dark brown beer.

They didn't speak.

They watched the door.

Always suspicious, *since Tania…*

Dorothy sipped her drink like a lady. Frank slurped his beer. Dorothy side-glanced him with disapproval.

Edith arrived late and the other two tutted silently. She waved as soon as she spotted them, by far the more animated and sunnier of the threesome. She wore a thin coat and looked as though she might melt from the heat. She wore tight curls on top of her head and her face was immaculately made up with elegance. Frank stared at her, and Dorothy noticed his longing had never cooled after all these years. She looked down her nose at the pair of them who were by far the most emotional of the group.

The fourth person, Tania, was missing and had been for many years now. They were here to raise a glass to her memory, like they did once a year, on a special anniversary.

Edith shuffled to the bar. For sixty-seven, she was in poor shape too. But her ailments were what kept Edith's conversations going; without them, she had nothing except memories, and bad ones at that.

'They told me I need to wait for my blood pressure to go down before I can have my other hip done,' Edith said as she approached the table with her drink.

Dorothy glanced at her with disdain.

'Maybe lay off the sweets, Edith,' she said.

Edith chuckled and so did Frank. They were both used to being told off by Dorothy, who'd always ran things.

'I do like my chocolate eclairs!' Edith said.

Dorothy rolled her eyes.

Frank raised his glass.

'To our absent friend,' he said.

Dorothy and Edith lifted their glasses to his. They held them suspended in the air as the glasses touched.

'Up the Gunners,' they said and lowered them, taking a tentative sip, except Frank who gulped his beer. They weren't Arsenal fans but that wasn't the point. Tania had been.

'To Tania.'

Silence descended as they each remembered their friend.

What else was there to say?

They sipped their drinks and Sookie came across to ask them if they'd like a top-up. They all nodded. They were in no rush.

'Do you think it's really her?' Frank said finally.
He wasn't talking about Tania.
'She's a policewoman now,' Edith said quietly.
'Shush!' Dorothy demanded.

The air felt claggy and Edith swallowed hard. Dorothy stroked her glass. Condensation ran down the sides and she wiped it away.

'If she's found us, we can find her,' Dorothy said.
'Why now?' Frank asked.
'What does she want?' Edith joined in.
'What they all want,' Dorothy said. 'Some kind of pity. She doesn't realise how lucky she is. Christ, we gave them bloody everything.'
'Right, so,' Frank said, gulping his beer.
'What do you think she meant by "others"?'
'She's bluffing. Ignore it. Just silly words. She wants attention, like she always did.'
'I always knew she was a watcher. She just sat there and said nothing,' Frank said.
'Stop it!' Dorothy demanded. 'Talking about it won't change anything. Even if she is with the others, we have nothing to hide. It all went away, remember? Nobody is interested in what a bunch of kids say happened thirty years ago.'
'And what about Tania?'
'What about her?' Dorothy shot Edith a vicious look. 'She's gone off and doesn't want to be found, that's all. Tania was always the weak one. She'd rather run away and let us deal with it all than face it herself. She's a coward!'

Edith sat back, deflated, and contemplated the desertion of their friend.

'What if she didn't just go away?' Edith asked. 'What if…?'
Frank nodded.
'What if she really disappeared and she's dead?' Edith whispered.
'Oh, behave! Don't be so dramatic. Tania has gone off and is living it up in Spain, knowing her, the selfish little madam she is, leaving us behind to deal with the fallout. Pull yourselves together.'
'For seven years? And no word?' Edith looked scared.
'What if it is her?' Frank asked.

'Who, Frank? You really expect me to believe that the bogey man exists? Don't be ridiculous! You sound like one of them! Crying into their pillows when no one came to save them.'

Dorothy cackled and the barwoman looked over.

'I think it's her,' Edith said. 'I'm with Frank, Dorothy. I'm scared.'

'Scared?' Dorothy snapped. 'Scared? Of what? Look at you, you're an old woman! They don't know who we are, it's all scaremongering.'

'They know where I live,' Frank said. 'I got a letter to my home address.'

'And me,' Edith said. 'I got a letter too. It's her.'

'She's right,' Frank said. 'It's Jill.'

Chapter 2

Few things said London like the black, dusty grit that stuck in your nose from the underground. It didn't burn or even smell funny, but Kelly still knew it was there. And it was worse in summer. Silent, invisible clouds bellowed through tunnels, pushed ahead of trains hurtling through them as the surrounding air whistled and whined, signalling for the passengers to stand back. She stood close to the tiled wall and mulled over her day: her final day working as a detective for Bethnal Green CID. But instead of making her way home through the Friday-afternoon crowds and the throngs of tourists, she had one last job to do for her team. On Monday, she'd begin her dream job, working for a murder squad: a post she'd pursued since becoming a detective six years ago. At twenty-eight years old, being selected to serve on a major investigation team (MIT) in London was the highest accolade of Kelly Porter's career so far.

As she watched the crowd and focused on a six-foot, skinny white male, she experienced a fleeting moment of unreality. Sometimes she could pinch herself that she'd come so far from the valleys and dales of Cumbria where she grew up.

The words of her father echoed inside her head as she readied herself for her mark to make a move.

'You're not London material,' he'd told her.

London material? She didn't even know what that meant, but she knew it was intended to hurt her. It was a put-down. A challenge to make her doubt herself.

But she was here now.

She studied the man's dark shaggy hair, and she knew without seeing his face that walnut-brown eyes shone from beneath a lifeless, menacing stare. She wondered what he had inside the khaki satchel strapped over his shoulder and hoped it wasn't a weapon. With the 7/7 London bombings only three years ago now, on a summer's day just like this one, it was difficult not to see every tube passenger with a hefty bag as a potential terrorist.

Kelly's colleague, a five-foot-one package of crime prevention called Cheryl, stood further down the platform. Known as Longstride to her close colleagues, as a sarcastic acknowledgement of her short legs, Cheryl nodded in Kelly's direction and they inched closer to their target. According to the Borough Intelligence Unit (BIU), Orlando Charles was responsible for a string of burglaries that had plagued Bethnal Green for the past year and Kelly and Cheryl had decided that Friday afternoon, in front of a few hundred commuters, when he least expected it, was the ideal time to arrest the bastard.

A last hurrah for her time in Bethnal Green CID.

A goodbye celebration with her mates.

They were a tight team and she'd miss them. Bagging Orlando Charles was her parting gift to them. She ignored the knot in her gut that warned her she was moving in prematurely. Orlando was a Harry Houdini character who evaded the law each time they got close. But this time she had an eyewitness.

Their colleagues were inside his bedsit in London Bridge right now, with a warrant, collecting evidence against him. He had no previous convictions and Kelly had never fathomed how he'd kept so clean in all the time they'd been tailing him.

They needed a confession. Without it, their case was flimsy.

And that's what they were here to put into motion. They'd keep him for twenty-four hours and pressure him in interview.

At least that was the plan.

The train arrived and Orlando didn't move at first, so Kelly and Cheryl closed in. Then without warning he made a dash for it away from the platform, through waiting commuters and disappeared into one of the tunnels leading up to ground level.

'Christ!' Kelly shouted, and set off running in the same direction. Despite the compact nature of Longstride's legs, she made up for it with speed and agility and she was soon overtaking Kelly and sprinting towards the elevator shaft.

Orlando peeked over his shoulder and made eye contact with his pursuers, sure now that he was in trouble. He sped up. Kelly took two steps at a time and reached the top just as Cheryl was jumping off the end of the stairwell. They took one flank each and reached him seconds before he went to launch himself over the barrier in the hall.

They grabbed one arm apiece, Cheryl manoeuvring herself between the turnstile and his huge body, and Kelly produced her cuffs. He struggled but Kelly mastered the arm weave takedown technique and Orlando crashed to the ground, squealing that she was hurting his arm.

'You're nicked, mate,' she whispered into his ear. 'Detective Sergeant Kelly Porter, pleased to meet you, you do not have to say anything…'

Cheryl stood in front of him and smiled. The man peered up in shock and Kelly could tell that he was more cheesed off at being caught by two women, and one as short as Cheryl, than he was about potentially going to jail. Bad luck, fella.

They dragged him to his feet and the ticket collector let them through the barrier. Orlando stopped struggling as they led him out into the bright sunshine. Somebody was playing a radio loudly and Kelly figured it came from a street vendor selling doughnuts. The smell made her tongue twitch and she swallowed hard, knowing she'd have to wait for a few hours before she could knock off and begin her weekend. The Ting Tings belted out *That's not my name*, and Kelly grinned.

'We know your name, Orlando,' she said into the bloke's ear as they led him to a waiting squad car.

People stopped and stared, half wanting the prisoner to make a run for it to embarrass the law, and the other half recoiled away from them as if the man's very size was testimony to his danger. It was moments like this that had brought Kelly to the capital and into the Met. And through the whole thing, she hadn't even needed to get her warrant card out of her pocket. The old leather wallet it was crammed into, beside her bank cards and cash, bulged in her pocket and the presence of it there, as well as the feel of the man in front of her, about to be booked into the station back in Bethnal Green when they eventually made it through the traffic, made her chest push out just a little further.

This was what she'd come to London for.

The thrill of the chase and the high of putting people like Orlando Charles in handcuffs. Already, she imagined walking into her new office, sitting at her new desk and opening her first case file, surrounded by colleagues for whom murder was their daily bread.

She said a silent *screw you* to her father.
I did it, Dad, said a voice in her head.
I did it and I didn't need your help.

Chapter 3

The CID, or 'upstairs' as it was affectionately known at Bethnal Green nick, was uncharitably warm and muggy. The few windows that opened were at full tilt and Kelly prepared a facsimile. She abandoned the broken chair and rifled underneath piles of paper, looking for the fax number she needed.

'We can't go to the pub to celebrate just yet.' Cheryl delivered the bad news. They'd been buried under paperwork since bringing Orlando in. He'd been processed, pending charges, and tucked into his cot bed in a cell for the night. But they couldn't raise a toast to Kelly's new job just yet. The Porter & Grape in Angel and Islington would have to wait for a few more hours, because another job had been called in.

Kelly gazed at her colleague with resignation, as if knocking off shift on time on a Friday was merely a distant dream anyway. But there was nothing wrong with fantasy. They were used to keeping unsocial hours. Kelly leant back on her chair, and it cracked. Nothing much worked as it was supposed to in the ancient office.

'Why? What's up?' she asked Cheryl, who was hanging on to her desk phone, covering the mouthpiece.

'Workers at the Olympic Stadium have just found a body, apparently.'

Kelly stopped what she was doing. 'Really?'

They received prank calls about human remains all the time and didn't rush to believe every story fed to their division. It wasn't entirely unusual for other nicks, say at Bow or Limehouse, to wind each other up on a Friday afternoon, just when they knew CID would be packing up to go to the pub. Kelly was sceptical.

'Sounds legit,' Cheryl said, hanging up the phone.

'Friday afternoon rush hour over to Stratford?' Kelly said, dismayed at the prospect.

They'd only been back in the office for an hour and Kelly had just started her notes on the arrest. Computerisation made their life easier, but unlike big tech in the city, with their rows and rows of brand-new hardware, the London Met spent heady sums on reconditioned versions. Transferring files to the digital age in CID was like digging for dinosaur bones, but they were getting there. Kelly's office computer was normally covered in ring files and dust. They took up enough space to hide a body, but the hard drives which stood on the floor provided a spare coffee stand when needed.

Kelly fancied a shower and a pint of something bubbly before embarking on yet another journey across their patch, but that, too, would have to wait.

'What about West Ham nick?' she asked Cheryl.

'Busy with the prep for tomorrow's football match. There's no one else, apparently. Hackney has two fresh murders.'

'What's the boss say?'

DCI Wallis sat barricaded in his office most of the time, emerging only to tell them when they'd screwed up. Kelly used him as a template of everything she didn't want to become, should she ever find herself a member of those dizzy ranks.

Cheryl answered with a hip-lock and a roll of her eyes. DCI Wallis followed the rules.

Kelly grimaced and rummaged around in her bag, looking for some tissues or anything she might use in the toilets to freshen up.

'Give me five minutes,' she told Cheryl. 'Has the HAT been informed?'

Each area of London had a twenty-four-hour homicide assessment team on call to review suspicious deaths, but on a Friday night, during rush hour, it was unlikely they'd get there first. Besides, it wasn't even confirmed if they had a body or something else buried under the building site over at the Olympic Park. They wouldn't waste their time until an area unit had checked out the call first.

'Yep, informed,' Cheryl said.

In the ladies' toilet, Kelly washed her face and reapplied a little makeup. A touch-up of mascara and lip gloss would do it, then she unbuttoned her shirt and washed her armpits, thankful she'd remembered to leave a deodorant at work after the last time she'd been called out to a chase at speed after a teenager was up to no good. London in summertime wasn't ideal for sprinting. She glanced in the mirror and smiled at the reflection. Detective Sergeant Kelly Porter stared back at her. She was ready to move on. There was something crazy about being squeezed into a bathroom in an office of the law, leg up on the sink, checking for bruises to her body after a chase, but that's why she knew she was alive. She felt her heartbeat in her chest and smiled before she left the room.

She was good to her word and reappeared in the office in under five minutes to find Cheryl arm wrestling with DC Pete Miller who was affectionately known as Windy, and they sure could have done with some breeze in the office today, particularly now to blow away the virile masculinity gathering in the corners along with the endless piles of paper. Kelly rolled her eyes. She knew Cheryl would win. Pete didn't work out, but he pitted his strength against his colleague because he loved to be beaten by her. It didn't damage his ego. In fact, he seemed to extract enjoyment out of being able to hold her hand for ten minutes, which is how long they could be sat there for.

'We really haven't got time for this,' Kelly said, gathering her things. The distraction worked, and Cheryl took advantage of Pete's sudden shift in focus to push his arm down to the desktop. They were lucky to find a space big enough between the dead plants, newspapers and spare traffic cones and nothing scattered to the floor with the impact. They high fived and Pete said he'd hold the fort until they knocked off.

Cheryl grinned all the way down the stairs to the front desk, where they passed a shoplifter being booked in. Outside, they peered at the Bethnal Green Tavern, wishing they could go in for a quick drink, but turned right instead and headed to the tube station. Getting stiffed with a callout on a Friday afternoon wasn't the end of the world, but when the sun was shining after a hard week, it made the job particularly disagreeable. Word was they were moving offices to Victoria Park Square soon, to an imposing Victorian-looking building. Like any change, it'd be a wrench, but Kelly would be long gone by then. She didn't envy them the task of sorting decades of paperwork groaning on the shelves in their current office. In her new one, she already had her own desk and her own modern computer waiting for her. And access to murder investigations across the capital. Her hands itched to get started.

The move to electronic data had been received with a general lack of enthusiasm at grassroots level. Some said it'd never catch on. Real police officers, face to face, working the leads, that's what police work was, and detective work even more so, which is why Kelly had sat her exams to become a detective as soon as she could, after two years in uniform.

'Don't be impatient,' her dad told her. 'A good copper needs to develop his nose, like a good hound,' he'd say. John Porter had worked in Cumbria Police since he was seventeen years old. To him the idea of Met detectives specialising in one crime or another was galling. He was a typical provincial old-school copper who believed in hard work and instinct. He didn't reckon that fancy badges and titles proved anything, and he'd laughed at Kelly when she'd told him her ambitions. Which is why she didn't tell him when she finally got accepted to Hendon and caught a train to London with one large bag to her name.

Maybe it was because he didn't back her that she did it. To prove him wrong and show that women could be just as good at solving crime and catching arseholes as men were. But whatever the reason, she'd rarely been back. She visited Cumbria when guilt forced her to return, but never stayed long. She'd traded sheep shit and mountains for concrete ghettos, and she didn't want to be anywhere else. She'd walked out on a fiancé too. Perhaps the clean Lake District air might have been welcome on a day like today, but the thrill of what she did more than made up for it and despite the pollution, she breathed easier single. She tried to concentrate on this now, as her body told her to strip off her sticky trousers and shirt and find a summer dress, with flip flops and sunglasses to accessorise, but she shrugged off the nagging doubts and pushed all thoughts of home away as they travelled across the capital city.

This was her home now.

Construction on the Olympic Park had begun in the spring and Kelly and Cheryl were amazed at the progress being made already, with the Olympics still four years away. They'd been told to go to site entrance D, at a project yard in Stratford, and they asked a few workers in hard hats for directions before they found the correct gathering of works vehicles, metal scaffold and cranes.

Building sites all looked the same to Kelly, but she had a feeling she'd seen this one before.

A portly bloke called Dennis Chapman, wearing a high-vis vest with nothing underneath and a yellow hard hat, greeted them gravely and handed them site hats. He led them into a partially constructed building.

The site was vast and they could just make out familiar shapes that hinted of its future as a sporting mecca in four short years' time. 2012 seemed a lifetime away but the capital was already gearing up for the event of the century.

'It's through here,' Dennis said, turning round.

'It' didn't sound human, and Kelly hoped their journey hadn't been wasted. Though at least then they could go to the pub.

Dennis Chapman was a typical foreman. He talked constantly and used his hands a lot. He seemed nervous, but then it wasn't every day you found a body at work.

'Thing is, we can't dig around it or do anything until it's taken out of there and no one wants to touch it. A few of the guys are religious and they said this used to be an old burial site, I dunno, it could be thousands of years old for all I know,' Dennis chattered on. A thousand-year-old body was all they needed but they kept an open mind.

Kelly had no idea what the land had been used for over the years and it wouldn't be the first time a building firm had disturbed an ancient graveyard in London. Romans, Saxons, Vikings and Normans had all at one time destroyed, raped and pillaged the land and then rebuilt around the port. Archaeological digs went on all the time.

There were layers and layers of crime under the capital city buried in the mud.

Dennis stopped walking and talking and Kelly noticed the birds singing, as if celebrating the opportunity. He pointed to a trough, roughly ten feet by ten feet, and Kelly and Cheryl peered over the edge of the lip.

'It's not right sending you girls, there should be a priest or something here,' Dennis said.

The birdsong stopped.

Kelly knelt down, ignoring his comment, and looked at a bone-shaped projection sticking out of the earth. It was possible she was looking at an arm or a leg, but whatever it was, it had fabric around it, and it was covered with something that reminded her of the beef jerky she shared with her dad in the mountains. Then she saw a skeletal hand and realised that Dennis was right. It was human after all, and Kelly's heart sank.

'It doesn't look like it's in a grave,' Cheryl said.

'No, it's wrapped in something,' Kelly said.

Part of being aspiring murder detectives was discussing the best ways to get noticed by a murder squad, and they talked their theories over incessantly, boring others around them with their conjecture. But a body, no matter how old, was as close as they got to being actively part of a homicide investigation and Kelly saw it as an opportunity to gather as much information before the HAT got involved and took the case away from them. Before she moved on to her own murder squad. Her adrenaline soared as she peered into the hole.

'We'd better get down there,' Kelly said.

They lingered on the lip of the trough.

London never failed to throw up a constant stream of victims of crime from hidden alleyways and dark ditches at all hours of the day and night, in a never-ending stream of deviance. And they had enough to do without a fresh body thrown into the mix. Kelly saw the clean break from CID to MIT slipping away from her. A pang of guilt crossed her furrowed brow as she saw herself leaving Cheryl in the shit over this, and alone.

But the body wasn't fresh.

Kelly was no expert in anthropology, but she could tell it wasn't a recent death.

'It might be a cold homicide case,' Cheryl said hopefully.

'Or it might be natural causes, or an accident.' Kelly brought her buddy back down to earth. 'Let's get the area taped off and call in forensics and an anthropologist,' she added.

'On a Friday afternoon?' Cheryl complained.

Kelly shrugged. 'You never know. We need to secure the area, whether it's a modern or ancient burial.'

'She can't have been missed,' Dennis the foreman said, nodding in the direction of the body.

'She?'

He shrugged.

'Or he. Who's the boss here?' Kelly asked him. But there was no answer. She turned to see Cheryl was already talking into her radio, requesting a forensic team and extra uniforms to seal off the area. Kelly looked for Dennis but he was nowhere to be found. Then she heard retching and spotted him bending over a barrel, vomiting his guts out.

Chapter 4

The toys were no ordinary playthings. They were original handcrafted dolls in the image of Jack and Jill from the famous tale, and Luther stared into Jill's eyes in awe as he held her gently in his gloved hands. Oils from human hands could wreak havoc on vintage specimens like this.

Jill alone, at auction, would fetch twenty thousand pounds.

Jack and Jill went up the hill to fetch a pail of water. Jack fell down and broke his crown. And Jill came tumbling after.

The rhyme's arrangement was strikingly simple to make the whole affair easier for children, and he whispered the verse under his breath. It was predictable, repetitive and comforting. Even for a grown man.

The pair was thought to date from around 1759 and extensive forensic examination of the clothing and glass of their eyes probably narrowed their origin to Germany.

His hands moved methodically and gently.

The way toys were treated said so much about a society. They were portals into the histories of children. If they weren't treated properly, well then, that said everything about the way kids were protected or not. If only he could take them all and put them in one of his puppet shows, where they'd stay forever, he could save them all.

Luther spent so much time in the museum that Oswald, the aged security guard, joked that he was born there. If he could sleep there, he would. In fact, one night he'd managed to escape Oswald's keen eye and had hidden in a cupboard until after lights out, and then he'd emerged into the darkness surrounded by thousands of toys, games, books and artefacts, and had continued his job of restoring and caring for them well into the early hours, contented and fulfilled. That had been a long time ago. Now he was too old. After the massive refurb, three years ago, the V&A kept him and Oswald employed more out of nostalgia than wise business acumen. They were more like museum artefacts themselves, and ones they simply couldn't bear to throw away.

His job was simple. He was chief curator at the Museum of Childhood in Cambridge Heath Road, a mere two-minute walk from Bethnal Green tube station. But it wasn't the title that made it straightforward, it was the fact that every day he could lose himself in the past of children whose only mission in life was to play. Play was the first and most precious thing a child learnt, and the most elementary, because it set the tone for everything else.

He recalled the times with affection that he'd been able to carry children off in a haze of animation, making up worlds for them to hide and stay safe in. Play was a refuge. He'd held the lock and key.

There were thousands, if not hundreds of thousands, of ways a young person could configure a game and remain transfixed by it all day long and it was Luther's job to keep those traditions alive. It was a serious task and one that couldn't be done by anybody with anything less than utter dedication to what made children happy. Their worlds, their fantasies and their wonder were the things that kept Luther coming to work late into his sixties and seventies. But today he was unpacking the final boxes which had been stored during the refurbishment. It had taken a whole year, but the place had been given a makeover and had dragged them all kicking and screaming into the new century. But these things couldn't be rushed and three years on, the artefacts were still being unpacked, relabelled and displayed.

He admired Jill's silk dress. She reminded him of someone. Her nose was worn away slightly but that was due to age. They'd found her like that. Both Jack and Jill were part of a house clearance in Stepney from the 1930s. They'd been tucked away like this together for almost eighty years, sleeping soundly and undisturbed until found by a clumsy removal firm and donated to the children's museum. Jill's body was made from a single piece of wood and her legs and arms moved at the joints. She wore a saque, an intricate dress of French origin, and the colourful lace embroidery had withstood the ravages of time because she'd lived in the dark, out of harm's way. Her hair was real, and Luther wondered if the ringlets had been taken from a living child or one who'd passed on. Her sleeves were the most delicate lace, like her bonnet. Her face was crafted from porcelain and her eyes of glass, and they stared at him, asking him if he would love her.

He carefully untied Jill's bonnet and held his breath without realising. Suddenly, his hands stopped, and a tear formed at the corner of his left eye. It came from nowhere and took him by surprise, but he knew it was there because his vision went blurry, and it took all his concentration not to allow it to drop onto Jill and contaminate her. The doll was almost two hundred and fifty years old and he wasn't going to be responsible for the degradation of the fabric so lovingly sewn around her bonnet. He looked away and blinked and the tear rolled down his cheek and onto the floor. Satisfied that there wasn't another, he looked back at the doll. Her hair was golden yellow, and he checked the roots. They'd been handsewn and they were all intact. She wore drawers under her skirt and a white pannier, or wooden hoop, which still flicked out the skirt, in the fashion of ladies of her time. It was dependent upon the era how Jill was depicted. Some portrayed her as a gentrified damsel, others a common milkmaid.

He turned to Jack who was usually illustrated as a younger helper. His innocent face was made more lovely with the bisque porcelain detail, and his blue eyes shone back at Luther questioningly. He wore cute little blue overalls and a chequered shirt with white pearl buttons. His bow tie was a nod to past societies' misunderstanding of childhood. Jack looked like a miniature adult, but he wasn't that at all. He laid them side by side, where they belonged and, no longer animated, they regressed to just being dolls again, like puppets without their masters, they stayed very still. If only they could dance and talk themselves, what a different world it would be, he thought. He knew that should toys take on a life of their own they wouldn't be tainted by the same dire blackness that plagued people.

He grinned at the romanticism of literature, and it calmed him a little. Fantasy always blurred the edges of reality and enabled stories to take on a dreamlike quality.

Luther remembered the faces of all the children who'd gained wonderment and freedom from the characters he helped preserve and also the ones who hadn't been so lucky.

That's where his tears had come from.

A crash made him jump and he almost dropped the box, but Luther knew that even if he was on fire, he'd save the artefacts before himself. He glared around to the source of the noise and a cleaner apologised. She was frozen in fear and Luther's face softened. He didn't like to be known as intimidating. He simply cared, that's all. It was a dying quality with the advent of modern notions of joy. Fewer and fewer children visited the museum to wonder at the toys of bygone years because all they were interested in was computers and electronic games which stunted brain cell generation and turned kids into zombies. Real amusement, that's what they needed, not some mindless junk stripping them of their reality. They needed to use their imaginations, not be spoon-fed graphics. There was a time when children visiting the museum looked on in astonishment at the array of playthings on offer, but now they yawned and fiddled because their brains were fried. He'd even seen some with the new mobile phone gadgets and it encouraged a rage inside him that produced a sadness he hadn't seen coming. He'd thought children would always play. It was the most natural thing in the world.

But they didn't seem to want to anymore. Not with real toys. Imagination was dying and all he could do was try to bring it to life for them when they were here, watching one of his puppet shows or learning how they were made, but it was getting harder and harder. He saw technology taking over the job of cognisance and it left him bereft.

Kids didn't want to be saved anymore.

Chapter 5

Kelly and Cheryl stood inside the hole, staring closely at the pile of rags. The scenes of crime officer had arrived and had climbed in too. It would have been cosy if not for the weirdness.

'What's that?' Kelly asked, pointing at a small patch of material.

'It looks like a hat with a feather in it,' Cheryl said.

'Crikey, we're dealing with an ancient specimen then, maybe a Victorian dandy?' Kelly asked. Whitechapel wasn't that far away and suddenly she had visions of Jack the Ripper stalking women around the dark alleys of the crime-riddled East End when bobbies chased ghosts through thick smog. She shivered. They were wearing gloves, coveralls, masks and black plastic bags over their shoes now the SOCO was here, and it made the heat all-pervasive as if somebody just turned up the dial, but Kelly's skin felt tacky and frigid.

Geena, the SOCO unlucky enough to be called to such a job on a Friday evening, looked up at them both.

'It's well preserved.'

'The hat?'

'No, the body. I'm not an expert in historic digs but I've seen enough of them. It looks old. The earth here is low oxygen and high acid, which can mummify them. I'm hoping that when we begin to remove it from the surrounding soil it doesn't fall apart on us.'

Geena looked at her watch, indicating her time was almost up. She sighed.

'We're going to have to move it if the bone man doesn't get here soon. I've got the mayor's office breathing down my neck.'

Bone man was their affectionate name for anthropologists.

With Geena's help, they'd moved enough of the fabric around the body to expose a whole human form. It was small, like a child's. Perhaps a teenager. Or a really old person.

'How did the mayor's office find out so soon?' Kelly asked.

'Press is all over it. Since you've been inside here, we've had three squad cars full of uniforms erecting a cordon. There's already calls to make him the Olympic mascot.'

The three of them peered at the remains.

'The skeleton bobsleigh team is interested,' Geena said, quietly grinning. Kelly and Cheryl stared at the SOCO then at each other. Gallows humour kept the Met ticking. They all needed a stiff drink.

The mayor's office was more efficient than the HAT, which still hadn't appeared. But Boris Johnson, as the newly appointed London mayor, was trying to make a splash.

'Is that skin?' Kelly dragged their thoughts back to the body. She pointed to a long piece of what had earlier reminded her of beef jerky. Geena leant over and looked closely. She reached down with a gloved hand and pushed her hand into the remnants of flesh they could see. It was a section near the neck of the deceased.

'That's not a natural tear, it looks like a wound to me,' Geena said.

Geena had explained that, in her opinion, the cadaver lay on its side, head to toe in line with the size of the hole, with clothing partially intact, and wrapped in some sort of material. From what they could see, it would appear that the victim had met with a violent death, given the lacerations to the leathery skin across the cadaver's chest area, which Geena now scrutinised.

Kelly recoiled, expecting there to be a slurping sound as the SOCO pulled her finger out of the hole. She imagined the horror of a fresh body spilling its fluids at one of the other crime scenes she'd been called to. But it was silent, apart from a snap of what seemed like elastic. Kelly assumed it was the age of the corpse that had desiccated it. Geena shone a torch onto the area. It was dark down in the hole. Then she pulled at something pink and it snapped back with a ping. Kelly and Cheryl looked on with macabre intrigue.

'It looks like a dress-up nose, you know like Pinocchio?' Geena said.

The SOCO held the item up so it dangled off her finger and they agreed that it looked like a model nose attached to elastic to keep it in place around the head.

'When was elastic invented?' Kelly asked.

'Ah!' Cheryl said. 'I know this one. 1820. It's made from rubber.'

Kelly stared at her.

'Since when did you eat a history book?' she asked.

'Pub quiz,' Cheryl replied, grinning, pleased with herself.

'That long ago?' Geena asked, alarmed. She gave Cheryl a doubtful look as though she didn't believe her. Kelly reckoned Geena was the type to take pub quizzes very seriously.

'How long was the hole open?' Geena changed the subject. 'This nose could be rubbish that's been thrown in, or at least trapped in another layer of earth. You know history in London is crushed on top of itself and sometimes you find Roman coins with coke cans,' Geena said.

She'd clearly seen it all.

'Let's bag it anyway,' Cheryl said, unwilling to enter a competition with the SOCO's expertise.

Their attention was diverted to a man arriving on scene who looked hot and flustered. He carried a briefcase and wore plastic gloves and introduced himself as Jonathan Hass, an anthropologist from Brampton Forensic Services, based in Romford Road. He reminded Kelly of Harrison Ford in *Raiders of the Lost Ark*.

'What were you saying?' Geena asked Kelly.

Kelly felt less qualified to contribute suddenly, in front of the expert, who peered down at her from the lip, expecting her to supply something of grave importance.

'We think that's a plastic nose, you know, like the ones you might find in a dress-up box,' she said.

Geena held it up for Jonathan Hass to study, which he did. Then he peered into the hole.

'Ancient or modern?' Kelly asked him. 'That's what we really need to know.'

'Impossible to say until I get closer,' he said. 'The soil here is oxygen rich and—'

'High acid?' Kelly finished for him.

'Exactly. Perfect for mummification, so it could be a thousand years old for all I know.'

'Great,' Kelly said. 'But not the nose, right?'

He looked at her as if in agreement.

'Murder squad won't touch it unless it's a missing person or a recent homicide,' Cheryl said.

'Which means you're stuck with him come Monday,' Kelly said. 'Sorry I won't be here.'

'Are you going on holiday and leaving us?' Jonathan Hass asked, as if they were old friends. His familiarity was cute, but it gave the impression that Jonathan Hass didn't get out much. He was trying to fit in.

'She's moving to murder squad,' Cheryl answered for her.

Jonathan raised his eyebrows.

'I'll have to leave Pinocchio with you,' Kelly said.

'Pinocchio?' It was Jonathan's turn to appear puzzled.

Kelly nodded. 'Yep, Pinocchio.'

Jonathan Hass looked at them oddly and then to the fake nose, then he caught up and realised what they were referring to and smiled.

'Is that why that's there?' he asked.

The three women followed his finger. The anthropologist jumped down into the hole and carefully lifted a lumpy object from beside the deceased. In the light, it was easier to see, and he held it up, turning it over. Bright colours reminiscent of a once vibrant ensemble of fashion flickered in the torch beam.

Kelly and Cheryl stared at the bone man, and Geena whistled, impressed with Jonathan's eagle eye.

He held in his gloved hands a small toy about the size of a pencil case. It was red and black.

'Is that who I think it is?' Kelly asked.

'Ladies, meet Pinocchio. I can tell by the nose.'

Jonathan turned it over in his hands. It wasn't like the character Kelly knew from Disney movies. This one was wooden, two-dimensional somehow and not appealing at all. It was ugly and sinister. Kelly shivered, despite the London night enveloping her in sweat.

'Is this what we refer to as a calling card?' Geena asked.

The four of them stared in silence until Jonathan spoke.

'No ID then?' he asked.

Kelly shook her head.

'Which MIT will you be assigned to?' he asked her.

'East,' she said, vaguely distracted by the unearthing of the hideous toy.

'Good, I work closely with them. We'll be seeing more of each other.' He smiled, with Pinocchio dangling off his finger from a loop attached to the top of his wooden hat.

Kelly had never been chatted up over a grave before but there was a first time for everything, she figured.

Children's toys, to her, were things of wonder and joy. Innocent symbols of a mind not yet grown. The thing before her was not like that at all. A memory of her reading a bedtime story with her father flickered through her mind but was then lost.

Geena coughed to get the anthropologist's attention and showed him the wound she'd identified. He stepped closer to take a more detailed look. Kelly and Cheryl watched him as he nosed around the body. He too stuck his gloved finger into the hole and Kelly recoiled ever so slightly. He took a ruler out of his pocket and measured the opening then revealed more of the body by pushing away fabric.

'It will have to be excavated here, I'm afraid. This part of the building site must cease working until we get the whole specimen out, there might be others beneath if it's an old burial site.'

Kelly nodded grimly.

Jonathan Hass stared closely at the potential wound identified by his colleague.

'I can see one end is tapered and one wider, indicating a classic sharp trauma wound, it's deep too. Possibly a stab wound,' he said.

'So it can't be that old then?' Kelly asked.

'It doesn't determine time of death or the age of the corpse. People have been stabbing each other for centuries. Though the colour of the skin indicates the cadaver has been here some time.'

'That's still skin?' Cheryl pointed.

Jonathan nodded. 'Oh yes. It's incredible, isn't it? We won't be able to tell for sure though until we can get inside and do a proper postmortem. If that is a knife wound, then it's likely that the ribs underneath will show signs of trauma. But first I'll recommend a scan for the whole body.'

'So, we've got a homicide,' Kelly said.

Geena nodded.

A light flashed and a camera clicked as a forensic photographer went about their business. Kelly looked around at the building site and saw Dennis watching them, then he turned away and a second figure followed him.

Somebody she recognised.

Then she suddenly knew why the building site was familiar to her.

Chapter 6

'Bradley?' she shouted.

Kelly climbed out of the hole and ripped off her coveralls, shoe covers and mask, thankful for the fresh air.

The two men stopped.

Kelly had a habit of taking boys like Bradley Fellcroft under her wing. She'd always felt instinctively motherly towards down-on-their-luck youths like him who found themselves on the wrong side of the law. Unlike the macho police chiefs in charge of putting them away without giving them a second chance. She felt protective of him somehow and wanted him to stay clean and succeed where countless others had failed. She wanted him to show the law he was worth valuing.

She caught up to him.

'Bradley?'

The young man nodded and fiddled with his hands in his pockets. Kelly knew why she remembered the site; she'd interviewed Bradley Fellcroft here years ago. The site belonged to his father.

'Hi, Kelly, I kind of still work here sometimes.'

He sounded nervous.

'Did you hear about us being down here?' she asked him directly.

'Nah, erm, yeah.'

He was typically noncommittal. Which was understandable given that she'd just discovered a body in his father's building site. Jason Fellcroft was currently absent from any of his sites across London because he was serving a term of seventeen years for murder, in Belmarsh Prison. His property and businesses were held in proxy for his release. The association made Kelly uneasy, especially as they stood ten feet away from a dead body. No copper liked coincidences and she looked from Bradley to the hole in the ground and back again. He was supposed to be estranged from his father and staying away from trouble. A creeping feeling settled under her ribcage.

'I hope you're paying him fairly,' she said to Dennis, who nodded, but she noticed a slight hesitance behind his eyes. Five minutes ago, when she'd witnessed the pair in conversation, they'd looked tense. It struck her that Bradley appeared as the foreman and Dennis the worker, not the other way around. She smiled.

'When did you take Bradley on?' she asked Dennis. She spoke like a concerned parent, but something didn't stack up and she could feel Cheryl's eyes in her back. She'd clocked it too. Bradley was a police informant against his father's associates but here he was, stood in the middle of one of his construction sites.

'Ah, some months back now.'

'Good worker?'

She knew she was making Bradley feel awkward.

'We know each other, don't we, Bradley?' she said.

The young man, who was only just eighteen, looked away and nodded. She watched as Dennis eyed both of them with interest and apprehension.

'How long have you worked here?' she asked Dennis.

He shrugged.

'Are you personally acquainted with the owner of the site?'

'Huh?' Dennis shrugged again.

'She means do you know my dad,' Bradley said.

'Oh, no, before my time. I don't have anything to do with the old fella, I just work here.'

Dennis shuffled off.

'That spooked him,' Kelly said to Bradley.

'Did you do that on purpose?' he asked.

Bradley looked twitchy. His employment for his father's construction company had been Bradley's only lifeline after the old man was sent down to do time. She understood it kept him afloat and out of trouble but only because his father was out of the way. But she wasn't aware he still worked here. Kelly peered across to where Jonathan Hass was standing over the hole.

'Do you know what's in there?' she asked.

'I think I can see.'

'Know anything about it?'

He screwed up his face. 'No.'

Bradley was a reformed serial offender who'd had a terrible start in life. Kids born into families riddled with crime, like his, rarely survived intact and almost always ended up following in their parents' footsteps, but Bradley was different. Kelly had seen in him a fight that told her he wanted to break away from his past. However, he was still vulnerable, and it was by no means certain that he'd make it on the outside going straight. The shadow of his father followed him everywhere.

Kelly had first met him when he'd been picked up for being involved in a robbery at the age of fourteen, four years ago. By sixteen, he'd graduated to money laundering and faced eleven years in prison. The judge took account of his age and gave him a suspended sentence pending rehabilitation classes. But he couldn't help himself and reoffended eighteen months later, allegedly beating a guard half to death at a private bank. Again, his age went in his favour, as did the fact that it couldn't be proven that his accomplice wasn't responsible for the violence and Bradley a mere bystander, which his lawyer successfully argued in juvenile court. This time he was sent to Feltham Young Offenders Institution in Hounslow and Kelly had seen the backs of enough boys heading that way to resign herself to never seeing him again.

But he'd surprised her. Bradley was an anomaly.

With two months to go until his eighteenth birthday, he'd sworn off drugs and alcohol and had committed to staying clean upon release. He expressed a desire to become a youth counsellor lecturing on the evils of knife crime. He also shunned his father.

Or perhaps he hadn't.

She'd believed him to be a reformed character. But now she wasn't so sure.

She felt a slight prickle of foolishness for being so compassionate with these damaged boys who went off the rails. Maybe it was because Bradley reminded her of a friend who'd gone missing in Cumbria when they were teenagers. He'd disappeared after a boozy night by a lake and hadn't been seen since. That had been more than ten years ago but she'd never forgotten him. His smile, his wink when he messed around in class and the softness of the skin on his forearm and how it went honey-coloured in the summer when they swam in the sunshine in Derwent Water. Bradley kicked the dust like a much younger child might have done when challenged.

Whatever the reason might have been, Kelly had taken Bradley under her wing and she took an interest in his rehabilitation. She knew that without help he stood little chance of making it. Reoffending stats for youngsters like him were depressing. The chances of him breaking free from the inherent badness of his father was slim, but she felt as if she must try to save him for some crazy reason she couldn't fathom, and if she did that, she might save others like him too, and more than ever, she felt, young people needed saving.

'Have you visited your dad recently?' she asked him.

He looked away. There'd never been talk of Bradley's mother on the scene. In his notes, it said she'd died shortly after he was born.

The Olympic Park would keep labourers like Bradley in guaranteed work for the next four years at least, should he stay clean. Hundreds of thousands of jobs were being generated by the Olympics in four years' time, and it couldn't have come at a better time for Bradley to keep him out of trouble.

She wanted to hug him but knew she couldn't.

Kelly had never suffered the affliction of maternal desire in her twenty-eight years on the earth, at least not yet, but something about seeing Bradley scratched the itch while at the same time reminding her that parenthood was something that could be kicked down the road for a long time yet. Teenagers were so full of unresolved anguish that they put her off having kids for life, but there was something about Bradley that also pulled at her heart strings. Perhaps it was because he wasn't hers and she had the luxury of stepping back and not getting too close. Or maybe it was because she knew his family history.

Her usual cool demeanour deserted her and she felt as though she'd stumbled upon something that wasn't at all right, but she couldn't put her finger on it. Bradley's hands were firmly in his pockets, which told her he was guilty of something.

'All finished here?' Dennis said, strolling back to them.

'No, you'll need to give a full statement to that officer over there,' Kelly said, pointing to a uniformed officer interviewing the men who'd been on site when they arrived.

'You too, Bradley.'

He nodded.

'Is everything okay?' she asked him when Dennis had disappeared again.

Grey clouds floated above them, blocking out the light, and Kelly noticed Bradley's face grow dark and distant.

'You said I wouldn't have to testify,' he said.

Now his sullen mood made sense to her.

'I said it might not come to that,' she said gently. 'All you have to do is tell the truth.'

There was no way they'd nail Orlando Charles for the crimes he'd committed without witness testimony but Bradley was proving hard to convince. She'd used him as a material witness in the case because he and Orlando worked together on a building site like this one last year, also owned by Jason Fellcroft. Suddenly, this fact seemed important to her.

'You have our full support.'

'You can't protect me,' he retorted.

'Protect you from who?' she asked.

They'd had this conversation before but here, tonight, after his chat with Dennis, he was more fearful than she'd seen him.

'They're going to turn me into a grass. What's the fucking point in any of this?'

He was angry suddenly.

'Has Orlando threatened you?'

He stared at her and shook his head.

'Forget it,' he said. 'I just want to be left alone.'

Kelly noticed him picking the skin around his hands, which had now been pulled out of his pockets, and his leg moved from side to side. His body was showing signs of deep distress and she felt helpless to stop it. Come Monday she'd be off the case and knee-deep in other more serious crimes, but Bradley wouldn't see it that way. If Orlando's case ever went to court, Bradley would make a terrible witness on the stand, but they were desperate. It wasn't lost on her that on the day of Orlando's arrest, she was stood in the middle of one of Jason Fellcroft's building sites, chatting to one of her witnesses who also happened to be his son. A warning alarm sounded in her head.

'I'm not doing it. I can't. He'll kill me.'

'Who? Orlando?'

Bradley shook his head.

'Your father?'

Bradley nodded.

'I'm guessing Dennis over there knows who he really works for?'

'No, he's harmless, he has no idea who my dad is.'

'Really?' Kelly asked, surprised.

'You think he would have told you lot about a body on my dad's building site if he knew who he really was?'

'Good point, but everyone knows who your dad is, Bradley, whether you like it or not, and the foreman being unaware doesn't really convince me,' she said.

Bradley stared at her.

Kelly realised that Dennis the foreman was in grave danger. It also explained why he'd looked so nervous when she and Cheryl had turned up. If he'd lied to them then she needed to discover why. She glanced over at Geena and Jonathan deep in conversation in the hole beside the remains of a mummified suspected homicide victim. Jason Fellcroft could be just as dangerous outside the bars of Belmarsh Prison as he was on the inside. She just didn't yet know how. She mulled over the possibility that the ancient body had anything to do with the convict. If the body turned out to be more recent than the SOCO suspected then it was a very real possibility, and her heart sank for Bradley.

She turned back to him.

'Did Orlando Charles ever work here for your dad?' she asked casually, the question just now popping into her head.

The lie was written all over his face, because he was so bad at it, he didn't even have to reply.

'I need to go,' he said too quickly.

'But, Bradley, you've just got here, I saw you arrive. I know it's a shock, turning up to work to see a body in the ground, but it'd help me a lot if you could answer my question.'

'Yeah, I think he did,' Bradley said finally.

The case against Orlando Charles just got more interesting and now she understood exactly why Bradley didn't want to testify.

Chapter 7

Kelly was quiet on their journey back to Bethnal Green nick.

She indicated to Cheryl that she was feeling guilty over her new job and leaving her colleagues to deal with the Orlando Charles case without her. But really it was Bradley who was on her mind.

It was late.

The sky still shone with orange and purple streaks of promise, but the day was drawing in and Kelly looked forward to the oily shroud of proper night, when she could walk away from Bethnal Green nick for the last time. But she had an unsettled feeling that she might not be walking away from Orlando just yet.

She reflected on how joyous it was to wander along a street like Old Ford Road, gazing across to Victoria Park and to simply watch cyclists, joggers, sunbathers and picnickers living life. People like Orlando didn't know how it felt to do such simple things. Criminals led parallel existences that didn't follow the same rules as everyone else. She hadn't got to know him before slamming on the cuffs, and she didn't want to. He was merely somebody she sought to arrest, but now it felt more personal. Orlando had got under her skin and she felt protective towards Bradley who'd been dragged in because of her.

As they neared the station, the atmosphere of the streets changed. The traffic grew louder, the demeanour of people on the thoroughfares grew more serious and the air seemed thicker. It was just one reason she'd chosen to live as far away from her patch as she could afford. Bow wasn't terribly upmarket, but it attracted a different clientele, or had done since the wharf had been developed in the late nineties. It was pleasant, busy, up and coming, or so they said. To her, more importantly it was anonymous and safe. The flats were full of young professionals like her, and the bars buzzed with abandon and hope.

A couple of teenage girls, dressed in tiny dresses and gossiping together, crossed Cambridge Heath Road, past the imposing Victorian building of the Museum of Childhood, and veered across the pavement right into Kelly's path. Cheryl stood alert immediately and eyed Kelly's crossover bag. The girls could be pickpockets. Their immediate instinct was to treat them as thieves, but they were simply two mindless girls, unaware of their surroundings and oblivious to the dangers all around them. Kelly's bag was untouched.

'Right, let's do this,' Cheryl said as they walked into the nick.

The station was cool, and Kelly poked her head around DCI Wallis's door.

'Sir,' she said.

'Kelly, can I have a word?'

She went into his office. The guy was a paperholic – a workaholic who never left his desk according to his two senior DSs. Either that or he didn't rate his homelife, one of the two.

'The CPS has rejected Bradley Fellcroft's testimony,' he told her. Wallis never dressed anything up.

'What? I've only just convinced him to give us a statement.'

It was a small lie but DCI Wallis didn't need to know that just yet.

'I know what you sacrificed for it. You worked your way into that lad's life and did a good job. Sometimes we have to accept a higher judgement.'

'Higher judgement? What does that mean?'

She was enraged. She reckoned the DCI needed to get out on the streets more. All his books made him philosophical, which was a euphemism for useless in Kelly's book.

'Apparently, he's already a protected witness for a case in town. An east major investigation team use him and won't hand him over, for his own protection.'

Kelly's blood boiled. Not only had she been kept in the dark by her own people, but she was losing Bradley as a witness. She felt powerless.

'Which MIT? Don't make me a mushroom on this, sir!'

He shrugged. Junior detectives often felt kept in the dark and fed on shit, like mushrooms, but Wallis simply grimaced at her and signalled an end to the conversation.

'The CPS won't touch his case, sir, we'll lose it.'

'Find yourself another witness,' he said and closed a file on his desk. Wallis liked to emphasise himself physically and she felt dismissed and ignored.

She stared at him but it made no difference to his apathy, so she left the room, heading back to her office.

'That went well?' Cheryl quipped.

Kelly sat down heavily on a swivel chair that twirled around with her in it, and she kicked a floor fan over, spilling a vase of flowers – which were already dead – onto a pile of paperwork. They'd been a gift from the mother of a teenager they'd saved from a drug den three weeks ago. Their wilted heads, now stuck to somebody else's file, reminded Kelly of how small she was in the huge cog of the Met machine.

To add insult to injury, she now had to face Orlando Charles and somehow get him to confess to a string of crimes they had little evidence on that could stand up to a clever defence lawyer. They had flimsy forensics, tenuous alibis which couldn't be proven one way or another and DCI Wallis had already warned her that the case against him was on a knife's edge, which is why they needed Bradley.

Who they'd just lost.

It looked like their case against Orlando Charles would become just another statistic of Met failure to get to grips with capital crime; a war Boris Johnson was determined to turn around.

'Good luck,' she whispered under her breath.

The body at the building site played on her mind.

She'd never made the connection before.

What did Jason Fellcroft have to do with Orlando Charles? She couldn't help feeling that Harry Houdini was about to evade capture again, and it was her fault. She was leaving her colleagues with nothing.

'Ready?' Cheryl jolted her.

Kelly sat back on the chair, which was now under control, and she wheeled herself to her own desk, and tapped her foot on the computer wires screwed up into a ball of dust gathering detritus underneath it.

'Bradley told me tonight that Dennis Chapman made a big mistake reporting Pinocchio's body. If he hadn't, we'd never know about it. Without that one mistake, police and forensics wouldn't be crawling all over one of Jason Fellcroft's building sites.'

Cheryl considered what she'd said.

Kelly experienced a sudden grip of nerves as she realised her theories and concerns would be aired in front of a new team come Monday morning. Perhaps they'd be disinterested in her input? Maybe she wasn't up to it? Not everyone had Cheryl's patience and willingness to test out supposition. She'd be on her own. She chewed her fingernail and Cheryl watched her.

'I wonder if Jason Fellcroft knows yet,' Cheryl said finally.

News travelled quickly from the outside world to those held at Her Majesty's pleasure. Convicts like Fellcroft were well informed. That was one conversation they'd like to hear.

The information sat at the back of Kelly's mind with other snippets of dialogue she stored there. It had been her father who told her that no information is ever wasted and taught her how to create a filing system in her head that selected fragments to pull out when the time was right. It meant she possessed an almost photographic memory, like a cardex system, of thousands of pieces of information, though jumbled. When they were needed, they jumped to the front of her mind, and Kelly was hoping that the same would be true of this case. All they needed was one undeniable forensic link. DNA profiling was continually developing, and the National DNA Database (NDNAD) was growing year on year, with more crime scene profiles linked to individuals on the NDNAD than ever before. But the European Convention on Human Rights was a constant thorn in their side. They had to be mindful of an individual's rights to protect their biological products before conviction, and Orlando hadn't even been charged yet, and it was unlikely he ever would be.

They had no legal right to take either his fingerprints or his DNA. Besides, DNA results took an age. And Orlando terrified witnesses. Or somebody did on his behalf.

Which was why she was so worried about Bradley.

Her brow furrowed. Something didn't fit, and her initial passion for starting work on a murder squad which had been building up for months since her final interview with DCI Leia Lord at MIT east now dissipated as she found herself pining to remain here until the Pinocchio case was solved.

'You're sulking,' Cheryl observed.

Pete walked into the office and she and Cheryl high fived him.

'Still here, Kell?' he said.

'I know, I volunteered for the Orlando gig, lucky me,' she said. Despite her conversation with the DCI, the man in their cells still needed to be interviewed before they inevitably let him go.

'Would a doughnut help?' Pete asked.

Kelly grinned.

'That would be magnificent for my mood.'

'Happy to oblige.'

He held a bag open and she took out a fat jam doughnut and the sugar fell onto the floor.

'Don't worry, you'll be sat in a Ford Mondeo this time next week, Queen of Fucking Everything,' Pete teased her. 'You won't even look back.'

Kelly laughed as she opened their file on Orlando Charles with her free hand and it spilled out across her desk, on top of other bits of paperwork in front of the computer console which took up the space that once would have been taken up with paperwork. They'd been told that one day everything would be digital and paperwork would be obsolete, but to Kelly she couldn't see how the mountains of paper could ever be stored inside a metal box. And nothing replaced instinct; there was no computer program for that. Though she'd heard the murder squads rated HOLMES, the state-of-the-art software which helped them collate evidence, and she respected the contribution of computers, real police work would never be replaced. Any government that cut the numbers of real human beings working cases in the future would be doomed, she thought.

She sighed as she tidied up the mess and found the documents she sought. There was nothing she could see on Bradley, nothing obvious anyway.

She finished her sweet treat and licked her fingers, then signalled to Cheryl that she was ready.

They headed downstairs, into the bowels of the nick, where Orlando Charles waited for them. Moving the Bethnal Green CID to a more modern site round the corner would be beneficial, she admitted. Their current building had bags of history and charm, but it lacked air conditioning and space. It was barely possible for Kelly and Cheryl to walk side by side comfortably as they approached the interview room.

She knocked and they went in.

Orlando sat back in his chair and looked as though he was waiting for a pal in the Bethnal Green Arms on a Friday night. He had a vacant stare, one that indicated he was either unwilling or unable to calculate the gravity of his situation. It was as if he knew about her conversation with Wallis. He was in his mid-forties, and should have a stable career, a wife and a couple of kids by now, instead of running away from coppers and wasting their time. Instead, he was a nomad who moved fast and loose and they'd yet to trace his roots.

'Orlando, hello again,' Kelly said.

She sat down and crossed her legs, pushing slightly back from the table. Cheryl fiddled with cassette tapes and switched the recording equipment on, and they got the pleasantries over with. In the small space, Orlando took up more room than was necessary and he used his size to try to intimidate them. He wasn't muscular but he was tall.

His body was surprisingly big and imposing, and although he dominated all available space in the tiny room, it was his eyes that unsettled Kelly. They looked as though they were portals to a different time; a warning not to get too close. He peered up at her through his long fringe, which covered much of his face. Kelly tried not to be judgemental, but Orlando Charles *looked* like a criminal. He *smelled* like a criminal. She'd spent years surrounded by men like him and had interviewed plenty of them too. He kept his hands buried in his sleeves and she noticed scars on his hands as well as a new wound. He followed her eyes.

Perhaps the arrest had been a bit rough. He had hit the ground like a sack of potatoes, as her northern family might say, and she couldn't help smiling at the recollection.

Like all coppers, she knew the golden rules of interview techniques backwards, but applying them was a different matter entirely when faced with a scrotum sac like the one sat in front of her now. But her job wasn't to respect him, it was to *pretend* to respect him. Her empathy hat was firmly on, and she set her voice to low and sympathetic, wishing that she was sat in Victoria Park with a beer. Better still, that she was an American cop with a gun. She knew that Cheryl bristled against him in the same way. Something about him told them he was dangerous. Orlando Charles was a wrong'un. Plain and simple, but that wasn't enough to lock him up.

'Let's start at the beginning,' she said.

She opened her files and read out dates and addresses of robberies. Each time he shook his head, denying any knowledge of the crimes. She was getting nowhere.

'And you've got witnesses willing to go on record saying I was there?' he asked her. His voice took Kelly by surprise. She'd expected a gravelly, mature menace, but instead it was soft, balanced and undeniably humble.

But it was confident too. Patronising almost.

She closed the files loudly. She sighed.

'How well do you know Jason Fellcroft?' she asked.

She saw his eye twitch and he adjusted the position of his body. Cheryl didn't move.

Kelly knew she'd hit a nerve.

'You worked on the Stratford Junction building site, yes? You know his son, right? Bradley? Can you tell me about your work there?'

'Correct. I worked for him. He's a good dad.'

It was an odd statement to make and took Kelly by surprise. She saw a flicker of humanity inside Orlando Charles that she hadn't seen before.

'And do you think Bradley thinks he's a good dad?'

'I wouldn't know, but I can tell you that having a father who is strong and fair, but who you don't agree with, is better than never having one.'

He held her stare, but he looked away first. He spoke with a certain morality that surprised her.

'Let me show you a map,' Kelly said. She went into her bag and pulled out a tube map, alongside an A–Z of London. She turned to the correct page for Stratford and showed him the tube he'd catch to work from his bedsit in London Bridge, as well as the changes he'd make, and the route he'd take to the site.

'You worked there labouring, Orlando. It's an indisputable fact. If you're going to argue with me about facts, then we have a problem, because that throws into doubt everything we discuss under caution.'

'I want a lawyer.'

She stood up.

'Sure,' she said. 'You will have been given notice that Bradley Fellcroft is a witness for the prosecution,' she said as she gathered her things, including the huge file on him.

'I was under the impression he'd been dropped.'

She stopped what she was doing and stared at him.

His swagger had returned.

She'd only just discussed Bradley's use to them as a witness with DCI Wallis. There was no way in hell that Orlando could know that Bradley had been dropped so quickly unless he had a contact on the inside.

'Let me ask you again, what is your relationship to Jason Fellcroft?'

She watched as he looked up at her slowly and brushed the fringe out of his eyes. She didn't feel as though she was facing a criminal on the back foot, somebody who'd been caught robbing a few businesses and knocking out the odd owner who shouldn't have disturbed him. To CID this sort of criminal was their bread and butter, but Orlando was acting as though she was beneath him. The paradox caught her off guard. He was good at what he did, and he was careful. He chose businesses without CCTV or any kind of security staff.

She felt as though she was looking into the face of somebody who had the upper hand and wasn't a criminal at all. She suddenly felt on the back foot. Immature, unprepared and in the dark. She'd never hated the term mushroom so much as she did right now.

A grin began to spread across Orlando's face, and it was unexpected.

'I'll have a lawyer called for representation,' she said.

She went for the door and Cheryl stood up.

With her back to him, she felt a sudden pull of maternal ferocity towards the young man who'd won her over. She felt a fool. Bradley was in deep but she didn't know how. Yet.

An unsettled sensation colonised her body, warning her to pull away from the lad she'd become so attached to. This wasn't her fight…

Then she realised what Orlando was getting at. It had been staring her in the face all along. Bradley was compromised as a material witness because of his family, despite swearing he had nothing to do with his convicted father, he was still controlled by him from within prison. Orlando was letting her know that Bradley would never give them what they wanted because his dad had something on him that he hadn't let on to Kelly. And for some reason unknown to her Jason Fellcroft was protecting Orlando Charles.

They were screwed, and Orlando knew it. He'd just told her everything she needed to know about how well Orlando Charles knew Jason Fellcroft, but she couldn't prove any of it.

He grinned again when she stole a glance over her shoulder and he saw her face change.

She felt claustrophobic suddenly and wanted to get out in the open to breathe. With the tenuous forensics and lack of witnesses, they could perhaps tie him to two, maybe three crimes, but it was nothing compared to the power of the whole, and he'd walk away with six months suspended.

And they'd never get the Jason Fellcroft connection, which was what this was all about.

Her face must have shown her momentary realisation because Orlando's smile broadened and it spread all over his smirking face, and she wanted to punch it.

But the worst part was that it was she who'd put Bradley in danger by pushing for him to be a witness when he didn't want to be, and now she understood that the reasons behind his behaviour were a mystery to her, but not to this man sat in front of her.

Chapter 8

The Porter & Grape pub was a five-minute walk from Angel tube station. The area exuded chilled London cool with its eclectic mix of second-hand boutiques, specialist interest markets and upper-crust eateries.

It wasn't just the fact that the pub boasted Kelly's own surname that made it attractive, it was a genuinely decent night out and frequented by coppers from all departments of the Met.

Kelly felt safe there.

It had been an exhausting day and by the time they'd knocked off shift, the sky was dark and London's underbelly emerged from the shadows. The HAT still hadn't contacted her about the body in the pit who they'd christened Pinocchio until they got a solid ID. But that wasn't guaranteed. Some bodies remained unidentified for years in cold files stored in CIDs across the whole of London. For now, though, and for the rest of the evening they had left, she and Cheryl agreed not to discuss the case. Or Orlando Charles. The bar was packed when they entered and they waved to colleagues they recognised. Kelly's social life since moving to London had been confined mainly to police colleagues because of the nature of her job. She struggled to trust people. Her social network consisted of people she met at odd hours in labs, mortuaries and hospitals. Making friends outside of work was almost impossible due to her working hours and the stuff that filled her head. She wasn't adept at discussing the weather, the news or the state of the global economy. She didn't follow sport, and she had no hobbies, apart from walking in the Lake District when she visited home. With her peers she could open up about the cases that bothered her and swap ideas. She had two close friends. One was Cheryl and the other was her flatmate, Molly, a SOCO who she spotted waiting for them at the bar. They squeezed past a group of people at the bar and hugged. Molly was also in her twenties and single and blessed with an inquiring mind and an independent spirit.

Their resolve to not talk shop didn't last long and they found themselves going over the details with Molly, who was eager to find out about Pinocchio and the plastic nose. News travelled fast. They took their drinks to a corner with a free table and pushed through a group of men standing near the DJ.

Kelly knew they were young coppers out of uniform. She could tell by the way they stood, the way they held their pint glasses and the honesty behind their eyes. They let the women through with good grace and didn't attempt to grab hold of them or create a scene. She smiled at one who caught her eye, and his stare followed her body as the people sitting at a booth decided to leave. Kelly, Molly and Cheryl headed for it and the coppers noticed and held back, letting the women take the seats. It was chivalrous and comforting after a day dealing with criminally deviant minds. Being treated with respect wasn't something she was used to in her line of work.

The three women nestled together inside the booth and Cheryl brought Molly up to speed on the details of the body in the pit.

'Pinocchio?' Molly asked.

'There was a wooden toy next to the body,' Kelly said.

'Ah,' Molly said, keeping up. 'Weird.'

Molly listened intently as Cheryl filled her in on the items pulled out of the pit by the SOCO. They also told her about Jonathan Hass and how he obviously fancied Kelly.

Kelly covered her face and shook her head.

'He looked half dead himself,' she said.

'Did he smell of corpses?' Molly asked wickedly.

They'd all agreed that dating anybody attached to a mortuary or any kind of institutionalised workers who encountered dead bodies, ancient or modern, were out of the question. It was something about their scent. When you came across death in work, often it lingered, especially on those who investigated them. The three of them saw enough destruction themselves without inviting it in a partner as well. However, thanks to their working hours and lifestyles revolving around violence, they often ended up dating fellow coppers. Molly had it the worst. She found it difficult to explain to potential lovers what she did for a living and they made jobs up for her. Teaching assistant, vet, flower arranger...

Anything benign. When potential lovers discovered her true calling, that she picked up pieces of bodies and photographed blood spatter, they were often put off, so she kept it to herself. Unless the suitor was a weirdo and then they told him Molly was an embalmer.

'Did joyful Geena come up with anything?' Molly asked.

Competition between SOCOs was keen.

'Not much,' Kelly said honestly. It wasn't a SOCO's job to solve crime. However, Molly was always looking at crime scenes with one eye on the future investigation. Her brain worked like Kelly's. They were deeply fascinated by the story behind each scene and what had led to it. It was why they made such great flatmates.

'Tell me about it,' Molly said, sipping her cocktail.

Kelly delivered what she had and Molly listened intently, stopping her to ask questions and then allowing Kelly to carry on.

They'd lived together in a housing association flat overlooking Bow Wharf for four years. Theirs was an easy friendship and Kelly considered herself lucky to have found someone so similar to herself to share accommodation with. They worried about the same things and shared similar habits. They were both simple cooks and each burdened food shopping and cursory cleaning in equal measure. They also understood each other's routines and odd time keeping. Neither was put out if the other crept in at weird o'clock, with or without a man. Neither judged. Cheryl completed the wheel and would move in with them if they had a third bedroom, which they did not.

Molly worked for Hackney area mainly, so she was inundated with gang stabbings, and her knowledge of blood spatter was spectacular. She also liaised with the murder squads all over east London, one of which Kelly was about to join, and it was partly Molly's stories of her long days spent at gruesome crime scenes that had spurred her on to apply. Together, the three of them attempted to solve cases before the murder squad did, and often their theories were correct, but they never got any credit for them. Murder squads were almost untouchable, like pods of superhuman beings, righteous and formidable, a breed of their own. They were fawned over and looked up to. But now Kelly was going to be one of them and her biggest fear was that it would change her friendship with these two women.

'So, whose case is it? CID or murder squad?' Molly asked.

Cheryl shrugged. 'I guess we wait until it's dated. There's no point opening up a murder investigation for a body that's two hundred years old.'

'Have you heard of Jonathan Hass, then?' Kelly asked.

Molly shook her head.

'The dead anthropologist?'

Kelly nodded.

'No sex yet then?' Molly asked.

Cheryl shook her head.

'I assumed it was a man when you called it Pinocchio,' she added.

Kelly told Molly some of the grimmer details knowing that Molly would want to hear them.

'Definitely a homicide then,' Molly assessed after Kelly told her about the wounds on the corpse.

The DJ played Exceeder's 'Perfect', and Cheryl slipped out of the booth and began to dance. Her compact frame made her moves more purposeful and she threw her arms up in the air and wiggled her hips from side to side. Molly joined her and Kelly watched the pub come alive as the dancefloor filled. The London club scene was not only late, hot and crowded, it also threw vibes of deviance and danger their way that off-duty coppers didn't like. Pubs like this one with a dancefloor and willing punters who danced anywhere, including in the beer garden in summer, thrived off a slightly older crowd who preferred to sit down and sip cocktails in between banging classics. Kelly watched her two best friends and wished she could shake off the nerves and dance like them, but her thoughts turned unhelpfully to her father as she imagined him sitting chewing cases over with old men down at the old copper's club on a Friday night, just like this, but in Pooley Bridge, at the eastern tip of Ullswater.

Suddenly she felt a million miles away from her native land, and the isolation of London made her even more unwilling to throw off her inhibitions and dance with her friends. The dancefloor filled to bursting and she lost sight of them.

A pang of nostalgia gripped her and a part of her pined for the hills and lakes of Cumbria. The Lake District seemed a world away from London, and in some ways it really was. Her childhood home was quiet and without ambient noise from incessant traffic and emergency vehicles screaming through the night. It was also dark, being without light from a thousand offices still burning through the small hours. She'd grown used to the nighttime sounds of Bethnal Green in the distance, with sirens and screams coddling her until morning came. A sudden flashback of the peak of a mountain stilled her racing heart and she smiled into her cocktail.

She missed them.

Growing up in Cumbria had become a tug of war in the end. Loving the endless beauty but yearning for something else created a battle inside her. Her parents and her sister were happy to live their days out in the tiny town where she grew up, but for Kelly, a voice inside her head had always told her she needed more.

She'd felt different to the other kids and assumed it was because her dad was a copper. Any talk of lawbreaking around her always turned to whispers and she was singled out. They all thought she'd turn them in. It wasn't true. She'd had no interest in telling on people, unless they hurt someone.

John Porter had a fierce reputation for taking no crap, and back in the 80s, he was a minor celeb in the area. Then it had been a man's world, the policing game, and Kelly had always gazed in wonder at his uniform, with its shiny buttons and confusing symbols, and dreamt of wearing it one day. John Porter told her that real policing was behind the uniform and detectives were just nominal actors, taking the credit for the hard work of those who walked the streets. He was traditional and set in his ways and not for turning, though she'd tried. It was only now she was in London and hundreds of miles away from him that she'd softened her view of his hard exterior. He had a quick fiery temper and spoke to her mother too harshly, but deep down she believed he was a good man, if old fashioned.

She had fond memories of being a little girl and walking behind his huge stride trying to keep up, when he took her fishing around one of the smaller lakes, after a long hike carrying all the equipment. They'd eat warm and wilted sandwiches and wash them down with lemonade from a real glass bottle. He'd point out features of geography and pass on his knowledge of flora and fauna.

Sometimes when she walked around the streets of Bethnal Green, or caught a tube or travelled in a squad car with blues raging, she'd think about those times of peace and quiet and wonder why she craved such noise and chaos when she was growing up. She examined herself as if she was broken, seeking answers that never came. Why hadn't she been satisfied with the glorious stillness and lesser pace of Cumbria?

She knew it was something to do with proving John Porter wrong. Showing him that she had what it took to become a detective in the Met, and do what he did but ten times more, louder and faster.

Her heart missed the tops of mountains and the bottoms of lakes. Both were equally able to soothe her restless nature. But in London they were nowhere to be found, and that was never going to change.

She sighed when she remembered an invite to attend her parents' wedding anniversary party next weekend and the thought of it immediately dispelled all the sentimentality related to her childhood home and she thought of reasons and excuses why she couldn't go.

Molly and Cheryl were jumping up and down now and holding on to one another.

The song changed and she saw her friends heading back in her direction.

Cheryl put her arm around Kelly's shoulders and Kelly saw that she was a little inebriated. For such a solid unit, Cheryl surprisingly couldn't handle her drink and when she became intoxicated, she became emotional.

'I'm gonna miss you,' she said, squeezing Kelly's shoulder.

'I'm gonna miss you too, and our beautiful office, and the paperwork, and the fire hazard which is the fridge in summer.'

'Don't leave us!' Cheryl shouted, feigning tragedy.

The three women laughed.

'It's all right for you, you'll get to see each other even more, as if living together isn't bloody enough,' Cheryl added.

Molly grinned. They were a good team.

The Shapeshifters blasted out of the music system and Cheryl boogied backwards, twisting her hands around each other, as if she was in some kind of eighties throwback disco. Molly and Kelly laughed at their friend and joined in.

As the beat took a hold of Kelly's body, she closed her eyes and allowed her mind to close off from her job for the moment. But it refused. As she swayed to the beat, she knew that somewhere, across the capital, in an alleyway behind a bar just like this perhaps, her first murder arrest was waiting to happen. It was a fantasy that kept her going. They didn't know it yet, because they hadn't done the deed, but the person who'd make her name was out there, perhaps unable to sleep, planning the crime that would get them nicked.

Chapter 9

Orlando Charles was released from police custody without charge on Saturday morning. They simply had nothing on him that would convince the CPS to lengthen his stay.

Kelly couldn't bring herself to attend Bethnal Green nick to look into his eyes as his gear was given back to him and he was allowed to walk out of the door without looking back.

Instead, she lay on the grass on a patch of hot, brown, sunburnt earth in the middle of Victoria Park and stretched her arms underneath her head, resting it on them, closing her eyes away from the piercing sun. It shone down on her as if asking her where it had all gone wrong.

'It's only one case,' Cheryl said, propped up on an elbow.

'She's right,' Molly chipped in.

They'd brought a picnic with them and Cheryl had bought a bottle of Lindeman's Rosé to cheer Kelly up.

'Let it go. It's just work. Scumbags walk away from what they deserve all the time,' Cheryl told her.

Kelly knew that her friends were right. She sat up and held her glass out for a refill.

'It's warm,' Molly said, indicating the almost empty bottle.

'I'll go and get another, I need to stretch my legs,' Kelly said, rolling over to get up. Grass stuck to her bare legs. Her skin felt hot and it tingled. London was shrouded in a blanket of heat and it made even the smallest tasks arduous.

There was a corner shop just outside the park gate. She slipped on her sandals reluctantly and headed to the exit, past lovers sharing jokes and families chasing dogs and children. Kids squirted water guns and old people sat on benches sharing memories. It was times like this that Kelly wondered what her job was needed for. London glowed with happiness and abandon. No one would ever guess, as a visitor in summertime, that people were evil to each other behind closed doors.

It was almost thirty degrees and even as far north as Edinburgh, the heatwave covered the country in surprise.

Cops were trained to expect trouble when communities enjoyed themselves. It was like a national celebration. The sunshine was the same as a win at the World Cup or a Royal wedding.

People took it too far.

She didn't envy those uniforms on duty tonight, who'd have to deal with the drunks and the inevitable violence as a result.

She passed an ice cream van and studied the people in the queue. She listened to their conversations as she squeezed past. A sunburnt kid whined. A teenager whizzed past on a bike, too close to a dog, which barked savagely. A stressed father with a pushchair dropped three ice creams and swore. Misery was so close beneath the surface of wonder. It made her cynical, some would say. To Kelly, she was simply observant and cautious. She'd already shared one bottle of wine with her friends but they'd eaten a picnic too. They'd taken a bag load of Tesco dips, chips, bread and cold deli goods with them and she didn't feel tipsy at all. They'd taken their time.

She made her way to the shop and waited in the queue. It was a little cooler inside and she stood in front of an open cooler selecting her wine. It felt like an icy caress on her skin, and she felt her heart rate lower a little. As she closed the door, she took the bottle to the counter and moved aside for a man who headed her way.

She stood to one side and froze, praying he wouldn't recognise her in a summer dress.

The tall man wasn't interested in her and he concentrated on the selection of sweets on the shelves opposite the booze.

He stood so still that Kelly stole a glance in his direction, confident enough he wasn't paying her any attention. She held the bottle against her skin and felt its chill. The man behind the counter broke her trance by shaking out a plastic bag and it sounded like gravel being thrown onto glass. She jumped and the man turned her way, but not before she turned her head towards the counter. She walked towards the vendor and placed the bottle on the till top. The whole time she fumbled with her purse to find the exact money, and the vendor made polite small talk, she could feel his eyes burning into her back. He wore a hoody and a gilet, as well as heavy jeans. No wonder he was so pale...

She thanked the man behind the till and risked a last glance at the man, who caught her eye this time.

In the half second it took for his eyes to meet hers, she saw that his basket was full of sweets and several small gimmicky toys. Kelly looked away and took the plastic bag with her wine, and it clunked against a shelf. She didn't think he had kids…

Then the man smiled, and she knew that she'd been rumbled.

But it wasn't the hawkishness behind Orlando Charles's grin, or the fact that he took in her body underneath her scanty summer clothes, and he did it so deliciously slowly. It was more that he'd invaded her personal space. He was inside her world on a Saturday – her day off – and close to her home and where she laughed with friends. It made her skin feel sticky and she turned to leave.

The door closed behind her and she ran across the road, not looking for cars, and one screeched to a halt in front of her.

'Jesus, love!' a man hollered from behind the wheel. It was a convertible, and he wore very little, baring his chest for all to see. Suddenly all the nakedness assaulted her senses and she longed to see no more flesh. She apologised and got to the other side intact. She peered back to the shop in time to see Orlando leave and he looked around as if searching for where she'd gone.

He caught her eye once again and then waved.

Angered, she raised her middle finger to him from behind the cold bottle and even though he couldn't see it made her feel better. She was incensed that he was allowed to ruin her peace in such a shameless manner. The guy was not only a burglar, but he was also a fucking weirdo and that never ended well. It was all very well saying *each to their own*, but who wore heavy layers of clothing during a heatwave? It just didn't sit well with her. It said everything about him. He was always hiding.

'Guess who I just bumped into?' she asked the girls when she returned to their sunbathing patch. Cheryl had turned over and Molly was smoking a cigarette.

'Give me some,' said Kelly.

Molly handed her the smoke and Kelly took a few puffs, inhaling deeply.

'Who?'

'Orlando fucking Charles. Brazen as you like. He must have just got out of the nick and he was buying sweets!'

Cheryl smirked. 'Not sweets! How dare he? On a Saturday?'

'Oh bollocks,' Kelly said. She sat down heavily. She'd allowed him to get under her skin.

'He creeped me out, he had plastic toys in his basket, who does that? And he must have had three jumpers on,' she added.

'Do you want your own cigarette?' Molly asked.

'No, I don't smoke,' Kelly replied.

''Course you don't,' Molly said, handing her one.

Kelly took it and allowed Molly to light it for her. She stared across the park in the direction of the shop. She saw no sign of him. He hadn't followed her, or at least she couldn't spot him if he had. Good robbers could be masters of subtlety and surprise. They were excellent hunters. Silent and invisible. He might be watching them now. It made her feel exposed.

'I see people we've let go all the time, so do you, what makes this one different?' Cheryl asked her. 'Are you going to open that bottle or just cuddle it?' she added.

Kelly passed it to Molly to open and she shared it around their plastic glasses.

Kelly turned to lie on her side and sipped wine and blew smoke but she couldn't help feeling that across the park, from a concealed hiding spot, Orlando Charles was watching her. Always watching. But for what, she had no idea.

Chapter 10

Kelly left her flat early on Monday morning and strode along Bethnal Green Road towards the tube, with her chest a little forward and her shoulders back. This was it. Her first day on a murder squad. Underground, the train swayed gently from side to side and she allowed her body to rock with it, grasping the bar for support, going over and over what she might say to DCI Leia Lord, her new boss. Formalities and scenarios flew through her head as she contemplated greeting her new team with a mixture of confidence and professionalism. In private conversations – never to her face – the DCI was known as *Princess Leia* and Kelly had yet to work out if it was because she was precious, stunningly beautiful or just hellishly brave, or all three. To Kelly, the princess was the single most important character in the whole Star Wars movie franchise. Kelly had watched the original on VHS video with her dad in the late eighties when she'd been around seven years old. People thought Luke or Han Solo were the heroes of the film, but they were told what to do by the only person with the bigger picture: Leia. The Force had already been harnessed by her. The evil of her enemies had already been revealed by her. She already had a plan. She was respected by Yoda, Obi Wan and ultimately her brother before any of the others caught on what it was they were fighting for. She was the unifying glue of the whole universe, and the significance wasn't lost on Kelly. She'd even once owned a doll of Leia – her hero – which was now probably thrown into the back of a cupboard somewhere or given away. Perhaps Kelly would give it to her own daughter one day and tell her about how important she was.

A smile danced on her mouth as she recalled the heroes she was leaving behind. Pete's gassy flatulence and Cheryl's resulting howls of disgust as she desperately opened windows. Longstride's filthy jokes. But she forced them away as she tried to keep her nerves under control.

Would her new team have a sense of humour at all? Would they be so serious that murder consumed them?

Would they be stony-faced and sober?

She recalled her first meeting with DCI Leia Lord, which had been deadly serious. Kelly had struggled to discern much personality behind the armour but that didn't mean there was none. She must be patient. She'd be the new kid on the block and must give it time. It was an opportunity to learn and grow. Lord was a role model. A female officer rising to DCI in her forties wasn't an easy feat and Kelly reminded herself that it was exactly where she wanted to be at that age. Already she was looking to DCI Lord as her mentor.

Kelly wore dark-grey tailored trousers and a matching jacket, but the lack of air on the underground forced her to abandon at least half of the ensemble as she reached street level. She carried the jacket over her arm and by the time she walked into her new office building in Barking, she felt as though she must look a mess. Her hair was stuck to her scalp and she could feel sweat sticking to her body and running down her back. A woman with a lanyard took pity on her and took her to the lift and explained which floor she was on. Once upstairs, she was whisked to another office by another junior clerk and she desperately tried to memorise all the names she heard being introduced. The place was huge and detectives sat in front of upgraded computers that put theirs at CID to shame. A few heads popped up and nodded at her but mostly they stayed glued to their screens. The atmosphere was terribly solemn and she was reminded where she was. This was the business of death.

There were no let-ups.

Only homicide was discussed here.

Then she spotted a brief in session and saw that DCI Leia Lord was leading it.

Kelly was horrified. Was she late? Her heart sank. She approached the door and was waved in by the DCI, who halted the briefing as she introduced the newbie to forty-odd officers. Kelly smiled and willed herself not to blush.

'Good timing, Porter, we've got a fresh body at a comprehensive school in Leyton. You're on. This is your partner, DI Seb Crook. SOCO's already there. Forensics on their way. It's a messy one.'

Kelly felt forty pairs of eyes on her and realised Leia Lord was not waiting for a response. DI Seb Crook waited for her at the door and held it open. As they left, a mobile phone rang and it was set to a personalised ringtone, which jolted Kelly from her mortification. She recognised it. It was the jingle they used on ice cream vans back home. The ragtime hit, 'The Entertainer'. No one seemed fazed by it but then she saw why. The phone belonged to the DCI. It made Kelly smile. Her mother used to play it. Perhaps it was a sign, though Kelly didn't believe in portents, but even so, it was a welcome one.

Things around here weren't too stuffy after all.

And that was that. Her first day had started. Everything she'd expected of it had been wrong. And she had been given a partner. A senior partner. A detective called Seb Crook. She wondered if it was too early to make a joke about his surname and when she saw him look at his watch she reckoned it was.

'Thank you,' she murmured as she walked past the open door and out of the briefing room. She'd spent all weekend – when she wasn't thinking about Orlando Charles – rehearsing her lines for Leia Lord. She detected a small smirk on Seb's face and realised she must look like a rabbit in headlights.

'Ready?' he asked.

'Can I freshen up?' she asked.

He nodded and pointed to a corner of the vast open-plan office. 'Ladies' that way,' he told her and managed to smile which made his face much warmer.

'I'll take you past your desk so you can dump your things,' he added.

She realised this was him being helpful. The man was busy and keen to get going. She was slowing him down. They had a dead body. A real dead body. *Her* dead body.

She grabbed her water and ID from her bag, looked at her deodorant longingly but decided against it and rushed to the toilet, closing the door swiftly behind her. She went to the sink and ran some cold water, dousing her face with it, careful not to ruin her makeup she'd taken time over it this morning to make a good impression. She smelled her armpits and was satisfied that they were fresh enough, then she wet a paper towel and wiped them for good luck. She took a few deep breaths and reset her mind, then she left the room and rejoined DI Seb Crook who'd waited for her patiently.

He was a good-looking man with piercing blue eyes. He looked like how she imagined murder squad detectives – or at least how she hoped they looked: kind and determined. Soft demeanours hiding steely interiors.

Within five minutes of arriving at her new place of work, she was heading for the door and racking her brain for a checklist of procedures to prepare her for her first murder scene as the lead detective with a real partner.

As they emerged from the lift and she nodded to the woman who'd greeted her only minutes ago, she concealed a smile which had sprung from her toes and caressed her with a warmth that had nothing to do with the mercury showing twenty-five degrees already at not even eight o'clock in the morning. It was all from inside her. Thoughts of Bethnal Green nick, what she was leaving behind, as well as Orlando Charles, faded into the background and she followed DI Crook to his Ford Mondeo. Her heart raced as he opened the door. But then he slammed it again after retrieving a satchel from the passenger seat.

'Let's grab the tube,' he said.

Chapter 11

The school was on the other side of Hackney Marshes and a five-minute walk from the tube station. The body had been discovered by the caretaker doing a sweep of one of the buildings after hearing an unusual noise. The man, in his sixties, was being comforted by specialist officers. Thankfully it was the summer holidays and so the school was deserted. No children had been there to stumble on the scene.

The victim was a member of staff.

'Suspected homicide,' Seb told Kelly as they walked through the police cordon. She recognised a few journalists from the Porter & Grape who routinely hung out with the murder squads and shared information.

Hearing the word 'homicide' out loud made her stomach lurch a little but she was ready to face it. The adrenaline was from excitement, not dread. Whatever they found, they must assess the scene for themselves before jumping to any conclusions, but initial responders and ambulance staff had confirmed life extinct and passed on the message that the death was obviously unnatural.

Kelly braced herself.

She switched into detective mode as soon as they entered the school grounds. The cordon was set up as much to prevent concerned and nosy parents and residents getting on site as well as to secure the area for evidence gathering. The headmaster had been informed and the scene sealed. The body lay in the drama studio.

She followed Seb Crook's lead but was itching to take over. Questions burst out of her head and she almost fell over with relief as they approached the classroom where the body had been found and she recognised Molly in coveralls. The familiarity gave Kelly warm assurance and Molly winked at her over her face mask, before raising her eyebrows at Seb. They'd discuss that later.

Seb passed her gloves, coveralls and bags for her shoes, as well as a mask for her face.

It was going to be a hot day. Working in these conditions was unforgiving and Kelly felt sorry for Molly who would likely spend all day here.

Despite the horror of what she expected to see inside the room, Kelly felt calm. It was partly because Molly was there but also because she was exactly where she should be and her mind had begun to function solely as an investigator dispelling all her doubts. Gathering evidence at a crime scene took time and couldn't be rushed. She tried to go through all the things she'd been taught about approaching such contexts. The setting of a crime was not simply what had happened and to whom, but also the things that had been left there, and the things taken away. The emotions, the moments, the thoughts, the baggage. It was a multi-dimensional stage: an arena of evidence from which to gather clues which would lead back to the person responsible.

Her mind was open.

Some detectives wanted to swoop in and pass judgement on what they thought happened, solely on what they saw, but much work was required before they could confirm or dispute theories. She hoped Seb wasn't the type to hustle after the end game. The facts worked on their own and spoke an indisputable narrative eventually, and the SOCO's work was vital. She knew Molly was exceptional at her job and felt in safe hands. Back in the day, everyone knew that evidence could have a habit of disappearing or being ignored or not accounted for to make sure it fitted with stories and supposition. That was the stuff of the pre-forensic age and nowadays juries only listened to science, and the odd convincing witness. So this initial stage was critical.

A blue tent had been erected at the entrance to the room, which was part of an additional annexe with its own access point, so the forensic van had pulled right up to the doors. There was no coroner's van yet. This was their opportunity to do the victim justice and gather every shred of evidence they could, to give a voice to their last moments: what they saw, touched, heard, tasted and felt. The final moments of a murder victim were the most harrowing events anybody could possibly imagine, but that's exactly what Kelly prepared to witness as she entered the drama studio, to give the victim life and dignity once more.

She felt Molly's gloved hand squeeze her arm.

That's when she knew it was bad.

In the corner, slumped on the floor, like a collapsed heap of stones, was what was left of a woman. She'd been mutilated and her face and body were covered in blood. But most disturbing of all was the staging of the whole scene.

The murderer had taken his time. The woman had suffered.

This wasn't just a homicide; it was an execution that had brought somebody great pleasure. Kelly didn't know what to concentrate on first, the body or the macabre theatre of the whole thing.

Then she spotted it.

The structure behind the woman was a booth for puppets, like the ones you saw at the seaside. She'd been to Blackpool enough times with her family to recognise it. It was covered in red-and-white-striped silk.

'It's called a castelet,' Molly said, who'd moved to stand beside her. 'Recognise it?' Molly asked.

'Like a puppet show?'

'Exactly,' Molly said. 'Can you see the puppet in it?'

Kelly looked closer, then it all fell into place. The puppet inside the booth, behind the dead woman, was Mr Punch, the hideous character who beat his poor wife with a slapstick in the tales that kept millions of children happy at the seaside for a century. He was positioned looking down on the body.

And the woman was dressed like Judy.

'The caretaker confirmed she's a teacher here,' the crime scene coordinator told her. Her voice echoed as Kelly concentrated on the body. She heard Seb chatting and asking questions and noticed with interest that his tone was nonchalant. She'd heard that London murder squads – because that's all they did – were in danger of becoming emotionless shells of investigation and thus at risk of losing their edge after a certain number of years of looking at scenes like this one. She heard it in Seb's voice. It was flat and... something else.

'Dorothy Amis, sixty-five years old. It's not too fresh, she's been here at least ten hours. That's all we know at the moment.'

'What was she doing here in the middle of the night?' Kelly asked.

The CSC shrugged. 'It's possible she worked late last night. Teachers don't take the whole summer off, contrary to public opinion.'

'Doesn't the caretaker lock up after everybody has gone?' Kelly asked.

The CSC shrugged again. 'He's being questioned now. Hope you had breakfast early, this one's been chopped up by a real nutter.'

They followed the CSC and approached the victim but maintained a distance from her because Kelly wanted to walk in ever-decreasing circles, until she got to the body last. What was around the body and inside the room was just as important as what had been done to the victim. But her eyes were drawn to her face, which was daubed in crude makeup, over blood, as if the teacher had rushed last minute to make herself look half decent for a visitor. Though Kelly couldn't work out if the wide smile across her face was lipstick or blood. But that wasn't the strangest thing about her. She had on a white cap, like the ones old cooks wear, and an apron, as if she'd been playing a dress-up game when she was killed.

Kelly stood mesmerised by the scene. She flashed a glance at Molly, who was busy drawing sketches of blood pooling and spatter. Kelly couldn't wait to get her flatmate's take on the death.

The whole scene was made sadder by the fact that the victim was an elderly lady, close to retirement.

'Throat slit,' the CSC said.

Kelly gazed at the gaping wound underneath the woman's chin, but she couldn't keep her eyes off the clothes and the huge painted grin on her face. But it wasn't until she got closer that she realised that the leer was cut into her, and she'd been given the smile on her face by a knife so it looked as though she was smiling, and the women would go into eternity like that in Kelly's mind. A Chelsea grin, they called it. The whole thing reminded her of something else, but she couldn't figure out what and she pushed the thought away as she concentrated on her job.

Because of the macabre makeup, it made the blood underneath her chin look like some kind of theatrical face paint and it matched the colour of her lips, which had been clumsily painted red too. The mortuary had their work cut out with this one, she thought.

Next to the body, labelled by a police evidence marker, was what looked like a truncheon, and it had matted blood and hair on it. The woman had suffered a terrible end. It appeared to Kelly to look exactly like Mr Punch's slapstick, and the matter adhering to it suggested the victim had been beaten with it.

'What do you know about Punch and Judy?' Seb asked her. He was stood next to her now and he wanted her opinion. She looked at him and remembered where she was. This was her chance.

'Mr Punch was a bully. He beat his nagging wife and their child, eventually killing both. People used to laugh at this stuff. It was a children's show. I used to love it. I sat along with all the other kids, licking my ice cream and bending over double when he slapped her with his truncheon.'

They both stared at the wooden weapon on the floor.

'I imagine it's banned now, it's a bit dated,' Kelly said. She couldn't take her eyes off Dorothy.

'Staging like this is usually a message. Her killer is telling us something,' Seb said.

'I agree.'

'Go on,' Seb asked. He waited for her reply.

'She was punished for something.'

Molly caught her attention by holding something between her gloved fingers.

'What is it?' Seb asked.

'I have no idea,' Molly said. 'It looks like a small whistle, or a toy, you know the ones you blow into at Christmas?'

'Where was it?' Seb asked.

'In her throat.'

'It'll be a swazzle,' Kelly said.

'What?' Seb and Molly asked at the same time.

'I had one as a kid. It made me sound like Mr Punch. My dad bought it for me. It makes the sound a bit like Donald Duck. It's reedy. It's ridiculous really.'

A camera clicked and the photographer imitated the voice modifier with one of Punch and Judy's most famous slogans. *'That's the way to do it!'*

They stared at him.

'They're behind here,' he said. When they walked towards the booth and looked to where the photographer had just been working, they saw two puppets. One of Mr Punch and the other of Judy. Kelly glanced at Molly but her friend didn't seem to be thinking what she was. Maybe it was because she hadn't seen the anthropologist in Stratford dangling a small wooden Pinocchio from his finger like she had.

Chapter 12

Luther opened the box carefully, even though the seal had already been broken. He'd found his private office in disarray when he'd opened up this morning and he'd spent twenty minutes on his knees, sobbing, before he'd called the police.

A slow creep of dread had gripped him when he'd found his door unlocked, knowing he'd secured it on Saturday. Then, as he'd explored further, he'd spotted a path of destruction and opened and upended boxes, knowing somebody had rifled through his most valuable pieces.

Oswald had found him seized up with cold and cramp.

The V&A had tried to modernise the staff at the museum as well as the exhibition spaces, but some things never changed. It didn't matter how much money they threw at the façade, curators and museum cleaners were thin on the ground due to their abysmal wages and so the V&A kept them on.

'Sir, if you could just allow us to preserve the scene, that would be helpful.'

The young, uniformed officer appealed to the curator's good nature as she gently tried to remove him from the scene of the break-in.

'Why would anyone do this?' he said to her.

She smiled warmly but it didn't make him feel any better. Two officers from Bethnal Green Station were on site, interviewing staff who'd come in early or the ones who'd also been here last night. They'd checked the security arrangements of the museum and questioned the guard who'd heard nothing.

Oswald was seventy-one years old and hard of hearing as it was. Luther, at seventy-eight, fancied himself a little more useful. He'd helped the police compile a list of the items that were missing. It wasn't much, and the list was curiously uninspiring, but to him it was a violation and a senseless act that spread misery throughout the place which was supposed to be a centre of inspired positivity. The museum celebrated play, joy and happiness through time. This was a stain on their history and Luther couldn't help thinking it had perhaps been youths looking to cause trouble because they were bored.

'If they played real games instead of turning their eyes square in front of those computers, we wouldn't be in this mess,' he said.

The female uniform nodded.

As far as she knew, no money had been kept in the tills overnight and nothing of any value was taken, but to him, everything in here was precious and the police weren't taking it as seriously as he hoped they would.

'The Charlie McCarthy was priceless,' he muttered.

'The what, sir?'

'The Charlie McCarthy. You're too young to remember, he was one of the finest dummies ever to have been made.'

The officer looked dumfounded, and Luther corrected himself.

'Ventriloquist's dummy.'

'Oh, was he American?'

'Yes, is that significant?'

Luther often found people judged him for his accent which had originated across the pond in New York. The Brooklyn inflection had softened but he was still assumed to be an anomaly for pursuing a highbrow career in conservation despite hailing from a nation with little history to speak of. White history that was. Of course the indigenous history of the USA went back thousands of years but there was no hunger for that, tragically, and he certainly wasn't descended from such illustrious stock. His grandfather had been Irish and dirt poor and had landed on Ellis Island in 1893.

'We invented puppets too,' he said. 'We're pretty good at TV, have you heard of Hollywood?'

He waved his hand at her and shook his head.

'I'm sorry, my toy recognition isn't great. I liked *Toy Story*,' she said.

Her offering only saddened Luther more and he bent his head despondently.

Another police officer entered the room where the robbery had taken place and approached Luther.

'We've taken the statements we need, sir, so we'll get out of your hair.'

'What about fingerprints and look, over there, there's a shoe print,' Luther appealed to the copper.

'Unfortunately, sir, this is a working museum with thousands of customers visiting every weekend,' the copper said.

'And weekdays, we're very popular,' Luther insisted.

'Of course, sir. My point is, I've been on the phone to my boss and she agrees, it's impossible to narrow it down. If there was CCTV in here...'

'It's disconnected,' Luther said.

'We saw that, sir. I suggest you get that fixed as soon as possible.'

Luther nodded. He hated the intrusion of machines into his world. The higher-ups at the V&A would be cross he hadn't reported it sooner.

'So, you're doing nothing?'

'It's not like that, sir, we have gathered the evidence we can. There is no forced entry, no break-in and no material damage.'

'What about the mess?'

'We'll be in touch when we've opened a case file and we'll let you know our progress,' the copper said.

Luther looked away and rummaged in a box.

'Typical of this generation,' he grumbled.

The two police officers ignored his ranting and backed out of the room.

'In the meantime, sir, if you think of any other details, or any witnesses come forward, please get in touch.'

Luther turned his back to them and concentrated on another box which had been overturned. The police had taken photographs of the scene, where boxes had been upended, a table had been moved and one of the storage cupboards had been left open. Luther knew his museum inventory and he knew his staff. This was a break-in, albeit a sophisticated one that left no trace, but it was a crime, and he was determined to find the perpetrator if he had to camp out all night lying in wait.

And it was targeted. Somebody knew what he kept in here. It was his office and he stored the most valuable pieces in here. Who knew?

The Charlie McCarthy that was missing was an artefact from 1937. Luther wasn't an archival snob, he respected toys of all ages, even if they were of the modern age, such as Charlie McCarthy. Of course, an Elizabethan doll, played with by the queen herself, was worth much more in monetary terms, but as far as heritage was concerned, Luther held all his exhibits dearly. Each item in his inventory was irreplaceable because it was unique.

He considered what type of person might steal such an item and it struck him that a young person wouldn't be interested in an old puppet from the 1930s, much less one that wore a top hat and monocle. He almost laughed but was gripped by another wave of sadness as he contemplated the violation of his space. He knew he'd left this room pristine last night when he locked up and set the alarm, so it couldn't have been a bored young member of a school trip up to no good, because by the time he'd closed, the museum was empty. It had been somebody with access to the place, and not just the corridors and public spaces but this room, which was where he'd been working recently to complete the unpacking of artefacts from the refurbishment. There'd been something in here that the robber wanted, and he'd taken it. Luther remembered that nowadays it might be a female robber too, because some of them were *ladettes*, or whatever it was they were called, though the very thought chilled his old bones.

But his instinct told him it was somebody like him; someone who knew the intrinsic value of toys and puppets. Charlie McCarthy was a classic, and part of the forgotten exhibits sidelined for the more modern cartoon-style rooms. Like the young police officers, mass taste had shifted to movies and churned-out toys, so the robber would be mature in years.

But he was no detective and the police had made it abundantly clear that they were not interested in taking the case further, if they ever opened one at all.

'No,' he gasped.

He searched a box that he'd closed only yesterday, sealing in three figures to be dealt with later this week. He retrieved the box from under a desk and saw that it was empty. To show he wasn't going mad he looked on the side of the box at the label and there in his handwriting, clearly scribed, were the names of the three figures. The box was empty, and they were missing. But the police had gone now. Would they even care?

Luther walked across to a sofa in the corner of the room. He'd had it installed there as a treat to himself, to make the job of cataloguing and accounting more pleasant for whoever found themselves in here at odd hours doing the task. He sat down heavily with the empty box in one hand and took off his glasses with his other, then rubbed his eyes.

Maybe the policewoman might have cared if she'd still been here, because the toys missing from the box were modern and from a film that she might have seen. But then Luther realised that the officer was probably lying to him to make him feel better. He was sure that she'd never watched any movies about toys at all. He put her age at about twenty-five which would put her in the right bracket to be watching children's movies in the nineties.

Surely she knew Kermit, Miss Piggy and Fozzie Bear.

Luther's body felt deflated as if somebody had pulled a plug out of him. He sat heavily on the sofa and he stared at the empty boxes which were once filled with joy.

That was the point, he suddenly realised.

Whoever had stolen his toys had really stolen his delight. It crossed his mind that perhaps the thief was trying to cheer themselves up and the thought made him feel less desperate.

Luther couldn't help the tears falling down his cheeks and he wiped them away and sniffed. He peered over at the computer on his desk and an idea made him get up and go across to it, logging on to his private account. A young intern had showed him how to create a Facebook wall. It frazzled his mind to think that people all over the world could connect via a computer which connected messages via satellites floating around the earth. Apparently a young American student had created the new way to reconnect with old friends a few years ago and Luther had been trying to find old acquaintances ever since.

He found the correct page and selected the option to send a message.

The icon on the person's wall was a puppet show, like a collage of historical legends, and Luther smiled. It felt familiar and homely. All the greats were there. Exactly as he expected. He could see each one of the puppets he was missing and now it all made sense. Fozzie, Kermit, Miss Piggy, Charlie McCarthy. All in a row like an ensemble at a Christmas panto.

He typed a private message.

> It's not your fault. I understand and I'm not angry. I forgive you.

An answer pinged back immediately, and Luther jumped back from his desk in amazement.

He'd been waiting.

> The puppet man is too greedy. You cannot keep them all to yourself. You must share with those you swore to protect.

Luther scooted back to the desk on his chair and his fingers hovered above the keys.

'I'm sorry,' he typed. Then waited. Another reply appeared.

> Always allow your conscience to be your guide between the right and wrong choices.

Luther stared at the words and knew it referred to Jiminy Cricket. In the original Pinocchio story, Jiminy, a lowly insect – a status which should have remained until Disney ruined it – was supposed to be the wooden boy's friend, but he wasn't. He was a traitor and Pinocchio ended up killing him.

Chapter 13

'Let's take a break,' Seb said to Kelly. She nodded and peeled off her mask and gloves.

Outside, Molly caught them up and dumped her coveralls. Kelly grinned at her friend, who wasted no time introducing herself to the DI.

'We share a flat,' Kelly explained.

'Handy,' Seb said flatly.

Kelly realised that her new partner was growing on her. She observed that he didn't feel pressured into filling gaps in conversation and she admired his skills in the field. He processed a scene methodically and followed many of the same methods she did. He spoke to the SOCOs respectfully and listened to what they said. Which was another reason Molly had suddenly developed an interest in him, she guessed.

'What do you think?' Seb asked Molly.

'Let's sit down, I need water,' Molly said.

Kelly took a couple of water bottles from the back of the forensic van and they walked behind the school building where they found a bench.

'Fucking weirdo,' Molly said. 'That's what I think.'

Death was Molly's bread and butter and Kelly listened to her. She was used to watching true crime with her flatmate and listening to Molly explain crime scenes, but this was the first time she'd shared one with her.

'Kinky,' Molly added.

Seb raised his eyebrows.

'You mean the costume?' Kelly chipped in. Molly nodded in between swigs of water.

'There's male violence in there but it's more personal than just a war between a man and his wife,' Molly said. Kelly listened to her friend, at home among chaos, and she brimmed with excitement at being involved. She was in the thick of it and she loved every minute.

'The emphasis on her mouth. Judy was a gobshite, wasn't she?' Molly asked.

Kelly nodded.

'So he's shutting her up but teaching us a lesson in control at the same time.'

Kelly noticed that Seb was impressed. Molly carried on as they cooled down and enjoyed some fresh air.

'That poor woman was cut up like a piece of meat. And a teacher too, in the school where she taught. It's a place where kids are usually safe. It's their territory.'

They sat in silence and Molly's outpouring was carried away on a light breeze, which was welcome after being stuck in coveralls for hours.

'Have you ever seen anything like this before?' Kelly asked Seb. 'It's a confident kill.'

Seb stared at her and nodded. 'Correct,' he said. 'He's done it before. And no, I haven't ever come across anything like this on my watch.'

'Sixty-five years old.' Molly shook her head. 'Dorothy. I mean who kills someone called Dorothy? She was a sweet old lady.'

'I think my mum would be horrified you calling sixty-five old. Besides, perhaps she wasn't so sweet,' Kelly remarked. Molly stopped sipping and looked solemnly at Kelly, realising her mistake.

'Of course, how stupid of me. I'm letting my emotions in,' Molly said. 'A revenge kill? I like it.'

They both looked at Seb, as the senior officer.

'There's no age limit on crime, and the worst offenders come from the most surprising places. Let's dig into her background to see what sort of a person she was. It might turn out that she was a very sweet old lady. But equally, she might have been up to her neck in unlawful activity. That's where we'll start. Who she knew and who she let down,' he said.

'It sounds like it was her own fault when you put it like that,' Molly said.

'If it's about culpability then that could be the message, or he's just a psycho. Do you think this is the scene of death or just the stage, Moll?' Kelly asked.

Molly nodded.

'The blood spatter says it all. She was carved up right there in the drama studio, very theatrical. It's just... she looks so innocent, and vulnerable. Why her?' Molly sighed.

'It doesn't look random. He took his time.' Kelly said.

'I'm going back to the office to get started, do you want to stay here and go over the SOCO report?' Seb said to Kelly.

She was suspicious of Seb Crook for the first time since their meeting. He was dumping her on her own. He was asking her to babysit the SOCO report for him while he went back to the office to get started on the Police National Computer. She wasn't sure which she preferred. In the field she could get her hands dirty and dig into the investigation her way but risk being forgotten back at the office. But back at MIT east, she'd feel bound by paperwork, though at least DCI Leia Lord would see her face.

'Sure,' she said.

He left them and Kelly watched his back as he disappeared around the corner of the building.

'I haven't worked him out yet, what do you think?'

'He's sexy, like a commanding older type, you know?' Molly giggled and Kelly slapped her arm playfully.

They grew serious and stared at the playing fields, which seemed to compound the innocence of the place and solidify the horror of what was inside.

'I don't want to go back in there, it's not like me,' Molly said. Kelly watched her friend. It wasn't like Molly to have a professional wobble, and it took Kelly by surprise.

'What's up? Has the scene got to you? It's okay if it has, Molly. Everybody has a limit,' Kelly said.

'It's not the blood, or the slashing of her face,' Molly said. 'She looks like a clown. It's so vicious.'

'More so than other crime scenes?' Kelly asked gently. She was well aware that different images caused shock in different ways. One person could be triggered by a hanging, another by knife wounds, like Molly now. But Kelly had never heard her flatmate like this. She sounded scared.

Kelly knew that Molly had seen plenty of victims of knife crime, like they all had in London, but wondered what it was about this one that was different. In fact, Kelly realised, she was holding herself up better than she'd expected. The horror of it had spurred her on to think about the perp rather than what he'd left behind, she guessed. She'd been so busy thinking about the evidence they found that she hadn't had time to process the human loss.

'It's like the killer is taunting us, you know, doing it on purpose to send a message, at least that's what I think in my humble opinion,' Molly said. The old Molly reappeared and Kelly squeezed her arm.

'My new partner agreed with you.'

Molly smiled.

'I literally met him five minutes before we left the office to come here.'

'He seems nice.'

'Is nice what I want?'

'No, you want competent, but I was referring to him as a guy. It's important you bring your own personality to cases, that's what we do. Everybody has a different pair of eyes and a different heart. But sometimes a bloke like him, who's easy to be around, even though he's a bit serious, is safe. And safe is good.'

Kelly finished her water. 'Are you okay?' she asked her flatmate.

Molly shrugged.

'Any hypothesis yet?' Kelly continued, trying to keep Molly grounded.

'You want mine? You're murder squad now.'

'Don't you dare!' Kelly said, pretending to slap Molly's hand.

'Okay!' Molly held up her hands in mock surrender. Kelly thought the colour was coming back to her friend's cheeks. She questioned her own reaction to the crime scene and worried that her lack of compassion showed callousness. She'd always been able to see past the human tragedy because it meant she got to the perpetrator quicker. Yes, the scene was shocking but she'd help no one by dramatising it. It was dramatic enough. But they were all allowed private moments when it perhaps got too much, but it passed.

'Okay, here we go,' Molly began. 'This is what I think. Personal knowledge of the victim, obviously. Staged to send a message of power over her. Revenge. Payback. Has the hallmarks of torture.'

'Maybe an ex-pupil?' Kelly suggested.

'The notes said the victim hadn't been a teacher all her career, she worked in nursing homes or something like that.'

'Can you switch careers so easily?'

Molly spread her hands. 'I guess before all the obsession with formal qualifications came in, it was easier.'

'Or the background checks?'

'Bingo.'

'And what about the dressing up?' Kelly said finally.

'You're thinking about Pinocchio, aren't you?' Molly saw where her mind was going and finally cottoned on to what Kelly had been thinking all along.

'Of course, I can't stop thinking about it.'

'But wasn't that a historic case?'

'That's what I intend to find out.'

'But it's not your case, is it?'

'Until Bethnal Green CID get the nod from the HAT, it's theirs, and Cheryl's asked for my help.'

Molly shook her head. 'That's a really bad idea, Kelly. Compartmentalise. It's a new job, for God's sake. This is what you've wanted forever.'

'Don't worry, I'm not moonlighting, I'm just helping Cheryl, call it a handover.'

Chapter 14

Kelly remained outside to take a call from Jonathan Hass. She needed the air. The line was dreadful.

She imagined the forensic anthropologist wearing a tweed jacket and brown corduroys, balancing tiny spectacles on the end of his nose, examining the remains of Pinocchio, where she'd left him underneath the Olympic Stadium, or where it was going to be built at least. The remains were moved over the weekend and were now laid on the anthropologist's table in a lab on Romford Road but the image of him in the dark hole was difficult to shake. The immediate site around where the body was found was due to be excavated under a court order and digging would start later in the week. The site had been in continuous use over several projects. A cycle of delays rescued by new investments had kept it chugging along and it had moved and expanded from the first development there back in 1998. They had no idea what they might find.

'It's the most interesting case I've seen for a long time. We normally get Roman bones, Anglo-Saxon remains, the odd skull and plenty of grave sites when big skyscrapers go up, but this is different. I suspect I will be able to give you confirmation that the body is not ancient very soon.'

'So, our suspicions at the burial site were accurate?' she asked.

'I'm not entirely sure, as always, I must wait for the data, but the clothes are modern.'

Kelly had seen for herself that the figure was dressed in modern tailoring, at least from the last century. It had been difficult to see in the dark hole, but Jonathan and Geena had pointed out touches of fashion that dated the corpse closer to modern day than not. Together with the toy and the nose, she expected confirmation would be more straightforward, but scientists liked to rule everything out before committing themselves.

'I need a date so I can pass it on to Homicide. How long do you think it will take?'

'I'll go as fast as I can but I can only produce what I'm given in the time frame. I'm afraid I can't rush this, there are certain soil analysis details and skeletal tests that must be done.'

'I appreciate that, could we possibly meet? I can come to your lab to determine if I can perhaps pass this on to another team that handles historic cases.'

'Yes, I agree that would be a better use of police time. When I say modern, I mean this century.'

'So, in the last eight years?'

'Ah, my apologies, I haven't got used to the millennium just yet, I meant the twentieth century.'

'Ah. No worries, so less than a hundred years old, would you say?'

Kelly's stomach sank. She could see Cheryl being saddled with this case and she'd left her with a thousand and one other things to do, without a replacement yet. She'd become roused by the prospect of being able to link it to more modern MOs, but now she reverted back to her original assessment that it was probably Victorian. A person who liked toys, or even somebody who made them, lying undiscovered for a whole century. The prospect intrigued her, but she wasn't being paid for fascination, and she didn't have time for history lessons. All she'd wanted was to give Cheryl a hand with what had turned into a compelling case, but now she wasn't so sure. There was no way Pinocchio could possibly be linked to her current case and she realised she was barking up a very misguided tree. What she really should do is confess to Cheryl that she didn't have time to delve into the death of a Victorian partygoer who probably spent New Year's Eve 1899 dressed up as Pinocchio until he or she was cruelly dispatched and thrown in a ditch.

'I'd be more than happy for the company. The police don't often take any notice unless it's a new one. The bodies usually end up here then the detectives never come back. But this one is definitely a homicide, I know that much.'

Kelly couldn't let it go.

'I can head over there at some point today if you give me your address,' she said. When he told her she realised that the lab was situated on the Stratford end of Romford Road, which was only a short walk away from the tube station. Seb had left her to babysit the SOCOs but they didn't need coddling. She made her way back to the crime scene and left a message for Molly. It could be hours before her flatmate was ready to hand over an embryonic report.

It didn't take her long to walk swiftly to the High Road and catch a bus to the Broadway which linked Romford Road to Stratford. The fact that she'd been going round in circles since Friday, literally over the same patch of London, wasn't lost on her. A pattern was emerging and she drew it in her mind. To the west, she had Stratford, where Pinocchio had been found, further north was Leyton where poor Dorothy had been carved up and now she headed southeast and she still remained inside the patch of MIT east.

When she got off at her stop, she made her way to the address given to her by Jonathan. The forensic lab was inside a nondescript building that looked like an old pawn shop. The window out front was smeared with dirt, and she could barely make out the fliers stuck to it advertising dentists, night schools and shopping trips. Paint chipped off the door and she rang the bell and examined her finger after for signs of bacteria multiplying at record speed. She wiped it on her trousers and waited for the anthropologist to let her in.

The intercom buzzed and she pushed the door, then spotted the sign inside confirming she was in the right place.

Inside was entirely different and she breathed a sigh of relief. It was clean, tidy and air-conditioned. Jonathan greeted her. She shook his hand, hoping he'd washed it thoroughly after examining the cadaver.

'We're up here,' he said, showing her through the door he came from. He led her into a lab that was bright white and steel, like an operating theatre. It was set up like a mortuary with microscopes, operating tools and gurneys lined up. A computer as old and cumbersome as hers back in the office at CID languished on a desk, and a young woman sat in front of it typing. She looked up and smiled.

'This is my assistant, Lorna.'

Lorna smiled and Kelly felt at ease with both of them.

Jonathan went to a gurney where a white sheet covered a lumpy-looking pile of something, and she realised that it must be Pinocchio under there.

It was. As he peeled back the sheet, she saw the mystery body in a new light. Out of context, and dug up, he looked smaller, alien-like even, all twisted and brown, his skin like leather. She could see the clothes now and saw what Jonathan meant. They were shaped to a professional cut but more than that, they reminded her of something. Then she realised what it was. She could make out red woollen overalls, a yellow shirt and a blue bow tie. The cadaver wore a hat too. It had a feather in it and Kelly was reminded of her earlier reference to Cheryl about a dandy. She'd said it in jest but now she wasn't so sure. But this wasn't the ensemble simply of a smart Victorian gentleman, it was a caricature of the doll left alongside the body. The corpse was dressed as Pinocchio.

'He looks different.'

'She,' Jonathan said.

'She?' Kelly asked.

Jonathan nodded. 'Definitely female, she's been scanned quite comprehensively, and she's definitely not a child, more a middle-aged woman.'

'So, I'll have to give her a new name, then,' she said.

'No, Pinocchio is good. I think you were spot on. Don't forget for as long as the human race has been dressing up, gender has never mattered to any culture until very recently. It makes me wonder if the dressing up is the most important part of this murder. Have you heard of agalmatophilia?'

Kelly stared at him and shook her head.

'It's sexual attraction to a doll, or a statue. I think there are signs that whoever did this was in love with the figurative character. Sometimes it's also called pygmalionism after the Greek legend who was in love with the statue he carved. I have books on it,' Jonathan said, noticing Kelly's interest. He pointed to shelves of huge reference books and Kelly registered his enthusiasm for the topic. She also figured he didn't get out much. Sometimes, listening to experts on the reasons why people murdered other human beings was a strange existence, she thought.

'It was quite common in the Edwardian period. Cross-dressing isn't new but I think in this case it could supply a motive for you. Unless the victim wasn't the one who dressed herself like this, of course.'

Kelly stared at him as she thought of Dorothy dressed as Judy.

'Are her remains too decayed to investigate sexual assault?'

Jonathan nodded.

'Why would you kill something if you're in love with it?' she asked.

'Ah, now that is a good question. My guess is to control it forever. If the victim was indeed dressed by her killer then she has been treated with love and reverence, in as much as time and care have been taken in the dressing. Her lederhosen and blouse are an excellent fit, don't you think?'

Kelly stared at him.

'Lederhosen?'

'Typical Italian mountain dress,' he said as if it was the most natural thing in the world for her to know. She'd read Pinocchio a thousand times and now what he was wearing made sense. She wasn't aware the little wooden boy was Italian, but somewhere deep in her psyche she knew he was European, like Hansel and Gretel, like the Pied Piper.

'I thought they were Austrian.' Her brain woke up. 'Do you think there's any significance to dressing a woman in a boy's clothes then?' she asked.

'I think the toy's sex is not as important as the reference to childhood. Sacrificing a victim to innocence inside a story, well, that is something I have not come across before.'

Jonathan Hass's input was academically masterful.

'And it's definitely not an accident?'

'No, your SOCO was correct, they are knife wounds, and they would have been fatal. The scan confirmed that but I also wish to delve deeper myself of course, forgive the pun.'

Kelly continued to watch Jonathan Hass with interest. She didn't entirely dismiss what he was saying but she also thought his story rather far-fetched. However, she was willing to listen because she was also thinking about Judy. The dates simply didn't add up but that didn't mean that the two cases weren't connected somehow. Even if it was a matter of learning an MO from an older case, it might be worthwhile mentioning this to Seb.

Kelly walked around the remains and tried to work out which body part went where. She could see now the contours of a woman's body. A small woman. A vulnerable woman.

A mature woman.

'She's tiny,' she said quietly.

Melancholy settled over her as she acknowledged that women had been victims for as long as history itself. This one was no different, apart from being dressed like a puppet. Kelly realised that puppetry was the very manifestation of power and control, and she shuddered.

'I looked it up, Pinocchio was written in 1883, so we're at least in the nineteenth century,' she said. 'It's very theatrical,' she added.

Jonathan nodded. 'It's meticulous and in my experience somebody who takes time to stage such a scene has much invested in it. There's care here.'

'Care? In a murder?'

'To get it right. This was important. The feather in the hat, the attention to detail. I don't think this is the first time your murderer has done this.'

Kelly's stomach flipped over and she looked at Pinocchio wistfully, wishing she knew who she was. Then she remembered how Dennis at the building site had referred to the deceased with a female pronoun. It could be nothing, but it popped into her head. She gave the foreman the benefit of the doubt. Men on building sites would be more demographically likely to assume a dead body is female perhaps. Also, it could have been a nervous mistake. Kelly parked the information for later.

Jonathan drew her attention back to the table. The fingers had nail paint on them and for some reason this brought her alive to Kelly more than anything else. He talked her through the woman's dental hygiene and told her he'd taken an imprint. Dental records were only kept for eleven years by law, but Jonathan was nothing if not thorough.

'I've even managed to get fingerprints, look, they're pristine.'

Kelly was genuinely taken aback.

'I can get prints from Roman remains too, it's all about the soil. This one is preserved beautifully. She's definitely not Roman though. Or last century.'

'Why?'

Jonathan grinned and Kelly knew he'd found something.

'This was in her pocket,' he said, showing her a folded piece of paper. He fingered it carefully with gloved hands and Kelly peered at it as he opened it to reveal what was inside. The paper looked glossy, like a modern pamphlet, and when Jonathan opened it fully, she saw it was a fixture list for an Arsenal season ticket holder, from 2001.

Chapter 15

The blood was up the walls, across the floor and smeared over the castelet.

'Putting on a show,' Molly heard her boss say as she spoke into a Dictaphone. It sounded obvious but it was also crass, just like the crime. Molly was rattled. Maybe it was something to do with the scene being in a school, or the victim being an old woman who reminded her of a grandmother. Her wobble in front of Kelly earlier had shaken her. School was a place for kids to go every day to learn and be safe while they did so. It was a sanctuary, a bit like a church, she guessed. Seeing the small plastic chairs and the books piled high on windowsills, and the smell of the halls, had evoked certain memories of a time in her life – in everyone's life – when she had been innocent and free. Seeing Dorothy Amis's body had sullied those pleasant recollections.

She tried to concentrate. It had been a relief to see Kelly walk in from MIT east, and the familiarity made her release some of the tension building up between her shoulders. Having a familiar face around and one that she trusted and cared for made her want to polish her notes and be meticulous with her detail so Kelly could have the best start possible on the case of Dorothy Amis's murder. This was her flatmate's chance to make a good first impression.

The forensic team would be busy all day with processing the immediate and wider scene for evidence. Molly's job was blood behaviour and she'd spent the morning setting up projections, measurements and models of where Dorothy Amis's five litres had gone. The teacher had a total of forty-three knife wounds and several of them were deep enough to kill her. To Molly, the scene was personal. Knife wounds in double figures usually indicated frenzy, and anyone who does that to a human body is on a desperately reckless mission to cause as much damage as possible, and people usually cared that much for a reason. The blood had been left where it dropped, splattered, ran and pooled. There'd been no attempt to clean up. It was a confused MO. It was both private and intimate, yet public and emotionless too. But considerations like that were Kelly's department now. Molly's job was to give her as much as possible to go on.

It was eerily quiet in the drama studio. Only the noise of people going about the business of death could be heard and the odd sarcastic quip from professionals versed in gallows humour to relieve the tension.

'*That's the way to do it,*' in a macabre Donald Duck–like voice pierced through the hush occasionally.

The school caretaker who'd found Dorothy had been interviewed and was an obvious first suspect until he was cleared on account of any alibi or physical evidence. Murder scenes were messy affairs. No one got off lightly. Knife shafts became slippery with oily blood during frenzied attacks, and victims fought back. People took a long time to die. It wasn't like in fiction, where an attacker closed in and sprung the fatal blow by surprise and took a life. It was drawn out, horrific, hard work and dangerous.

In a nutshell they all agreed that no killer could walk away from a scene like this without something adhering to their clothes or skin. They might have cuts, they could have lesions where Dorothy fought back and they could have a serious injury. Molly had already examined Dorothy's hands and her nails were stuffed full of matter. It meant that either Dorothy's hygiene was off (unlikely) or she'd fought like a dog. The tragedy of the scene was all consuming. Molly entered her findings into a sturdy notepad she carried and created a replica scenario for the MIT to examine.

In her humble opinion, Dorothy was knocked out with a blow to the head from behind somewhere else, then dragged to the drama studio. Molly estimated Dorothy to weigh around a hundred a fifty pounds at least, so it wouldn't have been an easy task. The perp was strong. Dorothy had carpet burns on her back, so she hadn't been carried here. The drama studio floor was covered in a prickly synthetic tile which was compatible with the marks, and they'd found hairs in a clean line from the doorway to where her body came to finally rest. The tiles were a hideous burnt brown and so the bloody drag marks were difficult to see until they viewed them under UV light.

Molly's opinion, backed up by her senior SOCO, was that Dorothy had then been stabbed until she was dead.

The disfigurement had come after that. It was a small blessing.

The perp had both time and freedom to achieve his aims. The knife work was crude but effective and he was no surgeon. Then there was the dressing-up to make her look like Judy, as well as staging the castelet, including placing Punch in an elevated position, looking down on his dead wife, with his slapstick close to hand, which Dorothy had been beaten with probably postmortem.

In many ways it was clumsy, because there was so much evidence to go on, so much left behind, they'd be forgiven it was hurried and accidental. But in other ways it was confident and accomplished. Reckless was a word that sprung to mind, because the perpetrator would be covered in corroborative matter. But who was she to cast judgement on stupidity?

'It wasn't his first time.' Her boss reiterated what the detectives had thought.

She spun around.

'I agree,' she said. 'He gained most pleasure out of using her body rather than the kill, which was brutal but quick. He spent a lot more time after she was dead, weird bastard,' Molly said.

'Weird indeed. They've got a real sicko on their hands.'

The SOCOs, despite the gruesome nature of their work, always felt they had the lighter end of the stick when it came to dealing with crime. They didn't have to catch those who dealt it out.

'The end result is what drives him,' Molly said, pointing back to Dorothy.

'Have you got a theory?' her boss asked. It wasn't their job to solve a crime but it helped to play the scene back and forth, as if they were standing there when it happened. It could reveal things missed in initial reports and aid police.

'I think he is trapped in his own childhood, and he's recreating a scene from it but he's entirely in control. Maybe he wasn't in control of it when he was a child, but he is now, or rather, this makes him *feel* in control.'

After a few seconds her boss broke the silence. 'Remind me again why you're not the detective here?'

But Molly, though appreciative of the compliment, knew she couldn't do what Kelly did. Her added concern was that, from what her flatmate had told her about Pinocchio, she was looking for an individual who not only had been completely taken by a crazed mind, but might have been practising for years.

Chapter 16

Kelly arrived at the office on Tuesday morning expecting to be thrown into the middle of a chaotic investigation with officers spread thin.

It wasn't like that at all.

'Let me show you around,' Seb said.

'Haven't we got work to do?' Kelly replied.

Seb laughed. 'I know you're keen, we all were once, but you burning yourself out won't solve anything, you need to pace yourself. Come on, I'll show you where the coffee machine is first, that's the most important thing in the office. You need to bring your own mugs and milk. The coffee is free and you wash up your own mess.'

She followed him, greeting officers working busily at their desks as she passed them but there was little interest in the new kid on the block.

'There's a briefing at three p.m. Leia doesn't like anybody being late.'

'What's she like? She's difficult to read.'

'Coffee? You can borrow my mugs today. Milk?'

She noted his evasion.

'Yes please, and one sugar.'

'Sugar is shared, there's a tin over there, you put fifty pence in per week.'

He still hadn't answered her question.

Back at her desk, Seb showed her around HOLMES, the software exclusively used by murder squads to collate information. He created her own unique user profile and showed her how it related to an ongoing inquiry and her role in it. A HOLMES room had already been created for the murder of Dorothy Amis and Kelly was awed by how much information was already uploaded onto the room. Seb explained that a team of officers create rooms for each individual case with every item generated being added to it as it was collated. She could see that the SOCO report was still pending.

'So, you can see, we're not sat here doing nothing after all.'

She smiled, accepting his harmless dig at her keenness but also noting his reliance upon technology, which galled her slightly.

'I suggest you spend the rest of your time today getting to know how it works and you've got a ton of reading to do, I've sent you links on your desktop computer. If you need a break, don't ask, there's a great coffee shop in the park and it sells the best cakes, but I guess you're one of those women who watches her weight.'

His eyes didn't quite assess her rudely, but she could sense he was pushing her. Misogyny in the Met was notorious, but she could tell he was toying with her and she wasn't biting.

'I eat cake if I want it,' she said.

He backed away, holding up his hands.

'Of course you do. Happy reading, I'm over here if you need me.'

'I might just go and grab some of that cake now,' she said.

Their eyes locked and he looked away first. He wasn't joking when he said she had a stack of reading to do.

But first, she rang Cheryl.

'Hey, how are you doing?'

'Living the dream, boss. Missing you. Even Windy is pining. What are you up to? How's the office in the sky? Do you have servants catering for your every desire?'

Kelly laughed.

'Not quite, I've had my first case already.'

'Not surprised. I heard on the news, is that yours? The teacher?'

'Yep. But it's all a bit… underwhelming.'

'Geez. I'd give twenty quid to be underwhelmed right now. I've still got Pinocchio, the HAT won't allocate it until they know a date of death,' Cheryl said.

Kelly told her about her visit to see Jonathan Hass.

'The football ticket could be explained as litter in the gravesite if it wasn't in her pocket,' Kelly said.

'That's pretty concrete,' Cheryl said.

'And the sex is confirmed?'

'Yes.'

Kelly had seen it with her own eyes, the jaw structure, the hips, the small, delicate finger bones. Hass had extracted DNA from her bone marrow and teeth, and she still had some hair intact on her scalp. The skin which remained was mostly leathery. Other parts of it were as delicate as paper. On the face, the makeup had remained like a mask and Hass had his work cut out to analyse the various chemical and material components present around what was left of her.

'Look, I know I'm not there anymore but I'm still technically handing this case over,' Kelly said.

'You can't let it go,' Cheryl said.

'You know me too well.'

'What's bothering you?'

Kelly told her about Dorothy Amis. Within the privacy of their home, they trusted each other with delicate confidentiality issues.

'Holy shit, they kept that out of the news. I heard it could have been a robbery or something.'

'I know, they won't release details yet. She was badly mutilated, Cheryl.'

'And that's your first case? You don't hang around.'

Kelly didn't think over the phone was the place to share with Cheryl the finer details of the murder scene.

'I'm not doing a lot to be honest, I'm sat at my desk reading about procedure and it's boring me to sleep, I've been advised to go out for cake because the shop in the park serves excellent Victoria sponge.'

'Ouch. You knew you'd have to start at the bottom again.'

'True. It's good to talk to you. Give Jonathan Hass a call. I'll butt out.'

'Not on my account, if you have time on your hands, we need all the help we can get.'

'I do need to pay Bradley a visit at some point.'

'You don't owe him.'

'I do. I feel responsible.'

'You can't save him, we all choose our own story,' Cheryl reminded her.

'I still need to say goodbye.'

'Good luck,' Cheryl said. 'Don't be a stranger to us though,' she added.

'Of course I won't, I'm still on your patch. Molly was the SOCO on the teacher's case, it's a small world.'

'That's so cool, I'm jealous.'

Kelly detected the melancholy in Cheryl's voice before they hung up. Then she reminded herself that everything changed. Everything moved forward. It must. Movement was the only way to stay busy and relevant. But her chat with Cheryl didn't change her mood. The sudden inertia of her work shocked her nervous system and she got up to make another coffee. Seb was in the small kitchen.

'Would it be okay, do you think, if I tied up a few loose ends that are bothering me?'

'We've all got them,' he said jovially. 'With the best will in the world, you can't just waltz out of CID tidily. I get what you're saying. Leia is pretty chilled. If you do your work for her and progress the case, she stays hands-off. She doesn't micromanage unless you annoy her, which is rare. Unless you're late.' He grinned.

'Thanks,' Kelly said.

'A word of advice. Put in the legwork but never tell her what to think. She makes up her own mind.'

Kelly stared at him. It was an odd warning.

'The DCI has final say on cases, it's not a team effort?'

'Keep your voice down. I didn't mean that. Just don't go drawing conclusions without her say so, that's all. She wants to know everything even if she's a step away from the rock face, if you get my drift.'

'Understood. Has she solved this one already then?' Kelly quipped.

Seb didn't smile.

Kelly assumed that Seb was warning her that Leia Lord liked to claim glory on the backs of her staff but he hadn't said it explicitly, though she knew that's what he meant. Suddenly she was wary of her partner. He could easily be misleading her to make sure she didn't stand out and take any praise away from him. He could equally have his own axe to grind against Leia Lord and resent her as a female senior officer.

'If you're going out, you can deliver some exhibits to the lab. They're over there, on my desk,' he said.

He was palming her off with menial tasks again, but it suited her own plans. She walked over to Seb's desk and grabbed the evidence bags. The lab was in Stratford and so it fitted with her intention to pay Bradley a visit.

'I'll bring cake back,' she promised.

Chapter 17

The tube was busy with tourists and picnickers, and Kelly chose a corner to stand in, holding on to a bar overhead. As always on London transport, she happily watched people's habits and assessed them from afar. There was a couple arguing over a snapped bracelet and Kelly reckoned they were in the last throes of their relationship. There was a man who kept staring at a group of teenage girls and he was thirty years older than them. The summer brought two things together: exposed flesh and perverts, and she felt like slapping him across his face. But watching wasn't a crime. A young mother rocked her baby in her arms and stared into her child's face the whole journey and Kelly reckoned she'd be robbed blind in a second, she was so taken with her offspring.

She got off at Stratford and after a short detour to a forensic lab, she walked to the Stratford Junction building site where she'd seen Bradley on Friday evening. The site where Pinocchio had been dumped. A police cordon remained around the dump site, but work carried on as normal elsewhere. It was a large site. She recalled Jonathan Hass saying he'd requested a warrant to excavate the whole location but it looked as though, so far, he hadn't got his wish. The site looked in perfect working order apart from the obvious inaction around the trench where they'd found Pinocchio, which was still sealed off with police tape.

She spotted Bradley straight away. For a young man who said he worked casually here, it was quite a coincidence that he was here again now.

He was a big lad who loved the gym and on a day like this she'd predicted correctly that he'd be stripped to the waist. Men wolf whistled to her and she ignored them. Bradley turned around, hoping to get a glimpse of an attractive woman to distract from his work, but was disappointed when he saw it was Kelly.

She walked to a portacabin where she flashed her warrant card and obtained a hard hat. Bradley waved begrudgingly, egged on by co-workers, who welcomed the sight of her, even if he didn't.

He climbed down a ladder and met her by a pile of bricks. She looked up to the sky and shaded her eyes.

'Working hard,' she said.

He smiled his wide grin and she reckoned he'd charm anyone with his youthful appeal and good looks. But she also knew his dark side. Could it be that he hadn't terminated that part of himself after all? He seemed calmer than he had on Friday night.

'Can I have a word?' she asked.

'I thought you might be back,' he said.

'Working here full time, then?'

'Only since last week,' he replied.

'Probation worker notified?'

'Of course.'

Bradley looked around. She knew it wasn't cool her turning up like this, and his peers might give him a hard time after, but it was important. She was under no illusion that everybody knew she was a copper. No matter how she dressed or the way she carried herself, bad'uns always knew who she was. It could have been the way she stood confidently without a feminine need to carry a petite handbag, or the way she eyed the workers for signs of the stench of illegality, or perhaps it was just because she was a woman with no inhibition, marching into a building site full of men, without a care about what might come next. It was that kind of self-assurance that had got Bradley on side in the first place.

'I didn't know if you'd be here, I came to see Dennis.'

'He's not here.'

'No?'

Bradley shook his head. She'd seen the gesture before. Something was up.

Bradley took off his hat and wiped sweat from his brow, then replaced it and led her to a couple of chairs set up for brews behind the back of a loading area and they sat.

'I spoke to Orlando,' she said. 'It was about your dad.'

Bradley looked at his feet. 'What about him?'

'I thought you might be able to tell me that.'

Bradley laughed but Kelly knew it wasn't genuine. He was stalling. He was nervous.

'I thought you were free of him?'

'I am.'

'So why the apprehension over testifying against Orlando? Is there more to his connection to your dad than working here? He called him a good dad.'

Bradley sighed. Kelly waited.

'My dad tried to contact me, well, in fact, he did contact me. A bloke who worked here delivered a phone to me and he called me and asked in his own unique way for me not to testify against Orlando.'

'You mean he threatened you.'

Bradley nodded.

'And what was your reply?'

'I told him to fuck off and leave me alone.'

'Ballsy.'

'It took a long time for me to understand that I had a right to stand up to him. If he wants to harm me, he knows where I work. I could get taken out by an old gang member for all I know, today, tomorrow or the next day. I'm always watching my back. Makes no difference.'

'You think he'd kill his own son?'

Bradley nodded.

'He said I'd better watch my step up on the ladders.'

Kelly felt her stomach twist over.

'Bastard.'

Bradley smiled. 'Thanks. You gonna save me?'

She stared at him and tried to be as open and honest as she could be, but she didn't need to try because he read her thoughts.

'Bradley, you can still fight against your past. If you've got something to tell me, I'm here.'

He looked at her and smiled and it was a smile of a thousand years. He didn't believe a word she was saying.

'I was told you're an informant for a major investigation team already, I didn't know.'

Bradley looked confused.

'Is that not correct?'

'Do they pay? First I've heard.'

Kelly had a sudden urge to hug him and take him home. *Come and live with me! I'll mother you! I'm broken too. I don't want kids, but I'll protect you.*

The moment was gone, and she stood up. She couldn't work out why DCI Wallis would make such a mistake. Perhaps she could ask Seb about it.

She watched Bradley close off to her then. The conversation was over and he transformed back into the angry young man she'd first met when he was fourteen years old and facing juvenile court for the first time. Since then, he'd experienced several psychotic incidents, having been sectioned three or four times. She couldn't imagine the trauma he'd suffered, which led to him being utterly on the periphery of society before he even reached puberty. But she saw the boy in him now. All the hard work, all the progress, the rehabilitation and the promises were irrelevant now. She saw the power that held him down and she knew she couldn't break through and felt a fool for ever believing she could.

He turned to leave. 'We're done?'

'One more thing,' she said.

He hovered, eager to get rid of her.

'Dennis, your foreman.'

Bradley looked away awkwardly again.

'He referred to the corpse in the hole as a woman.'

'Did he?'

'He did.'

Bradley shrugged.

'He was correct, she is a woman. Any idea why he might know that?'

Bradley sighed as if Kelly was soft in the head. Either that or he was extremely uncomfortable.

'I heard a rumour.'

Kelly waited.

'Back in the day when my dad was in charge around here, some said he got rid of his enemies under his sites.'

'What?'

'No, I won't say it under oath. And no, I won't give you a statement. I'm not going to court for anyone, and I know where this is heading.'

He walked away, leaving Kelly dumfounded.

And as she turned to leave, she knew that he was holding back more.

Chapter 18

Back at the office, after delivering cake to the desks of her new colleagues in a shameless attempt to court favour, Kelly accessed missing persons for 2001.

Each time she asked Seb to give her something on the Dorothy Amis case, he fobbed her off with something elementary, such as chasing evidence or worse, making coffee. She tried to soothe her unease by telling herself that perhaps Seb was just busy, or he wasn't a fan of working with younger females or even the possibility that Leia Lord had simply chosen a poor mentor and partner for her, but she wasn't about to demand a new one on her second day in her new role. She and Seb must get to know each other better, that was all. She shouldn't expect to be in charge of an investigation for some time yet and she still had much to learn.

Bradley was on her mind. Whatever was going on at the building site owned by Jason Fellcroft, she knew it wasn't good. Under UK law, being convicted of a serious crime didn't mean your assets were seized unless debts were owed to the state. On paper, Jason's construction empire would be there waiting for him upon his release. But who was running it in his absence? Not Dennis Chapman, that was for sure. She couldn't act upon rumour from a convicted criminal either. Had Bradley dangled the information on purpose, knowing she couldn't act upon it? If so, then why? If it was true, and Jason Fellcroft had buried secrets under the rubble at his building sites, then how many more were under there? And why the costume, assuming Pinocchio was one of them?

She tried to concentrate on her computer screen and a list with thousands of names popped up on her screen. It was a sea of human beings who vanished into thin air every year. To reduce the search, she entered key words, such as 'Arsenal fan', 'Pinocchio', 'Caucasian' and 'fetish'. She also typed in 'Pygmalionism' and 'agalmatophilia'.

Fetish got the most hits. She raised her eyebrows at how many missing white females had 'dressed up' written on their files, but it included hundreds of prostitutes because the coppers taking the statements had written that in their notes. But Pinocchio wasn't simply dressed up, she was staged for theatre. Like Judy was too. And as if it wasn't clear enough, the placing of children's toys with the bodies indicated a macabre ritual, possibly years apart. And, in her mind, neither MO fitted with anything Jason Fellcroft had ever done. He was a thug who ran an organised racket, not a perverted sex killer.

She added 'theatre' to the search, and it narrowed to a few hundred women for 2001. Those dealt with by east region numbered thirty-seven.

It was a number she could work with.

She glanced at the profiles of the women and discarded most on age, build, face shape and hair colour.

It left seven.

All of them were cold cases which had been closed. Her thoughts sobered suddenly, and she considered her job. All these women had disappeared off the face of the earth in the area where she lived and worked, just in one year, and everybody else went about their businesses. Life carried on.

Did anybody miss these women?

There were attachments to the files and she was able to access them via her new unique profile created for her by Seb. There were also photos.

Kink murders, it seemed, were not as rare as it might be assumed. She looked at a few of them and then went back into the HOLMES room for Dorothy Amis, who was unmarried, she learnt.

She also had no immediate family.

The staging of her mutilation and the wounding patterns struck her as significant when she placed Dorothy side by side with what she knew about Pinocchio. Suddenly the similarities were eerily obvious. The room wasn't cold but she rubbed her arms then noticed movement and peered over her computer. Detectives were making their way to the briefing room and she checked the wall clock noting that it was five minutes to three. She gathered a pad and pen and joined them, making introductions as she shuffled into the large room. DCI Leia Lord was already sat at the head of the huge table and Kelly tried to catch her eye.

The DCI was busy reading and eventually she peered over her glasses which were perched on her nose and she smiled as her officers filed in.

Leia Lord was a woman who had clawed her way to the top of her game in a man's establishment. She was hawkish and upright, and invited no nonsense. Her hair was scraped back off her face and her makeup was deliberate. She was of slim build but solid and she liked to place her hands on her hips a lot. Her jacket was flung over the chair behind her and it had shoulder pads in it. Kelly thought they'd gone out of fashion but for women in the city who wanted to assert authority, she stood corrected.

Leia didn't hang around and launched straight into the brief. Questions were fired out to officers on several cases before they even got around to Dorothy Amis and it reminded Kelly of her meetings back at CID. This was a different world. The casual camaraderie of Bethnal Green CID seemed dated and sloppy compared to this. This was more like the real deal, she thought. She spotted Seb and they exchanged glances. He'd mentioned going out for a drink after work and she wasn't sure she had the energy. At the same time it would be a good opportunity to get to know him a bit better. Finally, Leia Lord got round to the Dorothy Amis case.

'Sixty-five years old. Single. Lived alone, no family. Unattached. Long employment history working for schools in different capacities, mainly in support roles, which is how she moved seamlessly into classes of her own, I assume. The headmaster is checking. There's no evidence of a formal teaching qualification so it's potentially embarrassing for them. However, it's not the first time we've seen people fall through the CRB checks. It's a terrible system that needs reforming. Before that she worked in children's homes. I want to know if this is relevant.'

Kelly busily took notes and everyone seemed to know their role. Molly had told her it was nursing homes, not kids' homes.

'Punch and Judy?' the DCI said, writing the names in large letters on the white board behind her.

'In the puppet show, Judy was a long-suffering victim of domestic abuse. Why kill her off? Surely if it was a vigilante show killing they would have killed off Punch, not his wife? This isn't classic vengeance as we know it. Any ideas?'

'Maybe it wasn't about Punch at all, just Judy.' Kelly couldn't believe she was articulating her thoughts so freely, but she couldn't help herself. The whole room of officers looked at her.

'Elaborate,' Leia Lord said.

'Judy was weak. She never fought back, not properly anyway. Punch always subdued her and he killed her children. Maybe this is more about what Judy didn't do. She didn't protect.'

The room was silent until Leia Lord spoke.

'Detective Sergeant Kelly Porter everyone. This is why I wanted her.'

Leia gave her a broad smile and suddenly all Kelly's nerves disappeared.

Chapter 19

Any thoughts of feeling too tired after a long day in her new job had gone by the time Seb and a few other colleagues suggested a few drinks before going home, even if it was only a Tuesday night. Kelly wasn't familiar with the area around Barking so she followed the others and trusted their judgement. Some stopped off to buy sandwiches to fill their stomachs. The chatter was about cases and Kelly's performance in the briefing room. Apparently speaking so candidly on her first brief was ballsy and Kelly didn't know whether to feel proud or worried.

'Leia loves people who take risks,' one said.

Kelly thought the term choice odd. Detectives weren't usually associated with risk. In fact, it was much better for them if they were the opposite. Measure and purpose were needed to crack cases. Echoes of her father's words rattled in her head and her first drink turned down the volume. Tonight she had something to celebrate. Not only her first two days on a murder squad but the fact that she'd impressed her boss. Making a good impression was important to her, but the fact that Leia Lord was a woman made her feel more satisfied.

It was a shame, though, that the boss didn't accompany them out to drink. It wasn't her style, she was told. Leia Lord was tee-total. Always in control.

Kelly took in the company and assessed that drinks after work were a young person's game. Those who were older and married had disappeared and left the rest of them to it. She ordered a gin and tonic and cradled it, sipping slowly. She wasn't interested in getting drunk, or even slightly tipsy, just a few to soften her nerves. Her aim was to get to know her colleagues: the people who'd be cracking the Dorothy Amis murder.

They sat in the beer garden and the sky was still light and streaks of blue and purple hovered over Longbridge Road. Their group was made up mainly of men who drank pints. The majority had beer bellies and she saw they were turning into the stereotype of coppers everywhere. It was as if more time served equated to a larger waist circumference. But not Seb. He stood out as different.

She scanned the garden tables and saw other groups drinking and Seb told her they were detectives too, though she could have easily spotted them as a tribe with their serious glances and suspicious eyes darting about expecting danger. Murder squad detectives wore a certain uniform: blue jeans, open shirts, pump-like shoes (good for running on pavements when required) and loose-knit sweaters hanging off their shoulders. There were always few women. It might be 2008, but equality in the biggest police force in Great Britain was sorely lacking. Which made Kelly even prouder that she'd come so far. A shadow passed over her thoughts as she remembered she hadn't told her parents yet. She wanted to savour the moment before deciding how to tell them. It should be done in person.

She watched Seb Crook from across the table. As he relaxed, he became louder and she thought he might be one of those blokes who turns dominant after a few drinks. She hoped not. She didn't want to work with a dick. As the pub grew noisier with people, the music was turned up and a live DJ appeared. The tunes came thick and fast and she watched as Seb became more drunk and opinionated. He told stories of cases he'd cracked. Younger officers hung on to his every word and Kelly worked out the hierarchy. Seb did very little listening but a lot of talking and she watched the reactions of others in his inner circle. He gave the impression of being a long-celebrated success and an old sweat who knew his onions. But she wondered what Leia Lord thought of him. The garden was full to bursting and people danced around tables. Kelly assessed it was almost time to leave but she didn't want to be rude.

The music switched to Duffy's 'Mercy' and the throng went wild, throwing their hands up in the air and moving en masse to the vocals. People imagined themselves in a soul movie, dressed in fifties dresses, bumping and grinding on the set of *Dirty Dancing*. But Kelly couldn't lose herself tonight.

She was with people who were familiar to one another but not to her. Her guard was up and she placed her half-drunk gin down. Northern men were better dancers. She went to find Seb to say good night.

She went to where he was swaying at the bar. He greeted her like an old friend and threw his arms around her. He smelled of body odour. She manoeuvred herself around him and encouraged him to join her at a quieter spot at the bar. Suddenly, her awe of murder squad seemed grubby and misplaced. Evil did that to people. Too much of it made them look to escape and it seemed Seb liked to let go at the bottom of a bottle. It was none of her business, but disappointment sat on her like a rude, uninvited guest.

'When did you make DI?' she asked him. She found herself getting close to his ear to make herself heard. She was desperate to stop him necking so much booze.

'You want to talk shop?' he asked, smiling goofily. He excused himself and downed his drink. It was the third time he'd needed the bathroom and when he returned he was rubbing his nose and Kelly noticed his red, wide eyes. She was immediately wary but didn't want to jump to conclusions but, to her, he was showing the characteristic signs of snorting something. It wouldn't be the first time she'd witnessed coppers dabbling in recreational drugs, but for her to suspect it in her new partner was bad news. Perhaps there was more pressure than she anticipated at MIT east, but the others didn't seem out of control or volatile in any way. It was just Seb. She also noticed that no one else seemed fazed by his behaviour.

She spotted a few of the detectives talking to journalists. They were old bedfellows: detectives and journos, but Kelly wasn't as trusting of them as others. Details had a habit of leaking out in the press that weren't agreed upon before. They scratched each other's backs but, one day, Kelly thought, it'd land somebody in trouble and their romance would end, but they could equally be helpful and worth the risk at times. Journalists could piece together leads where coppers didn't have time. They often knew areas better than uniforms and could dig into histories further and deeper than detectives could. People closed up when faced with a copper, even out of uniform. But most people could be swayed by a skilled writer who knew how to turn on the empathy and turn anything into a story. It was how many perps had been caught in the past. News people were treated with respect, as a result, and loyalty was repaid both ways. If a journo found out something first, they'd hand it over as a matter of respecting the code.

Often, information was passed along in bars just like this one and Kelly wondered what the conversations were about. Current cases? Dorothy Amis? Seb slapped his arm around a guy's shoulders and Kelly could tell he was press. She watched them closely.

'You've got that look about you,' the journo told her. Seb smiled, enjoying the show.

'What's that?' Kelly asked.

'The nose.' He laughed.

'My nose?'

'I don't mean your nose, I mean, *the nose*. You look like you've got the killer instinct.'

'Killer instinct? I'm not a serial killer, just so you know.'

'You wouldn't be the first,' he said.

His nonchalance bothered her, and a shiver caught her off guard. Was he seriously making a joke out of the fact that predators were known to have been caught hiding among the rank and file of the Met? She decided to leave them to their bromance and downed her drink.

'So, are you telling me I have what it takes to become a DI like Seb?' she asked, playing the game.

'Is that what you want?' Seb asked, involved now.

She nodded.

'So that's why you're talking to me?' He rubbed his nose. The journo got distracted and moved away.

'No, not at all, you brought it up,' she said. She matched his stare and he finally relaxed and laughed loudly. He believed her.

'Yes, you look like you do.'

'Thank you,' she said. 'Maybe you could advise me how to do it, then.'

'I could.'

Kelly was becoming weary of Seb's games. Sobriety was never a great playmate of a boring drunk. The act of his knowing it all and her being kept in the dark was tedious and she'd seen it played out before in pubs all over London. She hoped he wasn't the type to expect something else in return for helping her up the ladder.

'Does it get to you?' she asked.

'What?'

'The stuff you see.'

'You mean like yesterday?' He nodded. 'I've seen enough kink to last a lifetime.'

'That's not just Homicide, I got that shit in CID all the time. A toast to the city full of perverts,' she said and raised an empty glass.

'Wackos and wankers,' he said.

She couldn't help but laugh but she also felt sorry for him. She'd heard of murder detectives burning out but now she saw it before her very eyes. This man who seemed to have his shit together professionally and had been given the task of welcoming her to her first murder investigation was actually no more than a shell and he was falling apart. She had a decision to make. She could stay and take care of him, but she barely knew him. Or she could leave and pretend she saw nothing.

Chapter 20

Luther bent over the last box, which was tucked under a pile of Elizabethan courtier's clothes at the back of the cupboard. It had taken him twenty minutes to find it and he'd placed the clothes aside, careful to fold them for the education team who performed reenactments for school groups. They role-played battles, weddings, scandals and executions to the wonderment of the youngsters. Luther used to be hands-on with the kids himself but he found it too exhausting now. They were insatiable for a start, asking incessant questions and wanting to touch the artefacts. They were also disrespectful and impossible to keep in check. But more than that, interaction with them brought back too many bad memories, and besides, nowadays they just weren't that interested.

It was the toys he loved. The children who played with them were ungrateful and undeserving. Nowadays, the kids who came here didn't appreciate the artistry and legerdemain that went into creating the phenomenal items that he handled and preserved with passion. They no longer believed in magic. For the puppets weren't simply inanimate objects d'art. They had the ability to truly exist. Luther believed that if a child's soul captured a puppet, then it would always be free. It could never die. But they'd always be bonded. Puppets were born barren and only children could give them life with their laughter and their innocence. Only the good became truly animated, like Pinocchio.

He took the box to a table and sat on the chair. His back was playing up again and it made him melancholy. It slowed him down and meant that he couldn't take care of the pieces like he used to, which is why somebody had been able to rob them blind. A younger version of himself would have fought them off. If he'd been on his game, and in the prime of his life, he would have spotted an intruder and chased him off. As it was, he didn't hear a thing and didn't even notice until he checked the boxes. The V&A kept him on at his ripe old age because he was irreplaceable. Nobody they ever interviewed matched his experience in the field. He had degrees in archaeology, history and art, and that was virtually unique in his field.

Which was why he was given more leeway than would ordinarily be extended to a curator of one of the finest establishments in the world. He'd had the CCTV camera in his office reconnected though, after stern words from the Director of Collections at the V&A.

Charlie McCarthy might have gone but in this box, hidden under the stage props, was his prized toy. The one he treasured the most. He'd been toying with the idea of not displaying it anymore, keeping it locked away purely for his own pleasure, but he knew that wasn't right or proper. It deserved to be seen.

It was a vintage 1939 Jiminy Cricket wooden doll.

He was cracking a little around his face, if Luther remembered rightly, but otherwise he was in pristine condition and Luther was thankful he hadn't left the box out like he had the others. No matter how much they'd rooted around, they hadn't managed to find him.

Jiminy cricket was unique in that he was a cartoon add-on to a classic tale but generated as much interest as the main character in the story. People thought the star of the show was Pinocchio, or even Geppetto, the naïve toy maker with a big heart. But to collectors, it was the little insect.

Jiminy Crickets, I've lost my hat… Luther chuckled at the memory.

He opened the box and put his hand inside to feel for the silk which Luther kept him in. He'd been housed in the collections department at a constant ambient-level temperature and lighting. But from there, when the refurbishment completed and Luther began transferring pieces to the exhibit areas, Jiminy had stayed in his office.

He felt around inside the box, but stared at his hand when he felt nothing.

He pulled out his hand and picked up the box, shaking it and realising that it was too light.

He ripped out the silk and the stuffing and emptied the box all over the floor. There was nothing inside.

Jiminy was gone.

Luther twisted his head in all directions to see who had watched him come in here, and who might have known what he kept in here, but there was no one there. He felt pain in his chest and a burning inside him that he interpreted as nothing short of bereavement.

It hurt like hell.

But it was his own fault. He knew that much.

He kicked the box across the office floor, where it crashed into a desk with a clatter.

His breath quickened and he held his heart.

Then he sank to his knees.

He felt around the floor to see if on the off chance, Jiminy had fallen under the table, out of his box, and had lain there waiting to be discovered. But he was nowhere to be found.

He'd been taken.

Luther balled up his fists and felt a rage so hot that he scared himself. He crawled to his desk and used the wooden leg to help himself up and turn to his computer. He logged on and saw there was a reply to his Facebook message.

It was too much. Luther's heart beat so fast in his chest that he had to put his head in his hands to calm down. He watched as the page opened and he read a new message. It wasn't a long one. The person hadn't taken time to construct a cheery note or a long catch-up after so many years having not seen one another.

How long had it been? Two years? Three? He couldn't remember. All he knew was that the last time he'd seen him he was scared. Frightened of what the man could do with his bare hands. Terrified of what he swore to do to those who brought him harm. The man had once been a boy; an innocent who loved his toys. He had once watched Luther create stories and animations with puppets, running away to distant worlds where they could both pretend to live, instead of the world here which was scary and busy, and dangerous. An innocent boy, turned into a monster by what they did to him.

The boy grew big, and soon, he outgrew Luther too.

Luther saw that the man's Facebook wall had changed. In place of the puppets, there was now a photograph of several vintage children's toys in a row. His artefacts. Luther grabbed hold of the computer screen and scanned the photo for signs of damage to his priceless antiquities.

Then he read another, more recent, message.

Calm down, Luther. I don't need your forgiveness. I don't need anything from you. I don't want your pity. I want your puppets. I don't need you anymore. I've found them. I never needed you.

Then he saw the user was live. It was as if he was in the same room, in Luther's office, watching him and reading his thoughts. Just like he used to warn the children that the adults knew when they were lying…

Maybe he had been in this room, Luther realised with horror. Perhaps he'd been watching the whole time. That's how he knew where to find Jiminy Cricket.

'Give them back to me,' he typed furiously.

'No,' came the almost instant reply. 'It's too late.'

Luther's fingers worked furiously.

'What do you want them for?'

Luther was in danger of suffering a full-blown panic attack.

'To tell lies and perform magic, just like you did.'

'I never lied to you.'

'Yes, you did.'

'I never hurt you.'

'No, but they did, and they'll get what they deserve.'

'I've called the police,' he typed.

The user logged off and Luther sat back but then he came online again.

A minute later, he read the reply.

'That's a very silly thing to do.'

Chapter 21

News of a robbery on Sunday night at the Museum of Childhood in Bethnal Green reached the MIT early Wednesday morning. It had come to the murder team's attention because a link on HOLMES had been picked up. Dorothy Amis had been busy organising a school visit to the museum for a small group of students, shortly before she died. The link between puppets and a museum full of children's toys needed checking out and Kelly volunteered to pay them a visit seeing as she was closest to the location. Cambridge Heath Road was close to Bethnal Green tube station and she had plenty of reading to keep her busy before it opened at ten a.m.

The first thing she did as she left the flat after sharing a rushed breakfast with Molly was call Seb to see if he'd made it home in one piece. Her sense of duty to her partner had spurred her to leave with Seb in a taxi to deliver him safely back home before he went too far. There'd been no phone call thanking her for her intervention yet and she didn't expect one. Her plan was to gloss over the evening and allow him to take the lead if he wanted to mention it at all.

She was doing it again: taking a broken person under her wing. Whatever was going on with Seb, she really shouldn't get involved in his personal life.

There was no answer and she tapped the Nokia phone against her top lip and walked towards the entrance to the museum. It was cool and bright. The place had been refurbished recently, she'd read, and it felt fresh. It had closed in 2005 and reopened the following year, at the cost of almost five million pounds to the British taxpayer. There was a playful atmosphere laid on for their biggest clientele: children. Kelly found herself smiling as she walked towards the main atrium as she was transported back to her own childhood. Memories of toys and games flooded her senses, and the noise of children everywhere lifted her spirits. Theirs was such an honest sound. Kids didn't hide their true selves like adults did, they hadn't learnt they had to yet. That came later.

The curator she wanted to see was in charge of acquisitions and collections and his name was Luther Zedric. It was an exotic name for a bizarre profession and she expected to meet a *Charlie and the Chocolate Factory*–type figure who lived in a cupboard upstairs and made sweets. She showed her warrant card at reception and the woman, called Diandra, picked up her phone and called the curator directly. It took him less than five minutes to appear in the reception hall and he almost shook her hand off. So grateful, he said he was for the police to take the burglary seriously. She didn't have the heart to tell him that wasn't the reason she was here. His American accent made him endearing, as if peeling back the stuffiness of his profession. He suited his job. He was jovial and over the top, and she could see him engaging crowds of kids as he enthused about the thousands of toys surrounding them. Some people had the coolest jobs, she thought.

'Of course, anything you can tell us that might help, can we talk somewhere private? Perhaps you can show me where it happened?' she asked.

'Of course, this way.'

Luther Zedric scuttled away. He was an older man, possibly in his seventies, and he wore a tweed suit. His white hair was parted in the middle and he wore spectacles on the end of his nose. Kelly reckoned she couldn't have met a more fitting stereotype. He and Jonathan Hass would get on well. Luther looked as though he'd lovingly looked after toys all his life, just as Jonathan looked after bodies. She questioned the reasoning of somebody who was drawn into such a career and, ever vigilant, she wondered if it might be somebody just as odd who had a fetish for dressing murder victims up as legendary children's characters. She studied the muscle structure in his back as she followed him, assessing if he'd have the strength…

She couldn't help it.

'They took Charlie McCarthy,' he said.

The man was forlorn.

'Who?'

He tutted. 'Why doesn't anyone know?'

She apologised for her lack of knowledge and promised to learn about anything he wished to share with her today, including his familiarity with Pinocchio and Punch and Judy. He didn't appear to hear her and carried on mumbling about his missing dolls.

As they approached his office, they passed exhibits of toys she recognised. Trains she played with, board games she set up for her own friends and family, dolls, bears and collector sets. There was a display of editions of Monopoly, another one dedicated solely to Smurfs, and another filled with vintage Fisher-Price classics. She spotted a plastic telephone, a school and a tree house. Her head filled with memories of playing with her sister, Nikki, and one in particular stood out. It was their farm toys, set up on the grass, by the side of Derwent Water. They took the set everywhere with them. The feeling it evoked stayed with her like a warm blanket as Luther Zedric talked and talked.

He explained how Charlie McCarthy became the biggest ventriloquist's puppet star of the last century and she found herself apologising again.

'I grew up on the Teletubbies and Pingu, I'm afraid,' she said, hoping he'd forgive her ignorance.

'Of course. I understand. We're trying to educate the new generations, but they don't have the appreciation for real toys like we used to.'

Kelly nodded.

'Progress, I suppose,' she said.

He grimaced at her. She followed him into a large room that, to her, looked like a dumping ground for paperwork and spare boxes. It reminded her of the CID office at the nick, but here, one man had more room to spread out. Back at Bethnal Green nick, five of them had shared the space, and fought over desks.

'Charlie McCarthy was in here. Jiminy Cricket in here. And the Muppets were in here.'

He showed her the empty boxes and she thought she hadn't seen a man so bereft since she'd informed the family of a robbery victim who'd sustained terrible injuries during an assault, last week. He had genuine affection for these toys, and he acted like the father of missing children.

'Why those in particular do you think?' she asked him. 'There are hundreds of toys in here.'

'They were the most valuable by far.'

Kelly's heart sank. It wasn't what she wanted to hear. She'd hoped there were other motives for the robbery, apart from money, such as sick fetishes linked to dressing up murder victims, or hidden messages of revenge behind their stories.

'How long have you worked here, Luther? May I call you Luther?'

'Of course,' he said. 'Please, sit down,' he directed her to a lovely sofa in the corner.

'I sit here to catalogue,' he said.

She got the impression that Luther didn't get out much. She nodded.

'I started working here in 1988.'

'Twenty years. That's a long time, you must know this place inside out.'

'I do.' He smiled and sat down next to her. 'Look,' he said, getting up again. 'This is one of my favourites. You must know Jack and Jill, the nursery rhyme?'

'Of course.'

He took a box from behind a desk and unfolded the flaps, showing her two dolls inside. They looked like any other models to her but Luther explained the rarity of these particular specimens.

Kelly showed interest but she really wanted to move on to why she was here.

'Can I ask what you know about Pinocchio? I'm here to ask your opinion on another unrelated case, if you'll be so helpful. You're obviously an expert.'

'Why Pinocchio?'

'There have been other crimes across the capital. Involving toys,' she added, trying to be a little vague on purpose. She felt this old man didn't need to be privy to the details of a murder inquiry if it wasn't necessary.

'Really? Well! A serial robber of children's dreams!'

Something in the way he referenced children, like from a Grimm tale itself, as if the child reading was the centre of the story and not the character, made her pause for thought. Children's dreams. Is that what her mysterious killer was doing? Her parents had read her Grimm tales when she was a kid and they came flooding back to her now. Hansel and Gretel, Rapunzel, Snow White; they were all set in forests or castles and there was always an evil witch who wanted to kill innocent little children.

Most of the evil characters would be called paedophiles today.

She thought back to Pinocchio and what Jonathan Hass told her about the corpse. She was small, and childlike. But Dorothy Amis wasn't a child, she just worked with children. She was supposed to care for children, like the evil women in fairy tales were supposed to. Kelly chided herself for being unable to evict Pinocchio from her enquiries but she couldn't help herself. The two cases kept crossing over.

'Do you have anything to do with school visits, Luther?' she asked.

'Not anymore. I prefer the company of the exhibits.' He grinned.

She nodded in conspiracy.

'I suppose school kids can be challenging in an environment like this, perhaps you could point me in the direction of the person who does brave them.'

'Of course,' he said absently. 'I have a Pinocchio from 1889, would you like to see it?' His eyes lit up.

Kelly smiled. 'Yes, please.'

Chapter 22

The room behind the exhibit stage was cool and dark. It had to be, explained Luther, to keep the artefacts at a constant temperature and limit exposure to light and other elements which could ruin them.

Kelly had asked him if he knew of anyone who worked at the museum who would know where the most valuable pieces were kept and might have stolen them to sell.

'I trust all my staff. I can't think of anyone who'd do such a thing.'

'We're tracking sales on antique websites hoping they might show up with a lead for us,' she said. It was a possibility that whoever had taken Luther Zedric's puppets knew other, more sinister, lovers of fiction.

'The original story was written in 1883 by a Tuscan called Carlo Collodi. The idea of a toy coming alive and being highly mischievous was way ahead of its time. Genius, don't you think? Children these days think fantasy was invented by Walt Disney.'

Kelly smiled. She was having difficulty concentrating but she must be patient to gain knowledge from this man who seemed to know everything about puppets and toys. She already knew a little about the history of the original Pinocchio story.

'A marionette is a puppet, right?' she asked.

'Yes! Well done. You're learning. But it is one that is manipulated by strings, not controlled by a hand inside it. It's an important distinction.'

'Like Mr Punch?'

'Exactly. You're fast to catch on, see.'

Luther was pleased.

'So, here he is,' Luther said, taking her to a dark case, where she saw a wooden toy, about the size of a toddler. The museum was cool but even so, the goosebumps on her skin were a surprise to her. She stared at the puppet, who seemed to grin back at her. The toy was sat still, even though she expected it to come to life at any moment. It smiled at her and followed her gaze as she moved around it. It looked just like the miniature one they'd found with the woman at the Stratford Junction site. A group of children behind the glass, with two adults – presumably their parents – pointed and laughed at them.

She examined the marionette.

His eyes were blue and matched his bow tie, just like the props used on her female victim. He wore red dungarees and a black-and-gold jacket. His yellow hat was trimmed with a blue ribbon and an orange feather, and he wore wooden clogs on his feet. She wanted to touch him to see if she could wake him up. His long nose seemed to point at her, casting judgement.

'He has this effect on everyone, which is the genius of the story. It's about a puppet that is reanimated in the hearts and minds of children, but also in reality, in the story.'

Kelly thought Luther might wipe away a tear.

'All he wanted was to have fun, but his lack of responsibility got him into terrible trouble.'

'And that's when his nose grew, when he lied?' Kelly said.

Luther nodded, but he didn't look at her. He was mesmerised by the puppet, as was she.

'And when he reforms his ways and sacrifices his material desires to look after his creator – Geppetto – he becomes a real boy and is able to live.'

Kelly watched as Luther transformed in front of her eyes and she felt swept away by his love of the stories that had kept children's dreams alive for centuries. Her own affection for the Disney version came rushing back to her and she felt an overwhelming sense of power radiating from the drama. She wasn't sure if it was children or adults who appreciated dreams more. Certainly, it was parents who spent the money on them.

'So, it's about rebirth,' Kelly said. She wasn't looking for an answer, simply stating the facts as she saw them. She wasn't even sure if she'd said it out loud. The message behind the journeys of the happy marionette was simple, and it had been staring her in the face the whole time.

'Exactly! They're vehicles to another world.' But soon after he said it, his face darkened, and he turned away.

'What can you tell me about Mr Punch?' she asked, trying to reengage him.

Luther's face remained murky, as if she'd mentioned a dark sinister force. It was like the music changes so familiar to anyone who loved classic kids' movies. The baddies were always accompanied by menacing music when they appeared on screen. Her favourites were Mr Hook, Jafar and Cruella de Vil. But Luther didn't look captivated by cinematic genius, he appeared fearful. Her nostalgia disappeared.

'Mr Punch? He started out as Pulcinella, a trickster and a thief.'

Luther led her back to his office. She followed and listened to him.

'The British version was supposed to have originated as a seventeenth-century gentleman of some standing, compared to his French and Italian counterpart who was merely a violent peasant and perverted opportunist, beating those who stood in his way. The seaside equivalent was a hand puppet, a lowly children's character who brutally assaulted his wife and child. He is the epitome of slapstick who charmed post-Cromwellian audiences, sick of puritanical rule, revelling in the newfound gaudiness of the restoration era which followed. To me, though, he'll always be just a thug.'

Kelly didn't know what to say. She felt as though she was going down a rabbit hole and looked at her watch.

'You must understand that he pretended to play the role of a family man, when really, underneath, there lived a monster. The violence unleashed by this one character made hundreds and thousands of families laugh until their sides hurt, and they went home from the beach with their children tired after a long day out, all together, talking and swapping stories of how Mr Punch got his comeuppance. But he never did. That was a myth. Punchinello always got away with it. He even beat the devil.'

Kelly noticed Luther's demeanour change from engaging historian to something else entirely. They reached his office, and Luther went to a drawer and took something out.

'Judy never fought back?' she asked simply.

'Oh, she did but she was never strong enough.'

A terrible noise assaulted her ears, and she recognised it as the same noise of her childhood. The sound she'd heard a thousand times on Blackpool beach after she'd ridden a donkey and licked an ice cream.

Luther beamed at her and showed her a silver gadget. He put it into his mouth again and blew.

'I know what a swazzle is, that's very loud!' She covered her ears.

'You do! How charming. It's the very same. It's merely a flat ring which goes between the tongue and the roof of the mouth. The resulting sound – a cross between a toy duck and a Christmas party blower – gave Mr Punch his voice. Genius.'

He blew it again and smiled. His dark shadow had gone, and she smiled back.

'So, let's see,' he said, going to his computer.

Their technology was as woeful as the Met's, and they waited for photos to load. He showed her pictures of the puppets that were missing. The three Muppets, Jiminy Cricket and Charlie McCarthy, who gave her the creeps. Then he showed her a video from the internet of Charlie McCarthy and Edgar Bergen, his puppeteer. They both wore tuxedos. The skit was funny and Kelly chuckled at Charlie's risky one-liners. His monocle made him look intelligent but his face was childlike, even if his top hat gave the impression of maturity. He was a curious combination of old and young and she couldn't help but think that Edgar Bergen, the ventriloquist, wanted to live through his puppet. She recalled what Jonathan Hass told her about puppeteers feeling real love for their muses.

'I may be a dummy but I'm not stupid,' Charlie said and Kelly smiled, watching Luther as she did so.

'And he was wildly popular?' she asked.

'Charlie had his own radio show from 1937 to 1956. He was awarded an honorary degree, and he even appeared on *The Muppet Show*. He regularly appeared with Kermit and Howdy Doody. As of course did the great Milton Berle.'

'Who?'

'Uncle Miltie?'

Kelly was none the wiser.

'His theatre in London was the most famous of all, well, if you like ragtime, that is. I went there many times.'

'Ragtime the music?'

'Of course,' he said, grinning. He hummed The Entertainer tune and the tiny hairs on Kelly's arms stood up as she recalled the last time she'd heard it. In the office on Monday.

She refocused.

'And you said the three Muppets went missing too?'

'Yes, exactly. Thank goodness you see the importance! The police officer who was here had no clue. I'm sorry, I don't mean to be critical, it's just that I need a specialist on this, somebody like you who appreciates the worth of these exhibits. They're real to us here. They're alive.'

His eyes were pleading and Kelly saw his obsession and it thrilled and disturbed her at the same time. He'd showed her a snippet of her childhood by spinning back to a time when she was unsure, hesitant, weak and uncertain. And it felt dismal and wonderful at the same time. She suddenly saw her father striding ahead of her, across the grassland below Helvellyn, shouting at her to keep up. She sensed confusion spreading across her body and the mountain's harshness came to life.

'It does that to you, in here,' Luther said, snapping her out of her own fantasy.

She smiled at him.

'Thank you, Luther. It's been... informative.'

'And my puppets?'

'I'll do everything I can to get them back, I promise.'

'Thank you, Detective Porter,' he said in a strange voice. When she looked back at him, he had a puppet on the end of his hand, and was communicating through it.

She smiled uneasily.

He showed her back through his office and escorted her to the stairs where she said she'd find her own way out.

Chapter 23

After her encounter with Luther Zedric, Kelly found herself too close to Bethnal Green nick not to pay them a visit. She needed to decompress. The curator's eccentricity stuck in her mind and it led her to thinking how strange and wonderful his world was. Strange because it involved dolls, toys and puppets which gave her the creeps, but wonderful because of what it did for kids. The walk was familiar, and she found herself growing nostalgic for something ordinary. Seeing Cheryl and Pete was just what she needed.

When she'd dreamt of becoming a police officer in the Met, often going for long hikes alone in the Lake District national park, she'd envisioned teams of detectives driving around the streets catching criminals, who would run away down tiny alleys, only to be caught after a hot pursuit, like John Thaw and Dennis Waterman in *The Sweeney*. But sat on top of Place Fell, overlooking Ullswater, or walking up a gorge in the Langdales, the solace and quiet afforded her space to yearn for another distant place, where she could also be anonymous and hide. People thought the Lake District an idyllic place to grow up but it was firmly rooted in England's provincial tradition. Everybody knew each other's business and school was a series of survival episodes as she navigated her way around the popular kids and fell in with various crowds to blend in.

But she never had.

Work opportunities revolved around tourism or farming and she fancied neither.

Then there was the growing crime rate. The nineties saw the explosion of recreational drugs on offer, but nothing like it was now. When she spoke to her dad on the phone, he constantly complained about county lines drug gangs who'd taken over the area. It was a very different county to the one she'd left behind, which is why she never wanted to go back.

But it pulled at her too, and she couldn't quite let it go.

She felt it. She couldn't ignore it and found herself daydreaming about its wildernesses and peace, as she did now as she approached her old office.

The noise of the station greeted her and she headed up the stairs to the CID. Pete and Cheryl were both at their desks.

'Surprise,' she announced.

'Kelly!' Pete said and Cheryl soon followed suit. They each greeted her with a warm hug and a dozen questions about her new job. It was a different sentiment entirely to the one inside the Barking office. She told herself it was just because she hadn't got her boots under the table yet, that was all.

'I was just at the museum down the road, I thought I'd pop in.'

Suddenly she felt awkward.

'The museum?' Cheryl asked.

'Of childhood. There was a burglary, it popped up on our inquiry because of the puppets, I guess.'

'Oh, you're handling the teacher they say was dressed up like Judy,' Pete said.

Kelly nodded, feeling a flicker of guilt as if she was betraying her new team. She pushed the thoughts away. She looked around the office and spotted the coffee tray on the windowsill. A jar of instant sat encrusted to the sides, and dirty teaspoons stuck to the plastic tray. She found a clean mug and flicked the kettle on.

'Nice weekend, Pete?' she asked Windy Miller.

'Sound, thanks. BBQ with the in-laws. Bit of DIY in the garden.'

'You've caught the sun,' Kelly observed.

Pete was from Liverpool, a land devoid of windmills, but full of criminals. He met his future wife in a cell, when she got caught up in a mass arrest at a nightclub. She still saw him as her saviour from that night. He moved to London to be with her but Kelly knew he struggled with the different crime dynamic. The stabbings, gun crime and sheer scale of the capital made him seem constantly under attack, which she guessed they all were.

Cheryl was also a migrant, like her. She hailed from Leeds and her no-nonsense charm suited London's need for savvy interviewers who relished getting into the suites to crack witnesses. It was an art form, and Cheryl, with her kind northern charm, won over the majority of them. They'd worked together on Bradley Fellcroft.

But now they'd lost him, and she couldn't help feeling as though it was her fault. If she'd stuck around then maybe the case would have been smoother. Had she missed something because her mind was on getting into a murder squad?

'Did you find out who Bradley was an informant for? I heard it was your one and only Leia Lord, do they call her Princess Leia?' Cheryl asked.

Kelly's face must have changed because Cheryl asked her if she felt okay.

'I suspect it's to do with Bradley's father,' Cheryl said.

'Jason Fellcroft?' Pete asked.

'Same,' Kelly said. 'He threatened Bradley and had a burner phone smuggled out of Belmarsh and had it delivered to him.'

'What's the connection?' Cheryl asked.

Kelly shrugged. 'He's not opening up to me. I went to see him again yesterday and he gave me nothing.'

Cheryl raised her eyebrows. 'Little fucker, what's he playing at?'

'Dunno. He gave me the impression he hated his father. Orlando knows he's got away with it again.'

'How did he know before us?'

'Exactly. Orlando must have a link to Jason Fellcroft, so I started going over Bradley's file and did some digging.'

'They not working you hard enough over there at murder squad?' Cheryl asked.

Kelly chuckled. 'I needed a break from all the policies they've got me reading, anyway, I feel bad for leaving you two with this, I thought I could help.'

Kelly shyly brought a piece of paper out of her trouser pocket and unfolded it.

'I put together a list of building sites owned or run by Jason Fellcroft before he was sent down, as well as those suspected of being under his control via friends and associates currently while he served his stretch. This one is where we found Pinocchio, in Stratford, and look who worked there between 2000 and 2006.'

Cheryl looked at the list.

'Orlando? So, Orlando and Fellcroft have history, but that doesn't explain why Bradley would be intimidated by his father.'

'Isn't the fact that he's a murderer enough?' Kelly asked.

'Bradley has faced worse. When we spoke to him about Feltham, he was transferred a few times, wasn't he? Last year, when he was still seventeen, he was included in a tranche of inmates who were transferred temporarily to free up beds for younger boys,' Pete said.

Kelly nodded. The penny dropped. 'He spent six weeks in Belmarsh.'

Cheryl put her head in her hands. 'Fucking prison service, honestly, they want shooting.'

'Lack of cash, just like us,' Pete chipped in.

'I'll look into whether he had any exposure to his father when he was in there. Jesus, minors in Belmarsh, no wonder they become institutionalised,' Kelly said.

'Bradley didn't,' Cheryl reminded her.

'Maybe he did,' Kelly said.

'Shall I call him or will you?' she asked Cheryl.

Cheryl pushed back from her desk and her chair ran into loose wires along the floor, causing it to falter and judder. Kelly picked up the desk phone and rang Bradley's number which she knew by heart. She held the receiver away from her ear so Pete and Cheryl could listen.

She tried three times before he picked up.

'Hi, Bradley,' she said.

'You again,' he said.

It wasn't aggressive, or moody, simply observational, and slightly humorous.

'It is me. I wanted to ask you a question about your dad.'

They heard him sigh.

'His building sites. He still owns stakes but that isn't on the paperwork, is that correct?'

'If you say it is.'

'I'll take that as a yes. When Orlando Charles worked on the same one as you, is that how they first met or do they go back further than that?'

'How would I know?'

'Come on, Bradley, cut me some slack. I need to find another witness.'

'Don't make me feel guilty.'
'Why not?'
'Jeez, you want shit, he wants shit, everyone wants shit…'
They listened.
'Yes, he worked for him.'
Another sigh.
'Thank you. One more thing.'
'I've got to go.'
'When you were transferred to Belmarsh on remand, did you see your dad?'
Kelly sensed his breathing go very quiet.
'Yeah,' he breathed.
'I'm sorry,' she said. 'We should be looking after you better than that. You were only seventeen.'
'Yeah.'
'We can protect you from him.'
'No, you can't.'
He hung up.
Nobody spoke. Everything made sense now.
'I'll request information on their visitor lists,' Cheryl said.
'Good idea,' Kelly replied.
'I wonder if he visits him still.'
'Orlando said he was a good dad,' Cheryl reminded her.
'Maybe he visits him too,' Pete said.
'That would be something,' Kelly said. 'The link between the inside and the outside we didn't know we needed.'

Chapter 24

When Kelly revisited Brampton Forensic Services, she found Jonathan Hass enthusiastically studying the data on his computer. He turned as she closed the door and thanked his assistant. Jonathan smiled broadly at her. He had the pallor of someone who didn't see sunlight very much and if Kelly was honest, he gave her the creeps. His lab reminded her of a case study she'd followed when she'd first become interested in detective work. It was a murder case where a woman had been chopped up by her husband in a lab just like this one. She looked around, making sure she knew where the exits were, only half tongue-in-cheek.

'Hi,' she addressed him cheerily. 'What couldn't wait?' she asked.

He'd called her at the Bethnal Green office forgetting she'd left, to tell her that she needed to see something that he couldn't explain over the phone. Cheryl and Pete were inundated with other cases, so she'd volunteered to indulge the professor, secretly glad of the opportunity to find out more about Pinocchio.

She found the whole business of cutting up the dead repulsive and doubted she'd ever get used to it, but she knew if she wanted to succeed on a murder squad then she better harden herself to the sight of bits of humans spread over tables, and much worse. She'd seen autopsies in lectures online, but never one in person and she was glad of it. Jonathan's job was slightly different in that he dealt with people who'd been dead so long they were barely recognisable, but Pinocchio was so obviously a woman to her now that it made her shudder to see her again. Jonathan had photos of the procedure on his computer, but her body was still there on his slab, beckoning her to take a peek. She glanced over at her. Her clothes had now been removed, and they'd been bagged and tagged and sent to another forensic laboratory for testing. Kelly found the sight even more sorrowful. The woman's body was twisted and brown and it reminded her of the ancient bodies found in the Alps, or similar, which had been buried in snow five thousand years ago. Each time one of them was discovered, forensic anthropologists like Jonathan got very excited. Like he was now. She reminded herself to switch off her tenderness, which didn't help in situations like this and just gave HR something to scrutinise if you got too emotional.

She approached the slab.

'I'm almost done with her,' Jonathan said, and Kelly found his word choice chilling but understandably practical. The woman had already been discarded once before, in a hole in the ground, and now she was being cast aside for a second time. The coroner's office awaited the verdict of the forensic service and an inquest would be held into how this woman had met her end. It didn't matter how old the remains turned out to be, the death was suspicious and so a report must be filed. That's how the law worked.

'So, we now have a stab profile from the scan. I have a new computer program that is cutting edge,' he told her proudly. 'Excuse the pun,' he added, and Kelly reckoned he was fond of delivering them. It wasn't the first she'd heard. 'There's quite a pattern, she was ferociously attacked,' he said.

Kelly thought about Dorothy Amis and her cause of death. The coincidences were mounting up but she knew that killers didn't often wait decades between victims and so it didn't make sense. She dismissed it. For now.

'I've matched the wounds to a knife like this one,' he carried on and showed her a photo of a seven-inch blade on his computer screen. It looked harmless enough, as if it would be well suited to peeling carrots, but Kelly knew what havoc even small blades could wreak. She hated knives. They caused so much pain. It wasn't just physical. The fallout threw hand grenades into families. She'd worked in London long enough to witness the horrors blades did to flesh. This was different but no less impactful. The woman on the slab had been vibrant once, just like Dorothy.

'There are so many nicks and incisions on her thoracic skeleton that it's my informed opinion that she was stabbed at least eleven times.'

'Good work,' Kelly said, her mind racing with possibility. They needed a date.

'She's also kyphotic and she had arthritis. Her pelvic symphysis is pitted and craggy.'

Kelly looked puzzled.

'It means that she's likely over sixty years of age.'

Kelly nodded, taking in the new information. She was around the same age as Dorothy, then…

'The cloth and dye results are back and they were manufactured around the 1920s, so that got me focused on around eighty years ago. However, look what I found when I got the hat off her.'

'But that doesn't explain the Arsenal fixture list.'

Jonathan grinned at her and Kelly waited. He showed her some files on his computer and gave commentary on what she was looking at. He went through the fibre bonds on the hat, as well as the DNA of the feather.

'The hat is Tyrolean. It took some time to trace. There were only two stockists in London and they both closed down in the 1930s.'

'Tyrolean?'

'Italian Alps. The Tyrol.'

Kelly nodded. An image of Austrian dancers flickered across her mind. It was the same one she'd had when she'd first spotted the dungarees and bow tie and learned the origin of the Pinocchio story from Luther Zedric.

'The feather is real but sprayed red. The dye is being examined to ascertain its date. The clogs are hand carved, but untraceable I'm afraid. We can't date wood. But this is what I called you for.'

He brought up a page on his computer screen and she stared at some kind of metal gadget. There was a ruler placed beside it for context and she saw that the item was about five centimetres across. It was an oval metal disc with wires stuck out of it.

Her stomach turned over with excitement as she realised what she was looking at.

'When was the first pacemaker fitted in this country?' she asked him.

'1950s. But this isn't that old. It's a modern design.'

'Please tell me it has a serial number,' she said. She was close to him now and Jonathan was as excited as she was.

'It has.' He grinned. He walked across to a plastic box and opened it and retrieved an item from it. He held it in his hand and she looked at it.

'How do we trace it?' she asked.

'We contact the manufacturer, which is Bionomic in this case, and access their database, but I'm guessing you'll need a warrant of some kind to do that.'

'Amazing,' Kelly whispered.

They had an ID, well, not quite, but as close as damn it. And they knew the woman wasn't ancient. Her remains were less than fifty years old, which qualified her for a homicide investigation.

Her heart rate forced blood through her wrist and the *tap tap* of her pulse reflected the excitement she felt. There had been a time when the thought of murder squad swooping in and taking over the investigation based upon all their hard work filled her with a deep depression, but now she knew that it would be her investigation. It was MIT east territory. Their patch. But her heart sank as she knew from bitter experience how Cheryl and Pete would feel.

It happened all the time. She was no stranger to procedure in the Met. CIDs did their bit and Homicide and Major Crime Command did theirs. The members of the MITs, who pulled up in in their fancy Ford Mondeos, and their tailored jackets (or casual V-necks), with their access to state-of-the-art software like HOLMES, was what had made her want to become a murder detective, but she felt guilty about her old team again. She and Cheryl had discovered Pinocchio together.

But she was getting ahead of herself. They still had to confirm an identification. This was still Bethnal Green's case, and the HAT wouldn't assign it until they had a firm date. The only person she was obliged to inform was Cheryl. But perhaps with Jonathan's help, she could still make herself indispensable.

Chapter 25

Visiting the home of a murder victim was always a solemn affair. Dorothy Amis lived in a third-floor flat in an old Victorian townhouse along Chelmsford Road. Kelly watched Seb dip under the police tape and followed him into the hallway. There was something distinctly sad about entering Dorothy's private space, knowing she'd never come back here. Kelly almost expected the woman to emerge from the kitchen and ask them if they'd like a cuppa.

'Forensics have been in to collect prints. They found no evidence of unusual activity,' Seb said.

He was firmly back in work mode. They hadn't discussed his erratic behaviour from Tuesday night. She'd put it down to him offloading. Coppers' need. And she wasn't about to push him. She was thrilled to be out in the field with him doing something important. She'd reported her conversations with Luther back to him and he'd nodded nonchalantly, asking her to write up a report to submit to HOLMES on Wednesday evening. That had been last night and now they must focus on something else. It had been deflating but she understood that investigations of this nature took time. Nobody was jumping to any conclusions, which though it didn't satisfy her need for immediate answers, it did remind her that there was a process that must be followed. Some murders in London took years to solve; others never were.

The house looked pristine. Dorothy was a proud woman and she also had scant taste. Everything was clean and tidy and the space was functional. The décor was dated like her parent's house in Penrith. The furniture was mismatched and inexpensive and there were few pictures or personal touches around the place. There was a pile of magazines in a stand and Kelly flicked through them, noting they were back copies of periodicals that she guessed any teacher might take an interest in. There were a couple on special educational needs, some on history, science, nature, teaching early years and serious policy matters. Dorothy was a personal and social education teacher – a vague epithet with ill-defined professional requirements. She supposed plenty of teachers were interested in general kids' welfare topics. The woman was passionate. Kelly moved to the bookcase and she heard Seb go upstairs.

She ran her fingers along titles of Penguin Classics that Kelly vaguely recalled from school: *Treasure Island*, *Ivanhoe*, *Black Beauty*. Her finger stopped on a beautifully bound book which was larger than the rest and caught her eye. She pulled its spine and it slid out and she read the title. It was a Grimm collection of fairy tales and Kelly couldn't help smiling as she recalled her father reading some of them to her. Every child her age must have been brought up on *Red Riding Hood* and *Hansel and Gretel*, though of course none of them knew at the time how dark they really were.

As she flicked through it, a brown envelope slid out onto the floor and Kelly bent over to pick it up. Inside, there were photos that looked to Kelly distinctly like surveillance images taken by intelligence departments of professional organisations. She scrunched her brow and examined them. Dorothy was the focus of the pictures, in all kinds of settings. There were dozens of them but no accompanying note. Kelly noticed the voyeuristic nature of the snapshots and she was certain Dorothy had no idea she was being watched until somebody sent her these. She flipped over the envelope, and it was postmarked three months ago, from a local postal area in Greater London. It could be evidence that Dorothy was being blackmailed for something.

She looked around. An armchair was positioned directly opposite the TV and Kelly figured this is where Dorothy spent her leisure time. Alone. They hadn't been able to trace any wider family and no next of kin. Teachers at her school said she kept herself to herself and didn't attend staff socials. She was polite, charming, but distant. Nobody really understood who Dorothy Amis really was and it had made them feel guilty. Especially the headmistress who said she assumed Dorothy was a private person.

Private or unpopular?

Or a recluse being threatened?

A book like a diary sat on a small coffee table next to the armchair and Kelly picked it up. It was a planner like many people have and it was filled in sparsely with odd appointments and dates of interest. There was nothing personal. She didn't find an outpouring of emotions and complaints pertaining to her killer. That would have been too easy.

Kelly looked carefully over the last few weeks and came across an entry which said 'Museum of C, TEN P.M.'. This must have been to confirm her upcoming visit, Kelly thought, but ten o'clock at night? She'd confirmed the trip with the school liaison officer at the museum yesterday, but a phone call was as far as they'd got in the planning stage, according to them. She'd need to double check. Another entry said simply 'pub'. This was more interesting because it indicated that Dorothy had been social and had ventured out to meet somebody. It indicated she might have a friend. Somebody who knew her. She made a note of the dates and flicked to the back of the book, where a few odd pieces of paper were covered in random scrawls which Kelly didn't understand. There was a shopping list on it, as well as a phone number, which they could try, and a doodle of stick figures, like a family, holding hands. Underneath was a photograph and Kelly saw that it was of four friends, three women and a man. By their fashion, Kelly dated it to the 1970s. They wore knitted jumpers, huge collars and flower prints. It was faded and Kelly smiled. Dorothy did once have a life. She turned it over and found handwriting. It said 'CSOLSC, 1983'. She'd got the decade wrong but it was close. She flipped it over again and studied the faces. She spotted Dorothy straight away. Her photograph on her employment file at school was just as severe and she wore distinctive makeup even back then, when Kelly worked out she'd have been forty-one. In both images, Dorothy had worn garish lipstick, making Kelly think of The Joker from the Batman films. The fashion struck her as retro 1950s, when women's glamour peaked after the war. In that era impressing a US serviceman was more important than taste. She studied the photo closer. The harshness of the colour didn't suit her, and Kelly was reminded of her Chelsea smile cut into her face in the drama studio. It struck her that Dorothy's killer could be commenting on the fact that she made her face up too sluttily, in an attempt to look younger. It struck Kelly that back then people aged quicker, they looked more mature in a way. Stiffer, less free, more shackled to an invisible set of standards. In the photo, Dorothy's hair was pinned up. Kelly considered a style like that at forty-one prematurely aging and recoiled. She held the photo closer. Dorothy's smile… She rushed upstairs and found Seb.

'Look,' she breathed.

She showed him the photo and pointed out what she thought about Dorothy's red smile…

'I think she was being watched, and she knew it.' She showed him the surveillance photos.

'Crikey,' he said.

Finally, Kelly thought, she'd managed to trigger some passion in the man. She'd found something that he was interested in and she swelled with pride.

'That smile is just like the gash across her face,' he said.

'Isn't it?' Kelly said.

'Where did you find it?'

'In this,' Kelly said, producing the planner.

'We must find these other people,' Seb said.

He turned away and Kelly produced an evidence bag.

'Do you know what this is?' Seb asked.

She studied what he held in his hand, and it looked like a squashed silver ring, but thicker. She peered at it.

'It was in her bedside cabinet inside a smart ring case so it must have been dear to her,' he said.

'It's not a ring,' Kelly said.

'No, I agree, it's too thick and oddly shaped. It could be a pendant.'

Kelly shook her head and gave him another bag to slip it into.

'It's not a pendant, either, it's a swazzle and I know somebody who might be able to tell us more about it,' she said.

Chapter 26

'Mum, I'll try my best to get there, I promise. I just don't know how long this case is going to take.'

Kelly took the call from inside the ladies' toilet at the Barking office after they'd spent much of the day at Dorothy's flat. She was expected to travel home tomorrow for her parents' anniversary party. The week had flown and she was reluctant to commit. Her mobile phone number was strictly supposed to be for emergencies, as opposed to her landline, but Wendy Porter didn't grasp the notion.

'That's what you always say. There's always a case on. If you wait until you have none then you'll never come home. Your dad wants to see you.'

Kelly found herself wishing mobile phones weren't a thing. Only a decade ago, people who owned them were thought of as wankers who either worked in the city or ran a criminal gang. There wasn't much in it and some of them in the Met saw the two as synonymous as the Northern Rock scandal last year proved.

'It's only three hours on the train, we'll pay for your ticket,' her mother said.

'It's not about the money, Mum. It's work.' *I'm not seven years old.*

'You're just like your father.'

That was the killer blow. Shame and guilt forced its way through the airwaves and into Kelly's ear and dripped down into her very soul, making her feel like shit.

'It's not a nine-to-five job, Mum.'

'I told him he shouldn't encourage you. It's a man's job.'

'Mum!'

She bit her tongue. Her mother was from a different generation who relied on their husbands for everything. Kelly was sure that part of her mother's disapproval of her moving away was that she didn't have a man. If she moved with a partner – a husband, like Dave Crawley, her ex-fiancé – she might not have such a problem with it.

'I take care of myself, Mum, I'm earning good money.'

'What's money if you have no family?'

Kelly imagined her heart strings as flimsy strands of overcooked spaghetti and almost made a joke. Her mother was being dramatic.

'This is the twenty-first century, Mum, women have jobs and they don't need men to say it's okay.'

'I raised you myself because I wanted to. It's natural. That's what mothers do.'

Now she'd gone too far. Motherhood was off limits. But that was the point. Kelly wasn't a mother because she didn't want to be. The thought of sacrificing everything she'd worked so hard for, for a baby and a man, made her blood boil. She could never envisage a day when she'd give everything up for that. They were made different. An image of Dorothy Amis, childless and alone in her flat, jumped into her peripheral vision and Kelly closed her eyes.

'I love my job, Mum. Can't you be happy for me?'

'Time is running out for you, Kelly. Your sister has two with another on the way.'

Another knife to the heart. She wondered if Pinocchio felt it when the blade went in…

She hadn't entered into any kind of serious relationship in London since moving there from Cumbria and leaving her future marriage in tatters. The guilt she felt after finishing her relationship with Dave was enough to put her off for life, but something inside her told her that Dave Crawley wasn't the man for her. She was terrified of ending up like her own parents, with two kids, and steady, average-paying jobs. Or like her sister whose bitterness at being chained to the kitchen sink consumed her. John and Wendy Porter lived in the same house she'd grown up in: a three up three down in Penrith on the edge of the national park. Life there was ordinary and regular. Even the crime was fairly predictable. The beauty was undeniable but more attractive to the middle-aged than to a woman in her twenties trying to make something of herself. The mountains would always be there for her, when, and if, she ever returned. But for now, the MIT east and the promise of being allowed into that world was pull enough to keep her head firmly in the capital. Nikki, her sister, had never moved away.

'I'm really sorry, I have to go.'

She hung up and felt miserable. Ordinarily at times like this she'd wander over to Cheryl's desk to share her despair but she could no longer do that. There was nowhere in the office in Barking to indulge herself. She was still on probation and on her best behaviour. She left the bathroom and emerged back out in the open-plan office, where people were filing into Leia Lord's briefing room. She caught Seb's eye and he beckoned her over.

'Something has come up,' he said.

She grabbed a pad and pen and followed him.

When the room fell silent, Leia Lord began to talk.

'We've got another body,' she said, and officers whispered and glanced at one another in shock. So soon.

'Another school, in Leytonstone this time. We don't have much but from first responders, the MO sounds similar to that of Dorothy Amis. Porter and Crook, get over there now.'

The DCI's use of Kelly's surname before her more senior partner's struck her as odd. Could it be a sense of female camaraderie?

'The body of sixty-seven-year-old Edith Callaghan was found in a school in Leytonstone by the caretaker early this morning. We've sealed off the area to the public. The headmaster has been informed and is cooperating with us on Edith's history. She has no family and lived alone.'

'Like Dorothy Amis,' Kelly said, a little louder than she intended.

'Let's not jump to conclusions yet,' Leia warned. 'But yes, it's obviously a red flag, two older teachers in the space of four days. The school was empty again, thank God.'

'Do we know anything about the scene?' Seb asked.

'It's messy. I'm preparing a press statement. The mayor's jumpy. The new term is not very far away and thousands of kids will be returning to school soon. Let's get going on this, please, report back to me as soon as you get back.'

They left the briefing room, grabbed their things and left the office, heading for the garages in the back of the complex.

They'd blue-light it in the Mondeo this time.

The traffic through Leytonstone was choked but vehicles parted for them and they entered the school gates before midday. Kelly couldn't help enjoy the frisson of importance she felt.

Seb seemed focused and alert. They still hadn't discussed Tuesday night and now Kelly knew they probably wouldn't. Men and women were different like that. Women addressed all of their feelings regardless of their surroundings, men shut them away.

He drove and she gazed out of the window. She wondered if Molly would be on scene. She hoped she was, because she wanted to see a familiar face, but equally she didn't want her to be there because Kelly was protective of her friend who'd been struggling lately. It was a silly thing to feel compelled towards. Protecting a SOCO from the dead was impossible. Only last night, Molly had insisted she was fine.

'Do you think we should be going public with this?'

It was the first time Kelly had dared question Leia Lord's judgement. Kelly believed they should be holding back.

'I agree but I'm not the boss. You're probably too young to remember Robert Napper and the terror he created in London in the '90s,' Seb said.

It was the first reference to Seb's seniority in terms of career and age.

'Why? How old are you?' she asked. 'And of course I know who he is, he's going down for another murder, isn't he?'

'Yup, trial date Old Bailey, November, bastard pleaded not guilty.'

He laughed and shook his head. 'And I'm almost forty,' he said.

'Young for a DI,' she said.

'I should be DCI,' he replied.

He fell silent and Kelly knew she'd hit a nerve. He'd allowed a part of himself to be revealed. Did he resent being overlooked in favour of a woman? He changed the subject unexpectedly.

'So, tell me about the pacemaker.'

Her heart skipped a beat. 'What?'

'I took a phone call for you from Jonathan Hass at Brampton Forensics. What have you been up to?'

She felt foolish, and deceitful.

'Don't worry, I'm not going to throw you to the wolves.'

There was a soupcon of a warning in his voice.

'You know you can talk to me anytime,' he added.

'I don't need somebody to talk to. I need answers.'

She told him about her final callout at Bethnal Green CID. She told him the HAT wasn't interested until the body was dated. She told him about their silly nickname for the body.

'It's not silly, though, is it?' he said. 'Look at what we're dealing with. Right now I'd believe pigs could fly if you told me.'

'Pigs can fly,' she said.

He smiled.

'The thing is, I don't want to lose the case,' she admitted.

'I know. I remember that feeling. I'd work weeks on a case only for the MIT to come in and take it all away from me because the victim died and it turned into a homicide. You said the HAT didn't want it?'

'It's not they didn't want it but they said not until they knew for sure when the death occurred.'

'Fair enough, they're not going to investigate a body that's been lying under a London street for fifty years, that's for the archaeologists.'

'Forensic anthropologists,' she corrected him.

'Those too.'

'I dealt with Bionomic a few years back. Let me know if you have trouble with them,' he said.

'Thanks.'

'But the point is you don't get to decide which cases you go after. You'll have to come clean with Leia. And she won't be pleased if it turns out Pinocchio is related to Punch and Judy, I mean, what are the odds?'

He was teasing her.

'I know, and I intend to, as soon as I have my ID.'

He nodded. It was a concession.

'Can we talk about Tuesday night?' she asked.

'We're here.'

'I'm worried about you.'

'You've no need. Worry about yourself.'

'What does that mean?'

'It means I don't need your sympathy. There's no room for worrying when we do what we do. Concentrate on the job.'

'But that's my point. How can you be operating to the best of your ability when you're…'

'When I'm what?'

He stopped the car violently and she lurched forward. He turned and glared at her.

'Don't ever question my integrity,' he said.

Kelly shrunk back in her seat. She felt like an idiot. Seb Crook was a good operator and she had no business speculating about his life outside work.

Chapter 27

Leytonstone Comprehensive had an illustrious history as a grammar school going back to 1911, though today might not be a day that made it into next year's prospectus for enquiring parents. Kelly and Seb made their way through the press gathered at the gates and batted away questions about the victim and the killer.

'Is there a serial killer on the loose?'

'Have you caught him yet?'

'Should parents be worried?'

'Will the beginning of term be delayed for kids?'

'How long have the police known about the killer?'

'Is it true he's dressing the victims up as puppets?'

They bent under the police tape which flapped annoyingly in the wind that had picked up. Deserted hubs of academia always looked strange to Kelly. She remembered her own school days and the throng of bodies crowding the playground at break. They walked across a deserted one now and peered up at a hundred windows looked through by a century of countless bored students.

The uniforms on duty looked grave. Word had got out about the nature of the killing.

'They're calling him The Puppeteer,' Seb said.

Between leaving the Barking office and arriving here, more details had been passed to the DCI, and she'd confirmed her suspicion the two murders were linked. That's why the press had gone crazy for particulars. Fresh from the home of Dorothy Amis, they braced themselves for what they might find inside.

'Well, at least Leia has her wish. People are talking about it.'

'You have a problem with her?' Kelly asked.

They walked away from the journos and towards the police tape. Kelly couldn't help thinking that Seb Crook thought the DCI's job should be his. He had an axe to grind. All might not be well at MIT east after all. She considered if Leia Lord was up to the job, as opposed to a man, and she decided that she was. The DCI might be distant, intimidating even, but bosses weren't there to be pals.

Edith Callaghan's body was in the gym. She'd been a part-time dance and movement teacher.

The team was considering the chosen locations and if they were relevant. In Kelly's experience, criminals this fastidious, this obsessed, didn't leave things to chance. Drama and dance. Two sides of the same world of entertainment.

'Let's see what we've got here.' Seb focused her mind. 'Leia wants this steered towards a vigilante ex-pupil scenario.'

Kelly stopped walking.

'What? Steered? Is that how she works?'

Seb stopped and stared back at her.

'I mean, I've never heard of that being an actual approach. What about the evidence?' Kelly asked.

'You want to take her on? Be my guest. She might look good but she's inexperienced. I reckon they were satisfying some positive discrimination statistic in the Met when they promoted her.'

Kelly stared at him and her mouth dropped open inadvertently.

'So, she doesn't deserve to be more senior to you?'

Seb shrugged. 'I didn't mean it like that. Female police officers are very good at what they do.'

'I sense a "but" coming,' Kelly said.

'Shit, this is all coming out wrong.'

'It is.' Kelly waited.

'What I mean is, like you, I'm surprised she's going down the route she is.'

'What I want to know is did they know each other? Did they have shared history?'

'I agree.'

'I mean is this a pattern, or was what they taught me in detective training untrue?'

Seb stopped and seemed agitated. He brought a small tin out of his pocket and opened it, dipping his finger into it and rubbing his gums.

Kelly watched him and didn't know what to say.

'Don't say anything. Your face is enough. I just need a pick-me-up. Crime scenes can be challenging, that's all.'

Kelly stayed silent. He'd let her in. In his way. He wasn't willing to talk about it just yet, but he'd acknowledged a potential problem to her. He'd admitted the job got to him and that was a huge revelation for a tough London cop. She got the impression that perhaps she was the first person he'd opened up to in a very long time. Further conversation about their boss could wait.

They pulled on overalls and gloves and covered their shoes with blue bags and went inside.

SOCOs and forensic officers moved about silently in white plastic suits with face masks covering their identities, making them look like a tribe of medics handling a global pandemic. It was otherworldly. She recognised Molly, though. She knew the silhouette of her body and the shape of her eyes when she glanced over at the new arrivals.

Nobody spoke. The scene was loud enough with Kelly's senses assaulted from all sides. She'd certainly never witnessed a scene of any crime like it and as she glanced at Seb, she reckoned he was just as shocked. She felt herself part of some perverted show, but she hadn't worked out her role yet.

She saw Molly working on blood-spatter patterns, which were extensive and told of a brutality which belonged in textbooks. Molly used weights and string to map out where Edith's blood had travelled, and she held a new gadget that calculated equations of physics and maths in a fraction of the time it took a human. Murder technology was a growing industry and science companies made huge profits from helping CSIs do their work.

'There are pools, trails, droplets, splashes and flow,' Molly said through her mask as she came to stand next to Kelly.

Kelly understood the language of blood thanks to living with Molly, but also by paying attention to every aspect of forensics. Kelly believed in following the science and what the scene told her. She wondered if Leia Lord might be problematic when faced with concrete evidence. Dictating a motive and an outcome before thorough detective work was an unsettling prospect. Only time would tell. Sometimes, those who put power over product, and left the coalface, where murder happened, removed themselves from the process and simply focused on results, but in Kelly's experience with all crimes, only the evidence could speak the truth.

She took in the scene and listened to Molly.

The victim had been dragged like Dorothy, and she'd already been bleeding by that point, so she'd been attacked across the room.

'Any witnesses?' they asked the SOCO in charge.

'No. Despite it being common for teachers to come in and work during the holidays, this went unnoticed.'

The very real prospect of interviewing ninety-odd staff here and at the school in Leyton Park was off-putting to say the least but it would have to be done.

The large gym was quiet. Seb didn't speak. Kelly saw he was looking at the victim, who was slumped over a beam which had been hoisted to about eight feet off the ground. It was appropriate for her attire. The murderer – who was indisputably physically capable – had tried to make her fly.

Kelly watched Seb and knew he was searching for the same thing, then they spotted it. A SOCO was photographing a doll close to where the body had been hoisted up into the air.

'Can we get her down?' Seb asked.

Kelly detected suffering in his voice and warmed to his humanity on display.

In among the blood spatter, and an otherwise spotless gymnasium kitted out with frames, tables, mats, benches, trolleys, balls and cones, Edith Callaghan was dressed in a green party dress, much too small for her, with wings on her back. They'd been attached to her by two holes which had been drilled into her body, like hinges.

Two uniforms in forensic suits took Edith's weight and she was lowered to the floor of the gym where she came to rest on her back next to the doll. It was a pixie little thing, smiling like a child, with big, amazing eyes. Her hair was blonde, like gold, and her green dress shone as if illuminated with light. The doll had no blood on it and was pristine and Luther's words drowned out the silence. Stories, and the characters inside them, were escape vessels for children. And she couldn't help thinking that whoever did this to Dorothy and Edith – and possibly the woman in the hole at Stratford Junction building site – blamed these women for stealing their dreams. Fantasies that were never realised.

'Let me guess,' Kelly said. 'Tinkerbell?'

Chapter 28

'We have a pattern,' Kelly said.

They were sat on a patch of grass behind the school taking a breather from the scene of carnage indoors.

'All life is about patterns,' she added.

It was something John Porter told her all the time. He said it when they were hiking and they watched Osprey over Bassenthwaite. Behaviour, including that of humans, was all about habit. Their murderer had formed his over years. He might even have been practising or copying from another for a very long time.

'We need to consider Pinocchio as part of the pattern,' she said.

Still Seb didn't answer.

'Are you okay?' she asked, sensing he was distracted. She decided to stick to the job at hand. Her partner would open up to her if he learnt to trust her.

'Let's spell out what we know,' she said.

She began by going back to the beginning, but this time she included Pinocchio in her analysis.

'You're good for me, Kelly Porter,' Seb said suddenly.

'I'm an asset already?' She slapped him playfully and he caught her hand, releasing it quickly.

'Are we searching through the files of all the youngsters Edith and Dorothy worked with, who would be between say twenty and forty years of age now?'

If the DCI wanted to go down the revenge route, then the first place to look would be ex-pupils.

'Not yet, the boss said it was a waste of time until we have more evidence. We have forty officers, Kelly. Twenty of those are on background, and the others are chasing physical leads.'

'Is any lead a waste of time? What I want to know is if there's anything in Edith's or Dorothy's past that might indicate a child would want to carry a grudge into adulthood. If she's serious about focusing on the vigilante route then surely we should be investigating the victims' connections to children? Did they pass vetting for example or were they of the generation that slipped under the radar of police checks before they came into force. There are plenty of them knocking around.'

'Good question. It was different back then and they still fall through cracks. The system isn't perfect. We need a service that combines all information about those who work with children, so institutions can access them directly without going through so many different systems.'

'An extension of List 99?' she asked.

He nodded. 'It all needs centralising. Look what happened in Soham.'

'So, is there any direct evidence that either Dorothy or Edith was abusive towards children? That's what we need to find out.'

'It means trawling through the Criminal Records Bureau and their employment files.'

'It's as if he's ridiculing them,' she said. 'The murders and staging are bold and brazen. The confidence is staggering. I'm optimistic there'll be something tying the killer to the scene, it'll just take time,' she said hopefully. 'Molly said the scenes are so messy that it would be impossible for the killer to not have left organic material behind, though whether they find it is another matter entirely.

'He's not just sending a message about how they deserved to die, but also he's asserting his control. They're women in a man's world. Children's stories are all about tradition and he's breaking it by giving us an alternative ending. He's rewriting the stories of our heroes.'

Seb stared at her.

'How the hell did you put all that together?' he asked.

'I need to tell you about a curator called Luther,' she said. 'And the story of Pinocchio.'

Chapter 29

'I can't confirm anything, it's a feeling. It's a...'

'Hunch?' Seb asked.

Kelly nodded. For the first time since they'd met, Kelly felt as though she was talking to a real partner. They were sharing something. He'd asked her to tell him everything she knew about Pinocchio.

'It's got the hallmarks of a practice run. She's a woman dressed as a children's character, there's innocence and playfulness but it's incomplete and immature.'

'And the planting of the doll?'

'The puppet? The curator was insistent about details. Puppets, marionettes and toys are all very different. We have a mixture left for us. That's an inconsistency. But we can let the public call him The Puppeteer for now.'

'And you haven't heard from Bionomic?'

'I'll check with Cheryl.'

She called the Bethnal Green office and Cheryl told her that there'd been a fax from Bionomic's medical technology department, she just had to find it under all the others. Kelly heard rustling and the sound of sheets of paper floating across the office to the floor and she envisioned Pete going mad at her, telling her to tidy up. Open-plan offices were all well and good when those who used them kept them equally neat. But that wasn't the case in her old CID. She imagined Cheryl hunting for fax paper under piles of casefiles, traffic cones and evidence bags.

'Here. Yep, there's a name. Sorry, Kelly, since you left, I've had DCI Wallis breathing down my neck.'

Kelly felt bad and nodded to Seb. He sat up straight, paying attention. Kelly thought he looked better than he had all day.

'It's registered to Tania Harrison, her NHS number is here and the device is dated back to 1989.'

'Brilliant, can you text me that and when you get time pull up her medical records and see if she's got a criminal one too.'

'Sure, there's a new development too,' Cheryl told her.

Kelly waited.

'Dennis Chapman has dropped off the radar. No one knows where he is, if he's missing, AWOL or on holiday. I've tried all avenues to trace him and there's been no sightings of him at his registered address. I think it's suspicious.'

'It's suspicious that he's the one who reported the body in the first place,' Kelly said.

'Exactly.'

'And Jason Fellcroft has long arms that reach out of prison.'

'Yup,' Cheryl agreed. 'Or he's running scared. I hope it's that. I've filed a missing person report.'

'Keep me updated,' Kelly asked.

'Sure. See you later.'

They hung up and Kelly turned to Seb.

'We've got a name. Yesterday, I compiled a list of missing women from the east of London area for 2001, I came up with seven, I'm sure I recognise hers from the list.'

'Why 2001?'

She told him about the Arsenal season schedule. He nodded and made a call on his phone and she listened to him request a background check on Tania Harrison to see if they had anything on her. It reminded Kelly that now she was murder squad, she had that kind of clout at her fingertips. Knowledge was power, for sure, but it still didn't make up for a detective's nose. When he hung up, he was grinning.

'Tania Harrison went missing in 2001.'

'Fucking bingo,' she said. 'Now we need a description.'

'And she was a nurse,' he added.

'But what was her history? How old was she?'

'She was fifty-nine when she went missing.'

'Which would make her in her sixties now. Don't you think that makes it likely they possibly knew each other? Do we know if she worked in care homes before hospitals? They might have worked together.'

'Or even if they were just friends.'

'Do you have a copy of that photo from Dorothy's house in the car?' she asked.

He nodded and they both got up and headed back through the police tape. Seb reached into a case in the back and brought it out, then they found a quiet spot away from the cameras. They studied it together.

Kelly squinted. The quality was typical of its age. But she was almost sure that one of the other two women in the photo was Edith Callaghan. She pointed at the third, who was smaller, like a bird.

'Do you reckon she's Tania Harrison?'

'We need to find out who the man is,' Seb said. 'And fast.'

Chapter 30

Kelly and Seb stood outside the door of DCI Leia Lord's office waiting for her to answer. They'd knocked quietly and Kelly looked at her shoes. It had been a long day.

'Come in!'

Seb opened the door and they went inside.

Leia Lord perched on the edge of her desk like a schoolteacher waiting for the excuses of her pupils as to why they were scurrying around the corridors, up to no good.

They stood in front of her, not asked to take seats.

Kelly waited for Seb to speak but he didn't and she glanced sideways at him.

'Is there something important?' the DCI asked. 'I assume you two are getting along? How's the investigation going? Is there something to add to the brief?'

Still, Seb didn't speak and for a tense moment, Kelly thought that he might be scared of her.

'One of my old cases at CID has come to my attention, ma'am,' Kelly said.

'Old cases?'

'Well, my last one. It was left unfinished in fact.'

'And?'

Kelly looked at Seb, who said nothing. She carried on.

'It was a body,' she said.

'A body? What was CID doing investigating a body?'

'It was a historic case, or so we thought. The HAT was informed straight away.' Kelly felt as though she was rushing her story and willed herself to slow down. 'They delayed referring it as a homicide because we had no idea how old the corpse was, but now we do.'

Leia Lord uncrossed her feet and stood up, walked behind her desk and sat down. 'Sit, please,' she said, indicating the chairs to the side. They were lower than Leia's and so Kelly felt distinctly at a disadvantage.

'So?'

Kelly took a deep breath but she had no idea why this woman made her nervous, apart from her rank.

'The body has been with Brampton Forensic Services and the anthropologist's report is here,' Kelly said, getting up to place the report on Leia's desk.

'I don't need to read that, you can tell me what's in it.'

'Yes, ma'am. She was found on a building site, in a hole, dressed up and she had a pacemaker, we thought she might be Victorian, but this type of pacemaker is very modern and she had it fitted in 1989. We traced the company and she went missing in 2001. She lived in the same area as Dorothy and Edith.'

'Dorothy and Edith? What has a body found in a ditch got to do with our teachers?'

'Because she was dressed up, and a doll was left with her,' Kelly said.

'What did you say her name was?' Leia asked.

'I didn't. She's called Tania Harrison and she was a nurse, but after looking at pictures of her from her employment file sent to us by Whitechapel Hospital, we think she knew Dorothy and Edith.'

Kelly detected a curious mix of quick-witted intensity in Leia Lord's face but something else too. It could have been fear or at least trepidation. And Kelly realised that they were on to something big. This was a high-profile case and Kelly had just given her something that might potentially lead them closer to their perp. She felt smugly satisfied suddenly, but then remembered that they were here because three women had died horribly.

'Who reported the body?'

The question caught Kelly off guard but she appreciated that Leia would want to know everything about the case.

'A foreman called Dennis Chapman, he's missing, we have reason to believe that—'

Leia stopped her by holding up her hand.

'And where was this?'

'A building site at the new Olympic Park, it's being excavated to make way for new foundations.'

'Where exactly?'

'I'll show you,' Kelly said, opening the other file she'd brought into Leia's office. She pointed out the site on a map of Stratford and explained that they'd got a warrant for the excavation of the rest of the site.

'Who authorised that?'

'DCI Wallis at Bethnal Gr—'

'I know who he is. Interesting...' She got up from behind her desk and paced around the office, thinking hard and scratching her scalp. Kelly knew she had some weird habits when she was deep in contemplation. Even after only knowing the woman a week, she'd made a strong impression. Still Seb hadn't spoken and Kelly took the opportunity to scald him silently. She felt hung out to dry. Seb spread his hands and mouthed it was her investigation into Tania, not his. Kelly realised then just how worried her partner was about speaking up in front of his boss.

'We also think this is the three women together in this photograph,' Kelly said, reaching out to hand it to Leia. The DCI stopped and looked at the photo, not handling it but staring at it, as if it was the first time she'd seen physical evidence of photographic technology. Kelly felt that she alone was the only professional in the room right now.

'Look, this is Dorothy, and we think she is Edith, and she's Tania, we're trying to identify this man as soon as we can.'

Leia went behind her desk again and sat down, she placed her hands in front of her and clasped them. 'Good work. What's your next move?'

Kelly looked at Seb, who finally woke up and took the invitation to speak.

'We need to go further than their current jobs, ma'am,' he said. 'We need to find out what they were doing in 1983, wherever this place was. CSOLSC.'

Kelly turned the photo over and showed Leia what she believed to be an acronym on the back.

'We have no idea what these mean yet, but it's vital we find this man,' she said.

Leia nodded.

'And your area CID were the responders on the body in the ditch?' Leia asked.

Kelly nodded.

'Lucky us,' she said, and smiled a wide and empty smile. 'Anything else?'

'We think she might have been blackmailed or threatened.'

The DCI waited.

'We found surveillance photos in her flat.'

The DCI's face was unreadable. Lord tapped her fingers on her desk and her phone rang. They were dismissed and Kelly walked out to the tune of The Entertainer, looking back once. She couldn't help her once affectionate memory of the tune dulling and becoming nothing else but irritating, and for that, Kelly disliked Leia Lord even more.

As Kelly and Seb left the office with a seemingly blank page to investigate the links between the women in the photo further, Kelly couldn't help feeling deflated, and a little miffed that her boss wasn't more impressed with her efforts on her fourth day in the team.

Chapter 31

'You knew Pinocchio was important, didn't you?' Molly said to Kelly. Cheryl had arrived laden with Chinese takeaway, and they'd eaten their fill. Talking shop was their only agenda when the puzzle was so intriguing.

They sat on the small terrace overlooking the canal and each gulped from a small beer bottle. The tiny French-style ones lasted two sips each before they were gone but they had the best flavour. Molly bought them in 20s from the Sainsbury's in Whitechapel and cycled them home in rucksacks at the weekend. Kelly went inside to pop open another three.

'You're giving me way too much credit, Moll.'

'So, Princess Leia bought it then, what did she say?'

'It was weird, actually. She looked shocked and I guess she was a bit.'

'She has no idea yet how good you are.'

'Thanks, Cheryl.'

She passed the beers out.

They clinked bottles and Kelly sat down heavily.

'Wouldn't it be better if every CID had access to HOLMES and we could share our input?' Cheryl asked.

'Like the good old days when cardexes went missing and you couldn't see the incident board because of the cigarette smoke?' Molly replied.

'Exactly!' Kelly laughed. 'The good old days. God, I can't believe it was only this time last year when we could have a smoke in the Porter & Grape. Bliss. What I mean is surely everybody benefits from as much transparency as possible. Provincial teams have it right.'

'Oh, hello, says you who thinks you'll have a nosebleed if you step out of London,' Molly said.

'No, that's just south of the river,' Cheryl teased.

They laughed. Kelly felt better after sharing her day with her friends. She needed to off-gas after processing Edith Callaghan's crime scene earlier today, and so did Molly. They'd filled Cheryl in on the gruesome details.

'Apart from the green fairy outfit that made her look like a drunk grandma at Christmas after too much sherry, who dresses a sixty-year-old as a fairy?'

'Her face was slashed into a smile, just like Dorothy's,' Molly added. 'And she was made up to look ridiculous, poor woman.' Molly referred to the garish cosmetics slapped on Edith's face, not only across her wounded mouth, but on her eyes too. Kelly guessed it was meant to be doll-like, but it wasn't; it was obscene.

The forensic team and the SOCOs had concluded that Edith had been stabbed to death then moved and hoisted up onto the bar after she'd bled out. The dress had been put on over the top of her wounds. The killer must have stayed with her for some time. It was puzzling he'd not been seen or heard, even during school holidays.

'She looked so peaceful and... sweet, under all that makeup,' Molly said.

'Always the romantic,' Cheryl goaded her gently.

'Dead people often look at peace, even when they're killed like that,' Kelly said. She yawned.

'Don't they all?' Molly said.

Kelly reckoned it depended on your perspective. People had different filters; Molly's was obviously sympathetic.

'Wolves in sheep's clothing,' Cheryl said, sipping her beer.

They looked at each other and the words tumbled out in sync.

'Red Riding Hood.'

'I can't even look at another kid's film the same again. I'll always be wondering which one is coming next. And those smiles, Kel, they were horrendous,' Molly said.

Kelly would never know if a grin was cut into Pinocchio's face because there wasn't enough skin left on the facial bones to examine after seven years in the dirt, acidic or not.

'If it turns out that Edith and Tania worked in kids homes too, do you think the perp was in their care and they read him stories, you know you hear about it, like perverts doing it to music and that sort of shit,' Molly carried on. She was the biggest theorist of the three. Cheryl and Kelly were more cynical and less likely to accept wild hypotheses until they were proven.

Molly was in her zone talking about what happened to Dorothy and Edith. She painted a picture of female predators, up to no good, begging for forgiveness from an ex-student. Kelly nodded. Nothing surprised her anymore. If she hadn't witnessed it herself in London, she'd heard of it. Fiction, like the stories that were the focus of this investigation, had nothing on the real thing. They were just props, but she had to find out why. Victimisation was the first step to a profile. But Kelly and Seb had already checked for Dorothy and Edith on the Criminal Records Bureau, and they weren't there. Neither was Tania Harrison.

No criminal records, no families, no children and, it appeared, no close friends or associates. Their employment profiles were still being pieced together and the same was true of their professional lives, they were like hermits. No strings. No echoes from the past.

Of course, all the MIT had to do now was compile a list of all the kids the two women had worked with in education over the years and narrow it down, but that could number in the thousands and even HOLMES couldn't beat clever police work. After that, all they needed do was see if Tania had a history in kids' care too.

Kelly told her friends about her visit to the Museum of Childhood and the recent robbery there. It was a promising lead but Leia Lord had been underwhelmed by it when Kelly had mentioned it earlier today. To be fair, Seb wasn't convinced either, though he was interested in the curator's weird obsession with toys and Kelly reckoned Seb might even go so far as to investigate the seventy-eight-year-old as a suspect.

'I get it. I know she's busy, Jesus, MIT east face almost forty murders a year, and her resources are spread thin but she's beginning to irritate me,' Kelly said.

Molly laughed.

'I can't wait until you're a commissioner. No messing around then. The shit will hit the fan, and people will get a surprise rod up their arses.' Cheryl laughed.

'Here, here,' Molly was becoming tipsy.

'I'm not saying I could do a better job, but she does seem to miss what is staring her in the face. There's something off,' Kelly added.

'What does she think about your curator at the museum?'

'Seventy-eight-year-old Luther?'

Molly nodded, swigging her beer. 'Dark horse.'

'Not much. A good sideline lead.'

'Really? A sideline?'

'Is it just me then, or not?' Kelly asked.

'No, I would have thought that was a good place to start,' Cheryl said. 'The robbery is recent, who knows if the muppets will be left at the next one? I mean, what did Luther say? He's the expert.'

Kelly had reached the point where the beer was talking more than sense now but she indulged her friends regardless.

'Pinocchio was a spoilt brat who lied all the time. He was a bragger. The thing is all these old tales had moral lessons attached, which fits with a punishment motive. The original story of Pinocchio ended with his fatal hanging, it was only the publishers who changed it to resurrect him. He was a badly behaved and selfish boy. Punch and Judy is a grotesque snapshot of Victorian views of women, but the original story was, again, Italian.'

'I thought Punch got eaten by a crocodile in the end? So he got what he deserved, not poor Judy who was the one who suffered. I looked it up.'

Kelly smiled. Molly would make a great detective.

'Actually, Punch is the one who survives, even when the devil himself comes for him, and always with audience help.'

'So, what about Peter Pan, it seems like a curve ball, or is that Italian too? Please tell me Robin Williams was in the original, and Julia Roberts!' Cheryl said.

'Afraid not. I talked to Luther over the phone today. I asked him about Tinkerbell. In fact, he was pretty angry with Disney over what they've done to beloved characters over the years. He emphasised that Tinkerbell wasn't a main character, but she was a tinker, in every sense of the word. A trickster, she was mischievous and deviant but the most interesting thing is that being a fairy and so small, Tinkerbell could only hold one emotion at a time and this made her volatile. If she was angry, she could be explosively vindictive and lacking in any sense of compassion which humans can show when balancing their feelings.'

Kelly leant towards her friends, as if relaying ghost stories around an imagined campfire.

'Which humans are you talking about?' Cheryl asked.

They laughed.

'Well, that's the point, the killer took away the victims' humanity and turned them into fictional characters loved by children, which tend to be simplistic. Kids dish out reward and punishment like little dictators, they rarely possess moral counterbalance which is why these characters were such a hit with them.'

'How long were you on the phone?' Cheryl asked.

Kelly rolled her eyes.

'I find him intriguing,' Kelly admitted.

'So, do you think it's about the most notable characteristic of each identity? Deceit, abuse and anger?'

'They're all quite destructive traits, aren't they? Something like that, but the MO has changed if we include Tania. And we have seven years between them.'

'So, it can't be the same person, could it be a copycat?'

Kelly shrugged and drained her beer. Her head throbbed with possibilities.

They sat in silence, each contemplating the complexity of a person's mind who could dream up such methods of torture. The motive in the end still remained elusive. Murderers must learn their trade after all, and some took years to reach perfection and even then they weren't satisfied. It was obvious that the murder of Tania Harrison wasn't like the others. She'd been concealed. The killer's work on her was obscured and they'd never know what actually killed her.

'If it is the same and this is a pattern of learning his craft, he wasn't as proud of his work then as he has become today,' Kelly said. 'Why the break in between? Or are there further victims we just haven't yet found?'

'Or was Tania his first and since then he's perfected his technique?' Molly said.

'Or was he forced to pause his work? I've seen it in other cases. Gaps of time due to imprisonment, moving away or illness even. Seven years is a long time to wait. And it's ample time to learn and grow, and build confidence,' Kelly mused.

Prison was a place where men were separated into two camps: they sank or swam. They either thrived or withered away.

To thrive inside, you needed a posse. A group of like-minded criminals to gather around like an entourage. You needed to fit in and be willing to do what it took to stay on the right side of those in charge, and she didn't mean the screws. Prison officers were no more in charge of prisons as the police were of the streets.

To survive well enough to be able to function inside society upon release, one had to earn the protection of the big boys. People in charge.

People like Jason Fellcroft.

Chapter 32

On Friday morning, Kelly took Seb to Bethnal Green to introduce him to the curator of the Museum of Childhood.

The SOCO report for the Dorothy Amis crime scene was finally ready and Molly had sent it through to them. It had been the blood work that had taken the most time, and now they had their work cut out over at the Leytonstone site where Edith had been found, looking for similarities. That investigation had entered its second day.

The entry and approach were certainly a standout focus point. The killer had access to both schools or convinced his victims to gain access for him, in which case, he must have known them. His ability to enter and exit both sites seamlessly pointed to him being familiar with them. The time lapse from death to mutilation was also close, as in the killer took his time enjoying the process with both women spending a similar amount of time staging the final scene. The SOCOs agreed that it was a matter of power and controlling what the police saw when they discovered his 'work'. Their words, not Kelly's. CCTV footage revealed no significant movement around the school, though in both instances, cameras did not cover the immediate vicinity and it was possible that the killer could have arrived from fields adjacent to both institutions. Both women were seen on camera arriving in the early morning and both looked in a hurry from what could be gleaned from the tape, which was grainy and unreliable. Molly told her that the photos were all collated in order and she'd noticed that aesthetically – a term used in-house and certainly not for juries – the scenes were balanced. Molly explained that in the drama studio where Dorothy was found, for example, she faced the door and they'd found evidence of blood being cleaned up there, which was new. Initially, they'd thought he hadn't cleaned up at all. This indicated the killer desiring maximum impact from those who discovered the victim. The same was true of the other site, where Edith was suspended mid-air and any observer's eyeline was drawn upwards. Blood had been cleaned from other parts of the gym, as if to make sure the police looked at the real show, the one that mattered.

Grandstanding was the official term.

Plenty of useable prints had been lifted from both sites but hadn't been processed yet. The same went for DNA samples from the victim's bodies. Their nails, orifices, hair and sweat would be examined closer at autopsy. At both sites, no murder weapon had been found, indicating control and planning. No panic. Several partial shoeprints had been recovered at both sites and initial estimation was that they were of similar size and tread. Footfall over the inner contamination barrier, that is the space where the bodies lay, was kept to a minimum and in total, one hundred and three items were recovered, packaged, sealed, labelled and recorded. Kelly knew that the next couple of days, if not weeks, would be taken up by trawling through this evidence and Molly warned her that it'd take hours of police work. It was why murder squads were so big. They needed officers raking through the detritus of every scene and as she'd seen only yesterday in her first brief, teams did not have the luxury of handling one case exclusively at a time. Kelly's job was to interpret the evidence, not trawl through it, and this was the most distinct departure from her old job to her new one. Murder squads were like giant machines. Each cog had its place. Then Leia Lord, like a factory foreman, made the final decision.

They held on to a bar close to the sliding door on a tube on the Jubilee Line to Mile End, where they'd change to the Central Line.

'I think you should go to your party,' Seb told her. The whistle of air screeched along the tracks and Kelly winced.

'I can't, not in the middle of this.'

Seb smiled.

'I'm trying to tell you that you must. You missing a family party will make no difference whatsoever to this investigation. Murder cases are slow. Grinding. We churn and we chase. You have to go.'

She eyed him with suspicion as if he had ulterior motives. What if he cracked the case when she was gone and took all the glory?

'I used to do that.'

'What?'

'Put my work first all the time. I ignored the people closest to me.'

He'd opened up to her again and she listened, paying attention to him. She held his gaze and waited.

'My parents died in a car crash. I hadn't bothered to visit them for seven months before that.'

'My God, I'm so sorry,' she said. It was a whisper.

'Don't give up your life for cases, it doesn't work like that. It's not worth it. It's just a job.'

The pressure to put everything else on hold while she threw herself into this case to prove herself to Leia Lord was overwhelming. Seb had just given her more insight into why he perhaps drank too much or even messed with recreational drugs than she'd ever expected him to. Waiting for him to trust her had been worth it, even though she'd only known him a week. Everybody needed to numb out occasionally, including her. It was just the same as alcohol addiction, or shopping, sex, gambling and sugar. He was anaesthetising the pain. It was nothing to do with Leia Lord after all. There was something about him that she saw in a new light. Something honest and she was glad Leia had paired her with him.

'When was the last time you took time off?' Seb asked.

'The weekend.'

'I mean, really off, like when did you last leave London?'

She shrugged.

'When was the last time you saw your parents?'

She looked down and the train swayed left and right. 'Christmas.'

'I take my days off every week. It's vital you do the same. We get too many officers sleeping under desks and never going home. There are no prizes for the longest shift. I'm pulling rank on you and ordering you to go home. You can take work with you if you like.'

It seemed a fair compromise. Besides, she could hardly argue with him after what he'd just told her.

'Besides, the force can't afford to pay you overtime, do as you're told,' Seb said, laughing himself. 'I know you've been travelling back to Bethnal Green CID after you finish with the MIT.'

Her shocked look made him spread his hands in a truce.

'All I'm saying is we all do it, but I've been doing this a decade more than you and believe me, busting your gut and making yourself ill isn't recommended.'

Seb looked away and down at his hand which was clasped around a rail as he held on. The tracks sang in a perilous pitch as they whizzed around a corner and Kelly felt her body sway with momentum. Two schoolgirls going home for the day stared at them and she smiled. They looked away.

Often she felt moments of parallel universes like now as she thought back to what they'd witnessed in the last two days and then compared it to the scene on the tube. People went about their business – tourists, families, old, young, angry and sad. They lived their lives. Across the capital in two schools, two women had been mutilated and most of the population had never seen what knives do to the human body, or what rage does to flesh.

And it was a good thing. They did their job to protect these strangers on the tube. The two girls in school uniform. Hopefully they'd never witness violent death in their lifetimes because major investigation units did it for them.

When they emerged from the underground at Bethnal Green tube station, Kelly indicated that the museum was a short walk away and she pointed it out to him. It was an impressive building and she felt a little pride at showing him around her patch.

His phone rang and he took a call, nodding and gesticulating in reply. It sounded important.

When he got off he smiled at her.

'What?' she asked him, knowing he had something to tell her.

'It's confirmed. They knew each other.'

'Dorothy and Edith?'

'Yup. They worked in a kid's home together in the eighties.'

'Bloody hell,' Kelly said. 'What about Tania Harrison?'

'I asked them to add her to the list and they're getting back to me, it shouldn't take long. They have a staff list from the home, it had a long ridiculous name after some religious saint or something.'

'You're not a believer then?' Kelly asked.

'After what those bastards did to hundreds if not thousands of kids? Never. Hypocrites, the lot of them. I'll never forget Sinead O'Connor ripping up a photo of the pope on Saturday Night Live. What a woman.'

It was the first time Kelly had heard Seb say something so passionately about the moral drive behind their work, and she admired it, and trusted it. It was also an insight into his fabric. She changed her mind about him being potentially misogynistic over Leia Lord. It wasn't her sex; it was her manner. And Kelly agreed.

Suddenly Kelly appreciated the fundamental value of HOLMES. It didn't replace coppers, it simply sped up connections. It was able to join dots that would take humans days or even weeks to work out, even if it was simply one employment record over twenty years ago.

That would make the women in their early forties, like in the photo. Details were lining up.

'What was the ridiculously long name of the kid's home?' she asked him.

'Wait, it's on my phone, she texted it to me along with the address.'

He searched his texts, clearly not used to the small buttons and eventually found it. 'The Charitable Sisters of Our Lady and Saint Catherine,' he said.

Kelly stopped still in the street.

'What is it?' he asked.

'CSOLSC,' she said. She walked away towards the museum.

'How the hell did you come up with that?' he asked, chasing her.

'My dad said my head is like a cardex,' she said.

'That's why you should go and see him, you get it from him, don't you? Is he a copper?'

'How did you know?' she asked. They were almost at the museum steps.

'The nose,' he said.

They heard screeching and turned to see a line of children walking past them. They were small, around eight years old, Kelly guessed, and they were holding hands. Perhaps on a summer camp. They looked so innocent, and Kelly almost wanted to reach out and touch them to cleanse herself from the case.

They filed past and Kelly stared at them. Partners held hands and volunteers led the way, appearing stressed and harried. She wondered if they felt like police officers: overworked and underpaid. The kids' attention was easily drawn elsewhere, they wandered and meandered and stared into space.

Then her eyes were pulled to two children who were in the middle of the pack and quietly doing as they were told. They held hands and stayed away from the roadside of the pavement and in their free hands they swung dolls. One held a Kermit frog and the other a Miss Piggy.

They made their way up the steps of the museum and lined up outside, waiting for their teacher's instructions.

Chapter 33

Luther Zedric stared at the computer screen lovingly, his fists clenched into balls.

It was the only way he could see his beautiful puppets again.

The private messages on Facebook had stopped for now. The last one was sent by Luther, inviting the man to meet him face to face. Every few minutes, Luther looked at the door, then back to his screen. They'd engaged in ferocious exchanges via the social media platform, and it had taken its toll on the curator. He sat back. The screen remained inactive. Had he really meant it when he said that those who'd harmed him would pay the price?

Finally, after he'd accepted that the conversation for today was over, he distracted himself the only way he knew how. With his beloved puppets.

Most of the episodes of the original *Sam and Friends*, the show created by Jim Henson featuring Kermit (not yet the Frog), were never recorded and thus lost in the historical wasteland of creativity littered with ideas, unreplicated to date. The tragedy still affected Luther. The 1950s, in New York, was a golden age of TV. Elvis Presley appeared for the first time. Quiz shows were born. The stampede to make westerns put the gold rush to shame. And Jim Henson's show first aired on WRC from Washington DC.

Luther hummed the melody of the 'Glow Worm' song and found a light-hearted chuckle in his throat, which made him feel better and he unclenched his fists. The Muppets might be missing but their comedy lived on inside his head and he imagined Jim Henson crouching behind a board making the noise of Kermit gulping glow worms.

But it didn't quite mask the sadness he felt.

Being robbed was like being physically violated. He felt *handled*. Worse than that, bereft.

Betrayed by one he loved.

A shadow of depression had settled over him since Saturday when he'd opened the museum and known instantly that something was wrong.

And he'd first suspected who'd done it.

And now he felt like the child he once knew. Only his stories could save the little ones who cried in their beds every night. Monsters weren't in books, they were real. They hid behind the masks of those who said they loved you. Those who wore the uniforms of the protector, the nurses, the policemen, the teachers and the jailors. All of them took off their masks at night and revealed their true intentions. Nobody was truthful. Everybody hunted the defenceless.

But it had been his toys that brought escape to them, just like the old-fashioned playthings of his youth gave adventure in journeys across distant lands, which didn't exist for adults. They weren't allowed in. Only those with innocent hearts were given tickets to cross the silent oceans and skies of the night, to travel to the safety of another world. The two were never allowed to cross. If they did, then the magic was lost forever.

And the realms beyond reality were exposed as fake.

But he ruined it all.

Luther had been through a list of people in his head. Those who had keys issued. Diandra on reception was an officious woman who viewed breaking the law akin to ignoring the place of history. Doing something so heinous wasn't in her DNA and she'd been almost as morose as him since the weekend. Fillippe and Cassie from Archives were so law abiding, they'd had Luther over for dinner several times and gifted him tickets to an exhibition about Germany to observe a complete set of Arthur Rackham's illustrations of the Grimm brothers' tales.

The caretaker, Oswald, was seventy-one years old and took two days to clean each department, often missing bits because there were too many boxes stacked which he didn't have the strength to move. The V&A for some reason took pity on him and would pay him until he collapsed on the job.

In effect, Luther had begun his own investigation because the police officers promised everything but delivered nothing. In a city where gangs were shooting each other to death every Saturday night and teenage stabbings were reaching record levels, it was no wonder that a few dolls going missing from an obscure niche museum in the East End might be sidelined. Nobody had been harmed. Nothing had been broken, except perhaps Luther's heart. Since Saturday, he'd tried to divert his attention away from the most likely culprit, until he admitted, finally, that he knew exactly who had taken his toys. And the Facebook messages simply confirmed it.

What he felt for his artefacts was a kind of love and he admitted that now. For what was love if not loyalty, commitment, care, passion and adoration? And that's exactly how he felt about his prize exhibits.

His phone buzzing from the desktop made him jump and the cup of tea that he'd allowed to get cold wobbled in its saucer, knocked by his hand. He grabbed the phone and answered Diandra.

'Luther, it's the police to see you.'

'Oh? Send them up.'

'I'll bring them up myself.'

Luther got up from his seat and held his back. He ached. It was funny how he noticed the nagging twinges in his body more when he was upset. The mind was a powerful thing, he knew. It could manipulate terribly, awesomely, completely. It could invade a host and change the brain to make an agent of chaos. He should know. He'd seen it with his own eyes. Which was why he preferred puppets to people.

He recognised the woman Diandra showed into his office and he held out his hand for Kelly Porter. He waited to be introduced to the man, who looked more serious, but in pain. Emotional pain.

'I was popping by,' she told him.

'I can't imagine you *popping by* anywhere, Detective,' he said.

'This is Detective Inspector Seb Crook.'

Luther took the man's hand and looked deeply into his eyes. He recognised in both of them a deep commitment to their work which reflected his own. Kelly Porter was a passionate person who treated her cases like he did his puppets. She took care of them, which is why she'd come back, this time with a senior officer, to prove her value. She had something on her mind and she wanted to talk, he could tell. For somebody who spent most of his time around inanimate objects, he read people very well indeed.

'You missed me?' he asked her. He liked toying with real humans when he got the chance.

She smiled again. It suited her. It was a pity she was in such a serious job.

'Why are you a detective?' he asked.

The question caught her off guard.

'Erm, because I want to stop bad things happening to good people.'

'That's a good answer.'

'Was it a test?'

'I am just curious why you choose to surround yourself with such negativity. Your face is open and kind. I fear ten years on your job will make you hard and cynical.'

He looked at DI Crook when he said this and the irony landed where it was supposed to. The male detective was already lost to hardness, though not entirely. There was hope yet.

'Oh, I hope not!'

'Yours isn't a London accent. You're an outsider like me.'

'I'm from the Lake District. It's in Cumbria.'

'I've heard of it. Beatrix Potter land.'

'Ah, yes. Lake Windermere. She's a pull for the tourists that's for sure.'

'You don't approve?'

'Tourists come with benefits and drawbacks. They bring in the money but not for the people who need it, young people and locals.'

'Which is why you came to the capital, to make your name?'

'I don't think so but I'd like to think I make a difference.'

'I've been thinking. About my robbery. The perpetrator has a key.'

'And you're quite sure about that?'

Luther nodded emphatically.

'So you know who it is?' DI Crook asked.

'No. I'm afraid security here is lax. I've given out so many keys I can't recall everybody. I've worked here for twenty years and in that time I've seen people come and go, students, cleaners, managers, post handlers, conservators and the list goes on.'

'And they all get their own key? Don't they hand it back when they leave?'

He screwed his face in an embarrassing apology.

'I see,' Kelly said. 'So, how many people could there be, ex-employees for example, with keys that work?'

Luther grimaced. 'I've calculated around thirteen.'

Kelly absorbed the information. 'Could you supply us with a list?'

Luther noticed the male DI snooping around.

'Of course. I was compiling a file of information to share with you before you arrived. I'm glad you came today. Happy that you *popped* along.'

Kelly smiled.

'We were talking about Pinocchio last time I was here,' she said.

'Yes, we were,' he said.

'I was wondering if I could get your knowledge on two other popular children's characters.'

'Really? Why?'

'I'm curious as to why somebody would break in here and steal toys.'

'So you want me to tell you about Charlie McCarthy?'

'Who?' the male DI asked.

'One of my puppets that was taken. Haven't you read the notes?'

'Of course, I'm sorry, yes, Charlie McCarthy, the Muppets and Jiminy Cricket, wasn't it?'

Luther didn't know if the detective was trying hard to be empathetic or was genuinely interested in his missing toys.

'What do you see when you look at old toys? You have great affection for all of them, I know, but do you think children see them all the same way?'

Luther thought carefully, it was an odd question but it made him think and he liked questions that did that. He must answer carefully, because she was digging for something, that was clear.

'Do you mean can they adapt stories to themselves? To their own experiences?'

'I guess that was what I was asking, yes.'

'I think toys save children.'

'From what?'

'Adulthood.'

'Like Peter Pan?'

'Exactly.'

'How important was Tinkerbell to him?'

'She saved his life.'

'Really?'

'Yes, at first she was jealous of Wendy and wanted to kill her, but ultimately, he chose Neverland and Tinkerbell over a life with Wendy. He wasn't ready to grow up.'

Kelly had forgotten about Wendy's role in Peter Pan. The fact that she shared her name with her mother inserted unwelcome emotions into the situation, as if confusing the two might hurt her. She pushed the thoughts away.

'Was she a love interest?' Kelly asked.

Luther chuckled.

'No, she was more like his sidekick, though Disney made us think she loved him, but Disney always must have romantic love. In fact, the real fairy tales and children's shows were very dark indeed.'

'Yes, like being raped and eaten by a fox and such like,' Kelly commented drily.

'So you know enough about children being lost in forests and the sexual connotations of red cloaks to hold your own. It's not pleasant, I admit.'

'Yet that's the world you are in. I wonder, what makes adults still believe in stories?'

He looked at her, trying to seek answers but her face was closed off.

'Hope,' he said. 'Just hope.'

He was becoming distracted by the male detective who was opening boxes and reading papers.

'And can a child fall out of love with stories and become a worse version of themselves?'

'Of course, we all can. Just because children are born innocent doesn't mean they stay that way. Stories merely remind us that corruption is everywhere and the odds of surviving are slim.'

He saw the detective rub her shoulders as if she was suddenly chilly. Her questions were scarily accurate, and he knew he was in trouble, but he faced a more terrifying dilemma.

'Do you have a Peter Pan exhibit?'

He glanced at her and caught her right eye flicker. She was keeping something from him. Her investigation was much more important than she was letting on and she was here to use him for information on something bigger than just his lost puppets. Every toy, whether it be a puppet or a doll, had a specific purpose. The female detective had come here snooping about Pinocchio and Mr Punch already. His next guess was the question about Tinkerbell held a more sinister purpose. They were the characters of his favourite stories, the ones which he'd promised him could save him, but they never had.

It was way worse than anything he had feared.

And it had already started.

Chapter 34

'Mr Zedric,' Seb spoke directly.

'Call me Luther, please.'

'Luther, we have some specific questions for you regarding a school visit that was planned.'

Seb was becoming impatient and Kelly realised she'd waffled on too long drawing Luther out.

'A school visit? That's not my department I'm afraid, it's school liaison you need. I put on the talks, they book them in and deal with the teachers. You'll find them in the education office on the third floor but they're not in on Fridays.'

'Fair enough, we'll come back,' Seb said.

Kelly could see that the two men had got off on the wrong foot. They didn't like one another.

'I spoke to them on Wednesday, Luther. They confirmed a name but not an itinerary. Is Dorothy Amis a familiar name to you?'

Luther looked up at the high glass ceiling and shrugged. 'No, I can't say it is.'

'We were also wondering if you could identify this for us,' Kelly said.

She held up a bag containing what she thought was a silver swazzle, found in Dorothy Amis's bedside cabinet, and Luther examined it.

'Well, well. Yes I do know it. It's a swazzle.'

He reached out his hand to touch it and Kelly allowed him to take a closer look.

'It's a device used to produce an unusual but distinctive sound when inserted between the roof of the mouth and the tongue. I have one somewhere.'

He went to a cupboard and began searching through drawers, making a mess as he rooted around.

'Here!' he said triumphantly.

They watched as he inserted the small ring into his throat and began to talk.

'*That's the way to do it!*' he said.

Seb glared at him. Kelly watched her partner. This was the reaction she was hoping for. She'd brought him here to bring the characters at the centre of their murders alive, and it was working.

The sound was the unmistakable noise of the seaside. It was the voice of Mr Punch.

'I hope that helps,' Luther said, taking the small item out of his mouth. 'Now where were we? You wanted to see some of my toys? Come with me, I can show you the finest example of an early Tinkerbell.'

Kelly and Seb glanced at each other and Seb shrugged. Finally, her partner had been taken under Luther's spell and she found it endearing. The old man was difficult to discourage. They followed him into an adjacent room where he stood on a ladder and took down a box from a high shelf and opened it.

'In my opinion, Tinkerbell is the mistress of trickery. Remember in the original novel she was a common fairy, no more. It was Disney who turned her into a star. Tinkers were ordinary folk in the fairy world, menders of pots and pans, not trailblazers like in the awful animation. Tinks was very bad tempered and not a nice fairy to be around most of the time. She was frustrated and stubborn. Her voice was the tinkle of a bell. But she was the teller of lies.'

Satisfied he had the correct box, he continued talking as he climbed back down the ladder and Kelly thought he might fall if he didn't concentrate, and she hovered around the base with Seb holding on to the rungs. Kelly found herself lost in Luther's world and it wasn't lost on her that, to date, each time she'd come here, the curator had revealed something awful about each of the characters central to their inquiries that dispelled the myths of childhood magic around them. Without Luther, she'd still be scratching her head wondering why such fabulous characters were being pulled into murder.

'I'm fine, you know, I'm only seventy-eight.'

Luther reached the bottom of the ladder and passed Kelly a tiny fairy dressed in green. She was smaller than the one left with Edith's body. More delicate. Pixie-like.

'She looks innocent, doesn't she?'

Kelly showed it to Seb who examined it. Her goal for the visit was for Seb to witness Luther's love for his toys and puppets. Then he might understand why they were here.

'Her biggest trick, and the most sinister I think, is her tricking youngsters out of their beds with her tiny light and making them believe they could fly.'

They stared at him. The last place Kelly expected to feel unusually alarmed was surrounded by toys loved by millions of children of all ages, and yet she did.

'Does it annoy you what Disney has done to your beloved characters?' she asked.

'They're not mine, but yes, I don't appreciate bastardisation of anything historical.'

'There are real stories behind these figures, aren't there?'

'Of course. They've been around for generations. Take Judy for example, you asked me about her, Samuel Pepys first mentioned the show in his diary over three hundred and fifty years ago.'

'Which is your favourite? The older ones or the modern?'

'I have affection for them all for different reasons, I suppose.'

Luther was back to his plain adoration of the magic of children's stories again, gone was his creepy conjecture and sinister tone. Even Seb breathed easier. But Luther's enthusiasm was infectious. Something about Luther Zedric was undeniably familiar and comforting. He cared.

'Judy could also be said to have been frustrated, but not with her job, with her husband. He's a terrible father and a bully and uses his slapstick with impunity.'

Kelly and Seb listened intently.

'That's the origin of slapstick humour?' she asked.

'Yes, it was the sound it made. It was two pieces of wood glued together but with a gap between so the air causes a great slap when it was wielded. It hurt more too.'

Kelly couldn't help but grimace.

'Don't take it too seriously. Mr Punch was a typical man of his time, be that Georgian or Victorian. A man kept his family in check with his fists. We can't judge another age by our standards, that's not fair.'

'That's controversial, to say the least,' Kelly said.

'I don't really care. I'm too old to worry about flights of fancy and fashion. I remember my mother slapping me with a shoe, she used to chase me down the street.'

Kelly folded her arms. She could feel Seb next to her wanting to chuckle.

'Don't feel bad for me. We knew no better, they were different times. Do you want to see an original slapstick from 1842?'

'Why not?' Seb said.

Luther delved into an open drawer and took out a velvet bag and opened it on a table in front of them. The bag was full of slapsticks. He lined them up in date order and told them where they'd been taken into care. They'd been rescued like orphans.

Kelly recoiled from one of them and she felt Luther watching her. He picked it up and thwacked it through the air. She stood back, shocked, and he realised he'd gone too far.

'We used to have a Punch and Judy show here but it was banned by the politically correct army.' He rolled his eyes.

'I guess we all have to progress,' Seb said. 'Child abuse is a real problem for the victims,' he added, failing to keep the sarcasm out of his voice.

'Victims grow up changed and not how they were designed to. It stunts growth in all sorts of ways, it's a good thing it's taken seriously now, even if it wasn't back then,' Kelly added.

She heard herself grow serious. Luther frowned.

She was appealing to his compassion, and she was convinced he had it in him somewhere, even if he was from a different era. She was trying to make him see that tradition was valuable but often misplaced if held on to for too long. But he was belligerent.

'Tradition is of its time and therefore perfectly appropriate in that moment. If we time-travelled back to 1842 and I hit you with a slapstick, yes, it would be appalling to you but back then it was accepted and after all, Punch often got his comeuppance depending on which version you watched. Even in 1842 there was only so much domestic violence that was tolerated.'

'I recall some audience participation,' Kelly said.

'That's the beauty of fiction, sometimes the audience gets to decide.'

'Like children get to decide?'

'No, but they don't sadly.'

'In their heads, maybe,' she said.

He glanced away. 'That would be nice, wouldn't it?'

He busied himself with exhibits and picked out a Kermit the Frog.

'The Muppets played practical jokes on each other. Tom and Jerry tried to kill one another. Popeye was a violent thug, even if he said it was in Olive's name. He was also a chain smoker. The Grimm brothers wrote about paedophiles and cannibals. What are children's stories if there is no balance? No light to contrast the dark. But for good to prevail, we must face the evil first.'

She smiled but she knew he'd hit a nerve. He was at it again, as if he were some puritanical preacher telling her off.

'Have you always been a museum curator, Luther?' she asked.

His mouth moved, as if he was preparing to tell them something else. The truth perhaps. But then the moment passed, and he launched into another story, this time about Kermit the Frog.

Chapter 35

Edith Callaghan had once lived in a smart two-up-two-down terrace not far away from Dorothy Amis, in Leytonstone. Neither woman owned a mobile phone, as per their generation, and so digging into messages and call history was restricted to landlines. They revealed that they called each other about once a month.

They were friends.

Inside Edith's home was rather different to Dorothy's. Edith was demonstrably a more outgoing person. There were examples of artistic flare in her choice of furnishings, paintings and decoration. She'd been a collector of porcelain dolls and it reminded Kelly of her grandma who collected similar figurines of beautiful women walking, dancing, laughing, posing and generally looking perfect. Kelly had been told off by her grandmother for wanting to play games with them.

'They're not playthings!' she'd been scolded. A familiar notion of being watched crept up on her and made her spine tingle as hundreds of eyes followed her around the room.

'It's like a freakshow,' Seb said.

They stood in the middle of the living room and tried to ignore them, but it was tough going. They seemed to pass judgement.

'Not as tidy as her pal,' Kelly said.

It was true. Edith had left a plate of biscuits on a small table and there were dirty cups in the fireplace.

'Looks like she had company,' Seb said.

Kelly browsed Edith's extensive book collection and found it to be mainly romantic novels, theatre and film guides and travelling companions with lots of pictures.

'She was a dreamer,' Kelly said.

On the wall above the table was a framed poster. Edith clearly loved her movies. The impossibly handsome features of Robert Redford and Paul Newman stared back at them.

'They were the pin-ups of her age, I guess,' Kelly said. Her own mother, Wendy, was madly in love with Paul Newman too.

'It's *The Sting*,' Seb said.

'What?'

'The movie. From the seventies, I think. It's a classic.'

Seb moved away and started humming a tune under his breath.

Kelly stared at him. Then she remembered that 'The Entertainer' was an overused theme tune to many productions. It just got more annoying the more times she heard it. Like an advert jingle, it was the type that stuck in her head, and she couldn't get rid of it. Clearly, it had stuck in Seb's too. It was why ice cream vans used it, after all.

Like Dorothy's house, there weren't many photos on show and Kelly thought of her own flat and how she plastered pictures of her life, in frames or not, all over the place. Anyone walking into her personal space would be able to piece together who she was, who she loved, what drove her and what she lived for. Not so with Edith or Dorothy. It was as if the opposite was true; they actively hid their lives, or kept them somewhere else where they couldn't be seen. But there was one photo, stood up on the bookcase, faded and worn, of two people, a man and a woman, and Kelly instantly knew who they were. The woman was Edith and the man was the one from the picture in Dorothy's house. The man they desperately wanted to talk to. The man who knew all three victims.

'Look.' She showed Seb. Thankfully, he stopped crooning.

'They were a tight group, that's for sure,' he said.

The song disappeared from her mind.

They both agreed that finding the man was key to their enquiries, and so far, they'd had experts enlarge his face from the other photo and release it to the press, with no luck. However, this one was better and they popped it into an evidence bag. So far, he was their prime suspect.

They also had a long list of men who'd worked with the three victims, from different institutions over the course of twenty years and each one needed to be checked out. The legwork was done behind a computer by a detective constable, grinding out hours and hours of menial labour until their eyes could take no more. It's how they all started. Kelly had done her time. Every detail was vital and somebody had to go through it. Computers couldn't do that job, it had to be a human being, but it took time.

They moved to the kitchen.

There were dirty pots in the sink and rotting food on the side. A mirror sat on the countertop surrounded by piles of makeup and Kelly thought of Edith's face as she dangled from the gym bar. She'd been heavily made up like Dorothy but the attempt to make her appear like a fairy had in fact had the opposite effect and made her look like a clown. She'd been made to look ridiculous. It was a message.

'Whoever killed her wanted to humiliate her,' Kelly said.

'I agree,' Seb said. 'The whole image is tragic.'

'It was a message. The makeup. I know much of it was her own blood but painting her face, whichever way, is a communiqué. It's telling us she was vain, that she loved herself too much. She put her appearance before other things and somebody resented it.'

Seb stared at her.

Kelly shrugged. 'That's what I think.'

'No, don't be shy, I agree, I'm just impressed. Profiling is overlooked too much, I think it's important.'

'Thank you,' Kelly said and smiled. She felt less silly for her outburst which had come instinctively. It had risen up as she stared at the makeup and turned into words. She couldn't help it.

'What's that?' Kelly asked, pointing to a calendar hanging up on the wall. It depicted pictures of cartoon characters and Kelly thought it distinctly infantile and odd. Seb noticed too.

'It could have been a joke present from a friend, you know the type who thinks they're hilarious at Christmas?'

'A stocking filler?' Seb asked.

'Exactly, you still get one?'

'No, do you?'

'I'm ashamed to admit that my mother still gives me one.'

'What does it have in it apart from stupid calendars?'

'Socks, sweets, fruit—'

'Fruit?'

'You know the old tradition of giving an orange?'

'No.'

'Oh. Well, it's a thing.'

'Up north?'

'Obviously. It's a note.'

'What?'

'A note, look,' she said. He came to stand next to her. Pinned to the calendar was an envelope marked 'Frankie'.

'Is that a woman's name?' Seb asked.

'It could be either, I'm sure people call men Frankie too.'

Kelly reached across and unpinned it, opening the envelope and pulling out a handwritten letter and some photographs.

'It's a nursery rhyme,' Kelly said. 'Jack and Jill.'

'As in, "went up the hill"?'

'The same.'

Seb's phone rang and he answered it. Kelly continued looking around and Seb soon ended the call.

'Tania Harrison worked at the Charitable Sisters-whatsit-place too,' he said. 'The kids home. They all worked there.'

'The man must have worked there too, get them to concentrate their search to there. He's our number-one suspect.'

'I already did.'

'What are the photos?' he asked.

'Surveillance, just like the ones of Dorothy.'

Chapter 36

Kelly reflected on her first full week at MIT east. She didn't yet feel as though she belonged and, like a frustrated partner, she took her woes to her old colleague.

Kelly walked into the Bethnal Green office early on Friday afternoon and plonked her tired body down in front of Cheryl. It felt as though she'd worked a whole day already. She had just over an hour before her train from Euston to Penrith, *if* she got on it. She'd been home briefly to grab an overnight bag and had packed reluctantly, not quite understanding what it was that was stopping her.

Cheryl looked up from her desk.

'Hey. Make me a coffee.'

London was in the grips of a heatwave, but there was no air conditioning in Bethnal Green nick. It was as incendiary in the office as it was under the full sun.

'I'm not going,' she said finally.

'Where? To make me a coffee?'

'Home. I can't, there's too much up in the air.'

'Don't be stupid, you're all booked and packed. I thought your boss said it was fine and your partner said you should go.'

'Why do they want me out of the way?'

'Now who's being paranoid?' Cheryl asked her. 'About that coffee.'

Kelly got up and went to the tray in the corner where she flicked on the kettle and kicked off her shoes.

'Make yourself at home,' Cheryl said.

'Any news?' Kelly asked.

'Jonathan Hass still doesn't understand that we no longer have the Pinocchio case and he sends everything to me which is fascinating but I'm tempted to report him,' Cheryl told her, grinning.

'You get everything before we do?' Kelly's eyes widened.

'He's old school, he asks after you every time.'

Kelly shivered slightly but it didn't cool her down.

'What's this about Tania working at a children's home called – wait a minute—' She read from her pad once she'd cleared a mug off it. 'The Charitable Sisters of Our Lady and Saint Catherine?'

'It's a mouthful,' Kelly said, pouring water into mugs. The last thing she fancied was a hot drink but she was sure she'd heard that hot drinks actually helped cool you down. It was something to do with tricking the brain into thinking it was even hotter than it was and making your body cool itself quicker.

'We've searched for it but it no longer exists, we're tracing it and as soon as we get a hit, we'll try to unearth their records,' Kelly told her.

'Any idea why it closed? Just asking for a friend.'

Cheryl was in a mischievous mood. It was almost the weekend.

'Come with me, I could do with the facile distraction.'

'Where? To the kids' home?'

'No, Cumbria.'

Cheryl took her coffee.

'I don't like the sound of it, all those hills and relatives I'd have to speak to.'

'Oh, come on, I need the company.'

'Sorry, somebody deserted my team and left me in charge, I couldn't possibly spare the time.'

'Are you working all weekend?'

'Not all but I have sleep to catch up on.'

Kelly sat down heavily and sipped the hot drink.

'How did you get a hit on those women working for the Charitable Sisters when there's no trace of an address? Was it affiliated to a church?' Cheryl asked.

'I guess the Church of England, though saints are catholic, aren't they?'

'Anyone can have saints, they're two a penny. Like staff without background checks in the 1970s, just saying.'

'I know, but I'm also just saying that probes of their more recent employment are all verified. No complaints, no disciplinaries, no warnings.'

'I once had to visit a priest, going back a few years now,' Cheryl said.

'Is this going to be a confession?'

'I'm beyond that. No, he was the fount of all knowledge, if there was a charity home for kids in London in the '70s, I swear he'd know it. He was about a hundred years old and knew everything, I just can't remember his name.'

'Well, let me know when you can.'

'I will. Fancy a proper drink?'

'Now you're talking.'

Cheryl shut down her computer and they turned off the lights and the two struggling fans blowing paper across Pete's desk. They left the office.

'Any news on Orlando Charles?' Kelly asked hopefully.

For coppers, there was always one case that disappointed, one perp that got away. For Kelly it was Orlando. It seemed so unfair as if he had a guardian angel protecting him.

'I'm still watching out for him. People like him can't stay clean. We'll get him one day. He's been really quiet lately, though.'

Kelly felt her guts turn over but she pushed the thoughts away. She already believed that Dennis Chapman had disappeared from the building site because of his error. What if Jason had that reach over Orlando? If he vanished too they'd never know who was behind half the robberies in east London. But that was Cheryl's problem now.

By the time they'd downed their drinks at the Bethnal Green Arms, Cheryl had convinced Kelly that she should go home. Cheryl echoed Seb's warnings to her of regret and missed opportunity, and Kelly acknowledged that it was dismal but true. Dorothy Amis and Edith Callaghan, and poor Tania, the nurse, would never get to go to another family gathering ever again.

It made up her mind.

Chapter 37

As the train to Penrith pulled out of Euston on Friday afternoon, Kelly looked at the pile of paperwork she'd brought with her to reassure herself that she wasn't skipping her duty. Gone were the days of John Porter when people took sleeping bags into work and smoked their way through long weekends trawling through evidence. But men back then had wives at home keeping their lives functioning. Nowadays, people had personal lives to tend to and Seb had already called her telling her he was knocking off for the weekend.

'I'll check in if anything develops,' he told her.

'Be careful,' she said.

He hadn't replied straight away.

'Thanks,' he said, eventually.

Kelly wondered when the last time Seb Crook had anyone watching his back and decided it must have been a long time ago.

A large file caught her eye and she pulled it out. It belonged to Fellcroft, Bradley's father. She still felt guilty about the young man. A small part of her thought she could still talk him round and perhaps get him away from his father's influence. The first step would be to find him alternative employment.

The journey home to Cumbria was just shy of three hours and her dad had insisted he'd collect her from the station. It was just as simple to get a taxi but John Porter was not to be moved. His decision was final. She couldn't help but feel fifteen years old again each time she faced going home. Like one of his suspects, she knew she'd be interrogated.

Her mum and dad's wedding anniversary brought mixed emotions, and they swirled in her head as she stared out of the window, avoiding Jason Fellcroft's file.

The folder on him was huge, as was only fitting for a criminal of his standing and experience. But she found herself not reading it as a detective bolstering a case for a prosecution team, but as a woman who couldn't help feeling pain when she imagined Bradley growing up with such a man for a father.

After all this time, the older man dominated his son who was soon to be an adult, making his own decisions and crafting his own life plan. But she knew that wasn't how these things worked. Which was another reason not to have her own kids. The life path of human beings, from tiny babies to men the size of Bradley, was wrought with danger. At every twist and turn there were adults corrupting them, persuading them, manipulating them and abusing them. The more they were surrounded from birth by deviants, the higher the odds of turning out exactly the same.

Bradley's life had been doomed from the beginning.

However, Kelly couldn't help but see the glimmer of hope inside of him every time she saw him, which was what had drawn her to him in the first place. Her desperate need to fix things confused her priorities.

She felt an overwhelming desire to scoop up all the kids in the world who were born to unloving guardians and whisk them away to a happy place, like the old woman who lived in a shoe. Weren't all fictional heroes and heroines orphans? Was there a message to that? Belle, Hansel and Gretel, even the Lone Ranger.

Pinocchio had no real parents, neither did fairies, they were created from the laugh of a baby or the tinkle of a Christmas bell… Punch and Judy were the most awful guardians.

Kelly felt her heart race as once again she found herself thinking about children's story characters. Suddenly, her own heroes took on extra meaning in her life and she recalled her favourite stories. In some kind of way she wished she could live a simpler life like Luther Zedric, wrapped up in stories and surrounded by heroes all day long. She guessed that in a way that's exactly what she did but in her stories the villains often got away.

A metal trolley rolled into her peripheral vision and stopped right beside her and the man pushing it asked her if she'd like any refreshments. The stale sandwiches, sugary drinks and plastic snacks looked anything but refreshing and she declined his kind offer.

She opened her case zip with a sigh and pulled out files, and began to read. She'd brought plenty of them, and her Nokia phone sat next to her, ready to be answered should Seb need her urgently. She had no idea what she might do in any such scenario, but at least she would be in the loop.

Jason Fellcroft first found himself on the wrong side of the law at just twelve years old, when he'd been taken to an armed robbery with his own father. The parallels of what he'd done to his own son were chilling. The year was 1978. Times were hard. The Empire was no longer the powerhouse of Europe, thanks to two world wars, and Fellcroft senior used any old story as an excuse for his crimes. He also had the morals of an alley cat when it came to his son, who'd been put into care in 1974, four years prior to his first offence. Jason had been abandoned to children's homes.

Perhaps he wanted to bond with the kid, like dads do…

Bradley, she realised, was up against generations of bad'uns, and the odds of him breaking the cycle were slim to none. Kids from those families didn't usually escape the patterns.

Unless somebody took them under their wing.

Then she saw it.

It was written by a senior detective in an entry from 1999.

> Fellcroft likes to give youngsters jobs to keep them off the streets, but often they become enrolled by him, swapping petty crime for organised, under a master.

Had Jason Fellcroft been a modern-day Fagin? Or Bill Sykes? Recruiting and teaching the waifs and strays he picked up to carry out his orders.

There were numerous examples in the file of apprentices associated with Fellcroft. Some had been caught, others hadn't.

All were on watchlists.

Including Bradley.

So where was Orlando?

It seemed that anyone connected to him became infected with his reach and power and ended up committing some form of crime themselves. Which would explain the family of ne'er-do-wells he surrounded himself with inside Belmarsh. It was nothing new to Kelly. She'd seen it a thousand times over. It was a well-trodden path for criminals who stuck together, but nowadays with the infiltration of foreign gangs, terrorist cells and drug money, control was harder to maintain. It was one reason for the explosion of gang wars in the last twenty years. For that reason, she was glad she didn't work in nearby Haringey. The Trident system was overrun with data on gang shootings and stabbings in London, with 2008 shaping up to be the worst on record.

Her eyes lingered on some of the names linked to Jason Fellcroft's nursery system, as one humorous copper had dubbed it. In other words, Fellcroft was suspected of nurturing lost souls, usually minors up to the age of twenty, and training them to become an invaluable part of his own thuggish empire. His preferred rendezvous point was his numerous building sites and he recruited young men who walked in off the street, as well as lads referred by word of mouth. Kelly became engrossed in the investigation into Fellcroft's business dating back to the nineties, and was astounded at how many young boys and men he'd groomed into his business with the promise of work, companionship and wages. It was just another gang model.

Which was why she was puzzled at not finding Orlando's name anywhere. He was the same age as Jason, forty-two, and they'd already established he'd worked on the sites owned by Fellcroft. So why wasn't he there in the numerous files along with the others?

Her heart sank.

Perhaps she was mistaken and Orlando meant nothing but her dad had taught her to think the opposite way to most people. In fact, it could mean that Orlando could be deeper embedded in Jason's business than she realised and he was protecting him. It would explain why Bradley was scared of him.

She called Seb and told him they must go back to the building site first thing Monday morning and arrange a visit to Belmarsh Prison to interview Jason Fellcroft.

'Are you going to do this all the way up to Scotland?' he asked.

'It's not Scotland! It's Cumbria.'

'Still cold.' He laughed. 'Enjoy the party.'

Chapter 38

John Porter strode towards Kelly with purpose. Kelly almost backed away, his presence was so forceful, but when he opened his arms to her, she smiled broadly at him and was thankful for somebody to carry her bags. He was a fit man still, though he was in his late fifties now. His arms rippled with muscle and he stood tall and proud.

John Porter had enjoyed much success in his career as a uniformed copper. He'd shunned the detective route, opting for 'real policing' and had been put in charge of serious crime for the north lakes area several times as a stand-in for superior officers. Lines were smudged in the provinces and uniform or no uniform, teams were more cohesive. In the capital Kelly still hadn't worked out if the wholesale contracting out of crime was working. There were talks of shutting local police stations and leaving work to specialist teams which were dotted around the capital. It all seemed crazy to her. She imagined, twenty years from now, desolate streets full of gangs and criminals where the police would be scared to even patrol, if there were any beat bobbies left. It was a desperately depressing prospect. They faced the ludicrous situation that if you committed a crime in Walthamstow, the investigation team would come from some central office, depending on the nature of the crime, perhaps based in Croydon or Dulwich, to take over. It was the parcelling-up of crime and in Kelly's opinion it was a gift to people like Jason Fellcroft.

She had to admit that seeing her father made her appreciate old-fashioned police work. His eyes sparkled with intelligence and his demeanour emitted the confidence of the successful. In Cumbria, a patch was a patch and local teams tackled local crime. It made her breathe easier without her even realising it. That, and the mountain air which floated in from the northwest. Penrith was on the very edge of the Lake District, but she could smell the lakes and mountains of her childhood, and she wavered between it comforting her and challenging her.

There had been so much to run away from but now she was home again, there were so many things she missed and she wasn't even in the car yet.

'You look tired,' John said.

'Thanks, Dad.'

'Your mother has made hot pot.'

'It's almost twenty-five degrees, Dad!'

'She doesn't like salad, that's for southerners, Kel, you know that.'

'Yes, how could I forget. You know southerners don't all eat salad,' she said.

He eyed her sideways and suspicion slithered out of his eye sockets.

'Where's the party?' she asked, trying to take the conversation away from her being brainwashed into bizarre southern ways.

'It's at the cricket club.'

She heard impatience in his voice and kicked herself for not remembering. Of course it was at the cricket club. Where else would it be? John Porter had been a member there since she could remember. That's where his school mates went, it's where his copper mates played in the same team and it was where beer was still one pound a pint.

How silly of her.

'You need some northern air, Kelly. You should have a good feed then I'm taking you up the fells.'

'What?'

'Look at you, you're disappearing! You've lost weight and you're dressed like a tourist. You need to get some shorts on and some boots and get your lungs working. I bet they're stuffed full of filth from the city.'

He almost shivered when he said it as if the city was where real people went to die.

'Dad, I just want to unpack and maybe go for a walk.'

'We are going for a walk. What about Blencathra?'

'That's a mountain!'

'No, it isn't, you've gone soft. Saddleback is a gentle hill. You're out of shape, I can tell. Are you smoking?'

'No!'

She said it far too quickly and he sussed her out. She felt fifteen again.

'Look at that sunshine!' he said as they pulled away and the cloudless sky beckoned her to her childhood home. Suddenly the car felt hot and stuffy and she opened a window to let the draught catch her hair and she closed her eyes.

'Got a boyfriend?'

Kelly rolled her eyes underneath her eyelids.

'No.'

'Your mother will ask.'

She groaned inwardly.

'You're not a lesbian, are you?'

'What?'

Kelly opened her eyes and stared at him.

'I heard London is full of them.'

Kelly wanted to laugh out loud at the backwardness of her father, but incredulity prevented her and she felt a bizarre affection for his ignorance.

'One day there'll be lesbians here too, Dad,' she said with a warning tone in her voice. She smirked.

'I know what your game is, Kelly. Laugh at me, go on. You'll see one day, when you want a baby and there's none there, and you come home to silence. Your house was full of life when you were little. Always somebody there playing and screaming and filling the air up with laughter.'

'Lesbians can have kids too you know, Dad.'

She watched him grip the steering wheel tighter.

'I'm too busy for a boyfriend.'

'Ah, go away. What is there to keep you too busy for courting?'

She found his old-fashioned phrases somehow appealing, and she was at once appalled and enamoured by it. She gazed at the contours of the mountains longingly.

Perhaps her dad was right. A hike was just what she needed to sort her head out. It was saturated with frustrating cases. Up here, everything seemed much simpler.

The drive across town was smooth and quick compared to travelling anywhere in London. The traffic moved freely and she didn't feel hemmed in by metal boxes. She could see the sky and the land looked far away. It helped her to breathe and it seemed that by the end of the journey, it didn't matter what her dad said, he couldn't rile her at all.

When they got out of the car in front of the terraced house she'd grown up in, she was smiling.

'That's better,' he said. 'Look, you're more relaxed already.'

Her mother, Wendy, came out to greet her and enveloped her in a warm hug. Kelly felt her shoulders unwind and she smelled cooking from inside. Her mother looked well and a pang of emotion stung Kelly's heart as she realised she'd missed them. And the place.

Her dad brought in her bags and took them straight upstairs to her old room, then her mother plopped a plate in her hands. A fat slice of homemade cake sat on top of it and Kelly gazed at it lovingly.

The radio played '80s music and announced news about sheep and mountain passes, as well as tourists getting lost on the fells and the sterling work of the mountain rescue. She put her bag down and her mother immediately moved it. Kelly eyed her and took a carton of orange juice out of the fridge and poured some into a glass.

She wasn't used to being policed. She and Molly left their stuff wherever they wanted. The kitchen was smaller than she remembered, and she pressed her body up against a cupboard to let her mother open the oven. A volcanic blast of heat hit her and she squeezed past her mother and went into the living room. Behind her, John Porter took her bag upstairs.

'Right, ready?' he said. He'd already changed into walking gear, and she stared at him. His face was so keen and she realised that he missed her too. He'd been looking forward to this.

'Yes,' she said. 'Give me a minute.'

She'd packed running gear which made suitable hiking apparel and changed quickly, trying to ignore the décor of her old room staring back at her. It was claustrophobic and dated. It hadn't been changed one bit, which made her sad and guilty at the same time. Wendy always said she'd turn it into a spare room when she left but it still looked like the room of a teenage girl, and it comforted her in a weird sort of way.

She trotted downstairs and her father handed her a water bottle.

The car journey this time was less fraught with unsaid platitudes and they headed west to the mountains in the distance. The journey took them over the M6 and in no time at all they were parking up at Scales.

'So what are you investigating in the capital at the moment? Knives? Guns? Drugs?'

It hadn't taken him long.

They sorted their bags and checked they had what they needed and set off. John's pace was as quick as she remembered it. He hadn't slowed down at all and she struggled to keep up at first. Her running had taken a nosedive in London because of opportunity but also the lack of beautiful wide-open spaces to inspire a nice long run. Soon, however, she found her mountain legs and she was determined to keep up with him.

'Actually, I'm on a murder squad now.'

He laughed at her. 'You sound like the bloody Sweeney! A murder squad, what's that? What about old-fashioned policing? Put it all in one place and you're asking for trouble.'

He paused for breath. She didn't answer; she didn't need to. This was why she kept her work life private.

'Want me to take a look?' he asked.

They'd barely gone a hundred yards and already he was muscling in on her job, but she breathed deeply and let it go. Realistically, she couldn't get enough breath to argue anyway.

They stopped to look back at how far they'd come and Kelly felt her heart rate settling into a rhythm. She swigged a few gulps from her bottle and John did the same.

'Have you got a profile?' he asked.

'Two female teachers in their sixties, four days apart, dumped and dressed as children's puppets.'

He snorted.

'I'm serious, Dad.'

'Crikey, those southerners are bloody off their nuts.'

'Quite. Anyway, one was dressed as Judy from Punch and Judy fame and the other as Tinkerbell – don't ask – but there's more.'

'There had to be.'

'Seven years ago a nurse was murdered, dumped in a building site and dressed as Pinocchio. The three of them were friends and worked closely together in the eighties.'

John stared at her and shook his head.

'See, this is what happens in the city. Weirdos everywhere. I used to read Pinocchio to you at bedtime.'

He set off and she caught up to him.

'Tell me about them,' he said.

Kelly knew what he was doing. He was focusing her mind and in that moment she loved him for it. She forgot about the times he'd scared her by shouting so loudly at her mother that her heart almost stopped. She forgot that he made her feel so insecure about her own ability that she almost became a secretary like he suggested. She overlooked the times he raised his hand to her when she was too noisy, too naughty or too much. In that moment, he wasn't a bully, or a domineering ogre. He was just her dad and he wanted to know about her job.

'The one from 2001 was a nurse. Single. Lived in a flat-share housing association.'

'What's housing association?' he asked.

'It's what I live in. It's housing funded by the government for government workers, and it's cheaper than private accommodation.'

'That's a good idea.'

'Isn't it? Anyway, she was single, no kids and worked in nursing and care homes.'

Suddenly Kelly regretted being so honest. John Porter would now tell her what she was doing wrong. But to her surprise he didn't say that at all.

She saw he was thinking deeply. She filled in the details for him.

'In London, murder is only investigated by murder squads. They're centralised in pods around the city. Once a case becomes a murder investigation, they take over. I thought mine was a cold case, perhaps even older, we didn't know if she might have been there since the fifties for all we knew, or even Roman times, but it turned out it was much more recent, so now it's part of a wider investigation.'

'How many officers?'

'Forty or there abouts.'

He tutted.

'Elites don't solve murders just because they're senior in rank. You need foot soldiers,' he said. 'Murder is about people. All policing is about people. There's no such thing as a unique crime.'

She felt strangely vindicated as though he understood. As if he'd been listening to her conversations with Cheryl and Molly. She wished Leia Lord could hear him.

They carried on and she saw the summit of Blencathra come into view. The sky was blue and wide and nothing blocked the serenity of the view. The land was still and she saw a single bird fly over Sharp Edge, wishing she could soar over peaks like that.

'Who is your superior? Get me a name and I'll phone him.'

Kelly smiled to herself. The notion that John Porter could tell Leia Lord what to do was at the same time comforting and silly, because he probably could, but it was hugely embarrassing too. But the idea that she needed his help hurt like hell.

'She. And no thanks.'

They stopped for another drink and they looked across the national park.

'God's country,' John said.

She'd heard him say it a thousand times, maybe a hundred thousand times. The feeling of getting to the top of one of the fells on a day like today was incomparable, she had to agree.

And if she believed in God, it would be godlike.

'Where did she drink?' he asked.

'Who?'

'This nurse, what was her name? All nurses drink like fish. They're like teachers and policemen. Where did she drink with her friends?'

'Tania. I don't know where she drank. But you're right, Dad, they often live together.'

'Who?'

'Nurses and teachers.'

'Well, she was taken from somewhere and somebody missed her. There's always a link. If they worked together back in the day before police checks and national records, who hired them and why? Did they have any discipline procedures against them? That's what I always check now, since 2002. Usually women who go off with men and end up dead do so from public places where they feel safe. And they've been watched for a while before that. By perverts. Especially the perverts.'

They strode up towards the final summit hike of Blencathra and Scales Tarn glittered beneath them in the sunshine.

Kelly's heart rate, though the organ was pumping blood madly around her body, felt calm in her body and she felt centred like she never did in London. The adrenaline necessary to keep her going, in between tube rides, taxi journeys, offices and tall, airless buildings which choked the light from around her, was absent, but in the background. Her body was working in a different way and she was fighting to climb to the top of a hill that was just as steep as what she faced in London, but the peak of this one got nearer as she grew stronger. John Porter marched ahead and she saw that the summit was empty. No one else was mad enough to spend their Friday evening up here when they could be at the pub. But that was the irony of the whole thing. This was where she wanted to be and suddenly London was a million miles away, not just a couple of hundred, and Tania, Edith, Dorothy and Orlando Charles, Jason Fellcroft and Bradley were players in the background. They made noises but allowed her to breathe for the first time in weeks.

She and Seb had read Tania's hospital notes, as well as her GP records, along with some statements made at the time of her disappearance from her colleagues and friends.

Now, with renewed clarity, thanks to a walk in the hills, the details in Tania's file came flooding back to her, and among them was the name of a Hackney pub where nurses gathered after their shifts in the late nineties to gossip and unwind after caring for the sick all day long.

As well as the fact that Tania had once worked on a children's ward.

Chapter 39

Saturday was filled with Wendy buzzing around like a whirling dervish finalising arrangements and popping in and out. Kelly carried flowers, wrapped food, addressed cards and wrote out place names. But this was her mother's comfort zone: she was busy but not connected. She was useful but not present. This was the real reason Kelly avoided home, not because her father told her what to do, which, she'd realised was actually good for her, but because Wendy could never bring herself to slow down and simply be her mother. It made her sad.

Kelly did as she was told and by the time the afternoon sped away from them, it was time to go to the party. She wore a satin dress cut just above the knee. The claret showed off her deep brown hair which was tinted at the front by the sun. It was warm enough not to need a jacket but Kelly slung a cardigan over her arm. Because the temperature was ten degrees cooler than London.

The cricket club hadn't changed since the last time Kelly had been there, which was about five years ago. The claret-coloured velvet seating still looked shabby and the floor was still sticky with last night's booze. A faint aroma of tobacco clung to the walls and fixtures and the fake Mahogony woodwork shone with polish. The barman hadn't aged any better. By the time Kelly ordered her first warm white wine at the bar and heard a familiar voice offering to pay, she realised why she'd left the lakes for good. She turned to see her ex-fiancé, Dave Crawley, stood next to her.

She recoiled inwardly and felt bad for doing so. They'd shared time together. They'd laughed, cried and everything in between. They'd planned houses, children, careers and holidays as a family. And it had all come crashing down when she woke up one morning and realised that marriage to Dave Crawley would be the same for her as one of her criminals felt about life inside one of Her Majesty's prisons.

Moving to London had been the escape which saved her.

The air in the capital might be thick with pollution but it was cleaner than around Dave.

Her announcement back then had shocked everyone. Her dad and Dave's dad were buddies. Dave's mother had planned and bought her wedding outfit, they'd already chosen a house, close to his parents, and had begun decorating and they even had plans to buy a dog.

Now, looking at him, with his grinning mouth plastered on to his drunken face and his belly protruding out of his shirt, and his shiny red nose, she felt terrible guilt that her dumping him had thrown him off the rails.

He used to be attractive.

Or at least that's what she remembered. He'd been alluring in a safe way perhaps rather than a classical manly good-looking way. There was a difference. Some men exuded a bright future for a potential mate, others promised excitement in the moment. Dave was the former but not anymore. His eyes were glassy and his teeth were bad. A funny feeling caught in her stomach as she suspected Dave was on the brink of becoming the sort of person who might pop up in one of her enquiries. She pushed the thought away. She was being cruel because he looked like shit. It was just her brain justifying dumping him.

'Kel, you look gorgeous,' he slurred.

They air-kissed but on the second cheek he turned his head so his mouth brushed hers and she felt nauseous. His breath smelled of booze and cigarettes and she was reminded of sexual fumbles when she was fifteen.

Then she spied her father grinning behind them and approaching like a great white shark, hunting for supremacy. He slapped Dave on the back and then grabbed his hand and shook it.

'Dave! Good to see you, lad, isn't our Kelly looking grand!'

Kelly cringed inwardly. Her skin felt tight.

Then she spotted Nikki, and Kelly was able to excuse herself to greet her sister. They hugged. Kelly stared at Nikki's belly.

'Wow! That's big!'

Nikki rubbed her baby bump proudly and Kelly felt slightly inadequate as a woman. Kelly was the one who'd got away, but she was also the one left behind, because everybody seemed to be having babies. Nikki looked well. She glowed healthily. Their relationship hadn't always been easy. They were very different people. Nikki was judgemental about how her younger sister lived her life. She saw her move to London as a betrayal of Mum and Dad.

But now she exchanged pleasant trivia with her sibling about baby names and coloured blankets. It reminded Kelly how peripheral she was to this life surrounded by mountains. Her concrete wilderness in London didn't compare and she felt the familiar tug and tear of emotion building up inside her. The very feelings she avoided when she threw herself into work.

Her parents looked blissfully average in their forty-year marriage. Apparently, forty years was marked by rubies and lots of people had bought fake silverware decorated with gaudy stones, as well as claret jugs, velvet curtains and wine. Mum looked beautiful in her green silk blouse and white flared trousers.

John had bought Wendy some ruby earrings.

The band struck up their first song and played some ELO as a livener and Kelly was transported back to when she worked behind the bar as a teenager. She saw Ian in the same seat he always took and saw that he still drank Guinness. Then she waved at Dora who'd been sipping port and lemon since God was a lad. Pete and Maureen nodded in her direction, and she saw they had one glass of cider and one pint of ale in front of them. Time had stood still.

Her dad and Dave were still talking and she felt her arm being prodded.

'I said Dave's haulage company has taken off since he took over from his dad, Kelly,' John Porter boomed over the band.

'Great!' Kelly said.

'You two should dance,' he added.

'No, I'm fine, I need some air, it's roasting in here,' Kelly said, backing away with her drink and fanning herself as if she was about to faint.

On her way out she passed faces from her childhood that had grown wrinkly but they all wore the same clothes and laughed at the same things.

Carelessly, she bumped into a large figure coming through the doorway and her drink spilled over her.

'Shit!' she said.

'Kelly Porter?' a deep manly voice boomed.

'Flash?' she asked.

Paul 'Flash' Gordon was a classmate of hers and Dave's best friend.

'You look amazing!' he said.

Kelly smiled. He was still as charming as when they were seventeen.

But she didn't feel amazing; in fact, she felt pretty useless. She'd been promoted to a murder squad, and they were making progress on a huge case, if slowly, and she was fond of her new partner. There was nothing for her to be miserable about but she tied herself up in knots because she was home, where she didn't fit in anymore because she'd chosen a new life. A life which moved from day to day, minute by minute, with new faces, challenges and surprises. It was as if the room closed in on her and she took a deep breath.

'Thanks, Flash. You've been working out,' she said, then she felt stupid because it sounded like a come-on. She wiped her top, but the damage was minimal. It was only a few drops after all.

Flash tensed his bicep for her, and she felt obliged to feel it. She nodded approval and feigned being impressed.

'Your old fella said you'd be here. Have you seen Dave?' he asked.

'Yes, I have.'

He nodded. They stood awkwardly for a few seconds, staring at one another.

'What's London like?' he asked.

It was a straightforward question, but it threw her and reminded her how far away she was from the capital.

'It's busy, and hot, and noisy,' she said.

'Sounds awful,' he replied. Then he was distracted by somebody else and moved away, waving to somebody.

The band was excellent. Just as good as she remembered and she stood watching them for a while, then she made her way outside to get some air.

Later, she drove her parents home because she'd only had one drink. John Porter read her discomfort.

'You didn't look very happy tonight,' he said to her. Wendy snoozed in the back seat happily.

'I was distracted, Dad, I didn't mean to be morose. I actually had a really lovely time.'

'You know you don't need to rush off, your mother would like you to stay, you've only been here five minutes.'

She drove in silence, staring at the road.

'I understand, love. I was always like that with your mother. When I sniffed a new lead, or I was close to catching somebody, nothing else mattered. But it was a mistake. I should have spent more time at home.'

John looked ahead at the road as Kelly drove.

Tomorrow, her mother would cry when she hugged her goodbye. Kelly would hold her close and wonder how quickly they were both aging. It was worse when you didn't see them every day. Wendy would insist on feeding her well before she left, constantly worrying about her being too thin.

'Would you have done it differently?' she asked him.

He didn't answer for a while.

'I want to tell you yes, but I'd be lying, Kel. The thing is I see your passion, and I understand your commitment, all I'm saying is that you'll sacrifice so much on the way that you might miss out on all the other stuff, the important stuff.'

His words echoed Seb's, and she was tiring of being lectured to. Her mother purred gently from the back of the car.

'But this is the important stuff, Dad. I thought you of all people would understand that.'

The guilt sitting between her shoulder blades wasn't entirely founded. She wasn't trying to hurt anyone. Sometimes duty was more important than anything else. There'd be other parties.

'You and Nikki seemed distant.'

'Did Mum tell you to say that?'

She had nothing in common with her sister anymore. They'd barely spent five minutes in each other's company in the last five years. They were as different as Pooley Bridge was to Bethnal Green.

But she still craved her father's approval.

He nodded. 'You know how she worries, Kel. All she wants is for you two to get along.'

'We do, Dad, but we have different lives.'

'I understand, lass,' he said, patting her knee. 'You've got an important career to look after. Nikki is content being a mother.'

Kelly gripped the wheel. She'd never heard him say anything about her decision to pursue her dream and not have a husband and kids in such a way as he did right now, and she felt her eyes burn.

Right now, all she could envisage in her future was doing well at her job, and only then would she be ready to give other parts of herself away, the part she kept hidden. She wasn't wholly without a mission. If she settled down now, half-heartedly and without fulfilling her dream, she'd be half the partner she could be.

Like her mum.

Wendy had settled for being a housewife and had become invisible because of it. That way wasn't an option for Kelly. Her life would have been very different if she'd settled down with Dave Crawley and she often wondered if John Porter had been her mother's only love.

They pulled up outside the tiny terrace and John got out. He was a little unsteady on his feet and she realised he was a little worse for wear. She walked around to his side, and he took her into his arms. She felt her body crush under the weight of his arms and for a moment she wanted to stay there, but the only way for her to grow and become the woman she always wanted to be was to walk away and get back to her job. Tomorrow she'd take the train to Euston and continue to build a life that didn't belong here in Penrith.

They got Wendy out of her slumber and into the house, and Kelly shut the door.

She felt a twinge of something in her gut, it was like pain, but it was warm and knowing. It came in waves. It was as if her childhood had just disappeared.

Chapter 40

Kelly woke on Monday morning to the buzz of her mobile phone, the sound of her pager and the sounds of Molly banging on her bedroom door. It took her a few minutes to realise she was back in London, in her flat.

She'd slept badly and she had a headache. On balance it had been worth going home to get her father's unfathomable wisdom on her case, which she'd talked Seb through last night late into the night. When they'd finished, her mobile phone had run out of battery and she'd plugged it in hoping not to hear it again until her alarm went off. She checked her clock. It was five a.m. She covered her eyes from the hall light and waited for Molly to explain to her what all the fuss was about.

'Body. Leyton. Man in his seventies. Your partner has called me asking why you're not picking up.'

Molly disappeared and Kelly sat bolt upright, then scrabbled underneath her bed for her phone, which she ripped out of its charger and called Seb back. He picked up straight away. It sounded like he was on the move already.

'I've got very little information. Meet me there.'

He gave her the address and she jumped out of bed to get ready, her head thumping as she padded into the kitchen to find tablets.

Twenty-three minutes later she was sat on the tube with Molly, silently staring across the aisle out of the window, deep in their own thoughts.

Kelly's were of the man in the photo. The one with Dorothy, Edith and Tania.

But she was getting ahead of herself. Seb had agreed it sounded like a similar profile but the first responders hadn't confirmed an ID.

They got off at Leyton tube station and walked the short distance to the property.

Seb was already there.

'Have you been in?' she asked him.

'See you inside,' Molly said.

'No, I waited for you,' Seb said.

'I shouldn't have gone away.'

'What? Stop it. What could you have done?'

She realised she was being melodramatic and took overalls, gloves and a mask from their packets and covered up quickly, regretting wearing jeans. It was cooler up north and the difference always caught her by surprise when she returned. The heatwave still gripped the capital and as a result, they smelled the victim before they saw him. The air was thick with death.

'All the doors and windows were closed. The alarm was raised by a new postwoman who said she couldn't get a letter through the door because something was blocking it. She made some enquiries and found out nobody had actually seen the resident for over a month. The incubatory qualities of the house have preserved the scene but the corpse itself is in a dire state, I should warn you,' a SOCO told them.

'I can smell it.'

'He's decomposed but not completely, the insect activity on his body is very advanced, the entomologist is on his way.'

Seb paused for breath as if this might be the last fresh one he'd get in some time. Kelly did the same. They passed a pot of Vicks between them and rubbed a pea-sized lump under their noses. The whiff of the effluvial was still strong and reminded her of other rotting corpses she'd witnessed in her career. Other than that, dead animals in the woods sprang to mind when she hiked through Grizedale Forest and came across dead deer.

They made their way through to a ground-floor bedroom. When they entered, Kelly couldn't help but gag at the stench.

Bodies in white suits stood over the figure on the bed, which was face up and had a terrible contorted grimace on its face. She couldn't think of male or female pronouns because all identity and humanity had been stripped off the cadaver in front of her.

A body in a white plastic suit held up a passport and Seb instructed him to read it.

'Franklin McKay, born 1933, aged seventy-five.'

They stared at the figure on the bed who'd now been confirmed as a male. Called Frank.

Frankie.

But what struck everybody more than the awful fact that the man had decayed all alone was how he was dressed.

Kelly recognised the outfit from the museum.

Luther had shown her, when he'd taken her to see his pride and joy. His favourite Charlie McCarthy had been missing so he'd shown her another puppet, this time one of Jiminy Cricket. Luther had explained to her his devastation at losing them both, but the museum possessed several, if not scores, of versions of each toy. He'd shown her an antique wooden doll and had beamed from ear to ear in excitement. She hadn't known what all the fuss was about, and to her, the wooden toy was a lifeless, rather ugly obsession, which no grown man should care about.

But here, looking at the man on the bed, whose skin seemed dried up like an old pig's ear, she saw Jiminy Cricket staring back at her. The blue top hat had fallen off and was on the floor where it had filled with worms, maggots and other insects called to the feast. His yellow cravat was filthy and twisted to one side as if an army of six-legged soldiers had moved it to hammer out a better invading path. It moved with activity. Was there anything left to eat? She wondered as she moved closer.

'How long?' she whispered under her breath to no one in particular.

'We need to wait for the entomologist, but in my experience, from the larvae I can see, it's about three weeks old. All the insect samples will need examining then he'll come back with an accurate assessment, he reckons, to within a week or so, when I spoke to him over the phone.'

Kelly nodded. 'That fits with nobody seeing him recently. And did he own this property?'

'Looks like it's registered to Frank McKay, he's a retired caretaker, the neighbour said.'

'A retired caretaker? I don't suppose he worked at the Charitable Sisters of Our Lady and Saint Catherine in the eighties?' Seb said to Kelly as an aside. The SOCOs got on with their grim work and Seb and Kelly discussed next steps. Seb took the man's passport and they looked at the photo together.

'Too good to be true?' Seb said.

Kelly shrugged her shoulders. 'I think it could be him, he's put on weight, but he was very portly in the photo, he's got the same round face.'

'Why in his home, not a school or place of work?'

'Could it be natural? He was our main suspect. Did he dress himself up as a last hurrah? Can you see any obvious injuries?'

It was difficult to tell when decomposition was so advanced. Bloat, skin slippage, rotting and explosive orifices could all present as wounds and they must be careful not to jump to conclusions.

'Let's talk about those clothes, do you recognise them?'

'Yes,' Kelly said. 'I know exactly who it is. It's Jiminy Cricket.'

Seb stared at the corpse.

'Is there a doll?' she asked.

They searched around the body and saw small feet sticking out from under the bed. They were too small to belong to anyone living. Kelly bent down and pulled it out. The character was full of joy and she couldn't help but feel affection for him, the young Jiminy of everyone's childhood.

'The MO is too similar, I say The Puppeteer has struck again. What we need to know is how much Leia Lord wants to release to the press this time. She's on her way apparently,' he said.

'What?'

Seb shrugged. 'I think she's under pressure on this one.'

'It took three bodies for her to feel under pressure? Where has she been for the last week?'

Chapter 41

Kelly and Seb walked into the sunshine and took gulps of air. Kelly's lungs felt tacky and rancid and she doubted she'd ever get rid of the smell of rotting flesh out of her nostrils.

Some said decomposition smelled sweet, others said it smelled like diarrhoea. Kelly thought it was a combination of both. Once whiffed, it was very difficult to dispel.

'DS Kelly Porter,' a voice said behind them. They turned around and saw DCI Leia Lord walking down the path under the police cordon. They spotted press on the street and turned to cover their faces.

The DCI looked perplexed. It was a side of Leia Kelly hadn't seen before.

'Porter, I've heard you're making progress. What have we got?'

Kelly stared at Seb.

'You don't want to see the victim, ma'am?'

'That's your job. Let's talk.' It was an order, and the DCI beckoned her away from her partner.

Leia was the type of woman who sucked the air out of a room, just in case a man was thinking about stealing it first. Kelly didn't know whether to admire or fear her. It was an ominous invitation but Kelly followed her boss nonetheless, casting a puzzled look back to Seb, who shrugged and followed.

'DI Crook, I don't need you joining in,' Leia said over her shoulder, so Seb hung back.

For a moment, Kelly felt embarrassed and she experienced imposter-like terror. She certainly didn't know anything more than anybody else at this stage, including her partner. She must be careful, she told herself, not to allow her ego to take over. Intuition warned her she wasn't being singled out by Leia Lord because of her talent. It was something else.

The DCI strode off around the back of the house and Kelly followed her, unable to get the Star Wars theme tune out of her head.

In the back garden, Leia Lord quizzed her about the investigation so far. Kelly tried to pay attention to the DCI's barrage of questions and wondered what had taken so long for her to take an interest. Perhaps her boss had requested a report. Or maybe this was just what it was like in a murder squad, you worked your arse off at the coalface, unearthing leads and racking up hours until one day, you revealed something so important and momentous that it caught the attention of those above.

This was her moment. She'd been on the squad for exactly a week, and her DCI wanted her ear.

'When did the importance of the cartoons strike you?' Leia asked.

'They're not cartoons.'

'They're all Disney films.'

'That's not strictly true. The original characters predate Disney by decades, sometimes centuries, and it's the originals we should be concerned with. And Punch and Judy was only ever made by independents.'

'Here I am thinking I have all the answers,' Leia said. Kelly had embarrassed her senior in their first proper one-to-one, and she felt a fool. 'Assumption is the mother of all fuck ups,' Leia said, using one of Kelly's favourite phrases. She smiled warmly at her boss.

'Easy mistake. It was only when I spoke to an expert that I changed my opinion of them too.'

'Which expert? It's not in your notes.'

Leia looked annoyed.

'With respect, it is.'

'Ah, my mistake. Carry on.'

Kelly could have sworn she'd mentioned Luther to her.

'It was an entirely different case. The Museum of Childhood in Bethnal Green was robbed on Saturday, perhaps Friday evening, the week before last, but that wasn't why we visited there to interview the curator. Dorothy Amis had a visit scheduled there, I thought there might be a link.'

'You thought?'

Kelly nodded.

'And DI Crook?'

'He agreed. We've been using him as a source.'

The DCI seemed needled and Kelly doubted her time here would last long if she carried on surprising her boss.

'I had no reason to notify you, all my sources were uploaded to HOLMES when the murder of Tania Harrison was confirmed as recent.'

'So how did you come about your line of inquiry?' the DCI asked her.

'Which line of inquiry?'

'You have more than one?'

'Yes,' Kelly said.

'Good. You're one of those types. I don't judge. All I want is answers. I swear Jiminy Cricket is fucking Disney, though.'

'He is, ma'am. Disney took the character from the original story of Pinocchio.'

'I know that!' Leia coughed and looked around. 'Sorry, I mean, everyone knows that. Just tell me if we're dealing with toys or cartoons?'

'Neither, we're dealing with puppets, ma'am. Which is why I think we have a specialist on our hands.'

Leia nodded intently. At least she was paying attention, though Kelly appreciated it was a complex set of MOs.

'And your main leads are? Remind me.'

Kelly looked over her shoulder at the house, keenly aware that her partner was excluded from the conversation.

'The dead guy inside there was our main suspect,' she said. Leia Lord tapped her foot. Kelly carried on. 'When I was working the Tania Harrison case before I moved to MIT,' she began.

'You mean when you were double-hatting and moonlighting at Bethnal Green CID, which you still are according to a certain forensic anthropologist called Jonathan Hass.'

Shit, she'd been rumbled.

'I couldn't leave them in the middle of something so important... I...'

'Don't panic, I admire your tenacity,' Leia said.

Kelly exhaled.

'Before the connection was confirmed, I had started to think that the two teachers might be linked through their current jobs. It's an obvious one. But when I looked into Tania's background, I changed my mind and began thinking they were perhaps tied by previous careers.'

'Such as?'

'Care home workers, ma'am. Children's homes more specifically. Tania Harrison worked for Hackney Council for twenty years or more before moving into nursing before you needed a degree to do that. She trained at Whitechapel Hospital. We did a bit of digging and came across some interesting information.'

'We have their bios and there's nothing there.'

That evasion again, thought Kelly. Now she was becoming hacked off. Her skin tingled. The woman didn't listen.

'But there is.'

'Dorothy Amis was an ex-nurse. Edith Callaghan worked in an old people's home,' the DCI said.

'Yes. But both became teachers before police checks on background were introduced. My dad reminded me to check the Criminal Records Bureau from before 2002 to see if there were any notes alongside their names. DI Crook rang around a few London councils this morning and checked. Dorothy Amis and Edith Callaghan worked together in a children's home in Hackney before it was closed in 1987. We discussed this in your office, ma'am, it was called the—'

'Yes, I know, the Charitable Sisters of Our Lady and Saint Catherine. I'm keeping up, Porter, don't you worry. What exactly has your father got to do with a major investigation?'

'Yes, sorry, he's with Cumbria CID.' Kelly felt the urgency in the DCI's voice and wondered if her boss was chronically stressed.

'And what does Cumbria have to do with my case?'

'Erm, nothing, ma'am, I just run things by him occasionally, he's very experienced.'

'I see. What else did Hackney Council tell you?'

'That Tania Harrison worked there too.'

'So, all three worked in the same NHS institutions, not exactly a game changer, is it?'

'Erm, no, I suppose not.' Kelly frowned. Maybe she'd missed something. She thought it was a strong lead. She felt embarrassed.

'You suppose? And what about the excavation at the site where Ms Harrison was found? Who authorised that?'

'DCI Wallis took care of it, ma'am.'

'Of course, your old boss. Do I need to remind you that he's no longer your line manager, I am.'

'Yes, ma'am.'

Kelly felt thoroughly told off, like a teenager. The feeling was awkward and her cheeks burned. She'd never in her whole time at Bethnal Green CID felt so insignificant, so useless, so... discarded.

DCI Lord stared at her and Kelly felt examined.

'If you want my opinion...'

'Yes, I do,' Kelly said.

'Like I said, if you want my opinion, it's this. Until we have evidence to prove that we have a vigilante on our hands, it's a waste of police time and resources to go supporting theories that frankly belong on telly. You're walking a fine line here, Porter, and it makes me think you don't like rules.'

The DCI had, in the same breath, told Kelly that she admired her but that she was also disappointed in her. Kelly's head spun.

'It depends if the rules are sensible, ma'am.'

Leia Lord stared into her soul and Kelly felt naked. It was an uncomfortable place to be, on the end of Leia Lord's wrath, and she hated it. But then Kelly saw a sparkle in her boss's eyes, and she recovered herself. Princess Leia wasn't pushing her because Kelly had made any mistakes, it was because Leia Lord had just spotted some competition.

Chapter 42

The man dead in his bed and desiccated with just enough flesh adhering to his bones to be autopsied, affectionately known as Frankie, had, they learnt from a helpful member of the public via their Facebook page, frequented a watering hole in Hackney. It was a pub called the Grain & Grape, on Mare Street where groups of nurses and teachers had hung out since the early 1990s and 2000s.

An old colleague of Tania's from Whitechapel had come forward as a result of the public appeal and recalled her spending time there. It was just as her father had said: look at the habits and there's always a pub; and the same pub Edith Callaghan hung out in. Kelly thought it highly unlikely that it was coincidence and still smarted from Leia's earlier rebuttal. Either there was a silver-haired oldies scene happening in Hackney or they'd been drinking there for many years. Now they'd established more than one link between the women, they now needed to work out how Frankie fitted in.

Hip bars and international eateries, as well as world-famous theatres, dotted the area, and Hackney Old Town boasted some of the oldest pubs in east London.

'This was here in my day,' Seb said as they approached the Grain & Grape early on Monday afternoon.

'Your day? You can sound so old sometimes,' Kelly said.

He laughed and pushed the door open. 'This job does that to you. I meant when I was training.'

'You make it sound like you're an old man, is that what murder squad does to you?'

'Something like that, especially when Leia Lord is your boss.'

The bar was busy, which was always the case when the sun came out in the capital. The bar staff looked young and transitory.

Kelly had called ahead and managed to speak to somebody who'd worked here seven years ago and hadn't moved on.

Sookie was the only name she gave and when Kelly looked around, she reckoned there was only one woman who fitted the description of an independent, no-nonsense bar worker who kept on top of the place and knew everything about everyone. She had that look about her. A keen eye and something about the way she chewed her gum. The Grain & Grape was the sort of place where secrets were kept and anonymity was easily bought. The barwoman stared at them and smirked. She walked towards them.

'You the coppers?' she asked. Kelly stretched out her hand and smiled, introducing herself. Seb did the same after Sookie had assessed them from head to toe. Kelly wondered how she came across to somebody like Sookie. Dull? Vanilla? Plain? Two-dimensional? She suddenly cared what the woman thought. Sookie was dressed in tie-dyed dungarees and a white vest. Her wrists jangled with jewellery and her nose was full of rings. Her arms were tattooed with animals and Kelly was drawn to them. They promised an insight into a different world, one which Kelly rarely explored. It was a realm of no rules and freedom. One where the line between criminality and anarchy was a fine one and, she'd been taught, threatened the way of life she was trying to protect. In reality she admired the woman for her liberty. After all, wasn't that what all revolutionaries fought for? They were supposed to live in the city of the brave, in the land of the free, but she suspected Sookie didn't see it that way.

So why had she been working in a bar in Hackney for seven years if she was such a free spirit?

There was a soft murmur of patrons on the thick air and fans whirred in the corner. Sookie's skin had a layer of perspiration covering it and Kelly was reminded of bars abroad but those were by beaches and the staff were able to dive into the ocean after their shift.

'Can we sit down?' Seb asked.

Sookie led them through the bar, past staff pouring pints and mixing cocktails, and they received stares of derision more for their dress sense, Kelly reckoned, than anything else. Most of the punters wore casual clothes and didn't look as though they planned to work anytime soon. Kelly wore light trousers and a T-shirt-style blouse. Her pockets bulged with cards and her phone and she had her hair tied back in an officious manner. Seb wore jeans and an open-collar shirt, his pockets strained under the same kit.

They looked like relatable politicians or consultants. To East Enders, they were obviously coppers.

Sookie led them to a quiet table out the back and offered two stools for them to sit on. She took one herself and folded her arms.

'I spoke to you on the phone about Tania Harrison?' Kelly began.

Sookie nodded. 'I saw it on the news. I haven't thought about her for years.'

'She went missing seven years ago. The last sighting of her was near here,' Kelly said.

Sookie nodded. 'She'd just left here. She used to hang around with the lot from the hospital. And a group of older pals. They were tight. That one stood out because she had a particular style of dress.'

'Go on,' Kelly encouraged.

'Old fashioned. Smart. Ladylike. It's unusual round here. She never caused trouble, she'd come in after her shift, sit with anyone she knew, get a bit loud, tell stories about the good old days like the old timers do and leave.'

'She was fifty-nine years old when she disappeared, that's not exactly old.'

Sookie looked vacant. To a woman in her late twenties, fifty was ancient.

'And her associates? Anyone stick out?'

'I told the same to the police at the time.'

Kelly had read the file, and Sookie's statements, which they'd pulled from the archives. Her dad had been right. Tania had socialised here, inside this pub, and somebody who knew her must have known where she'd gone the night, she never made it home.

'Do you recall the last evening you saw her and who she was drinking with?'

'It's all in my statement. It was busy. A Thursday I think. She was with a few teachers, I think. Jed. Billy. Caitlin.'

Kelly recognised their names from Sookie's statement. They were being checked out.

'Do you recognise these women?' Seb asked Sookie, showing her photos of Dorothy Amis and Edith Callaghan.

'Her, yes, definitely, that's Edith, she came in to meet Tania.' Sookie pointed. 'The other one came in once or twice, she sat with Edith.

That's Dorothy. There's no messing with her.' Sookie laughed but Kelly and Seb didn't join in. Sookie's face darkened.

'What do you mean exactly?'

Sookie shrugged. 'She was old school. Reminded me of my gran. Fierce. Garish makeup, like a drag queen, but she was standoffish. She called the shots with the smaller woman.'

'And this man?' Seb asked, showing her a photo of Frankie McKay.

'Frankie? Of course, he's still a regular here. Dorothy doesn't come in as often, they changed after Tania disappeared. They were her pals.'

Seb fell silent and Kelly grimaced. Sookie looked between them.

'Shit, you're here to tell me Frankie's dead, aren't you?'

'Sookie, we're here to tell you that Dorothy and Edith are dead too. And we think Tania died shortly after she disappeared.'

'Jesus! You guys know how to ruin my fucking day.'

'You knew him well? Frankie?'

'He's a good customer. Shit. Sorry, I need a minute.'

Sookie looked away and shook her head. Then she looked back at the two detectives and stared at them accusingly. 'They were murdered, weren't they? This is why you're here? Fucking hell.'

'Sookie, when you're ready, can you tell us about when you saw them drinking together and if so, who else they were with?'

Sookie looked at them both and nodded, biting her lip.

'Yes, I can. Frankie and Tania seemed to go way back. They chatted like they were an item. I actually thought they had a thing going at one point. He idolised her. Sorry, this is so sad. They were like a pair of old lovers who'd found each other later in life, you know? But then Tania disappeared.' She paused. 'Sorry,' she said again. 'It was only after she went missing that Frankie told me Tania thought she was being stalked. And she was scared.'

Sookie paused and coughed. Kelly could see that the shock was causing some distress.

'He told me Edith felt the same way and I laughed and told him they were old women fantasising, God, I feel such a bitch.'

'Are you sure?' Kelly pointed to Edith's photo. 'Edith Callaghan?'

'Yes, Edith, she said she was being followed too. She mentioned letters and photos, it creeped me the hell out. I didn't think anything of it at the time, old people like to talk. He was lonely and I thought a bit delusional. That's why I joked about it. Was he telling the truth? Were they followed and... Oh, my God.'

Kelly ignored the direct question. 'Did they mention names?'

Sookie shook her head. 'Sorry, that's all I remember.'

'Do you recall them discussing this stalker? Any distinguishing features or theories about where the letters came from?'

'No, I don't remember. There was a guy who I didn't like, he hung around with them for a bit but then fell off the radar. I didn't think anything of it.'

Seb and Kelly looked at one another. Sookie noticed. Good barmaids never missed anything.

'Did you mention this to police at the time?'

'No, I just remembered now. They didn't ask me about Frank or Edith. Or Dorothy.'

'Can you tell us about him, the younger man?'

'Creepy, a lot younger than them, I assumed he was a work colleague, they all knew him. Leather jacket, shaggy hair. Tall. Dark eyes, like really dark brown eyes.'

Sookie looked away.

'Poor bastards, were they murdered like Tania?'

'We're following the leads we have but the cases are linked, yes,' Seb said.

Kelly thought he spoke like a pro: evasive and aloof. Sookie wasn't fooled.

'So that's a yes then. Some sicko going around bumping off old people who are single and like to play kids games?' Sookie sniffed and wiped her nose.

Kelly and Seb exchanged glances again.

'Sorry, did you say children's games?'

Sookie smiled. Then she nodded. 'They loved them. I keep them in the bar for the oldies. They played Cluedo, Monopoly, Risk. Buccaneer was Frankie's favourite.'

Sookie became wistful and looked away.

'The man who you said was "creepy", did he play with them?' Kelly asked.

Sookie thought for a bit.

'No, that was the thing. I reckon that's why he got bored, or something, and didn't come again. They argued. He got mad when he lost a game. He threw it across the bar. The pieces went everywhere. Funny, I never recalled him until now. Because he came with Edith. I joked that she had a toyboy and he threw me the most disturbing stare. I can remember feeling unsafe and I don't usually experience that here. This is a busy light-hearted pub with locals and passing trade, pleasant, you know. He didn't fit in.'

'Did he ever pay by card?'

Sookie laughed. 'In here? We only got a card reader two months ago.'

'You've been really helpful,' Kelly said.

'Wait, he always used the same cab company to take Edith home.'

'He took Edith home?'

'I don't know but he always called her a cab, so he could have done.'

'Do you think you could aid police with an artist's impression?'

'You bet.'

Chapter 43

Belmarsh appeared like something out of a dystopian movie from the seventies. It reminded Kelly of *Mad Max* or *Blade Runner*. It was all brick, flat roofs and Victorian judgement. The ghost of Dostoevsky sat at the entrance telling them to turn back. *This way lies madness*, he told them. Even in the sunshine, Belmarsh was bleak. The wire commanded the clouds to magnetise themselves to the microclimate to punish the prisoners even more and she could almost hear their sighs as they were squeezed into seven-foot rooms in threes and even fours.

People blamed the Tories. Others blamed Labour. It really didn't matter. In her work, governments were all the same. They took the glory and screwed the services until they bled. Boris Johnson was now London mayor but nobody expected him to make a difference either. Those who held the purse strings were all the same at the end of the day.

Called the Guantanamo Bay of the UK, or *Hellmarsh*, Belmarsh housed around six hundred men, serving time for category A offences, including terrorism.

At close to half a million square metres, the prison was huge and was built on top of the original Woolwich Arsenal, which Kelly found curiously amusing, seeing as kings and queens of old had relied upon the reserves of weaponry there for centuries, and now it housed those who would do them harm in a heartbeat.

She looked at the dull walls and recalled an article she'd read about local residents saying they could hear the screams of inmates at night.

Did their perp come here? Had he served time? Perhaps with Jason Fellcroft? If so, how did he survive?

She knew how Jason Fellcroft survived, for sure.

Like a king, Fellcroft sat on a vast network of thugs and sycophants. Inside he could get anything and as long as he behaved himself, he was left alone. Nobody could expect screws outnumbered ten to one to control such a population. The UK prison service was firefighting, pure and simple. And the less intense the fire, the more likely the foundations were to survive.

There was talk of getting permission to build an adjacent young offender's institute next to the gigantic prison, which would make the area a virtual prison town, much to the disgust of local residents. The country couldn't cope with the exponential rise in its prison population, and one day, they'd blow the roofs off and whichever government was in power at the time would regret not planning them better.

As they buzzed through security and surrendered their ID, keys, phone, warrant card and other personal effects, Kelly thought about Bradley and how he survived his dad.

Seeing the place where his father was incarcerated made her doubt he had. The more she thought about it, the closer she came to admitting she'd got the youngster wrong, and he was still controlled by Jason. It wasn't difficult to get an interview with him. Jason Fellcroft loved attention. The governor insisted they were accompanied by two prison officers at all times but that was a relief to Kelly. She didn't trust the man they were about to meet.

They were shown into a large room that Kelly guessed was used for visiting at the appropriate time, but it looked like it could be used for training as well. A large white board was hung on the wall and a flip chart sat unused. Prisoners weren't often brought in here, she figured, because there was too much that could be weaponised. They'd made a special effort for them.

Two officers brought in the prisoner and the door opened with a jangle of keys and a clash of metal: two sounds that classified prison life. She watched as he was brought to his seat and they placed him down as if he was an invalid.

He didn't take his eyes off her. It was as if Seb didn't exist. Perhaps he'd heard that Kelly sought a close relationship with his son.

Fellcroft was dressed in a grey tracksuit and Kelly could tell that he spent time working out. He looked hard, as if his body was made of metal and he sported tattoos across much of his body. They were the usual smorgasbord of cobwebs and dots arranged in a square that most inmates boasted on their skin. It was difficult to place him as Bradley's father.

They'd agreed she'd do the talking, given that Orlando Charles had been her case and also because of her closeness with Bradley. She introduced them both.

Fellcroft remained cuffed and stared at the shackles. Kelly wondered what it felt like to be incarcerated and watch people from the outside invade your world. Was she like an alien from outer space? Had he forgotten what normal people looked like? Real three-dimensional people?

And especially a woman.

She watched his eyes move up and down her body and she regretted not covering every inch of her skin.

Jason Fellcroft was a dangerous man and she wondered if it was possible for Bradley to outsmart his DNA.

Or had she been hoodwinked? Was Bradley just the same?

Both had come through the care system, forgotten by the rest of society.

'We've come to talk to you about your building sites.'

For all his hardness, Jason Fellcroft was a small man and she wondered at the modern evolution of men of average stature raising giants. Apparently it was something to do with modern food. She imagined five-year-old Bradley left in his mother's flat for four days on his own as she lay dead in a pool of her own vomit after a heroin overdose and shivered slightly. His six-foot frame hadn't come from being spoilt.

'You've been talking to my boy.'

Kelly bristled.

'He wants nothing to do with me and rightly so, I'm a bad dad.' Fellcroft grinned.

'I was given the impression that's not the case at all, by a suspect in a string of violent burglaries.'

'Really?'

'Yes. Orlando Charles. Heard of him? He also worked for you on your building sites.'

'I know Orlando, how's he doing?'

'Pursuing your line of work. Did you give him a job working with your son on purpose? To make sure he didn't testify?'

Jason's face didn't change.

'You're in for a long stretch, seventeen years, less if you behave. Are you behaving?'

He nodded. He rubbed his plastic cuffs as if the chafing bothered him.

'Is this what you want for your son?'

'What?'

She looked around. 'This existence. Inside, like you. Taking after his old man, being assaulted every few weeks, not sure if he'll survive another night. Forced to watch while friends are punished for grassing. I've read your prison records.'

He glared at her. She felt as though she'd touched something deep inside him.

'You don't want Bradley to be a grass, but at the same time, you don't want him perjuring himself either. Either way, he might end up in here, and you might not be able to protect him.'

'You can't make him take the witness stand.'

'No, you're absolutely right, but what I want to know is what Orlando Charles has over you. He's calling the shots here. That got me thinking. Was he just a casual employee of yours or something more?'

Jason looked away, seemingly bored.

'What has he got on you? We're not here for a cosy chat. We're here to give you one chance to tell us who had access to your building site in 2001, and who might have wanted to dump a body there. Was it Orlando?'

Jason turned back to her and smiled ever so slightly, making Kelly's body go stiff with a shadow of something she felt rarely and only in the presence of people like him: evil, or how she reckoned it felt.

'What does he know that would make you threaten your own son?'

'You're struggling in your case against Orlando because you've got the wrong guy. You're looking in all the wrong places.'

'Enlighten me, who should we be looking for? And what do you know of my case?'

'I'm afraid you're clean out of bargaining chips, DS Porter.'

'Why can't you stay away from your son?'

His face broke into a look of surprise then and even shock.

'You care about him! You care for my lad! Jesus, this is what it's all about, you want to protect him, not see him end up like me. That's so sweet.'

He chuckled and the sound of it grated on Kelly's nerves, and she knew he was right. She felt humiliated but at least her discomfort was true and came from a good place. She stared him out.

'If you were any kind of father you wouldn't want him ending up like you either.'

'You bitch,' he said, jutting his head forward. 'You people. You create criminals like me because of your rules, and then you lock us up and then you lock up our kids because they were raised by no one.'

'Calm. Down. Son,' Seb intervened. Jason sat back.

'Why was there a dead body discovered on your building site?' Kelly asked.

'The Romans?'

'Do you know this woman?'

Seb produced a photograph of Tania Harrison. Jason didn't look at it at first, and when he did, Kelly watched his face for signs he knew her.

'What about her?'

Seb showed the photograph of Dorothy Amis, followed by Edith Callaghan and finally Frankie McKay.

It was the last that elicited the most visceral response. Jason's brow twitched when he saw the face of Frankie McKay and his Adam's apple bobbed up and down as he swallowed hard.

What a web we weave...

'Tell us,' she demanded, but she'd gone too hard too fast. Jason closed up and flicked them the bird. Then he took a huge snorkel of spit inwards and gathered it in the back of his throat and spat at her feet.

She moved away just in time and then the guards intervened and dragged Jason to his feet and back through the door he'd come.

Seb jumped up and pushed out his chest.

'You were supposed to look after people like me!' Fellcroft shouted over his shoulder.

Kelly wanted to kick something but instead all she could do was look at the brown, stained mucus in front of her on the floor. It was impenetrable and soiled, just like their case.

His last words stung her skin. Her head ached and her shoulders felt as though they had lead weights attached to them. Who did he mean when he said 'you' were supposed to look after people like him? The state? Coppers? Women?

'He's a care home kid,' Seb said simply, and a creeping feeling spread under her ribs.

'Thanks for letting me lead,' she said.

'You did good,' he said, trying to reassure her. But it didn't feel like it.

Not at all.

Chapter 44

Their journey back across London to Stratford was hot and long. By the time Kelly and Seb arrived at the Stratford Junction site where Tania Harrison had been discovered, they were both irritable. They had more questions than answers and they'd hit the moment of an investigation commonly known as the wall. It was still early enough to expect revelations, but too soon for forensic results and all the things that make a case come together. Kelly grabbed a hard hat and walked through the site. Seb followed. The excavation that Jonathan Hass had recommended had been delayed and it frustrated Kelly that things weren't moving quicker. Dennis the foreman still hadn't been located. He'd been missing for ten days.

She felt out of place like she did every time she visited a site like this one but today was harder because Seb was watching. There was no one in charge, the site was chaotic. It was no place for a female yet, despite talk of equal rights. Little girls weren't encouraged to dream of building stuff, which was sad and Kelly hoped that one day it might change.

Finally, they found someone to escort them into a mobile hut and he offered them strong cups of tea, as if reminding Kelly she was in a man's world here. She accepted and peered into the mug for floaters that inevitably accompanied offerings in such environments. She was thirsty as hell and she felt as though all she'd done all day was talk to people unwilling to tell her the truth. Anybody but Seb, that was. It was hot on site and the sun beat down on the cabin. They'd agreed that she'd take charge today and it was her moment to prove herself but, so far, she felt she was failing.

'Has anyone heard from Dennis?' she asked.

He shrugged. 'Nah.'

'Do you know where he is?' Seb asked.

A shake of the head.

'Did you work here seven years ago?'

'Nah.'

'Northern?' he asked.

Jesus, she thought, he was coming onto her. She felt rather than heard Seb snort into his tea.

'I think it's time we were off,' he said.

The foreman looked annoyed at the interruption.

'Northern born and bred. Listen is there anyone here who worked here back in 2001?'

'Nah.'

'Is Bradley working today?'

'Nah.'

'You know Bradley? You're not that unfamiliar with the site then.'

'Nah. So, then, the body was from 2001?' he asked.

Now they had his interest.

She nodded.

'So, it was murder then?'

Kelly raised her eyebrows at him. 'Armchair detective?'

'I love Bergerac.'

'Bergerac! Jesus, that's a blast from the past. I loved that show. Did you pick up any tips?' she asked, trying desperately to get him onside and catch him out.

'I'm suspicious of foreigners' was all he offered.

'You must employ a lot of visa workers for the Olympics.'

He nodded. 'Mostly don't cause trouble but you get the odd one demanding more money. I'd prefer to give our boys the work but they don't want the hassle, do they? It's all Europeans who are the hard workers.'

'Your boys? That sounds like you've been here a while then. Was it the same in 2001?'

'Back there again. I know how this works. You're trying to piece together a picture of what the site was like back then, who worked here and who could have buried a body here.'

'Buried?'

'I've heard rumours.'

He smiled at her. She gazed at him in conspiracy.

'I heard the gangsters who owned this place got rid of enemies, if you know what I mean.'

She felt Seb stiffen.

'How?' she asked, intrigued.

She was close to him and she felt as though they were discussing plotting the downfall of the government, Guy Fawkes style.

'It's easy to put them in the foundations, if the boss turned a blind eye.'

'So, gangsters used to own this place? Come off it, if you were here in 2001, then you know that Jason Fellcroft owned this place, now, why don't you tell me about your relationship with him?'

'*The* Fellcrofts?' he whispered.

She could tell he was toying with them.

He leant back and smiled. 'Don't know them. Heard of them, of course. Who hasn't?'

'We'll soon find out. The diggers will be here soon, I have all the warrants to start the excavation.'

Kelly saw his right eye twitch and he brushed imaginary dirt off his trouser leg. She had no doubt that her information would be passed to Jason Fellcroft at the earliest opportunity. She also knew that digging was unlikely to start before the weekend. Leia Lord wasn't convinced it was the best use of their budget just yet. DCI Wallis had been overruled. It was no longer the remit of CID. They needed more.

But the workmen didn't need to know that, and neither did Jason Fellcroft.

They left armed with nothing new, least of all an explanation of what had become of Dennis the foreman who'd unwittingly called the police to Jason Fellcroft's door. Kelly couldn't help but suspect that he wasn't simply taking a few days off in the middle of one of the busiest periods for building London had ever seen and she worried that he'd perhaps had a nasty accident. A squad car had already been sent to the address they had for him and nobody was home, and hadn't been for ten days.

Chapter 45

On Tuesday morning, Kelly walked into the psychiatric ward of the Royal London Hospital. Bradley Fellcroft had experienced a psychotic episode and hers was the only name they'd been able to get out of him as he was restrained.

An ambulance had been called to the building site where he worked when Bradley began to display unusual behaviour.

'What kind of behaviour?' she asked the secretary on the front desk as she showed her warrant card.

'You'll have to speak to the doctor on call.'

Kelly nodded and was shown through two sets of locked doors and it reminded her of prison.

At the moment, Bradley was a prisoner of his own mind. It was a devastating indictment of what happened to kids who went off the rails. Last week, Bradley had seemed fine, but she knew that he harboured this demon inside him and occasionally it reared its head. With a father like Jason Fellcroft, she wasn't surprised.

'DS Porter?' a voice asked. She turned to see a woman in a white coat and a stethoscope around her neck and assumed she was the duty consultant.

They shook hands.

'What happened?'

'We assumed you were his mother or sister, he kept asking for Kelly. You're difficult to track down. It was only when we passed his name to the parole service that they suggested he might be talking about you.'

'Are you keeping him in?'

'He's on a section three, so we've got him for twenty-four hours. He's showing signs of less agitation, I'm hopeful he's making progress. Sometimes the brain shuts down in order to allow it to sort out a specific problem. How long that takes is impossible to gauge. How long have you known him?'

'Four years.'

'Were you aware he has a history of psychosis inside juvenile prison? We're treating him with a general round of meds to stabilise him.'

'Yes, I was aware. Is that necessary?'

'To protect our staff, yes. It's like emergency care, think of it as triage. We need to take the sting out of the tail and make the situation safe before we decide on a long-term strategy.'

Kelly nodded.

She'd witnessed plenty of psychopaths in her time but few actual psychotic patients. There was a difference. Psychopathy was a personality disorder as she understood it. Psychosis was a medical emergency. But as for long-term strategy, she couldn't help thinking that they'd simply discharge and lose him again.

'Can I see him?'

'Yes. I've authorised it because I think it's always in the patient's interest to anchor to somebody familiar. He requested you and so that means you're a safe presence around him. I'll supervise though.'

'Of course.'

'Have you ever witnessed any trauma suffered by Bradley in your presence?'

'No, why?'

'Sometimes they grab on to a name for negative reasons and the consequences can be rather different. I had to check.'

'Sure. Is that what you think this is, he's locked inside some kind of trauma?'

'The brain is complex, Detective, but psychosis is usually a protection mechanism in layman's terms. It's protecting him from something which could have happened yesterday or a long time ago. At the moment he's locked in there, wherever that may be.'

Kelly was taken through another set of locked doors and the buzzing of codes and jangling of keys, as well as the distant sound of trauma, made her anxious. She was in a place full of broken people and it crushed her heart to think of Bradley in that way. He was getting back on his feet. He was rehabilitating… The doctor kept talking.

'It's important to listen to any cues that might be revelatory. I'm compelled to make the decision to override the patient's right to confidentiality in this instance,' she said and stopped walking. Kelly faced her.

'Oh?'

'He's mentioned the killing of a woman. Now, I need to advise caution, this isn't a confession. It may be he's simply seen it on TV, but it's also possible he's witnessed it in real life, and that might account for this episode.'

'Witnessed it recently?'

'Not necessarily, it could be from years ago.'

Kelly was shown into a private room and the sight of Bradley strapped to a bed and asleep made her heart leap.

The sins of the father...

His eyes flickered at the sound of the door closing and she smiled at him and sat next to his bed.

He recognised her. It was a good start. She reached for his hand and covered it with her own.

'Hey,' she said.

Tears filled his eyes and she knew how much effort it would be taking him to hold them back. He'd never cried in front of her before. Had he ever cried? It was a strange experience but also one that humbled her, watching a grown man of six foot two become a boy again. She wondered what event had triggered this episode and sat patiently, waiting for him to do the talking. The consultant stayed in the corner of the room.

Kelly sucked in her breath as Bradley moved and the top part of the sheet covering him exposed a lump underneath it. He was cuddling a toy. It was a soft toy. She stiffened, trying not to alarm him. She recognised the red dungarees, the bow tie and the Tyrolean hat with a feather in it. Bradley was holding a soft toy of Pinocchio.

'Is he yours?' she asked.

He looked down.

Then he glanced towards the consultant.

'You chose it, Bradley. You've been holding it since you came in,' the consultant said. 'It's an option we have to offer comfort, if the patient wants,' the consultant explained. Kelly was touched. It reflected the depressing fact that many people who broke down had no one to hold on to.

Bradley looked at Kelly, as if seeking approval that her question had been answered.

'Did you want to tell me something?' she asked gently, trying not to stare at the toy.

'Everything is black,' he said.

Kelly concentrated on his face and tried to be patient with him.

'Where am I?' he asked.

'In hospital.'

The doctor had told her not to lie.

'Why?' He stared at his restraints.

'You had an episode, they brought you in here for your own safety. You were at the building site, do you remember?'

Bradley became agitated.

'What sort of episode?'

She could tell he was ashamed, and she wanted to comfort him, to tell him not to be embarrassed, but what could she say to an eighteen-year-old man who she barely knew? She knew she couldn't save him.

'Bradley, you've been sectioned. That means you weren't well enough to make decisions yourself.'

Kelly had promised the doctor she'd probe as much as she could, within reason, to unlock some of the mysteries inside Bradley's head. They needed something to work with: a starting place. It was her job to make him feel safe enough to speak out.

'It was the sand pit,' he said.

'The sand pit?' she asked.

He nodded. 'At school.'

Kelly waited.

'It was like the sand at the building site. They were digging. It reminded me of the digger at my dad's work.'

'When was this? When you were a kid?'

Another nod. 'I went to his building site after school and hung out there. But I saw them…'

He stopped and Kelly soothed him and stroked his hand.

'It's all right, you don't need to force yourself. They'll take care of you in here.'

'I want you to stay.'

Kelly nodded. She couldn't help but be drawn to the cuddly toy, and the black eyes seemed to accuse her of something.

'What made you pick Pinocchio?' she asked him, her heart racing.

'Because that's what they threw in the hole.'

'What hole?'

'The hole they dug under the house. It's where they put her body.'

Kelly held on to his hand.

'Can you remember where?'

'The pit. They threw her in and she wore a yellow hat with a red feather.'

'And where was this, Bradley? Where was the hole?'

Bradley shouted something unintelligible and pulled at his restraints and the consultant rushed to him to check his vital signs. She fiddled with tubes and switches and soon the boy was still again, and his eyes closed. It was horrific to watch. It made Kelly question her own sanity and every decision she'd ever made about criminals.

'Have you any idea what that was all about?' the consultant asked Kelly.

'I might do, yes. He's had a traumatic childhood to say the least. I think he might have witnessed a murder when he was only eleven years old.'

Chapter 46

The CCTV was patchy and lines ran up the screen, but it was definitely Tania Harrison on the screen, buying her season pass at Highbury Stadium, on the twentieth of May, 2001. Kelly vaguely recalled they'd moved to a new venue recently, owned by Emirates. Windy Miller was a huge fan. The old cassettes were transported to a lock-up at the new stadium and forgotten about. Until they asked for them. They sat in the Barking office, side by side, watching the grainy footage.

Tania went missing the same week she bought the programme.

Kelly and Seb sat next to each other. Leia Lord had been absent from the Barking office all morning. Kelly had toyed with not telling Seb about where she'd been this morning but in the end her conscience won out.

'Is he a suspect?' Seb asked. 'Given my impression of the father and his capability of giving orders from behind bars.'

It was a fair question but they had no motive apart from Bradley was an angry young man who had endured life in and out of the care system since the age of seven. The fact that he chose Pinocchio as a comforter inside the psychiatric ward was a red flag too. But Kelly struggled to believe that Bradley could be a killer. *Their* killer.

They turned away from the screen and Seb read from Tania's notes.

'No family. Pastimes: football and beer. Born in 1942 to a shipwright and a dishwasher, she was fifty-nine years old when she went missing. We can't trace any living relatives. Her father passed away in a machinery accident in Vickers shipyard in 1964, and her mother was admitted to a mental hospital in 1971, where she died in 1980. Tania became an apprentice typist for Barrow shipyard in 1958, then she began working for the council in 1962, who put her into the admin staff of several children's homes after that. At some point she moved to Hackney and she next pops up in a children's home in the borough from 1970 to when she qualified as a nurse in 1987, which is when she went to work for the Royal London in Whitechapel.'

'Pretty comprehensive,' Seb said.

Kelly carried on.

'The Charitable Sisters of Our Lady and Saint Catherine closed in the early nineties, or rather was shut down when care in the community took over. It was an institution for orphans as well as disturbed emotional cases of abuse.'

She stopped reading.

'I'm sorry, Seb, this is just a bit triggering.'

'All those kids? I know, it's tough. It's why I don't work child protection anymore.'

'You used to be on the paedophile unit?'

He nodded.

She could think of nothing to say because she didn't want to say something trite, like 'that must have been awful'. He talked instead.

'The home would have been thought of as a place of safety and rehabilitation, but records stop in 1988 and there's no access to anything before. In all the years I worked child protection, this makes me smell a rat.'

'Closing down suddenly?'

He nodded.

'And why might that be?' she asked.

'In those days, they were being found out, en masse. They were dark days, and frankly, they still are. There's a culture of cover-up,' he said. 'A handful of dedicated officers never gave up and got some of them closed. Maybe that's what we're looking at here.'

'Jesus,' Kelly whispered. She considered their four murder victims and saw them in a very different light suddenly. It was difficult to have empathy with injured parties when they were bastards, but she reminded herself they had no evidence of that yet.

They had a staff and residents list and that was about it. As a result, they still had thousands of names to trawl through.

'Oh dear,' Seb said.

'What?'

'It was part of Operation Daisy.'

'What was that?' she asked.

'An inquiry into historic abuses launched under Tony Blair.'

'You were part of it?'

Seb nodded. 'I didn't deal with the Charitable Sisters, though, my remit was north London at the time, it was split into sections because...'

'Because the abuse was so widespread?' Kelly asked.

He nodded.

'The Charitable Sisters underwent a staff culling in 1987,' he read, 'but it couldn't prevent the momentum of accusations gathering pace.' He stopped reading. 'That place was a hell hole for those kids.'

'Might we have our motive?' she asked and he nodded sadly.

'Bingo,' Seb said. 'Dorothy Amis began working there in 1975 as an assistant auxiliary nurse. Edith Callaghan worked there from 1979 as a nursery teacher. Frankie McKay worked there from 1980 as a caretaker. They all had their employment terminated in 1987.'

'But they were each able to stay in social care of some sort, and education services. Perhaps they weren't involved.'

She studied Seb's face. He was a natural cynic, and she could tell he didn't buy it.

'Thank God for geeks who inputted all this stuff to digital,' Kelly said, trying to lift him out of a slump he got into occasionally. As she got to know him better, she'd witnessed his consideration for others more. He was a good guy.

'Thank God for computers!' Seb agreed.

'So, do we agree that our prime suspect could be an ex-resident?' Kelly asked.

Seb nodded. 'One hundred per cent.'

They high fived.

Kelly stared at the screen, absorbing information. She calculated dates in her head.

'Somebody who'd be around forty years old now,' she muttered.

'In my experience, these types of traumas leave awful wounds on these kids,' he said. 'It wouldn't be the first act of revenge on an abuser,' he added.

'Put in Orlando Charles,' she said.

'Your man from the building site?'

'Same.'

'I can see where you're going with this,' he told her.

'Just humour me, he's a slippery character I've been trying to nail, and he keeps popping up working at building sites all over east London.

He has anonymity. He has opportunity. He's a care home kid. And he's about the right age. They both are.'

'Him and Jason Fellcroft?'

She nodded. 'His pal.'

He stared at her but typed it anyway.

'Nothing,' he said.

'What about Jason Fellcroft?'

It was another long shot because Jason had committed murder in Kent and so the Met would have no record of him, recently at least. HOLMES had to be instructed to search other police areas and CIDs; it didn't do it automatically. Counties had to request to share information with each other, so if Jason kept clean within the remit of Greater London, he wouldn't be known to any of the major investigation teams.

They stared at the screen and Seb whistled.

'You just hit the jackpot,' Seb said.

Kelly read from the screen.

'Holy shit. Jason Fellcroft lived at the Charitable Sisters of Our Lady and Saint Catherine's children's home, between 1974 and 1982, that makes him only eight years old when he moved there and sixteen when he left.' Her voice tailed off to a whisper and she became aware of Seb staring at her. She sat back and covered her mouth.

'I'm sorry, I need a minute.'

Kelly had no idea what terror Jason had suffered inside the Charitable Sisters but one thing she was sure about was that he couldn't have committed three of the puppeteer murders because he was inside HMP Belmarsh. The question was, did he have an alibi for Tania?

And was Bradley telling the truth when he said he recalled a woman being put into the bottom of a building trench in the middle of one of Jason's sites, when he was eleven years old?

And was the man he saw do it his father?

Chapter 47

The Fairview Nursing Home had not always had such a pretty façade. The site in Stoke Newington, close to a church, had been in continuous use since the nineteenth century, and had originally been an alms house for the poor. It had developed into a lunatic asylum of sorts, because that's where the Victorians liked to put anyone who was trouble. Single mothers, women who answered back, problem children who talked too much and the bereaved were all squeezed into the hospital-like wards and left to rot. It was called Begbie House back then. After Lord Alfred Begbie who donated half a million pounds to philanthropic gestures. By the 1950s it had become used solely for the elderly, many of whom had lived there all their lives, which is why they were elderly. And a lifetime of institutionalisation had turned them crazy. It was renovated and revamped in 2001 and reopened as Fairview.

Tania's mother had been moved into Begbie House in 1971 because Tania got a job in Hackney, close by. They thought if they started there, they might be able to trace people who'd worked with Tania. They'd discovered that the Charitable Sisters children's home had closed after the inquiry and had been bulldozed in 1999, and a supermarket stood there now. This was the next best thing. At the time, Tania had been twenty-nine years old and her mother forty-nine. Kelly thought about the forty-nine-year-old women she knew and couldn't imagine any of them being considered aged or insane. It was a shocking indictment of what society did to women when they became spares.

On the bus to Hackney, Kelly eyed a potential pickpocketer two seats in front of her and Seb, and kept a close watch on his hands as he fiddled with his bag, the buttons on his oversized, extremely unnecessary coat and his wide-brimmed sun hat. Kelly reckoned if he wasn't about to rob someone then he had other intentions to cause aggro. But London, she found, did that to her. It stimulated her imagination and created wild narratives in her head. The guy could be completely harmless and they got off the bus before he did, still watching him as the bus pulled away.

Fairview Nursing Home had been given a facelift which had transformed it from the building she'd seen in the ancient photos of Begbie House on her computer back in the office. It looked like a stereotypical nuthouse from a Hollywood movie. Kelly and Seb fully expected to turn up to screams from the basement and old people wandering around with crash helmets on for their own protection, but it wasn't like that at all. The front was glass and concrete, with modern planters outside and the entrance was reached through modern sliding doors which brought them to an intercom. A cool breeze wafted through the foyer and the staff wore casual green scrubs. It was nothing like she imagined the old days when nurses wandered around in their vintage white caps, made all the more sinister by *One Flew Over the Cuckoo's Nest*.

They were buzzed through and showed their warrant cards to the woman sat at the reception desk and were told to wait.

Soon, the nursing manager walked towards them with an outstretched hand and Kelly knew he was going to be the type who was extra helpful. He was in his forties and tall, with a mass of ginger hair and a wide smile. He gravitated to her first and Kelly reckoned this was a good sign. Old-school misogynists always communicated male-on-male.

'I've checked out some files for you, you're lucky, we started keeping the records from 1970 onwards and a couple of years ago we made the move to digital so you should find what you're looking for on our database. You said you had a warrant?'

'Yes,' Seb handed him the document. Kelly had marvelled at how quickly murder squads could get their hands on warrants for almost anything if they deemed it relevant to a murder inquiry. He scanned it quickly and led her away. They took the lift down to the basement and he took them to a filing room, where a woman was busy tapping away on a huge computer which reminded Kelly of the ones in CID. The private sector had begun using ultra slim ones, but government-run institutions were always playing catch up.

'These are the detectives I was telling you about, Moira,' he told her. The woman smiled sweetly and Kelly wondered if Moira liked her job stuck in the bowels of an old lunatic asylum filing terrible life histories away to be forgotten.

'Hi, Moira, I'm Kelly,' she said. She introduced Seb as Detective Crook. Moira didn't seem to mind having her day interrupted.

'I've got the files ready for you if you'd like to come around and take a seat.'

The manager left them alone and Moira talked them through the software and it was like other programs Kelly had used before. She soon got the hang of it.

The details for Maude Stamford, Tania's mother, came up on the screen and they had even uploaded an old black-and-white photo.

'Impressive bookkeeping,' Kelly said.

'We often get people looking for family histories and the like. It's sad what happened to a lot of them. After the investigation, we had to make our records watertight.'

'Operation Daisy?'

'Yes. I assumed that's why you were here. The hospital closed in 1987, along with a few others across London. It was a massive police report on accusations of abuse. Sadly, I don't have a copy, it was hush hush,' she said, holding her finger to her lips.

Moira spoke the last sentence so quietly that Kelly squinted to hear her. It was obviously taboo around here. It was as if the residents hearing it would certainly make them go mad.

'I've got things to do but shout me if you need anything, I'll just be over there, in row nineteen.'

'Is that why the home was renamed?'

Moira smiled and nodded, then left her to it. Kelly took her time and started at the beginning. Maude Stamford was transferred from Lancaster Moor asylum in 1971 and her medical history was attached. She'd been sectioned twice for 'mania' and was noted as destitute with no fixed abode. Kelly scanned forward to the therapies Maude received under the care of the Moor and read with interest that more humane psychiatric therapies were coming into the NHS by the 1970s and Maude's treatment was mainly sensory stimulus. Kelly read on to see what that meant and found that Maude liked to dance and sing and watch plays.

But the main reason for coming to the facility was to see if her relationship with her daughter, Tania, was mentioned as a factor in her treatment. Kelly searched visitor notes and again was impressed by how detailed they were. She supposed that if the state was going to lock you up then they had to have good justification for it. But the more she read about Maude, the more she found that the staff found her sweet and amenable, with several requesting her release all the way through the 1970s up to her untimely death in 1980, which was logged as 'an episode in her sleep'.

Then she came across notes from a meeting with the consultant psychiatrist in 1972, about how Maude was settling in. It was signed at the bottom by the witness, Tania Harrison. Kelly scanned the notes and found the meeting was about keeping Maude in solitary confinement as long as her therapy continued. Tania specifically requested creative arts therapy as a way to ease Maude's suffering. She read that *The process of making puppets creates opportunities to externalise, represent and explore problems at a safe emotional distance; while playing with puppets connects us to our feelings and enables dynamic expressive interaction designed to facilitate change.*

Kelly and Seb both stared at the page on the screen.

'Are you reading this?' she asked him and he simply nodded with his mouth open.

She read out loud for them both.

'Puppet therapy was experimental at the time but got the go ahead more widely in the hospital, endorsed by the consultant and countersigned by Tania Harrison, who wasn't qualified in either psychotherapy or psychiatry. Holy shit.'

'This is gross negligence on a corporate scale. The power she wielded... She was a council secretary and typist. What was she doing recommending and endorsing groundbreaking mental health therapy?'

'Look at the name of the company they used,' Seb said, pointing to the screen. The typing was old fashioned and grainy but they managed to read it out.

Happy Puppets, based in Leyton.

Kelly's face froze and she moved closer to the screen, unaware if she'd made a mistake.

It couldn't be...

The contract name on the document, and the main puppeteer at *Happy Puppets*, who treated Maude Stamford, was a man called Luther Zedric.

Chapter 48

Luther was hunched over his desk when Kelly and Seb walked in. She'd sweet-talked Diandra into letting them go straight up to the curator's suite.

He jumped suddenly and twisted around.

'Sorry, I didn't mean to startle you,' Kelly said. Seb hung back.

Luther looked tense.

'Were you expecting somebody else?'

Luther's mouth twisted gently and he smiled, but before the gesture became benign, Kelly had seen something else. Fear? Warning?

'If I'd known you were coming I would have made tea,' he said. Luther switched into entertainer mode and Kelly saw a glimpse of the puppeteer.

Kelly felt a fool for accepting his innocent demeanour because he was an old man and realised that it was how Nazi SS officers got away with their crimes decades after they'd been committed too. She'd been hoodwinked by his age.

'How did you start in museums? What did you do before?'

She walked around the other side of the room gazing at exhibits and imagining them through the eyes of either small children or the very mentally sick, or both. Their division caused Luther discomfort, which is what they intended. Seb walked the other way.

Luther didn't answer so she turned to him and leant against a desk with her arms folded.

She waited for him to decide if he was going to speak. He appeared to be floundering and she could tell that he was unnerved.

'Are you all right, Luther?'

He slid his glasses up his face and blustered about, tidying papers and opening and closing boxes.

'I mean, I was wondering if you always worked in museums or you did something else first? When did you leave New York?'

He relaxed a little, seemingly believing that she'd gone off tack.

'I was only ten years old but I still have memories. They say children can remember from two years old, I believe it. I can still smell the fresh waffles baked at the end of the block, and the money was different. The Brooklyn Bridge towered over our house…'

Kelly wondered if his American accent was genuine and if anything he said could be trusted.

He stared off into the distance and Kelly wondered if he'd turned to puppets because he was lonely. The man before her didn't seem like a killer but he needed to explain how he knew Tania Harrison and her mother. Murderers come in all shapes and sizes. They can be old and kind, or young and innocent; thin, fat, poorly or weak.

Luther knew a thing or two about disguise. Wasn't all puppetry mere play?

A trick.

'So what did you do when you first came to London?' Seb asked.

Luther glanced at him and went mute again.

'Have you always loved puppets and dolls, Luther? They can help people, can't they? Unlock their minds and help them deal with trauma. Is that why you visited homes around London, with your puppets, promising to heal people?'

His mouth opened but no words came out.

'Yes,' he said simply. A tear rolled down his cheek and Kelly witnessed his removal from time again. A moment where he disappeared and left his body behind for her to fathom.

'Begbie House?'

He flashed her a look of what Kelly took as pure fear. His eyes widened and his face set in stone. She'd only seen Luther Zedric as a man with a soft visage to match his personality. The creases in his brow she'd only associated with the loss of his beloved toys, but this was different.

'Did you work with Maude Stamford?'

He nodded and the shaking stopped.

'And her daughter, Tania?'

'She was a cruel bitch, is that why you're here? What has she said about me?'

'Nothing. In fact, Tania is dead. She was murdered seven years ago. Her body has only just been discovered under a building site in Stratford. Not far from here in fact.'

Luther's face dropped and his body went very still, as if he was waiting for a puppeteer to put a hand up his arse.

'Was she cruel to her mother?' Kelly asked.

'Yes.' It was a whisper.

'Did she like your puppets?'

Nodding.

'What were her favourites?'

'Her what?'

'Her favourite puppets, Luther. These characters are your life. I know you take notice of it when another person shares your passion. I've got all day.'

More tears rolled out of Luther's eyes and Kelly didn't expect this turn of events. She'd expected denials, regret, pleading, but not this; not an outpouring of emotion.

He cared for Maude.

'They loved Charlie because he was funny.'

'Charlie McCarthy?'

He nodded. It wasn't what they wanted to hear. They wanted evidence for the significance of Pinocchio, Judy, Tinkerbell and Jiminy Cricket. They needed a closer link.

'The toys that were stolen from here, Luther, were they *your* favourites?' she asked.

He stared at them and nodded. 'Of course they were, how did you know?'

She moved on.

'What was your relationship with Maude?'

Finally, he moved and slumped into a chair.

'I made her laugh. I tried to get her out of there but I knew Tania would never allow it.'

'Why?'

'Because she was punishing her for what happened to her.'

'For what happened to Tania?'

'Yes. Maude was a single mother and in those days it was a heinous crime. Tania was raised in shame and with several nasty surrogate fathers: people in Maude's life who were fraudsters and villains.'

'Go on.'

'She blamed Maude and had her committed.'

'Just like that?'

'There was a list as long as your arm of why else Maude was hospitalised. She led a very unhappy existence but she always did her best for her daughter.'

'I'm sure she did.'

Kelly couldn't imagine what it must have been like for a destitute woman raising a bastard child in what would have been the 1950s.

'When Maude took ill and ended up in Lancaster Moor, Tania did everything she could to keep her there, when that became unworkable she moved her to Begbie House, where they kept her drugged and bedbound. I did my best to help, but in those days, the governor of those places was the law. I did as I was told, I came in with my puppets and put on shows, and left.'

'And did Tania get you work at the Charitable Sisters of Our Lady and Saint Catherine children's home when she left Begbie House?'

It was a long shot.

Luther's face went pale.

'A nod or a shake will do.'

He nodded slowly.

'They didn't investigate me.'

'Operation Daisy?'

'Yes. I was questioned and cleared. It was awful what went on there.'

'You knew?'

'I heard.'

'Exactly what did you hear?'

Luther pulled at his collar.

'Physical abuse?'

A nod.

'Verbal abuse?'

Another nod.

'Sexual abuse?'

Luther's eyes closed tight. 'It's what I heard.'

'You didn't witness it?'

He shook his head so hard she thought it might come off.

'And can you remember Frankie McKay, the caretaker?'

Another nod.

Kelly knew they'd unearthed gold, but she was sad it had been discovered this way. It was like finding a nugget of pure grade-eighteen carat only to find a huge turd inside it. She didn't feel like celebrating.

'Dorothy Amis?'

A nod.

'Edith Callaghan?'

A nod.

Luther's head dropped to his chest and he stared at his hands. He behaved like a criminal under arrest and about to spend the rest of his days incarcerated.

'Were they implicated in the abuse?'

He dropped his head, and his shoulders slumped.

'Oh yes,' he said. 'They were the worst.'

'They're all dead,' Seb said.

Kelly winced but she knew Seb was reeling inside and she understood that's where some of his demons came from. Anybody who'd worked the paedo unit never let go.

'What? Who?'

'That's why we're here, because we think you know who,' Seb said.

'Was it you?'

'No! No! indeed, absolutely not!' Luther loosened his necktie and wafted air over his face, which had turned purple.

'Can you recall any of the children, Luther? Who lived at the Charitable Sisters. This is really important.'

'Is this about Operation Daisy all over again?'

'Try to remember any of the residents who lived at the home when you took your puppets in to put on shows. Any who took a keen interest in your work? One that stood out, perhaps, who might have something against the staff I've mentioned.'

Luther slowly nodded again and Kelly's stomach churned.

'Jason,' he said. 'Young Jason Fellcroft hated them, and he said he'd kill them one day.'

Chapter 49

Back at the Barking office, when Seb and Kelly strode confidently back in, they found groups of officers stood huddled together silently.

Kelly spotted movement in the corner of her eye and they turned towards Leia Lord's office.

Had somebody had an accident?

She'd never seen a police investigation unit this quiet. Judging by Seb's reaction, the same was true for him too.

And then they saw them.

The DPS.

They were crawling all over DCI Leia Lord's office and Kelly and Seb looked at one another.

The Directorate for Professional Standards unit didn't mess about.

They were here for a reason.

Kelly's mind whirled and Seb took charge. He ushered everyone to a back office and closed the door.

'We're not allowed to use our computers,' one said.

'But we can go to the lower floor and use theirs,' said another.

'They won't tell us what's wrong.'

'They haven't started interviews yet.'

Seb was met with a barrage of emotionally charged enquiries, but Kelly saw him grab control and a leader emerged. He guided everybody through what the rest of their day might look like. He told them he'd seen it once before. He told everybody to be calm, then he left the room, and Kelly watched him through the clear divider approach one of the investigators. They chatted for long minutes and Kelly felt her stomach turn to stone as she imagined her first few weeks at MIT east turn to disaster. The DPS investigated misconduct and complaints, and they had just one brief: to drive out corrupt and prejudiced officers. What could they want? Who'd reported them?

She wanted to call Cheryl and Pete, or Molly, to hear the voice of a friend. Irrational fears skipped through her mind. What if they were here for her? She racked her brain to determine if she'd done anything wrong. All her inappropriate conversations with Molly sprang to mind. She shouldn't be privy to anything the SOCO did outside of Bethnal Green CID. She thought of the times she'd contacted her father for advice, and the chats with Cheryl since she'd left the area nick. Her guts gurgled and she thought she might throw up. They were in Leia's office. Was that significant in itself?

Then Seb returned.

Officers were gathering their things and moving to the lifts, disappearing, she guessed, to other floors.

'What will happen to our investigation?' she asked him.

'Don't worry, we can work downstairs, I've secured us a room. It's activity on this floor they're looking at.'

'Is that what they told you?'

'Not exactly,' he replied.

'You know the guy you spoke to?'

'Really well, actually.'

Something in his voice made her stare at him longer than normal.

'You knew this was happening?'

He didn't answer but his face said it all.

'I had my suspicions,' he said.

She looked outside and back to him.

'Leia?'

He nodded.

'I can't say too much but yes, she's their focus.'

'Did you report her for something?'

Kelly felt herself becoming riled now and suddenly protective over a fellow female copper being investigated by a bunch of blokes.

'No. It wasn't me. I merely watched out for a few things.'

'You what?'

Kelly walked away from him and stared through the clear divider, watching the turning over of a fellow copper's office. She heard John Porter's voice in her head. *You never grass another copper.*

'You've been monitoring her. You're a plant!' she said when she turned around.

'No, I'm not. I'm a DI and, like you, I work murder squad. They've had their suspicions about her for a long time, I merely confirmed some of them.'

'What did she do? What suspicions?'

'I can't say.'

'Fuck you! You can't say. I thought we had a good relationship forming here. I really started to trust you.'

She didn't know what else to say. It was like cycling into a brick wall.

'What the fuck is going on, Seb? Who are you?'

He held up his hands and pleaded with her to keep her voice down.

'I'll be quiet if you tell me what the hell is going on.'

'I will, I promise, but not here, not now. There's more important shit to get done. Follow me.'

Chapter 50

Seb took her into a private office on the floor below and closed the door. The computer was already set up and a profile stared back at her from the screen. Seb waited for her to read the title of it.

HOME OFFICE

OFFICIAL-SENSITIVE

OPERATION DAISY

1998

She stared at him.

'Where did you get this?'

'It's a part of the DPS inquiry into Leia Lord.'

Kelly felt prickles up her back. She couldn't help thinking she'd been used, but she had no idea how or by who, or why.

'Are we on our case now or am I part of something else?'

'It's never been about you, Kelly. We had no idea you'd turn out to be so valuable.'

'We?'

'The DPS.'

'You're DPS?'

'Kind of.'

'Kind of? What does that mean?'

'I promise I'll tell you everything. But I need your eyes on this, then we'll talk. Being your partner was my cover. I never expected for you to be so damn good.'

'I'm good?'

'You're better than good, Kelly Porter. If it wasn't for you, we'd still be scratching our heads. We're close to cracking this because of you and I know you don't understand, and I appreciate you probably feel played right now, and used, and all of those things, but I swear to you that you're not any of them. But we don't have time to go over it now. Please, just read the report and then I'll fill you in on where we are.'

He left and closed the door quietly.

Kelly stared at the screen. He'd just said she was valuable. He'd said her input was pivotal. She stared at the door. She had no idea what was going on, but one thing beckoned her. A document that was hush hush. Perhaps she'd get some answers from Op Daisy. There was only one way to find out.

She began to read and soon after skipping the contents page and the introduction, she was glued to the words and found herself straightening her back and rubbing her shoulders, so focused was she on what she was learning about the children in the care of the Charitable Sisters of Our Lady and Saint Catherine. She sat with her hands over her mouth, as if drawing comfort from the warmth of her own flesh, or maybe a protective barrier between her and the words. Institutional grooming for sexual solicitation… Beatings… Punishments…

None of them were words anyone wanted to read when associated with the lives of children. Kids who had no choice but to exist in a world without carers. The vulnerable and impressionable residents of the CSOLSC until its closure in 1987 were victims of abuse so vile that Kelly felt tears pouring down her cheeks as she read. But she couldn't stop. She couldn't look away, because if she did, then she'd be abandoning them all over again.

There were individual casefiles on children. Hundreds of them, going back decades.

One of them was Jason Fellcroft and another was his foster brother Tomas Kovac.

Kovac had been made an orphan in 1970 when his parents were shot on a London quay. Executed. There was no more information than that. It was dramatically blunt and brutal, and Kelly wanted to know more. Young Tomas was then entered into the care system and virtually grew up with Jason Fellcroft, it seemed.

Before the Charitable Sisters, they'd been living in the same foster home together. The file said the two boys were inseparable. But after a house fire at the home of their foster parents, they'd been transferred to an institution because the foster parents refused to take them back.

The implication was the two boys were responsible for the fire. Fellcroft and Kovac were the same age, both born in 1966, now aged forty-two years. They moved into the Charitable Sisters when they were eight years old. Kelly closed her eyes and her throat felt tight. Her head filled with visions of children around that age and she thought of their round faces, their keen eyes and their trusting nature. Hansel and Gretel were around that age when they were fattened up for a witch to eat. Alice got lost in wonderland when she was seven and a half. Red Riding Hood couldn't have been much older visiting her grandma. Pinocchio was thought to have been around six years old. Innocence lost... It's what all fairy tales were about.

She forced herself to read on, for the sake of the children who'd gone like lambs to the slaughter into their own hell.

Seb was in the paedo unit...

That was his background.

Now he was DPS.

A dawning lingered over her as she flicked the pages and read about what happened to Jason Fellcroft and Tomas Kovac and all the time she read, she wondered what the hell had happened to Jason's best friend.

Operation Daisy had been conducted in secret. It hadn't been reported in the press. It was ruled at the time, by the Home Office, that it was in the public interest to investigate in-house. There were still too many people close to power to go after every privileged person who'd abused their position in the media, the police and the judiciary. The Met was still in the pocket of politicians, who were puppets of vested interests, and Kelly dreaded to think how many kids had been let down by the institutions supposed to protect them. She was about to find out.

Her eyes scanned the information. The verbal testimony, the witness statements, the pain and anguish. The habitual beatings...

Worse. The perversion of predators given legal access to minors. There'd been a sniff of institutional cover-ups last year when Jimmy Saville had been interviewed under caution about indecent assault. She'd heard rumours that everybody knew he was guilty as hell but there was no evidence. She read on.

A rage boiled inside of her, and she felt her hands twitching to snuff out those responsible. The sentiment caught her by surprise.

She was fantasising about murder.

Was there, in fact, some primordial justification for it? Was her job to uphold the laws of the land, which, it appeared, were mere illusions created to protect those in corrupt positions of power? Those willing and able to abuse children.

She felt sick.

Seb knew it'd be rough. It's why he'd left her alone in the room. To absorb the gravity of it.

To sense all the raw emotion of it. To leave her to cry, or scream, or simply give up and walk out.

Then one of the witness testimonies caught her eye.

She read on.

The children had sometimes made up names as if that might protect them from the adults who were supposed to care for them. Jason had called himself Jiminy Cricket. Young Tomas had referred to himself as Pinocchio. Seb had read this before her. He knew. He saw what was coming. These kids had pretended they could escape by flying away on fantasy. She'd heard about it before from victims of torture and kidnap. It was called cognitive dissociative disorder. The pain of molestation was so great that the human mind had zoned out and taken the child away, somewhere safe.

It was harrowing.

Princess Leia...

What? She did a double take.

She read the passage again. Jason and Tomas had a special friend. She was called Princess Leia. Images from Kelly's favourite films replayed in her head and the tragedy unfolded before her. She'd never be able to see them in the same way ever again. Household names. Toys that littered every child's bed. The comfort of holding a fantasy friend. A protector.

These children, living through untold horrors, had hidden in the comfort of historical characters. Some fictional, others not. They spent years together making up stories to escape the hell they were living in. It was little comfort.

Her eyes misted over as she skipped over the testimony of Jason and Tomas, both interviewed when they were grown men, in 1998, a decade after the home closed. It was almost impossible to read but she forced herself.

Op Daisy was shelved in 2002 and no one ever faced prosecution.

Added to the back of the document were several appendices and one of them was the employment record of a young detective. Kelly stared at it, not understanding why it was there, until she read on.

The officer had joined the Met police in 1987, at twenty-one years old. She was exactly the same age as Jason Fellcroft and Tomas Kovac. Her career trajectory was nothing short of stunning. She'd made DS in 1998 and had worked on Op Daisy, making her name as a standout officer. She'd become DI in 2005. Then she joined a murder squad in 2006. It was a meteoric rise and Kelly felt envy biting her.

The name on the employment record was Leia Lord and now she was in charge.

Chapter 51

The mobile phone jangled Kelly's nerves. She looked up from the screen and felt terribly alone.

The caller was Jonathan Hass from Brampton Forensic Services. She answered, eager for distraction, and he told her he had information on the Tyrolean hat placed on Tania's head by her killer.

Kelly stretched and listened, giving her eyes a break from hundreds of pages of notes. She rubbed them and listened to him. His enthusiasm had not waned once, unlike hers which was now deflated by Seb's revelations, as well as what she'd read. Compared to that, Jonathan Hass now sounded normal to her.

'Kelly, I have some further news on the hat's label. It was too soiled to read but I found a cleaning specialist who's managed to reveal enough of it without compromising evidence and it was bought from a milliner in Burlington Arcade, the one off Piccadilly.'

'Yes, I know it. I thought you said the factory shut in the 1930s.'

'They were made on-site.'

Burlington Arcade was a very smart row of shops which were as much for tourists as the very wealthy. Kelly had wandered down there herself to marvel at the jewellery and shoes on display. The prices were eyewatering, but it was where dreams were made, and, in her case, remained.

'I checked, the shop is still in business. Can you believe it opened in 1928 and is still selling hats?'

'Amazing,' Kelly said, in her best enthused voice. 'I'll get somebody over there to check receipts.'

'I can do better than that. I've already called them. They do bespoke hats that aren't available across the counter. The current milliner, who is the grandson of the original, remembers making a hat the same as ours and he swears it's the only one, it's one of a kind and besides he said he'd never forget the chap he made it for. It was his name.'

'His name?'

'Yes. It was Wimbledon that did it. The milliner is a big tennis fan. The name reminded him of Novak Djokovic.'

'Who?'

'The Serbian tennis player.'

'I know who Novak Djokovic is,' Kelly said.

'Of course. Anyway, I wrote it down. The hat was made for a Mr Tomas Kovac back in 2001.'

Kelly sat up straight.

She got Jonathan to repeat himself in case her tired brain had misunderstood.

'Did the milliner recall what he looked like?'

'Yes. You see, this is why I should be a detective. I knew you were going to ask me that. He was tall, with dark eyes. He wore a leather jacket, and he was young, around mid-thirties. Athletic but not big.'

Kelly had heard the description before, from Sookie the barmaid. The mystery man who'd thrown games across her pub. The one who'd escorted Edith. The true gent. Was he the same man who worked his way into the lives of those who abused him? She thanked Jonathan and they hung up, then she logged into a new window with her own profile and checked her emails. Sookie had been visited by a police artist and the image was ready. However, when she clicked on the link it wouldn't open, then her screen went blank. She stared at it and blinked a couple of times, knowing she was exhausted but that didn't satisfy her as explanation enough. She checked the wires behind the monitor, then tried again. The email was there but not the link to the image.

She entered Tomas Kovac's name into the PNC, knowing that by now, whoever Seb was really working for, would have done already. How long had he known about Leia Lord? And more to the point, what else did he know?

The result came up blank.

Chapter 52

In Stratford, diggers rumbled throughout the day at the building site where Tania's body had been found. They only stopped when several layers of surface dirt had been removed. It was the job of the forensic officers on site to sift through the debris. They'd been instructed by Brampton Forensic Services to remove a layer at a time, and Jonathan Hass stood on the edge of the pit waiting for signs of extinct human remains. Groups of men stood watching, though the police had erected a cordon to make sure they didn't get too close. Press interest had heightened too since the discovery of a third recent body and the leaking of information that Frankie McKay was linked to the three other women.

It was being reported as a historic gangland-related turf war, with the convicted felon, Jason Fellcroft, at its centre. Rumours swirled in the dust and construction work stopped completely at the site. Jonathan couldn't recall telling him this line of inquiry, or that it had been given to the press.

The fumes from the machines were choking and suddenly a technician held up her hand and Jonathan, thankful for some clean air, walked across to see what had happened. The technician bent over and then stood up, pointing to the ground. To Jonathan's trained eye, he saw what the forensic expert saw. To any layman it might look like a pile of mud, turned to stone with the sun. But to anyone who knew what they were doing, it was cloth that shouldn't be there. The technician moved the fabric to one side and Jonathan saw a bone that looked like a femur.

Across town, close to London Bridge, another group of plastic-clad officers conducted a search of Dennis Chapman's flat, under the watchful eye of the lead SOCO, Molly. The apartment was a tip. To an untrained eye it would appear that the forensic team was terrible at its job and had thrown all the belongings around, but then they were informed that a neighbour had reported a burglary last night, which had alerted the authorities to the address. They walked through the flat with shoe covers on and listened to Molly talking. They discussed diagrams of the rooms, projections of the burglary blow by blow and if there'd been anyone home at the time. They found scuff marks in the hall, along the skirting board and a shrivelled half-cooked chicken in the oven in the kitchen. They had no idea if anything had been taken because they couldn't ask the resident himself. They seized electrical equipment and noted the date of the post that had built up behind the front door when they'd entered: Monday last.

Then a neighbour said they'd seen the resident the Sunday before, when he came home from work.

In the bathroom, under UV light, Molly found blood spatter consistent with a possible dramatic bleeding event. The largest stains were next to the bath and inside the tub, not visible to the naked eye. Technicians put swabs in bottles and sealed them in plastic envelopes.

Then an officer shouted from one of the two bedrooms. Molly made her way there and when she got there, she was presented with the contents of a bedside drawer.

Inside it were four small doll-like puppets.

Jiminy Cricket.

Pinocchio.

Judy and Tinkerbell.

She left the room and removed her gloves and called Kelly straight away to tell her. The news didn't seem a surprise and Molly was disappointed at her friend's lack of enthusiasm.

'Are you there?' Molly asked. 'Is everything okay?'

'Yes, I'm just thinking.'

'Are you any closer to finding this weirdo? I'm assuming they're linked?'

Molly told her about the evidence of catastrophic blood loss in the bathroom.

'He's playing with us. He loves games.'

'What?' Molly asked.

'I've got to go, Molly, thanks for calling, let me know as soon as you get any results,' she said, ending the call.

Chapter 53

'I'm here to see Mr Zedric, the curator, I have an appointment.'

Diandra looked at her book, stalling for time. 'I'm sorry but I have no record of an appointment today. Mr Zedric is very busy.'

'Please double check. He knows I'm coming.'

Diandra didn't want anyone to know that her boss was in a police station, having slept there in his suit. She wasn't even allowed to take him his slippers or a pillow. She'd told the staff he was sick. They'd told her that Mr Zedric never got sick and she'd responded by telling them well this time he did. She was deeply worried about him. He hadn't been himself lately.

'I'm sorry, I can't help you.'

The man smiled and turned away. He walked into the museum and Diandra shouted out to him, catching the attention of the security guard, Oswald, who was unlikely to be able to stop a toddler. She caught his attention but by the time he'd approached her window, the man had disappeared upstairs. Diandra threw her hands up in the air and emerged from her booth.

'I'll take care of it, Oswald,' she told him.

She followed the man upstairs and saw that he was making his way to Mr Zedric's suite. She was angry he'd not only lied to her about having an appointment but was now trying to deceive her. But then she stopped. What if he was the man who'd broken in and stolen from them? He didn't look like a robber but then she wasn't entirely sure what one looked like because she didn't know any. She didn't like him, she knew that much.

She felt stuck and anxious. Whenever she had a problem she called Mr Zedric, but she couldn't do that.

She looked at her watch. He'd been held for eighteen hours now. He'd be exhausted. Her plan was to leave work at one o'clock and head straight over to the police station where he was being held and demand to see him. She'd already packed some food for him, and a bottle of water.

She peered along the corridor, above the heads of people milling about, and spotted the man trying the door of Mr Zedric's office. She hurried along the landing, making her way around paying guests and their children, excusing herself and apologising, and approached him breathlessly.

'You can't go in there! What are you doing? I'll call the police.'

'Where is he? I'm an old friend of Luther's and I need to see him, it's important.'

'So you lied to me?'

'I think he's in danger,' the man said.

Diandra noticed that the man had a similar underlying note in his accent to Mr Zedric. It was barely noticeable but she had an ear for these things.

'You're a friend?'

'Yes,' he smiled and Diandra softened.

'But how do I know?'

'Look, I brought him a gift,' he said, pulling something out of the large bag he carried over his shoulder, a bit like a shipping bag but much smarter.

Diandra covered her mouth.

'Where did you get him?' she asked.

'You see how important it is now? A gentleman tried to sell it to me. I knew Luther had been robbed and I could tell just by looking at it that it was his.'

'Charlie McCarthy! He'll be so pleased. But he's not here.'

'Not here?'

Diandra shook her head. She bit her lip.

'He's been arrested,' she whispered.

'No? What for? Luther is the nicest man I have ever had the pleasure of knowing, he's my dear friend.'

'Of course. I don't know. It's something to do with the police coming here all last week. It's about the puppets and I think it's something to do with those teachers who were found dead.'

Diandra wrung her hands.

'Goodness. Where is he?'

'He's in a cell, he's been there all night.'
'Do you know which station?'
Diandra nodded.
'Tell me, I have friends who might be able to help.'
'Friends?'
'Legal friends.'
'Ah, I see.'
'Can I put this in his office?' he asked.
'Of course. I didn't catch your name,' Diandra said as she found the correct key on her bundle. She opened the door and he followed her in and shut the door behind them.

Diandra turned to the sound of the lock clicking shut and she backed away towards Mr Zedric's desk.

'You remind me of someone,' he said.

Chapter 54

Seb returned to the office where he'd left Kelly. She told him about Molly's phone call, but any urgency had disappeared from her body.

'How long have you known about this?' she asked, indicating the file on the computer screen.

'When we discovered it together at Begbie House.'

She believed him.

'And you've read it all?' she asked.

He nodded.

'So, you're investigating Leia Lord because you think she was the Princess Leia who lived in the Charitable Sisters alongside Jason Fellcroft and Tomas Kovac?'

'Exactly that. I knew you'd piece it all together. That's why I left you to yourself. To absorb it all. I'm sorry.'

'You can stop saying sorry. It's trite and unnecessary. It insults my intelligence.'

He smiled. 'Of course.'

'What's she said?'

'I don't know, I'm not privy to the interviews.'

He blew out air and folded his arms. She saw him in a new light now. Gone was the vulnerable, struggling and resentful officer jealous of his boss. Instead, here stood a duplicitous professional.

'Was the story about your parents true?' she asked.

'Yes. It was. I haven't lied to you.'

'No, you just haven't told me the truth.'

'I couldn't.'

'What do you think she's done?'

'Honestly, I think she's been covering for Jason Fellcroft from the inside. As she rose through the ranks, she was able to wield more power. They've no doubt planned their revenge on these people for a very long time. Did you read the shit they went through?'

'Yes. It makes me sick.'

'All of it?'

'Yes.' Kelly forced images away that assaulted her mind. Leia alone in her room, visited by the caretaker in the middle of the night. Jason in solitary confinement, naked, scared and taunted by monsters. Tomas, crying out for help when he was beaten.

'How the fuck did these monsters get jobs in schools and hospitals?'

'It's an endemic failing. It's a mess. It's partly why I'm on this case. It will take years to weed all of them out, you know that.'

Kelly conceded. Rome wasn't built in a day, but she reckoned in her current mood she could destroy it in one.

'When was DPS notified?' she asked.

'They've been on to her since they were alerted to strange activity coming from her desktop computer.'

'You guys can track that kind of shit?'

Seb nodded.

'Holy shit, in ten years they'll be listening to private conversations.'

'They look for patterns. Her PNC was odd in the light of the cases she was in charge of. She also ordered various surveillance resources used on the victims.'

'The photos we found in their homes. You think she was harassing them?'

'It's possible. As SIO there are certain basic norms you'd expect an officer to be following. Her working protocols didn't stack up. You picked it up on day one.'

'You were watching me?'

'We monitor everyone, surely you expect that, Kelly?'

She nodded.

'What norms?' she asked. She wasn't sure if she was genuinely interested or filling gaps because she felt betrayed. It wasn't Seb's fault. Anti-corruption was vital in the force. It was a sad indictment of the temptations luring officers away from their jobs.

'Norms like procedure, search history and the way you called her out in briefings, for example. I saw you struggle with divided loyalties between what you knew and what you saw.'

She could have asked him why he hadn't let her in then, but she knew the answer. Those in anti-corruption trusted no one.

'So, you're not really my partner. That's a real shame, I quite like you.'

He smiled.

'Lord used HR computers without anybody's knowledge to gain information about people and we suspect she manipulated evidence.'

'Was she using Bradley Fellcroft?'

'We haven't established the exact link yet, but we have a fake informant file on him.'

'Yeah, you might want to talk to DCI Warren at Bethnal Green CID about that. I was prevented from using him as a witness.'

'On the Orlando Charles case?' he asked.

'The same.' She stared out of the window. 'Why didn't she use her position to bring the Charitable Sisters to justice? Are you sure she wasn't using her position to collect intel on them?'

'It's a strong case against her, Kelly.'

The silence between them said almost everything but she needed it spoken out loud.

'They went through hell.'

'I know,' he said. 'But there are ways to get vengeance.'

'Are there? Really? She was on the inside, about as embedded as you could be, and she knew there wouldn't be justice. This is about them doing it their way.'

Kelly looked away. Her eyes were moist. Sometimes a case came along in police work when, morally, it just didn't stack up. She took a deep breath and pushed the emotions aside. She wasn't a victim, and she had no right to wallow on anybody's behalf.

'So how long have you been here? Are you a new plant?'

'No, I've been here for years. But she got involved in a paedophile case and red flags were raised then. I know most of them over there still.'

'Is that what triggered the investigation?'

He nodded.

'Why did you leave the unit?'

He looked at his feet.

'Sorry. Stupid question.'

'No, it's not. Burnout is common over there. I'm not ashamed. I'm proud of the work I did for them. People think the paedophile unit is where police souls go to die but actually it's a place of huge hope. We nail more fuckers than any other department and there's lots of historic stuff.'

'Like Op Daisy?'

'Yeah, but that's only just come up on their radar.'

'Has she been arrested?'

'No, she's AWOL.'

'Holy shit. No contact?'

'None whatsoever, phone's switched off, the works. Her car is missing and she's not home.'

'Wait a minute,' Kelly said. The sensation of imminent discovery gripped her and suddenly she knew why.

'Her phone,' she said.

'What about it?'

'The ringtone, it was "The Entertainer" from Ragtime. Surely you recall. Remember the poster at Edith's house? The Sting! You were bloody humming it.'

She did her best to recreate the tune though music wasn't her strong point. He nodded at her.

'Luther told me about Uncle Miltie,' she said.

'Who?'

'Christ, I can't remember.' She sat at the computer and entered a search on him. The results popped up straight away.

'God, I love the internet. Here. Milton Berle. Luther said there was a theatre in London named after him.' Her fingers typed furiously.

'Here, look. It closed eight years ago. Damn.'

He stood behind her chair, leaning over.

She sat back. It was a dead end.

'Do you believe Leia had something to do with the murders?'

'We won't know that until we find her.'

'Do you think Kovac went rogue?'

'That's what you want, isn't it?' he asked.

It was true. Kelly didn't want to believe that Leia Lord had suffered as a child in the ways outlined in Op Daisy, only for her to throw her life away on revenge. It wasn't fair. Kelly believed that power was a force for good and if you were lucky enough to wield it, then you should.

'We haven't located him either. He's a ghost. And we have no idea what he looks like.'

'I might be able to help you with that.'

Seb raised an eyebrow.

She told him about her conversation with Jonathan Hass and the missing email attachment.

'Good work, we've seized Luther Zedric's computer equipment and he's waiting for us downstairs in a cell. Ready?'

Seb had been one step ahead the whole time. She felt used but knew that if she put her ego aside, she saw that they wanted the same things. She stood up and straightened her skirt.

'I'm sorry,' he said.

'What for?'

'Lying to you.'

'Did you lie about everything?'

'Actually, no. You're the first person who has taken enough of an interest to have your eyes open. You care about people, even those you don't know.'

She turned her back to him.

'Ready,' she said.

Chapter 55

Kelly walked into the interview room and sat down opposite Luther, who exhaled deeply when he saw her. But he soon tensed again when he saw Seb come in behind her.

'Morning, Luther. Let's put the tape on and I'll read you your rights, shall I?'

'Am I in trouble?'

'You haven't been charged but we need to ask you some questions about your involvement with Tania Harrison and Jason Fellcroft. We'll make a decision going forward after that. This is an interview under caution, which is why I'm reading your rights. You didn't want legal representation?'

'Why would I? I have nothing to hide.'

'Fair enough, let's get started shall we?' she said.

Luther studied her and she wondered if he could tell she'd been reading about predators who destroyed children's lives and those who did nothing about it. She saw him in a different light now. She stared into his face and hoped he wasn't involved in the vile things she'd read in the Op Daisy file, but predators never looked like evil. Often, they were just like everybody else. Carers, fathers, brothers, sisters, aunties, teachers and nurses. Police. It broke her heart.

Luther's belly hung over his trousers and he sweated profusely. He'd clearly enjoyed his food over the years. Cataloguing toys and organising exhibits could potentially be a taxing affair but it could equally be done from a chair. However, there was no accounting for strength when, old or young, fit or not, somebody had the crazed will to snub out another life. They had yet to make up their minds about him.

'Did you manage to get some rest last night?' she asked him.

Luther always had a worried look about him, or at least he had since she'd first met him. Kelly couldn't imagine him happy or contented.

He carried the weight of stress around with him, as if he was always looking over his shoulder. Only when she'd seen him with his toys did he look settled or anything approaching happy.

'Take a few deep breaths, Luther. You're here because you haven't been entirely honest with us about your connection to some persons of interest to us.'

He looked at her then and held her gaze.

He understood.

She smiled at him and suddenly she thought he was going to cry. She wasn't used to grown men tearing up in front of her but she didn't think it would harm anyone if it happened more often. He was carrying a lot of burden inside of him and she was hoping now was the time to get it out.

Luther did as he was told and inhaled deeply.

'Ready?'

He nodded and she started the recording, asking him to confirm details of his name and address.

Seb then asked him about how he got into puppetry and when he started the company *Happy Puppets*.

The purpose of starting gently was to relax him and get him talking. The strategy of taking it in turns to ask questions was to confuse him and increase the chance of him making a mistake. She knew Luther was holding something back but she also assessed him as an open individual who was fundamentally honest but scared.

She might be wrong, of course.

They chatted for about ten minutes about his history and how he came to establish a reputation as a puppet master in the 1970s in London.

'Word of mouth is a powerful thing, it's the most important marketing tool for any business.'

'I believe you're right,' Kelly said. 'You built a reputation.'

He nodded. 'I came to the attention of Begbie House, who offered me work.'

'What year was this?'

'Around 1971.'

'And that's where you met Maude Stamford?'

A nod.

'For the tape.'

'Yes.'

'And Tania Harrison.'

'Yes.'

'What was your job?'

'I put on puppet shows for the residents.'

'Maude Stamford?'

'Yes.'

'Did you have any dealings with Frank McKay, Dorothy Amis or Edith Callaghan there?'

'No, they didn't work there. It was only when I began to work at the Charitable Sisters that I met them.'

'And when was that?'

'Around 1975. Tania Harrison recommended my work. Dorothy worked there and Edith and Frank came later.'

'So you began working there in 1975. Did you remain working for Begbie House during that time?'

'Yes.'

'What did you do at the Charitable Sisters?'

'Puppet shows.'

'Who for?'

'The children, supervised by the nurses and doctors.'

'How many children did you perform for?'

'The shows were watched by all. I did a few private ones too.'

Kelly stopped and peered at him.

'Private ones?'

Luther looked terribly uncomfortable. He nodded. His mouth clamped shut as if his brain told it to. Tears formed at the corners of his eyes.

'Are you all right, Luther?'

He nodded.

'Which residents did you perform private puppet shows for?'

'Some boys.'

'Can you remember names?'

A nod.

'For the tape.'

Luther took a deep breath and listed several names until he got to six or seven, then he added Jason Fellcroft.

'And how old was Jason?'

'About ten when I first met him.'

Silence sat between them like a thick fog. Kelly's heart rate elevated and a feeling like hot prickles settled in her throat.

'What about Tomas Kovac?'

Luther closed his eyes and nodded. Tears dropped to his knees and he wiped them away.

'Can you tell me the source of your distress, Luther?'

'Those boys. I think something bad happened to them there.'

'Something bad? You *think*?'

Another nod.

'Could you be more specific. Take your time.'

Kelly wanted to be anywhere else but in the interview room.

'I saw bruises and I noticed them change from little boys to… something else.'

'Something else?'

'Shadows. I think my shows were the only time they were allowed to be boys. They loved the puppets, both of them. It was their escape. They even made up names for themselves, to hide.'

'To hide?'

'To pretend they could disappear.'

'Make themselves invisible so they wouldn't be abused?'

Luther nodded.

'Can you tell us the names they had for themselves?' Seb asked.

Witness testimony for Op Daisy had recorded some of them.

'They called themselves Jack and Jill…'

'Go on.'

'Oh? Nothing. I'm confused.'

'Take your time,' Seb said.

'Who was Jill?' Kelly asked.

Luther looked at his hands.

'I didn't know her real name.'

Seb produced a photograph of Leia Lord though Kelly had no idea where he'd got it. He hadn't warned her beforehand. He showed Luther.

'Could this be her? She's a little older now. They all are.'

Luther nodded.

'Yes, I think it is her. Is she safe? Please don't tell me she's dead too?'

'No. Nothing like that,' Seb said.

Luther visibly relaxed.

He cared for them.

Seb was more experienced than she was at interviewing predators, but Luther was convincing. All the studying she'd done on body mores and signals convinced her that he was telling the truth, though she knew that could be because she willed it.

'And did the children disclose anything to you that specifically concerned you regarding their safety during the time you visited?'

He nodded.

'Can you describe, in as much detail as possible, what they disclosed.'

Another nod.

'Jason fought a lot. He was beaten for it. He told me they tied him up and beat him.'

'Who?'

'Frankie.'

Kelly felt her blood boiling. The notion that a caretaker had access to medically and emotionally vulnerable minors was excruciatingly painful. It was wrong on so many levels but she knew that in the 1970s it was commonplace. She got the impression they were scratching a stinking scab off something. And at least four members of staff had been free to pursue other careers working with children undetected.

'They used the puppets to tell me about it.'

'Which ones?'

'Punch and Judy,' he whispered. A small noise escaped from his throat and Kelly found herself holding her breath.

'Any others?'

Luther gazed around the room, as if reminiscing about those times but not really believing they were real. Fantasy was everywhere.

'Jack and Jill. Tomas showed me how they touched him.'

'Did you report what they told you? Using the puppets to tell their version of events?'

'I tried.'

'You tried?'

'I went to the senior consultant but he said they were delusional, and kids like those have deviant needs. He said that. *"Deviant needs."* He said they made it all up.'

'Did you pursue it?'

Luther shook his head. 'I tried to be there for them when they needed me.'

'What does that mean?'

'I looked after them when they left the home.'

'How?'

'I stayed in touch with Tomas, we have a common ancestry. He's ethnically Slavic, like me. His parents were assassinated in a hit on a quayside in London. I felt duty-bound to watch over him.'

'When was the last time you had contact with him?' Seb asked, and as he did, his voice merged into background noise as pieces of a puzzle fell into place for Kelly. The twang at the back of the accent, the dark eyes and the floppy hair. Tall but not big.

Luther looked away.

'We've got a warrant for your computer and phone, Luther, so if you lie, we'll find out.'

'He sent me a message on Facebook. Am I in trouble?'

'When was this?'

Luther told them about his Facebook altercation with Tomas, who, he suspected, was the thief of his toys.

'Can you describe Tomas to us?'

'He's tall, very handsome. His hair is big and billowy. His eyes are unforgettable.'

Kelly was drawn back to the room and felt as though Luther was describing the love of his life. If she hadn't known better, she might have thought that the curator was actually talking about his favourite puppet. But Luther's eccentricity wasn't a crime.

'Does he live in London?'

'I don't know.'

The answer was far too quick, and Kelly knew he was lying. She knew that Tomas Kovac was right here, among them.

'We would like you to make a statement for us on this pad.' She pushed a large pad towards him with a pen.

'We understand it's painful, Luther, but we need to know exactly what the boys told you, and who they accused. The members of staff they told you about.'

Luther looked into her eyes and wiped them with the backs of his hands.

He nodded and began writing, slowly at first then furiously. He filled three sides of A4 in less than ten minutes.

When he stopped, his tears had dried up and he looked unburdened somehow.

She scanned what he'd written and made sure to set her face so he couldn't read it. Inside, her heart was bursting.

'Can you identify anything in these photos, Luther?' she asked him, showing him photos of the puppets found at the flat of Dennis Chapman. He gazed at her with glassy eyes.

'These are mine! Where did you find them?'

'I'm afraid I can't share that information with you. You're sure they're your missing puppets?'

'Absolutely, yes. Can I have them back?'

'Not at the moment, they're being held as police evidence.'

'Who had them?'

His voice was small suddenly, as if he was scared of the answer.

'Who do you think took them?' she asked him.

'Tomas?'

Chapter 56

Tomas walked away from the Museum of Childhood towards Victoria Park, along Old Ford Road. This side of London was quiet and there was nothing he'd rather do than stay here and sit under a tree, gazing at children playing with their parents and carers. That was the term now. Parent *or* carer. Guardian, caregiver... Whatever. The point was somebody should be looking after them and it probably wasn't their parents. They shouldn't navigate the world alone.

They should never be abandoned to face the terrors of humankind alone. But he knew that instead of sitting silently and smiling with joy in his heart, he'd walk silently by and take a bus to Stratford, because he had a long journey. From Stratford, he'd take the DLR to Woolwich Arsenal and then a bus to the Princess Alice stop, a five-minute walk to Belmarsh Prison.

Their time together in care homes had forged a bond unbreakable by any restraints imposed by society and its punitive laws designed to make the masses suffer. Justice was for people who claimed the spoils, not those who won them.

But the time for philosophy was behind him. He'd spent years at the mercy of his mind, tortured into trying to discover why. Why him? Why, why, why? It was so unfair.

It had taken decades to work out the universal truth that his life didn't matter. There was no fairness in nature. Dog ate dog until a bigger one came along. And that was that.

Only when he accepted that did he find peace from his demons. They'd been all-powerful and dominated his every waking moment, but once he'd defeated them with a mere flick of his hand, and banished them to where they belonged – nowhere – he was free to live, for the first time in his life.

Jason didn't live.

That's why he'd ended up inside Belmarsh. He'd never found the true meaning of existence, which was to say, what it meant to be insignificant. For only when one realises that life is transitory and unremarkable can you then feel true freedom to stop caring.

He'd almost cared too little and the key was in balance. He'd been frivolous, cocky, too confident. He'd made mistakes too. But Jason had allowed his rage to rule every decision he made and that's why he posed a threat to society. Not because he hurt people, but because he hurt the wrong people.

He visited his friend – his brother – as much as he could.

Today wasn't a good day but he needed to see him, face to face, to tell him it was all over. The prison visit had been arranged for weeks, as they always were. He still followed rules.

Tomas attracted stares everywhere he went, but today more people than normal looked at him and it wasn't until he got to Stratford and saw the front of the newspapers that he saw why. The police had put a photofit together of a tall man with dark eyes and floppy hair almost covering his eyes.

There was only one person who could have given it to them. That's why Luther had been absent from the museum. He'd been ratting to the police.

He turned around.

His mission wasn't over after all.

Chapter 57

Kelly and Seb entered the Museum of Childhood to find a chaotic scene. They hadn't planned a visit, but officers had been dispatched there with a warrant to seize the electrical equipment belonging to the curator, but when they'd arrived they'd faced a commotion and a seriously injured woman.

Luther had arrived back only an hour before they'd got there, after being released without charge, for now. He was traumatised and in a state of shock, as was Oswald, the old caretaker. Seb directed uniforms to sweep the place for evidence of who had attacked Diandra in the curator's office.

'What happened?' Kelly asked. She knew that Diandra was in hospital but nothing more.

'Oswald called me soon after I was released from the police station. I stopped to buy a hot chocolate. I should have refused to leave here, he was looking for me.'

'Who?'

Luther stared at her. He looked terrified.

'Who is looking for you, Luther? Who wants to talk to you? Is it one of the boys?'

'He died in the fire,' Luther said.

'The fire?'

Luther nodded.

'Which fire?'

'Tomas started it.'

'Where was the fire, Luther?'

She desperately tried to get him to focus, his mind was wandering all over the place and he was confused. None of his sentences were coherent.

They called them Jack and Jill...

'Jason was such a good boy, he was never supposed to turn out bad.'

Kelly looked at Oswald who shook his head and spread his hands as if to say he had no idea what, or who, the old man was referring to.

'Who hurt Diandra?' she asked.

Luther glanced at his desk, where the monitor had been before the police confiscated it. She turned to Oswald.

'Oswald, is there anywhere we can watch the CCTV for Luther's office? Did you have it fixed?'

Oswald nodded.

'Downstairs. We've already watched it,' Oswald said.

'And?'

'Diandra followed him in here, she challenged him. He hit her.' Oswald broke off, distressed. 'I found her on the floor in here. I called an ambulance, I thought she was dead there was so much blood.'

'Did you watch too, Luther?' she asked.

Luther slowly nodded.

'You saw who attacked Diandra?'

He nodded.

'Show me,' she said.

Oswald led her downstairs and she heard Luther following.

The caretaker took her to his office and she sat in the chair in front of several monitors. Oswald flicked some switches and rewound footage on one of the screens and she watched.

'This is the man?'

A tall male figure could be seen entering the museum, but he kept his back to the camera. The same was true when he took to the stairs and when he was inside Luther's office. It was as if he knew exactly where the surveillance was. She couldn't see his face but the small hairs on her arms stood up, despite the museum being sweltering hot, as if warning her about something, and a creeping feeling spread under her ribs. She knew his body. She knew his gait.

'Do you recognise him, Luther?'

Luther nodded.

'Who is he? Is it Tomas?'

Luther stared at her, then he nodded.

She watched the screens as the man who broke into Luther's office picked up a heavy object which he then used to smash Luther's desk drawers open. He took something out of the middle drawer and looked behind him. Then Diandra appeared on screen.

'What was in that drawer, Luther?'

'He was looking for this,' Luther said. She looked at him and he held something out towards her. It was a doll. 'It was the only thing that used to calm him down. I made up stories about her. Jack fell down and rolled down the hill, spilling the water but Jill didn't fall too, she stood her ground and survived. He loved that. That Jill survived and didn't smash herself to smithereens like Jack did. She was saved. She took care of them.'

Kelly stared at the doll of Jill. It was beautiful but it was only a doll. She realised in that moment that these damaged children, with Tomas at the centre of them, truly believed the make-believe world they'd created. The dolls had become animated and real. It was disturbing and sorrowful at the same time.

'Are you telling me that he thought this doll was real?'

Luther nodded. 'He became fixated on her. On her surviving. It was like a drug to him. It still is.'

'A drug?'

'Taking care of her.'

'So why not just buy a doll, take care of it and leave everybody else the fuck alone? Sorry for the swearing. I'm stressed,' she said.

Oswald and Luther fell dumbstruck. She apologised.

'Luther, who is Jill?'

He stared at her.

'I know they gave themselves names, to escape from the worst of the pain. Was Tomas Jack?'

A nod.

'So who was Jill?'

His eyes were like balls of glass, like the ones you'd find in a Victorian puppet from long ago.

'Was Jill Princess Leia, Luther?'

The old curator's face crumbled and Oswald put his hand on her arm.

'I think he's had enough, please.'

'Are you in on this too?' she said sharply.

'Me? No. I have no idea what this is all about. I know Luther's son visits him occasionally and he's, well, aggressive, but I certainly do not know who attacked Diandra.'

'Your son?' she faced Luther, who shrunk back.

'Luther, now would be a good time to tell me if you have a son.'

Luther shook his head.

Her shoulders sagged and she turned to Oswald.

'Is it possible, Oswald, that Luther was visited by the same man in the CCTV and he told you it was his son?'

'Why would he do that?'

'Why indeed,' Kelly said and walked away from both of them.

'They made up names because when they called each other by their real names bad things happened.'

It was barely a whisper.

'What?' Kelly swung around. He'd alluded to this in interview. Now she understood that what he meant was that the children had pet names for each other because it protected them. In their heads, they couldn't be hurt if they fantasised about being heroes.

'It was their special place,' he said. His head hung to his chest. Oswald shook his head.

'Their special place?'

It struck Kelly that children rely on having special imaginary places to run to. Their refuge, their haven, their Neverland… Kelly recalled feeling the same about a place on Derwent Water close to Calf's Bay, where she went alone, when she got the time.

What if these kids who were now adults had a real place too?

And that's where Jill had gone to confront Tomas. To tell him he'd gone too far. Or to apologise for failing in her mission, to punish their abusers from the inside. It struck her that Tomas could potentially be after Leia next. After all, she'd let him down too.

Chapter 58

'Luther, think!'

Kelly grabbed him by the collar and stared into his eyes.

'Now, Miss, I must ask that you stop…'

'Get off, this is none of your business, Oswald, unless you can tell me where Jack and Jill are?'

Oswald stared at her and she knew how medieval women felt when they were accused of witchcraft. Or at least the old woman who lived in a shoe. She turned back to Luther.

'You gave up on them once, don't do it now, have some spine, Luther! Think! They must have told you their safe place.'

Seb walked in as she shouted at the curator and stood still in the doorway.

'What the hell?'

'I know, I told her, she's assaulting the curator,' Oswald said.

'Oh, please,' Kelly sighed.

'Is everything okay, DS Porter?' Seb said.

'Luther has some information for me, don't you, Luther?'

Luther sighed.

'There might be a place,' he said.

'That's better, now if you could tell us sometime soon because we have reason to believe that Frankie McKay wasn't the last person on Tomas's list.'

'What?' Seb asked.

She went to him.

'Why would Princess Leia's best mate go on a murder spree right under her nose?'

'What? Who's mate?'

'Jack and Jill? Tomas and Leia, or Jill, or whoever she called herself then. This is not the work of a controlled pair. Tomas went rogue and now he's got her. I stake my career on it.'

'That's a stiff shout,' Seb said.

'Isn't it?'

'Can I have a private word?'

Kelly shrugged and glanced back to Luther, who was about as communicative as a hungry teenager.

They moved into the corridor.

'What was that all about?'

'There's no way this was planned from the inside. Okay, she might have been covering for him, and she pulled my witness, and she covered his records, but this? Horrific mutilations all in the space of a couple of weeks? He's gone rogue and I think he might be going after her. We find him and we find her.'

Seb stared at her.

'It's come to my attention that Tania Harrison was assaulted back in 1999 on shift, at the Whitechapel Hospital.'

'Go on.'

'Well, the guy who was arrested and questioned but released without charge because Tania refused to press charges was somebody I think you've mentioned before.'

Kelly waited.

'Orlando Charles.'

'Orla—'

'He was admitted on New Year's Eve. Drunk. It was a chance meeting.'

'Chance?'

'Is it possible he recognised her from when he'd—'

'Spent time in a kid's home?'

'Exactly.'

'Is he on any of our lists?'

Seb looked grave.

'Tell me.'

'He was at the Charitable Sisters?'

Orlando's profile came rushing back to Kelly's head in full ten-foot-tall technicolour. She'd memorised it for a whole year. He was born in 1966. He was forty-two years old. The same age as the others.

Now she knew why she felt a shadow walk over her soul when she watched the CCTV footage.

The person Luther was telling them was Tomas Kovac was in fact Orlando Charles.

'It's him.'

'Who?'

'Luther identified the man who attacked Diandra as Kovac but it was Orlando Charles.'

'How is that possible?'

'They've spent their lives reinventing themselves, right? They take on names then shed them like second skins.'

'Kids who've been through what they went through never get over it. If he saw her that night for the first time since they left the home, that'd be over fifteen years. The rage would have been overwhelming. Do we know how long his leg was in plaster and when he was mobile again?'

Seb nodded. 'I looked. I knew you'd be three steps ahead of me. He resumed work in March, 2000. But Tania didn't go missing until the following June.'

'Profilers would say that was his preparation and planning period. Orlando was into petty crime, he would have escalated. He found Tania by accident, it awoke in him a rage he couldn't control and finally he snapped.'

'Why the gap?'

'He was finding the others. They drank together. He inserted himself into their group. The man with dark hair and piercing eyes who ruined the games?'

'Of course.'

'He would have told Jill. I mean Leia. That's why she was involved in Op Daisy. They didn't get the results they wanted when Orlando/Tomas found Tania, he hatched a new plan, but it's my guess Leia didn't go for it.'

'She's got too much to lose, she would have suggested the legal route,' Seb said.

'And that wouldn't be good enough for Tomas.'

'When did Jason go down?'

'Christmas, 2001.'

'Was he on remand before that?' Seb asked.

'Only for three months.'

'Which makes him a suspect for Tania's death.'

'And Bradley a witness. Jill promised to save them all but she didn't. She was supposed to make sure Op Daisy ended it all, but she couldn't. She wasn't powerful enough.'

'She let her buddies down.'

'They thought she covered it up like all the others.'

'I don't know how you put this together but I'm willing to go with it for now. It's worth a punt in the absence of any other feasible theory,' Seb said. 'Did Luther give any hint of where they might have gone? Tomas, or Orlando? Christ, I can't keep up. Why Orlando anyway?'

'Walt Disney World? The most magical place on earth?'

She knew they were short on solid answers.

'We need to find Leia Lord before she's turned into the next puppet.'

'I agree she's in danger,' Seb said.

Kelly's phone buzzing startled her, and she saw that it was Jonathan Hass calling. She answered.

'Jonathan? Do you have news for me?'

'Actually, I do. It's about the paint used to spray the feather in Pinocchio's hat.'

'I'm listening. What about the paint?' Kelly couldn't help feeling deflated, she was hoping about news from the dig at the building site.

'It's a unique brand which was discontinued over a decade ago. It's very expensive and made of female kermes insects from Egypt.'

Kelly looked at her watch.

'Only a museum would be able to get their hands on it now.'

'Did you say museum?'

'Yes. It was too expensive to make and really fell out of use when the cochineal beetle was discovered in Mexico in the 1500s.'

Kelly peered over at Luther, who might have been more complicit than he was letting on after all.

'Thank you, Jonathan.' She went to end the call.

'I have some more news.'

'Yes?'

'We've removed a whole skeleton,' he told her.

'From the dig?'

'Yes. It was in a makeshift coffin. A wooden one, so not very stable. There was much decomposition. We found him over four hours ago, and we're working on another one now.'

'Another one?'

'Yes, there are at least four others in there. The gossip on the site is that the owner settled his debts here. You know, business deals gone wrong, debts owed, that sort of thing. They were chucked in holes for punishment and covered up with new buildings. It's genius really, if you're looking to get away with it,' Jonathan quipped.

If the conclusion had come from anyone else, Kelly would have squirmed, but from Jonathan it seemed normal. And he was correct. Somebody, in all likelihood Jason Fellcroft, had got away with it for years.

'We've got ID for one of them, the fella had a photocard in his wallet. Name of Orlando Charles.'

Chapter 59

Molly rooted through another box.

She'd been at the museum for five hours now and her body was covered in a thick layer of sweat and grime under her coveralls.

They'd recovered a laptop inside a silk bag. It had been buried beneath items that would be better placed in a craft shop. Luther Zedric's office was like a den, set up for a sleepover of kids at their favourite play area. Molly had never seen anything quite like it. It was more like a child's bedroom than the office of a grown man who'd worked in conservation for forty years.

It wasn't her job to analyse people's lives, just what they surrounded themselves with. Molly dealt in things not feelings, but she couldn't help thinking this man had an unhealthy obsession with children. There was passion, then there was neurosis.

She stretched her legs and bent backwards to give her back a break and it felt great to change position, and as she did so, she spotted a box underneath a sofa. It was a long, slim one, like those that posters came in. She slid it out from under the sofa and saw that it was sealed. She took a knife and opened the packaging carefully, sliding the lid off.

The box was stuffed with drawings and at first, Molly thought they were probably kids' drawings from school classes run by the museum. Or another antique. She handled them carefully with her gloved hands. Kelly had given her very specific instructions on what to look for before she and Seb had left, and as she examined the drawings, she suspected her flatmate might want to see them.

The drawings were juvenile.

Penned by children, for sure.

And they were aged.

They smelled old, and the colours had faded. Molly could just tell that they'd been in the tube for a long time, but she couldn't figure why they'd been neglected. There were names on the back, as she turned them over, and she assumed they belonged to the young artists.

The sketches were mostly of landscapes but some of them were of characters or cartoons, acting out scenes from what looked like fairy tales or stories that were familiar to her. She recognised Little Red Riding Hood and the wolf. She saw the three pigs. One depicted the fox and the hound. Others showed Pinocchio and Geppetto. Some were of Jack and Jill. And others were impressions of Looney Tunes characters. Given the cases currently under investigation, Molly reckoned she'd found something important but not incriminating. The artwork of a few kids revealed nothing to her, but that was up to Kelly to decide.

So far, she'd unearthed plenty of evidence that Luther Zedric loved toys and puppets, but none whatsoever that he used them for any other purpose than to study.

But then she read the final names on the last couple of illustrations. Tomas, Jason and Leia. They were all there.

She photographed the names and then dialled Kelly's mobile number, but she didn't answer.

Chapter 60

Kelly leant over Seb's shoulder, and they watched CCTV footage of DCI Leia Lord visiting Jason Fellcroft in prison. The DPS had found no evidence to support the visits in a professional capacity. She'd gone to Belmarsh as a personal friend. It was more damning evidence that Leia had a relationship with a felon outside of work. And she wasn't his only interesting visitor. They'd found footage of another guest, the man they thought was Orlando Charles but who they now suspected was really Tomas Kovac, who had stolen the identity of a dead man.

The tech department had explained that if you knew your way around a computer, then it was easy to change records, paper trails and photo IDs to create new identities. It was an up-and-coming method of crime that was catching on and had exploded since the widespread accessibility to the World Wide Web. iPhones, laptops and new gadgets kept digital criminals one step ahead of the Met. It boggled Kelly's mind.

They'd also had confirmation of at least one identity of another body found at the Stratford Junction building site, in a shallow grave underneath a set of joists about to be put in place over the foundations in an area slightly adjacent to where Tania had first been discovered. The body was that of Dennis Chapman. He'd reported a crime and paid the price. Tania Harrison was never meant to be found. Dennis's crime was getting in the way. It was evidence that their perpetrator was not only a murderer of those who'd harmed him in his life, but also of those who got in his way, and Kelly and Seb strongly suspected that Luther Zedric was in grave danger.

The man who spoke through dreams and promises was one of two things: either he was an associate of Tomas's or he was a potential victim. By Luther's own admission, he'd tried to save the children, and he'd kept in touch with Tomas, they had the emails to prove it. The young man had found it impossible to shut the curator out of his life. The man who'd kept him alive and shown kindness when the world forgot about them all.

Luther had turned a blind eye to Tomas 'borrowing' his toys. He'd failed to report this to the police. He was in trouble enough, but Kelly and Seb now must figure out if Tomas was working alone, or with Jason and Leia. And what role Luther Zedric played.

Under caution, Luther had offered them some suggestions of where Tomas might be. This was their top priority. The press was hounding the publicity department hourly. The Stratford Junction building site was surrounded, as were the two schools, and now they had an internal investigation going on. Kelly's second week on her new job made her wish she was still back at Bethnal Green CID. Inside Belmarsh, Jason Fellcroft's counsellor was tasked with pressuring him into revealing his safe childhood places. So far, he'd been belligerently dismissive and unhelpful.

Back at the Barking office, Kelly kicked a waste basket over.

'Do you think she's in real danger?' she asked Seb, referring to Leia. If she was with Tomas, they had no way of knowing if it was as a friend or foe. The relationship between the threesome went back years and nobody could second guess how enmeshed they were in each other's lives after the trauma they'd suffered together. Uniformed officers had been sent to all known addresses for Orlando Charles, as well as Leia's flat, and the registered addresses still affiliated with Jason Fellcroft's businesses and interests. So far, they'd found nothing, not even Leia's car.

'She'll understand better than most about how to avoid the city's CCTV cameras.'

Seb looked at her and she knew she was antsy.

'Let's have a break,' he said.

They walked out of the office and over the road to a coffee van.

In the distance she heard the distinctive ragtime piano of an ice cream van playing 'The Entertainer'.

She stopped walking and stared in the direction of the van, which she spotted about a hundred yards away.

'Kelly?' Seb asked. But she was zoned out in another place entirely. The sycophantic forerunner of jazz went round and around in her head as if taunting her to run fast, anywhere, but here. It was the kind of tune that stuck in your head in the middle of the night and wouldn't leave. The type of melody that haunted childhood dreams with its threat wrapped up innocuously as whimsy.

But Kelly wasn't fooled.

She walked away, back to the office, without ordering a coffee.

'Kelly, where are you going?' Seb shouted after her, but she ignored him.

Chapter 61

Kelly's stride turned to a jog, as she made her way back to the office and instead of waiting for the lift, she straddled the stairs in twos making fellow officers gawp at her. When she reached their floor, she panted, and the other officers stared at her. Seb wasn't far behind, and she heard him approach. She turned and they gathered their breath.

'Are you okay?' he asked.

'The Entertainer,' she said, her chest heaving up and down. Seb drew a long deep breath.

'What?'

She rushed to her computer and tapped in the title of the song and a video option came up. She played it and the tune filled the small office. Its hauntingly simple arrangement sat between them as Kelly got her breath back.

'Leia's phone ringtone,' he said. 'You mentioned it before. You think it's important?'

'Exactly. I do.'

He spread his hands. 'I know, you already told me, I thought we'd been here. I recall the poster. One of the best films ever, I appreciate Edith's movie acumen. *The Sting*, with Robert Redford and Paul Newman.'

'I think I dismissed it too easily.'

'I'm trying to keep up, Kelly, and I want to give you credit, I really want to be on the same page as you but you're speaking in riddles.'

'Exactly! Luther has been telling us this whole time.'

'What?'

'It's all theatre! It's all play acting, that's what children do to pretend they're somewhere else.'

She tapped furiously on the keyboard then read out loud: 'The most famous run of Ragtime in London was the one which ran at the Milton Theatre in Hackney until 1998 before it finally closed for good in 2000.'

'Yes, I remember,' he said.

Kelly's finger hovered over the computer mouse.

'What's this?'

It was a rhetorical question, and she opened the link before Seb could attempt to answer.

It was of Milton Berle performing 'The Entertainer' with Fozzie Bear from an episode of the Muppets from 1977.

'I read about this theatre in the notes you left me, when you gave me access to Op Daisy.'

'What?'

'It was a single reference, but I recall it because I loved the Muppets so much.'

Kelly glanced up at Seb. She was sat at the desk and they both turned to the screen when the tune came on. It opened with the beautifully simple piano introduction to the song. Fozzie was sat at the piano and Milton Berle stood over it, wearing a tuxedo. Then Berle began to speak. His voice was gravelly like a classic Hollywood legend who'd smoked a hundred thousand cigars. He spoke the lyrics. Deliberate, smooth and suave.

He explained to Fozzie what the song was about. The stars, the performers and the entertainers of the past. Kelly watched as Fozzie looked up at him, in awe, like a child would to a carer. Berle is his hero.

The mouse stuck and the screen froze.

'Fuck!'

Seb reached his hand over and placed it on top of hers.

'I get you. It's enough, Kelly. Come on, let's go. I'll alert armed response on the move.'

The screen jumped to life and the whole ensemble of the Muppets burst into a song. Kelly and Seb stared at them, speechless.

She stopped dragging the mouse about as if it had done her harm in a past life and clicked the performance to stop.

'An abandoned theatre?' he said. 'It's perfect.'

'Jesus,' Kelly breathed. She felt emotion surge through her body. The overwhelming sense of innocence lost, and the memories brought back in her own head a time in her own life when everything had been so simple. She'd grown up because that's what normal kids did. Adults put aside childish things when they moved into a new world, but those who were abused and derailed as a result never forgot the things that kept them safe when they were all alone. They held on to them. They made ringtones, and they collected dolls and puppets. And they made marionettes of their own.

'Come on, let's go. I've got the address,' Seb said, and she stood up. They left the office.

Chapter 62

The Milton Theatre had once graced a prime location along Mare Street, not far from the Grain & Grape pub where Dorothy, Edith, Tania and Frankie had once met. Kelly wondered if they went there to discuss the show after they'd seen Ragtime. As Seb drove, Kelly rifled through the Op Daisy report and found what she was looking for.

'Here, I knew it. The children were taken to the Milton Theatre to see ragtime. It stuck in my head because my dad used to sing it when the ice cream van came around in the summer.'

'Well done, Kelly, I'm right behind you.'

He glanced sideways at her as he used blues to navigate tricky traffic. Nobody stared. Crime and those chasing it were pedestrian in London.

'You're worried about being wrong,' he said, reading her mind. She nodded.

'You've got an old-fashioned nose, Kelly Porter. If it turns out you're wrong, then we'll start again. But I trust you.'

Armed response mobilised within nine minutes, and three cars had parked to the front, side and rear of the old theatre. Seb parked across the street.

The theatre was boarded up but the grand façade could still be made out.

Water stains from the last decade ran from the flat roof down to the walls, which boasted ruined posters from yesteryear as well as new ones plastered over the old by touts promoting the very latest in West End shows. Graffiti covered dilapidated walls, made new by adverts for *Les Misérables, Jersey Boys, High School Musical* and *La Cage Aux Folles*. Their corners hung loose and flapped in the breeze as cars sped by full of people with busy lives, completely unaware of what might be behind the crumbling icon. Layer upon layer of entertainment clung to the ruin. The letters of Berle's name hung precariously off long-rusted hooks and some of them were missing. They'd once been illuminated and proud, no doubt like the performers inside.

Seb and Kelly wore body armour and stayed close to the armed response group which entered by the rear. The place stank of piss and inside was just as unloved as the outside. Drug addicts and kids up to no good had got in and made a makeshift home which had been abandoned long ago. Mattresses, chairs, bottles, buckets and rags littered the floor of what looked like an old storage facility. They made their way up a flight of stairs and the red carpet which must have one day been luxuriously special was worn, drab and torn.

The lead officer stopped suddenly and indicated that he'd heard a noise. Another team met them on the stairwell. They'd come from the front.

Then they approached the main stage doors.

The third team was already inside and Kelly heard shouting.

Demands to freeze and put hands up. Her stomach did flips and her heart pounded.

Their radios crackled with the voices of the officers who delivered their assessment of the situation and if it was safe for Seb and Kelly to enter. There were three people in total inside. One woman and two males.

Seb made the final call for them to approach. One of the unidentified males inside was injured.

Kelly followed Seb and walked into the main theatre and then stopped in an aisle and looked up at the stage.

There were no lights, no dramatic music and no building excitement as people found their seats. There were no velvet curtains. No ice cream sellers. No volunteers handing out programmes.

The first person Kelly saw was Leia Lord.

The DCI was strung up by her hands and slumped motionless in the middle of the stage, tied by strings rising up to the ceiling. Kelly froze and stared at her body. Leia was wearing the same clothes she had on when they'd last spoken in her office. She wasn't dressed up. There was no visible blood or any evidence at all that he'd tortured or mutilated her body.

But she was motionless, and Kelly had no idea if she was dead or alive. Twine was wound around her wrists and ankles and one of her knees was bent upward in an awkward position.

Like a marionette's.

Seb walked past her. Then Kelly noticed Tomas. She'd known him as Orlando Charles for the best part of a year. A long investigation into burglary that had led her to believe he was a career criminal. Nothing in their searches had indicated that Orlando Charles used an alias. The name Tomas Kovac hadn't appeared in any of their inquiries. She'd been chasing a dead man all this time. Kelly had sat opposite him in the interview suite at Bethnal Green nick. She'd looked into his eyes. She'd jumped onto his body when she and Cheryl had put him in cuffs outside Mile End tube station, was it only a couple of weeks ago?

But now wasn't the time for questions.

'Tomas,' Seb said gently.

In the shadows behind Tomas, on the stage, she saw now that Luther was kneeling behind him. He stared at Kelly, then spoke. The man was terrified.

'Help me,' he said.

'Shut up, Luther!' Tomas shouted.

The whole auditorium echoed with a boom.

Behind them, radios hissed. Seb put his arm out behind him indicating that the situation was not critical. Yet. Kelly's heart thumped in her chest. She'd witnessed armed response firing their weapons only once before in her career. She didn't want to see it or hear it ever again.

'There's only one way to play this, pal,' Seb said.

Tomas eyed him. Kelly tore her eyes from Luther and watched Tomas and the way he moved his body, trying to work out what his intentions were.

'You don't want any more blood on your hands,' Seb said.

'Can I come and check on her?' Kelly asked, taking one step closer to the stage.

Tomas eyed her.

'Kelly Porter,' he said. She looked into his dark eyes and recalled Sookie's description of him. A connection nobody had made at the time.

'Orlando,' she said. 'I know that's not your name.'

'Who cares?'

'We do,' Seb said.

'We care about Operation Daisy,' Kelly said.

Tomas's eyes darted between the two of them and Kelly was desperate to rush up on stage to check on Leia, but she knew that Tomas was highly volatile. His killing spree had started a long time ago. The burglaries and petty crime CID had been involved in were paltry stuff compared. Mere time filling. She knew now that those burglaries of flats and houses around the Bethnal Green area were only a side hustle, designed to keep him occupied as, no doubt, his mind kept him running away from the demons which told him to kill.

'She's dead,' Tomas said.

Kelly caught her breath.

'Why?' she breathed.

'Because she turned into one of them! One of you!' he screamed, and his voice rattled around the vast space, reminiscent of a grand performance by a legendary bard.

'We understand, Tomas,' Seb said quietly.

Kelly stared at both of them. Then at Luther. Radios fizzed and popped.

'There's an ambulance on its way, and she really needs our help,' Seb added.

Luther began crawling towards them and Kelly went to put her hand out to make him stop. Tomas was unpredictable and they had no idea what he might do next. They couldn't see a weapon but that didn't mean he didn't have one. But to her surprise, Tomas let him go, and Kelly helped Luther get off the edge of the stage and she held him up as he staggered towards the coppers watching from the back.

'I tried to stop him,' Luther sobbed. Kelly watched as he was taken by a uniform and cuffed. He'd known all along. He'd known it was Tomas taking the puppets, he'd known what these kids went through and that they sought revenge. He'd known about this place. And he'd known all along the connection between her victims and the missing puppets. And he'd chosen to remain quiet.

It was then she saw the automatic weapons pointing at Tomas. Everything she'd read in the Op Daisy report rushed into her mind and the tragedy of Tomas dying here today overwhelmed her. But just because he'd suffered didn't justify what he'd done and perhaps today was his destiny.

'Leia was trying to help you, Tomas,' Seb said.

'She was trying to make things right from the inside,' Kelly added.

'Did you kill Tania Harrison?' Seb asked.

'No!' Tomas spat back. 'Who told you that?'

Kelly watched as Tomas moved towards Leia. He eyed the back of the room and knew the guns were trained on him. He used Leia's body as a shield. But Kelly saw her move slightly. Or it could have been the strings. A trick of motion and light. After all, they were in a theatre house.

Tomas began to laugh.

Kelly crept closer to the stage, toe by toe, holding her breath.

'But you did kill Dorothy Amis, Edith Callaghan and Frankie McKay?' Seb continued as Kelly inched forward.

Tomas didn't answer.

In the distance, from outside, Kelly heard the whining of an ambulance.

'I'm going to speak to the paramedics, Tomas, and I'm going to tell them they can come in and check Leia. Okay?' Seb asked.

Tomas still didn't say anything.

'The Entertainer was my first piano lesson,' she said.

It was a lie. She'd never learnt piano in her life.

Tomas watched her.

'Can I come closer?' she asked.

'I'm going to radio the paramedics, Tomas,' Seb said.

Tomas glanced at Leia. From her position now Kelly could see that Leia's face looked grey and lifeless. Tomas nodded.

Kelly moved to the stage and felt the wood of its boards beneath her hand. She brought her knee up to the rim and held on with her hands and hoisted herself up. She knelt facing him. She felt Seb behind her and knew he was unhappy. But still she inched closer to Leia and finally she was able to touch her. She reached a finger out and placed it against her face.

It was warm. Tomas didn't move.

Then she ran her finger down her cheek, across her neck and felt for a pulse.

There was a tiny thump of blood flow, but Kelly's face didn't change.

'She's just the same as them,' Tomas whispered.

His voice made her shiver, and she recalled feeling her body on top of his as she and Cheryl had apprehended him. He was a large, strong man but to Kelly he was still the little boy at the Charitable Sisters who hatched a plan with his friends to take their revenge someday against the people who'd never been brought to account.

'No, she wasn't, Tomas,' she said. Her face was two feet from his. She knew that she was putting herself in danger but she looked at his hands and she could see both of them and there was no sign of a weapon. She imagined the calibre of bullet that was loaded into the weapons behind her and willed Tomas not to make any surprise movements.

'They've got you in their sights, Tomas, let me show them that you're not here to harm anyone else. What you went through was unforgivable.'

He looked at her and she could smell his body. She'd smelled the same cologne when she'd arrested him with Cheryl. It was a juvenile scent that a teenager might choose.

'What happened to all of you was criminal.'

She gazed into his eyes and saw him for the first time. Really saw him. Inside his soul. When they'd sat opposite each other in the interview suite at Bethnal Green nick she'd questioned him, judged him, willed him to kick off, make a mistake, hang himself... But now she saw the human behind all that and realised that his eyes were the same ones as the little boy who'd been at the mercy of adults who were bigger, stronger, more powerful and untouchable. The system had protected them and not him. Op Daisy being brushed under the carpet was like being betrayed all over again. She couldn't imagine the pain.

But the law was the law and Kelly knew that Tomas would be punished. Again.

'Did you kill them?'

She wanted him to be innocent and her moral compass suddenly wavered. She was saving lost souls again.

A noise disturbed them, and they both turned to see two paramedics enter the hall.

She turned quickly back to him and whispered.

'Tomas, if you come with us now, I promise I'll get Operation Daisy reopened and I'll get justice for you and all those other kids. You have my word. I'll give it everything I've got.'

'Jill promised the same thing.'

'Jill?'

Tomas turned to Leia then she understood. Her name had been Jill at the home.

Kelly turned slightly towards Leia and in the split second she did so, a thwack passed her head, and three bullets slammed into Tomas's chest. He fell backwards and Kelly covered her ears, then she stared at his body. In his hand, he grasped a long machete-looking knife. She hadn't seen it. She hadn't even known it was there. Thick oozy blood began to spread from underneath him and she moved away. Bodies rushed past her and medics shouted emergency orders. Kelly sat on her knees and watched the scene in slow motion, willing it had gone differently. She didn't know if Tomas had intended to go for her or finish Leia off.

'We have a pulse.'

'Airway clear.'

'IV going in.'

An armed response approached.

'I'm sorry, ma'am,' he said. 'I had my eye on his hands the whole time.'

She heard words but couldn't feel them.

'It's okay. I know that was your absolute last resort. I trust you.'

He held out his hand and she took it to stand up and he helped her off the stage. It had been the only time she'd ever been on stage in her life. And she didn't ever want to be up there again.

She walked to the back of the hall and went through the curtains towards the remaining ambulance staff and saw Seb. Leia Lord had been cut down and was wheeled out behind her and loaded into the ambulance, which sped off at speed, with blue lights blaring.

Luther had been taken away.

It was over.

Suddenly, her body felt shaky and she rested against a stairwell. It had once been a grand feature in the entrance but now it looked as though it belonged in a horror movie.

'Let me help you,' Seb said. 'You're in shock.'

'I'm okay,' she said.

They walked outside into the sunshine and Kelly peered up to the sky. Murder squads earned their reputation. Her dad was wrong. They *were* experts.

In some peculiar way she felt as though she'd earned her place here. But the road to the truth was only just beginning. Her job wasn't about justice, she realised. It was about catching criminals. But not all offenders got what they deserved. And they bred new ones.

Her hands shook and Seb held them. It was as if his wisdom, and years on the force, were literally guiding her and helping her process what she'd just witnessed. He led her to a low wall, and they sat together in the sunshine, oblivious to the majority of Londoners who would be discussing how to make the most of the weather this weekend. It was forecast to be a scorcher.

'Take a breath, you did well,' he told her.

They remained in silence for a while, each contemplating what just happened. A uniformed officer approached them and handed Kelly a bottle of water, which she took gratefully. The cool liquid slipped down her throat and soothed her racing mind. As the uniform walked away, Kelly turned to Seb and squinted in the sunlight.

'Is this why you do what you do?'

'Do what I do?' He smiled and nodded in acknowledgement of the sentiment. 'You mean the thing that we didn't talk about?'

'Yes, that thing.'

'Kelly, half of London is taking recreational uppers, and most of them work for the government. Society is broken. We can't fix it. So, I cope. You're the only person I've ever told this to.'

She reached out her hand and placed it on his. She didn't feel it was over familiar or at all flirty. It seemed the only way she could show her respect for him in the moment. He smiled.

'We *can* fix it, one bastard at a time,' she told him.

He glanced at her and took her water bottle and chugged what was left.

'You know what, Kelly Porter, I might just believe you.'

Chapter 63

TWO MONTHS LATER

'Hi, Dad.'

'Kelly. When are you coming home? If you want a job up here, you know there's one for you.'

Kelly smiled into her Nokia.

'Thanks, Dad.'

'Your mother has something to tell you.'

Kelly walked along Bethnal Green Road, gazing at the fruit stalls and examining bundles of cherries, late in season and fat with juice.

'Kelly?'

Wendy sounded grave.

'Yes, Mum, are you going to ask me when I'm coming home too?'

'Your dad's not well.'

Kelly stopped walking and moved to the side of the pavement where there were fewer people. It was something in her mother's voice. Something she didn't recognise. A seriousness she didn't ever expect to hear.

'What's wrong?' she asked.

'Nothing. He won't let me help, but he wants you to come home and spend some time with him.'

Kelly closed her eyes. She couldn't work out if John Porter was being stubbornly cantankerous because he was jealous of her success, or Wendy was warning her that something awful was afoot.

The only way she'd know for sure was if she got on a train and went home.

She was due a holiday.

Perhaps she could take Molly or Cheryl with her this time and take them for stunning walks ending with a pub meal and a pint of Wainwright. Both her friends had promised to accompany her when she next went home.

'What has the doctor said?' she asked. And she wished she didn't because for the first time in her life, Wendy Porter was instantly honest with her and the pent-up rage of hearing that her husband was struggling to survive the worst diagnosis came tumbling out.

'They say six months.'

Kelly's world went numb and black and she held on to the wall behind her.

'Are you all right, love?' a man's voice asked her. It was the shop owner.

She smiled and nodded.

'Sorry, yes, I'm fine.'

'Pregnant,' she heard behind her. She walked away.

'Kelly, are you there?'

'Yes, Mum, I'm here. Can I call you back?'

'He said he hopes you come back to work here, it's his final wish.'

She managed to end the call amicably and blindly found her way back to the street.

She carried on along Bethnal Green Road and cut behind the Tower Hamlets high rises, home along Old Ford Road, across the canal and into her flat, where her friends waited for her.

They were celebrating.

Seb had been promoted to DCI. He'd chosen to transfer from DPS to MIT east.

They were going to be real partners.

It would either be a perfect union or the duo from hell. Technically, Seb had more experience, but Kelly had the better nose. He'd told her so enough times. With her instinct and his intellect, they were a formidable coalition.

Tomas Kovac had survived his gunshot wounds and would stand trial for murder. Leia Lord was recovering and had been charged with conspiracy to commit police corruption and knowingly disclosing data to be used in a crime. Jason Fellcroft had been charged with conspiracy to commit murder under the principle of joint enterprise, a law dating back hundreds of years allowing accomplices to face jail time, even though he was inside already.

Nobody was arrested for historic child abuses detailed in the Op Daisy report and the London mayor had not commented on it.

This time, Bradley promised he'd stand as a witness.

Molly and Cheryl thrust a beer into one hand and a cupcake into the other. Seb had been forced out of his shell and accepted an invite to celebrate his promotion grudgingly. He emerged from the balcony with a bottle of champagne.

Kelly shelved the feelings swirling in her chest about her father.

The tug of Cumbria stilled for a moment, but she knew that it would be back and one day, it would be so strong that she wouldn't be able to resist it. John Porter couldn't bring himself to tell her himself that he wanted her there, that he was proud of her and she should work close to him. But she knew that's what he felt. For now, London was her home, and there were plenty of criminals to keep her busy.

For now.

Acknowledgments

There are lots of people who I'd like to acknowledge for making this book a reality. Firstly, I'd like to thank Frankie Westoby for a two-hour coffee and cake session, over which the seed for policing in London in 2008 was planted. Her knowledge, hilarious anecdotes and experience of the Met eighteen years ago was invaluable to me and it really made Kelly's younger world come alive. Also, Adrian Priestley, for his constant support with technical questions.

To all the original Kelly Porter fans who've supported the books from the very beginning, I'd like to say I really hope you love this new perspective on Kelly's early life and where she came from. Writing a prequel was both a challenge and a privilege and Louise Cullen at Canelo has been a huge supporter of the concept from beginning to end. Huge thanks to Alicia Pountney too for her editorial input and tireless work on the book.

I want to give a huge shout out to my Aussie mate, Kristy Horne, who works endlessly behind the scenes on our podcast, *The Killer Storyteller*, to bring Kelly to new fans all the time. She's imaginative, has boundless energy and has dragged me into the technological age kicking and screaming. I'm quite good at Instagram now. Also to my daughter, Mati, for her educational tips on how not to look like an idiot on social media. She's my wingman behind the camera and works wonders with reels.

I'm eternally grateful to people who buy my books from all over the world, and the ones who send me messages on social media, asking questions, sharing thoughts and generally sharing their love for crime fiction at every opportunity. It's an honour to be anchored in such a community. Also my writing buddies who keep me sane. It's a tough industry and my pals keep me grounded and positive when things don't go as they should, which in writing is often. They understand the ups and downs and make me laugh just when I need it. Marion Todd, Shiela Bugler, Jeanette Hewitt and Sarah Ward, you're truly awesome! Massive thanks too to my agent, Peter Buckman for championing all my ideas and pushing me to produce my best work. Books are the product of hard work from all those involved, from agents, publishers, artists, proofreaders and editors, and I'm so proud of *First Act* and the opportunity it gave me to introduce Kelly Porter as she was in her early career.

Do you love crime fiction and are always on the lookout for brilliant authors?

Canelo Crime is home to some of the most exciting novels around. Thousands of readers are already enjoying our compulsive stories. Are you ready to find your new favourite writer?

Find out more and sign up to our newsletter at canelocrime.com